Anonymous

Puck His Vicissitudes, Adventures, Observations, Conclusions,

Friendships, and Philosophies Related by Himself and Edited by

Ouida

Anonymous

Puck His Vicissitudes, Adventures, Observations, Conclusions, Friendships, and Philosophies Related by Himself and Edited by Ouida

ISBN/EAN: 9783742830340

Manufactured in Europe, USA, Canada, Australia, Japa

Cover: Foto ©Andreas Hilbeck / pixelio.de

Manufactured and distributed by brebook publishing software (www.brebook.com)

Anonymous

Puck His Vicissitudes, Adventures, Observations, Conclusions, Friendships, and Philosophies Related by Himself and Edited by Ouida

COLLECTION

OF

BRITISH AUTHO

TAUCHNITZ EDITION.

VOL. 1119.

PUCK BY OUIDA.

IN TWO VOLUMES.

VOL. I.

"Je vous ai dit ce que j'ai vu. Si vous ne l'aimez pas, ne dites pas du mal de moi. Blâmez, plutôt, votre monde dans lequel j'ai trouvé ces balourdises, ces friponneries, cette beauté qui escroque, ces femmes qui dévorent, cette passion qui ne cherche que du butin, ces amours qui ne cherchent que de l'argent."

P U C K:

HIS VICISSITUDES, ADVENTURES,
OBSERVATIONS, CONCLUSIONS, FRIENDSHIPS,
AND PHILOSOPHIES.

RELATED BY HIMSELF,

AND EDITED BY

O U I D A,

AUTHOR OF "IDALIA," "TRICOTRIN," ETC.

COPYRIGHT EDITION.

IN TWO VOLUMES. — VOL. I.

L E I P Z I G
BERNHARD TAUCHNITZ
1870.

The Right of Translation is reserved.

DEDICATED

TO

𝔄 𝔍𝔞𝔦𝔱𝔥𝔣𝔲𝔩 𝔉𝔯𝔦𝔢𝔫𝔡 𝔞𝔫𝔡 𝔞 𝔊𝔞𝔩𝔩𝔞𝔫𝔱 𝔊𝔢𝔫𝔱𝔩𝔢𝔪𝔞𝔫,

SULLA FELIX.

CONTENTS

OF VOLUME I.

P U C K.

INTRODUCTION.

I am only a dog.

I find in all autobiographies which I have ever heard read that it is considered polite to commence with self-depreciation. But for all that I do not consider myself the inferior of any living creature: I never heard of any autobiographist that did consider himself so. According to their own account they are all *incompris;* and I suppose I was also; for I was always held in contempt as a "dumb brute." Nobody, except that wise woman, Rosa Bonheur, ever discerned that animals only do not speak because they are endowed with a discretion far and away over that of blatant, bellowing, gossiping, garrulous Man.

"Only a dog," indeed! However, the phrase has a pretty, modest, graceful look, so let it stand. Men never are taken at their own valuation by others; and so I suppose dogs cannot expect to be either.

"Only a dog!" Well, dogs cannot lie, or bribe, or don a surplice, or pick a lock, or go bull-baiting in share-markets, or preside as chairmen over public companies; we can only, if we are dishonest, run off with a bone in a most open and foolish fashion, and get instantly whipped for our pains. So that there is one art, at least, in which men are decidedly in advance of us; and in deference to that super-excellence in stealing I beg again to state, in my humility, that I am Only a Dog.

Such a little dog too. I can go in a muff with a scent-bottle, or in a coat-pocket with a meerschaum. I am very white, very woolly, very pretty indeed; covered all over with snowy curls, and having two bright black eyes and a black shiny tip to my nose like patent leather. I have heard myself declared a thousand times to be "thoro'-bred;" but I really do not feel any more sure of my paternity than the public can be of the authorship of a prince's periods or a bishop's charge. I have in my own mind very patrician doubts as to my father; and can, with truly aristocratic haziness, trace my ancestry up to an O.

· I have studied life, I assure you; and widely too, though I am only a tiny Maltese. I am called Maltese, you know, though I never saw Malta, just as your nobles are called Norman though they do not own an acre of land in Normandy.

I have studied life; we little cupids usually belong to the fair sex; and for a vantage-point from which to survey all the tricks and trades, the devilries and the frivolities, the sins and the shams, the shifts and the scandals of this world of yours, commend me to a cosy nook under a woman's laces!

I remember once hearing a big Alp-dog and a small King Charles disputing with one another as to which knew best the world and all its wickedness. Mont Blanc narrated most thrilling adventures amongst the snows of his birthplace, told how he had rescued travellers from midnight death, and dug a child out of an icy grave, and guarded a lonely old château through a whole dreary Swiss winter; and wound up by declaring that he must have seen the game of life best since he had once belonged to poor Grammont Caderousse, and now lived with a Guardsman who had rooms in Mount-street, where they played hazard till the dawn was up, and told all the naughtiest stories that were about on the town.

Little Charlie heard patiently, shivering at the mention of snow, then winked his brown eye when Mont Blanc talked of his Guardsman.

"My dear Alp," said he, "I see a trick more than you for all that; for I live with the ladies. As for your owner in

Mount-street,—a fico for him! Why—*I belong to the woman that ruins him!*"

The coterie of dogs that was listening declared the little fellow had won. Mont Blanc lived in the sphere of the tricked; Charlie in the land of the tricksters. Ice might be cold, but not so cold as the souls of *cocottes;* chicken-hazard might be perilous, but not so perilous as the ways of *cocodettes.*

You must be spider or fly, as somebody says. Now all my experience tells me that men are mostly the big, good-natured, careless blue-bottles, half drunk with their honey o pleasure, and rushing blindly into any web that dazzles themf a little in the sunshine; and women are the dainty, painted, patient spiders that just sit and weave, and weave, and weave, till—pong!—Bluebottle is in head foremost, and is killed, and sucked dry, and eaten up at leisure.

You men think women do not know much of life. Pooh! I, Puck, who have dwelt for many of my days on their boudoir cushions, and eaten of their dainty little dinners, and been smuggled under their robes even into opera, balls, and churches, tell you that is an utter fallacy. They do not choose you to know that they know it, very probably; but there is nothing that is hidden from them, I promise you.

They were very good to me on the whole (except that they would generally overfeed me one day, and forget to feed me at all the next), and I do not want to speak against them; but if ever Metempsychosis whisk my little soul into a man's body, hang me if I will not steer clear of my ladies!— that's all.

For viewing life,—all its cogs, and wheels, and springs, —there is nothing so well as to be a lady's pet dog. To see the pretty creatures quarrel with their mirrors, and almost swear over their hairdressing, and get into a passion because the white powder insists on resting in little tell-tale patches, and sit pondering grimly for an hour over the debatable question of more or less rouge; and then to trot down on the edge of their trailing skirts, and go beside them as they sweep into the drawing-room, radiant with smiles, and brilliant

for conquest, and hear them murmur prettiest welcome to the
rivals whom they could slaughter were only their fan a dagger.
Why, there is nothing in the world beats that for a comedy!

Ah! you scowl at this, and say, "What a dissolute dog
is this Puck; he has lived with Phryne, and Laïs, and all of
them!" Not at all, my good sir, not a bit of it. I have had
mistresses in all classes of society; I have dwelt with peasants
as well as with peeresses; and on my honour I have belonged
to young girls that rouged like any lorette, and to matrons
that intrigued like any courtesan; and I have seen as genuine
spurts of spiteful chagrin, or impulsive good-nature, in the
greenroom as in the schoolroom, and as matchless pieces of
impudent acting in the salon as on the stage. "*Souvent femme
varie;*" well, I don't think it(though they were always variable
about my meals); I have found female nature very much the
same all the world over. And a dog knows as a man cannot
know; when "only a dog" is with her, she *thinks* she is all
alone, you see!

You fear I am *blasé* and cynical? Perhaps I am. My
curls fall off a good deal, and I am forced to have my food
cut up in a mincing-machine; the world naturally looks dark
to us all when we come to this. But I have very often found
living agreeable enough, even though I have lived sufficiently
long to realise what Brummel felt at Calais: and I *have* met
noble women without rouge, and with truth on their tongues.
I have! And when I met them, I admired them, I loved
them, as your dogs (and men) of the world always do, with
an astonished reverential admiration that your country bump-
kins, your ungenerous youths, never feel.

We are ill appreciated, we cynics; on my honour, if cynicism be not the highest homage to Virtue there is, I should
like to know what Virtue wants. We sigh over her absence
and we glorify her perfections. But Virtue is always a trifle
stuck-up, you know, and she is very difficult to please.

She is always looking uneasily out of the "tail of her eye"
at her opposition-leader Sin, and wondering why Sin dresses
so well and drinks such very good wine. We "cynics" tell

her that under Sin's fine clothes there is a breast cancer-eaten, and at the bottom of the wine there is a bitter dreg called satiety; but Virtue does not much heed that; like the woman she is, she only notes that Sin drives a pair of ponies in the sunshine, while she herself is often left to plod wearily through the everlasting falling rain. So she dubs us "cynics" and leaves us—who can wonder if we won't follow her through the rain? Sin smiles so merrily if she makes us pay toll at the end; whereas Virtue—ah me, Virtue *will* find such virtue in frowning!

However, I fear I am getting a trifle too French-Memoir-esque, all epigram and no memoir. Living so much in the cream of society I have got a good deal of its froth. It is not wit, but it passes very well for it—over a dinner-table. Put down in black and white you may find it a trifle frivolous. As for printing wit—even my wit—you might just as well talk of petrifying a *vanille soufflée*. So I am afraid even I may seem dull sometimes; and I have as great a horror of seeming stupid as of seeming edifying.

How I hate that last word! It always brings to my memory a gentle dean who preached most divine platitudes, but invariably trod on my tail. I recollect the reverend gentleman had a playful habit too of pitching biscuits at me, which, when my innocent mouth opened for them, burnt it with a horrid hidden dab of mustard. And he tricked an old commissionnaire too, who once took me about, out of a shilling for a message. By the way, commissionnaires hate to do work for the cloth. "Nobody else cuts 'em down so close to a penny as them parsons," they will always tell you. What we poor dogs have lost by being shut out of church by the beadles!

But I am running out of my autobiographical track again, just as Montespan and Bussy Rabutin, and all of them always do. I will try and hark back again to my earliest reminiscences. They are humble ones, I must admit. The world always feels a savage pleasure in tracing its Shakespeares into a butcher's shop, and its Voltaires into an attorney's office, and its great men generally into paternal pigsties; it is a set-off to it for their disagreeable superiority. So it will be at once familiar and soothing to it to learn that I—the spoiled pet and idol of its oligarchy—first consciously opened my eyes in a cottage. You see I am as thoroughly honest as Rousseau in his *Confessions*.

Poor Jean Jacques! he only got called a scoundrel for his pains. I wonder where the man is who, telling the naked truth about himself, would not get called so?

Polite lies, polite lies! They are the decorous garment and the fitting food of the world. To be in the fashion, I shall have to treat you to them before I have done. But at the present moment I feel truthful. I am aware of the vulgarity of the admission; but I make it—I feel truthful.

So here is the account of my earliest home.

CHAPTER I.

His First Memory.

THE first thing I distinctly remember is lying on some
straw, in a wooden bed, and hearing the sound of voices
above.

"Do'ee think 't 'll live?" said one, the full gay voice of a
girl.

"It 'ull dew," said the slow soft tones of a man. "Git a
bit o' summat softer, lass; the straw, it do nashen of him."

The straw was truly nashing of me—North-English for
pricking and hurting me; and I took a liking to the man for
his thoughtfulness accordingly. The summat softer came,
in the shape of an old wool kerchief; and he laid me gently
on it, put me in the warmth of the sun, and fed me with some
new milk. It was the man who did all this: the girl stood
looking on, amused.

"How came 'ee to be gi'en him, Ben?" she asked, with
her hand on her side.

"It seems as mother's dead," he responded;—my mother
he meant, I found afterwards. "And pups was such a
trouble like to kip i' the quick, that up a' the Hall they'd no
away wi' 'em, and Jack he was a-goin' to put this little un
i' the water. It's the last o' the litter. 'Gi' he to me, Jack,'
says I; and he gi'ed him. 'He's o' rare walue,' says Jack,
'but he wunna live.' 'I dunno 'bout waluc,' says I. 'He's
no bigger than a kit; but he 'ull ha' a squeak for life anyhow
wi' me.' And I tuk him. Poor beastie, he's o' walue surely
i' God's sight!"

The girl's eyes sparkled.

"M'appen we might sell him after a bit?" she cried
eagerly.

I shivered where I lay; already I was regarded as a goods

and chattel, purchasable, marketable, and without a vote in
the sale! Mark you: it was a woman first proposed my
barter. It may have coloured all my subsequent views of the
sex; I do not deny it.

"Nay," said the man in his slow gentle voice. "A drop
o' milk 's all he 'ull cost awhiles—we shanna be harmed i'
that—and he'll grow to us, and we'll grow to him belikes.
Dogs are main and faithful. Look at auld Trust. It 'ull be
time eno' to talk o' turnin' this'n out o' door when he have
misbehave hisself. I likes the looks on him."

"But Jack told 'ee he was worth summat?" urged the
girl impatiently. "It was the old madam brought them wee
white dogs to the Hall first o' all, and they allus said as how
those little uns 'ud fetch their own weight i' gold."

The man shook his head a little sadly.

"Ah, ye allus thinks too much o' gold, my lass," he said,
with a soft reproach.

She laughed a little fiercely.

"We ha' got so much, to be sure!"

"We ha' got eno'," said he, with a patience very gentle,
and a little dogged. "We ha' got bit and drop, and hearth
fire, and roof tree. We ha' got eno'."

She gave a peevish, passionate twist to her dress; it was
woollen, homespun, and without grace or beauty.

He saw the gesture, and rose from his knees beside my
bed.

"'There was a dead woman found o' Moorside yester-
night," he said quietly. "And the bones were thro' the skin;
she's been clammed along o' want o' mill-work. You ha'n't
got to ga ta mill, lassie."

The rebuke was a very gentle one; but it displeased her.
She stood silent, in a yellow breadth of sunlight streaming in
through the leaded lattice of the long, lancet-shaped, creeper-
shaded window.

She was very lovely, this girl—strong, and lithe, and tall,
with a cloud of hair that would have glistened like bronze
with a little care, and great brown sleepy eyes that yet could

flash and glitter curiously, and a handsome, pouting, ruddy mouth.

She wore a russet-coloured skirt that reached scarce below her knees, and a yellow kerchief over her white full breast, and in her ears she had two tawdry brass rings and drops, and a string of red glass beads round her throat. She was quite young, exuberant though her growth had been; and the man, whilst he reproached her for her discontent, looked at her as if she were the thing he loved best under the sun. He himself was very unlike her; he had a homely, gentle, thoughtful countenance, and rough-hewn features, and gray patient eyes; on the whole there was a great resemblance between him and a shaggy sheep-dog that stood on the threshold, a sheep-dog who became my first friend, and who was the creature he had referred to by the name of Trust.

"'Take care o' him, Trust," said the man, as he left me and went through the door with his hoe and his spade, out to his garden work in the still evening time; and Trust came slowly to my side, and touched me good-humouredly with his great red tongue, and stretched himself down beside my box. Trust had a shrewd, kindly, black and white face, and I was glad to be in his charge instead of that of the girl who had spoken of selling me.

She, indeed, never looked at me any more, but betook herself to the window, where, by the sunset light, she began twisting an old hat about, and bedizening it with some shabby rose ribbons that seemed to please her but little, to judge by the dissatisfied, passionate way in which she pulled them one from another, and stuck them here, and twisted them there, and finally flung them all aside in a tumbled heap.

When the twilight came—the soft, sudden, gray twilight of a mild November's day—she still sat by the lattice with her elbows on the little deal table, and her hands twisted among her hair, staring vacantly out at the shadowy wood beyond, and doing nothing at all.

The man came in again, bringing in with him from his garden a sweet fresh scent of virgin mould, and of damp moss, and of leaves and grasses fragrant from late autumn buds that blossomed amongst them.

The girl never stirred.

"Eh, Avice," he called cheerily to her. "Ha' ye no' a bit of supper for us, my lass? I'm rare and hungered; them clods is hard to turn, the land's so drenched-like wi' the wet."

He gave himself a shake just as sheep-dogs do, and seemed to shake off him, as it were, fresh odours of flower-roots and dewy earth. Avice rose without alacrity, and took down a black pot from where it swung by a hook and chain in the wide brick chimney, and emptied its contents into a pan; then set the pan, with some flet milk and oat cake, on the bench that served them as a table.

"They've took the smoke," he murmured, as he ate the burnt and blackened potatoes; but he said it patiently, and made his meal without further lament; apparently used to the state of his kitchen. Avice ate her own supper without tendering him any excuse for the mischance that had come to the potatoes whilst she had been sorting her rose ribbons; and indeed she had a little sweet cake for her own eating, of which she did not offer him, nor even myself, an atom.

"All praises be to God as gi'es us our daily bread," said the man with sincere and grateful reverence, as he bent his fair curly head over the remnants of the smoked potatoes.

"Daily bread!" muttered the handsome girl. "It's main and fine what He do gi'e us, niver a bit o' wheat-loaf, mayhap, for weeks and weeks togither."

But she muttered it under her breath, and she did not dare let him hear it. I heard it; but then dogs hear and see a great many things to which men, in their arrogance and their stupidity, are deaf and blind. Wherever yet was the man who could tell a thief by pure instinct? We smell dishonesty on the air, but you only ask it to dinner, play cards with it, appoint it executor in your will, trust in it as your attorney, your priest, and your brother, and set it in high places exultingly.

Even your clever men are such fools: your best worldly knowledge is only on the tip of your tongue as parrots carry their jargon, and your Rochefoucaulds writing their aphorisms make asses of themselves over their Longuevilles.

But I am straying afield again.

I remind myself of what old Trust, when I came to know him well, told me: "Sheep and men are very much alike," said Trust, who thought both very poor creatures. "Very much alike indeed. They go in flocks, and can't give a reason why. They leave their fleece on any bramble that is strong enough to insist on fleecing them. They bleat loud at imagined evils, while they tumble straight into real dangers. And for going off the line, there's nothing like them. There may be pits, thorns, quagmires, spring-guns, what not, the other side of the hedge, but go off the straight track they will —and no dog can stop them. It's just the sheer love of straying. You may bark at them right and left; go they will, though they break their legs down a limekiln. O, men and sheep are wonderfully similar; take them all in all."

This was a favourite saying of Trust's, and I think he knew, for he had been sheep-dog to several farms, and had seen a deal of mankind in the little towns on the market-days, where the drovers haggled over their flocks, and fought over their ale. Trust was now far on in years, and his present master kept him only out of good-nature, but he was a valuable dog still, so far as shrewdness and faithfulness went.

When the man and the girl had gone up the little creaking dark stairway that evening, seeking their beds like the fowls with nightfall, Trust told me a little about them.

He had the garrulousness of old age. From a sense of chivalry and loyalty he was cautious about what he said about Avice; but I saw that he did not think very well of her.

"She's a feckless thing," he averred. "Always running

her head on ribbons, and rings, and gay rags, and such-like,
all out of her station. She's a bit selfish too—all young things
are; you are, I don't doubt. Only you can't get out of that
bed yet, to fight for yourself as it were. She is rare and
handsome; she thinks too much of it; she'll sit for hours
staring at her face in that little bit of broken mirror, and she
is full of discontent; but it will pass by and by, perhaps, all
that. She is so young and so spoiled; she was the youngest
of ten, and Ben the oldest. All the others are dead, and the
father and mother as well, and these two are left all alone.
Ben don't think there's her equal on all the earth; every little
thing as he can scrape together he saves for her. Why, I
know, she doesn't, that he's saved a matter of five silver
pieces this year, and put it in a hole under the old apple-tree;
and he is trying hard to save a whole pound by Barnaby
Bright (midsummer-day, that's her birthday), that he may
buy her a gown she set her heart on, when she saw it in the
shop-window in Ashbourne this Candlemas. A great pink-
coloured thing, very ugly I thought, but she cried for it like
a child, and it vexed him sorely because he could nohow get
it for her; he had only a few coppers by him. It is a very
difficult thing to lay money by in these times, you see; quarry
work brings ill pay, and the garden don't do well because it
is rocky and damp; and the fowls haven't laid all the winter,
and it's trouble enough to put by ten shillings a quarter for
rent."

And Trust shook his head like a dog on whom the economies of the world weighed heavily.

"Does she earn nothing?" I asked; I was acute for my
age, even thus early.

"Lord bless you, no," said Trust. "Flinging a bit to the
poultry, or mixing a little meal and water for cakes, is all
that lass ever does from morn till night. There is a deal for
a woman to do, let alone earning money; a woman that trims
her place tidily, and looks after the live stock, and is handy
at needle and thread, can save a power of money. She don't
need to go and earn it. But Avice, she just lets him labour

for her, in season and out of season, and does nothing herself,
and then turns round and mutters at him because she can't
eat off silver, and be shod in satin, and carry a train after her
like the peacocks. There are lots of women like her; lots,
my dear. You will be sure to come across them."

Now Trust had, of a surety, never in his life known any
other women than drovers' daughters and shepherds' wives;
but when I grew older, and went into the world, I could not
help thinking that those drovers' daughters and shepherds'
wives must have represented the female sex very completely
and very faithfully.

"Ben is good, is he not?" I asked, a little piteously; for
there is nothing that seems so dreary to the young as doubting or condemning those to whom they belong.

"Good as gold," said Trust emphatically. "And far
better indeed; for gold has done a swarm of harm in this
world; and Ben has done nothing but good all the days of his
life. He is the kind of man that does good—to everybody
except himself. I have known him ever since he was a lad of
fourteen. His father was dead 'and his mother ailing; and
Ben was about the farm where I lived, and he had the old
woman and the babies all to keep as best he could. My old
master helped him a bit, but it was Ben alone that kept the
mother and the children off the parish. He was always a
quiet, cheery, still sort of lad, but with a wonderful force of
work in him, and as strong as a young bull. He has always
had queer tender kind of thoughts too, about beasts and
birds, and flowers and weeds, and all manner of things that
he sees. There is much more in Ben than anybody thinks.
When he's been sitting on the hill-side with me, all alone
with the sheep, I've seen an odd, bright, wondering look
come in his eyes, just as if the bracken and the thyme had
got talking to him, and he was hearing beautiful stories from
them. He can't write a word, you know, and can only read
just a little, spelling it out as sheep hobble over a rutty road;
but I can't help thinking that Ben, if he only could express
what he feels, and say all that the water and trees and things

tell him, would be what I once heard some artistmen when they were at work painting on my moor-side talk about for an hour and more—I think they called it a poet. At least one of them read aloud, and it was out of a book that they said was a poet's, whilst the others were sketching; and the sound of what they did read was very like the look in Ben's eyes when he was alone on the hills, gazing at the clouds and the mists."

I listened, much impressed, but not at all understanding him.

"You must have thought a great deal yourself?" I said timidly. He looked very thoughtful with his old wrinkled and shaggy brows.

"Of course," said Trust calmly. "Dogs think a great deal; when people believe us asleep, nine times out of ten we are meditating. But men won't credit that, you see, because if ever they happen to hit on a thought themselves, they rush and set it all down in black and white, and cry out to all the others what wonders they are. You must think, among the hills and the dales; they make you, whether you like it or not. Even the sheep think, I do believe, though they look so stupid. Everything in creation thinks, that's my idea. Look at a little beetle, how clever it is, how cunning in defence, how patient in labour, how full of disquiet;—but you cannot understand, you are only a nurseling. Go to sleep until day-light. Myself I never do more than doze; that comes of habit when I used to have my sheepfolds to guard. Here there is nothing to take care of, for there is nothing to steal, unless it be those brass earrings of Avice's!"

With which smothered satire he stretched himself to enjoy that semi-slumber which the French call "*entre chat et loup;*" and I curled myself in my box to pass my first night under the roof of Reuben Dare.

CHAPTER II.

Under the Rose-thorn.

It was scarce daybreak when Trust went up the steep ladder-like stairs, and scratched loudly at the door on the top of them.

"I always wake them so," he explained when he descended; and I saw afterwards that he never was too soon or too late a single minute, though there was no village clock within hearing,˙ no clock at all in the house, and the sun at that time was as irregular and as little to be depended on as the sun usually is in the British Isles. "Only a dog!"—ah, "only a dog," with no watch in his pocket, will keep time with a punctuality that men seldom attain, despite all their best chronometric aids!

Soon a slow heavy step sounded on the stairway, and Reuben himself came down into the gloom; patted Trust, spoke to me, and undid the single shutter. There was not very much light even then: it was a chilly morning. He went out to a little shed, brought in an armful of peat and brush-wood, made his own fire with a great deal of labour, and got out his own breakfast. It was only a draught of cider and a bunch of rye bread; the diet on which most of your hard rural labour, your sowing and reaping, your ploughing and hoeing, your hedging and ditching, is done after all.

To Trust he gave more of the bread than he ate himself; and for me he heated a bowl of flet milk, talking to us both in his kindly and dreamy fashion.

Later he took down from the cupboard a single little dainty white china cup, and a small black china teapot; and a very tiny white wheat loaf, and pat of sweet amber-hued butter. He put some tea in the pot—weighing it as heed-fully as some men weigh gold, for it was terribly costly to him—and left them all ready together, on the table under the lattice.

Then he waited a moment or two, listening for a step on the stair: there was none—it was all silent above. A shade of disappointment stole over his face, but no anger; he took his huge pickaxe and other tools from their corner, put them over his shoulder, and went out through the door, lingering a moment with a backward look up the stair.

Then he drew the door after him, and I heard his steps growing fainter and fainter as they trod down the moss. Trust had gone with him.

I was alone a long time, a very long time; so long that I whimpered and cried, unheard, till I was tired, and held my peace for want of breath. When the sun was quite high, the girl Avice at length appeared.

"Be quiet, will 'ee, little wretch!" she cried to me; and went straightway to the table. Her eyes glistened a little as she saw the butter and tea, and she sat down and ate; never casting the smallest morsel to me.

Beautiful she was by the morning light; with her fair, rich colour, and her gleaming eyes, and her crown of half-bright, half-dusky hair, like the bronze in which there is much mixture of gold. But I thought I never saw anything of so much greed, or so intensely selfish. There was a vivid animal pleasure in the sight of what were dainties to her senses; but there was no sort of gratitude or feeling at the generous and thoughtful affection which had been thus tender of her in her absence. She ate all there was on the table, seeming to like to draw the pleasure out to its longest span; when ended, she washed the things and set them away, and did a little house-work, all in a very idle slovenly manner, like one whose heart was not at all in her occupation.

Then she went and fed the poultry, calling them round the door-sill. I could see them fight, and peck, and beat each other over the disputed grain; and when one helpless little speckled hen, who had scarcely a feather left in her body owing to her merciless sisters' unremitting onslaughts, was finally driven away from the mash-pan without having tasted so much as a barleycorn, I heard Avice laugh,—the first good-humoured and amused laugh that I had heard from her lips.

To feed the martyred hen she made no attempt: she left it to mope upon a rail.

When she came within, she drew her spinning-wheel to her, and began that ancient, graceful, classic work, old as the days of Troy. But she only tangled her yarn, and spoiled her web, and at last she pushed the distaff impatiently from her, and took up her piece of mirror, and fell to twining her string of red beads in and out of her hair, and knotting them round her arms, and wreathing them on her breast above her low-cut leathern bodice.

This little cottage of Reuben Dare's was quite alone, in the heart of the Peak country, on the edge of a great wood, chiefly of pines, at the farther extremity of which was the stone quarry where he worked, fair weather and foul; whilst in his leisure time he reared a few hardy flowers and simple fruits in his damp mossy garden, to which nothing but the indigenous ferns, and burdocks, and coltsfoot, took really kindly.

At the back of the cottage rose a hill, all grown over with ash, and larch, and firs; whilst, beyond that, there stretched the great dreary steppes of moorland, with a Roman tumulus, or a Druidic rocking-stone, alone breaking here and there the monotony of their brown, level, sheep-cropped wastes. Ashbourne was seven miles away, and the nearest hamlet was three; a scattered farm or two stood on the moors, and the Hall on the other side of the wood, where my forefathers had been reared, was utterly deserted by its owners, and left to the care of three or four superannuated servants, under whose neglect my delicate, high-born mother had perished.

Reuben's cottage was pretty; a square stone place with a pyramidal red roof, the whole enveloped in ivy and lichens, and the shade of spreading yew boughs; the same yews from which, in Robin Hood's days, the famous bowmen of England had been served with their weapons. Although it was midwinter, the cottage had a rosy glory that depended on no season, for it was covered, from the lowest of its stones to the top of its peaked roof, with a gigantic rose-thorn.

"Sure the noblest shrub as ever God have made," would Ben say, looking at its massive, cactus-like branches, with their red, waxen, tender-coloured berries. The cottage was very old, and the rose-thorn was the growth of centuries. Men's hands had never touched it. It had stretched where it would, ungoverned, unhampered, unarrested. It had a beautiful dusky glow about it always, from its peculiar thickness and its blended hues; and in the chilly weather the little robin red-breasts would come and flutter into it, and screen themselves in its shelter from the cold, and make it rosier yet with the brightness of their little ruddy throats.

"Tha Christ-birds do allus seem safest like i' tha Christbush," Ben would say softly, breaking off the larger half of his portion of oaten cake, to crumble for the robins with the dawn. I never knew what he meant, though I saw he had some soft, grave, old-world story in his thoughts, that made the rose-thorn and the red-breasts both sacred to him.

Avice would only laugh; and if he went away to work before the little birds had eaten all his gifts, would drive her chickens under the great thorn-tree to steal their oat-crumbs from those shy, pretty, russet songsters.

Midwinter too had other beauties in that secluded place. At least I heard old Trust say so many times; and it was true.

There were such grand tempestuous sunsets, with one-half the sky like a sheet of steel above the brown round hills, and the other half all dusky, red, and gold, behind the driving purple clouds. There were such beautiful wondrous snowstorms, that falling down past the great ivy-covered trunks and the dense net-work of auburn-hued branches, and drifting by the dim, soft, solemn shapes of the hill-sides and the bleak shadows of the fir-woods, mingled so strange a phantasy of dying colour, and made the earth seem dim, and sweet, and distant, even as in a dream.

Then one could see so easily the coming and the going,

the joys and the terrors, the loves and the strifes of the rooks, high above in the tallest trees that stood on the highest crest of the rocks. One could see the foxes' earths under the leaf-less brushwood, and the rabbits' holes under the withered bracken. The little ouzels, when they found their shallow ponds and freshets frozen, grew very tame, and fluttered close to the garden wall in hope of catching a stray crumb from the hens or a stray bone from the cat.

The cat herself—an unamiable creature when the weather was warm—grew sociable and good-natured when the snow drove her in-doors; and she shared with Trust and myself a place on the hearth-stone, before the cheery, brightly-burn-ing fire of "cobbles," that flamed up under the round swing-ing kettle into the wide black shaft of the old-fashioned chimney. For if she spit or scratched Trust drove her away from the fire; and she soon learned—what indeed is the rule for us all, from cats to court-beauties, from dogs to diplomatists —that the way to get the warmth of the world (and to give a sly safe pat to your neighbour) is to sheathe all your claws under velvet, and to keep in an excellent temper.

All living things seemed to draw closer together in the perils and privations of the winter, as you men do in the frost of your frights or your sorrows. In summer—as in prosperity —every one is for himself, and is heedless of others because he needs nothing of them.

The cottage was very pretty at all seasons, as I say, with its two long quaint windows and its wide door, through which the sunshine seemed for ever streaming, and a little brook singing close by, right under the garden grasses. It was very pretty, standing down as it did at the foot of the hill, with the dense green of the wood all before it. But it was very lonely, and no sound ever came to it save the sound of the water-freshets, and of the birds in the branches, except when now and then the thunder of some louder blast than common rolled faintly from the distant quarry, followed by the rumbling echo of the loosened falling stones.

It was lonely, certainly; and dull to those for whom the

brown silent moors had no grandeur, the ceaseless song of
the brook no music, the old gray hoary stones no story, the
innumerable woodland creatures, for ever astir under brake
and brushwood, no wonder and no interest.

And the girl Avice was one of these. The poetic faculty
—as you call the insight and the sympathy which feels a
divinity in all created things and a joy unutterable in the
natural beauty of the earth—is lacking in the generality of
women, notwithstanding their claims to the monopoly of
emotion. If it be not, how comes it that women have given
you no great poet since the days of Sappho?

It is women's deficiency in intellect, you will observe.
Not a whit: it is women's deficiency in sympathy.

The greatness of a poet lies in the universality of his
sympathies. And women are not sympathetic, because they
are intensely self-centred.

As Avice sat one day, when winter had grown into earliest
spring, pulling her beads about, and gazing at herself in her
bit of glass as usual, there came in sight in the distance, under
the arching boughs of the pines, a little old man with a pack
on his back. I found afterwards that he was a pedlar called
Dick o' tha Wynnats (i. e. of the gates of the wind), who
journeyed about on foot within a radius of twenty miles or so
round Ashbourne, and who came through this wood to the
Moor farms about once in three months—one of the very few
new-comers that ever disturbed the solitudes round Reuben's
cottage.

Avice's eyes sparkled with eager delight as she saw him
approach, and she darted through the open door and down
the glade to meet him with more welcoming alacrity than I
ever saw her display to any living creature.

I knew nothing about lovers in those days, or I might
have thought he had been one of hers, so gleefully did she
greet him. But if I had done so I should have been unde-
ceived on his entrance, for an uglier little old fellow never
breathed, and he was over seventy in age, though tough and
hard as a bit of ash-stick.

"What ha' gotten tha morn, Dick?" asked Avice eagerly, longing for a sight of his pack.

"Eh! ha' gotten a power o' things," said Dick, leisurely unstrapping it' and letting it down on the brick floor; "but m'appen ye' ull gie me a drop of summat to wet my throstle wi' first, Avice; canna, my wench?"

Avice, somewhat impatiently, brought him a little jugful of cider.

"Ben, he wunna ha' ought else to drink i' the house than that pig's swill," she said, with a sovereign contempt for what she offered.

"And hanna a mossel o' vittles wi' it?" asked old Dick with insidious softness. "I darena tak' this stuff a'out eaten of a mossel; it 'ud turn e' my stomach, it would."

I wished it might turn in his stomach, for I had conceived a great dislike to him, and had a horrid idea that he might take me away in his pack.

Avice, however, supplied him with the desired "mossel," and he appeared to have disowned all idea of danger in the cider, for he drained the jug to its last drop. Meanwhile Avice, fallen on her knees, was swiftly undoing the leathern straps of his portable warehouse, and feasting her eyes on all its wondrous treasures.

They consisted of glass beads, small mirrors, rolls of ribbons, gaudy cotton handkerchiefs, many-coloured woollen fabrics, penny illustrated periodicals, and all things of the cheapest and of the finest that could allure the eyes of country maidens, and the silver coins of their saving-boxes. But they were a million-fold more attractive to Avice Dare than the dainty robin's nest in the ivied wall, or the delicate bells of the dew on the leaves, or the marvellous sunset-colours in the western skies, or the exquisite heath on the broad brown fells, or any one of the many beauteous things in her daily life to which her sight was blind.

She lingered in rapture over every one of the tawdry worthless pieces of apparelling, and laid each aside with a sigh of envious longing.

The pedlar let his goods work their own charm whilst he
enjoyed his "mossel;" then he sang their praises, and spread
them out freshly before her.

"Look'ee lass," said he; "here be a many things made
right on to please ye. There bean't such a lot as this'n anywhere else our side o' tha Peak. Bless ye, afore I've been
half across moor-side I'll ha' emptied my pack o' 'em all, down
o the littlest spool o' cotton. But I'd rayther sell 'em to you;
'cause there bean't such a well-looking lass as ye anywheres i'
tha country. Ye set tha clo'es off, that 'ee do. Now' what'll
'ee fit on tha morn, Avice?"

Avice shook her pretty curly head.

"I ha'n't gotten no siller," she said with sullen sadness.
"Tha ten pennies I got for tha eggs ye had last time ye
come; I ha'n't got no more, not a brass farden, an' 'twas iver
so. Tha things is lovely; but ye wunna let me hev 'em on
tick, as 'twere?"

To this hint old Dick gave a sturdy denial.

"Canna, my dearie; canna, as 'twas iver so. I gies allays
ready money myself—allays; and if 1 was kep' out o' it I
should ha' to go to workhus. I'd do a deal for ye—ye're so
pretty wi' yer gowd hair—but I darena do that, let alone how
wild Ben 'ud be wi' me: ye's aware o' that."

"Ben's a gaby!" said Avice savagely, spreading out before her longing eyes a shawl of bright scarlet and orange,
and then folding it around her lovingly. "Lots o' folk go on
tick, and why na we? We'd be sure to pay sometime—when
tha garden was forrard, or the bins got well a-laying. What's
that there blue ribbon? That's beautiful!"

"An 'ud look beautiful in yer hair, my pretty," said the
subtle Dick, holding it up against the light. "And then
there's this red handkercher as 'ud go lovely over it—there
bean't a nicer 'sortment than blue and red togither. That's
a rare bargain too, that there lot o' jew'lry. I git it straight
from a born lady, as had come down i' the world, and was
obleeged to part wi' it. Them's real jew'ls, they is, and all
dirt cheap—only five shillin' for the lot. Real dimonds; fit

for the Queen o' England. Why, if ye hev them on at tha wakes i' this simmer-time, there wunna be a lass as 'ull hold a candle to ye, and a' the lads 'ull be dazed-like wi' yer glory. Pit 'em on, my wench, pit 'em on, even if ye canna take 'em; I long to sees 'em upo' ye."

All this, uttered in the soft sleepy "tongue o' the Peak," that slurs over every harsh word, and rolls its phrases all one in another, took its due effect upon Avice. Intensely ignorant, and honestly believing in her simplicity that she saw real "dimonds" before her, she yielded to the temptation, and clasped the brazen bands, sparkling with their bits of white glass, on her arms and about her throat, gazing at them and herself entranced.

Old Dick clapped his bony hands in admiring ecstasy.

"Lord's sake!" he cried; "ony look at yersel! Why, lord-a-mercy, no queen could ekall ye!"

The old hypocrite was most likely half-sincere. Avice was a very pretty picture then. Her arms were too fair by nature to have ever become sun-browned, and they were shaped to satisfy a sculptor; her throat was long and slender, though it denoted physical strength; and her neck, white as the driven snow, was the full blue-veined bosom of a goddess. Nor were these beauties much concealed by the low-cut leathern bodice that enclosed them; and as she breathed, quickly and feverishly, with longing and self-love, her eyes gleamed, her face flushed, and the mock diamonds really lent to her a curious kind of glittering transitory lustre.

"O, if ony I had 'em!" she cried, tossing her arms above her head, and unconsciously giving more beauty to her disclosed charms. "O, if ony I had 'em! They'd look at nobody else at the wakes!"

The wakes are the rural feasts held over the Peak country at every town and village on the anniversary of the building of its parish church. This religious commemoration takes the form of feasting, junketing, drinking, dancing, and eating very big, thin, round sweet cakes; and it was the only form of public festivity that Avice had ever in her brief life enjoyed,

To her the wakes seemed the pivot of the world, and all
the seasons rolled only to bring the wakes round again to re-
joice the souls of their worshippers.

"Ye must ha' 'em, my dearie," murmured old Dick be-
guilingly. "Ye must, somehow or ither. I should na ha' the
heart to see ony body else a-sportin' of 'em now I've once
seed 'em on yer bonny brist. Just 'ee think a bit—ha' na ye
got the littlest hantle o' siller?"

Avice glanced towards me; and I trembled in my box.

"There's tha pup as Ben had gi'en be tin week agone,"
she said. "They tell us as how 'tis a deal o' walue. Would
'ee tak' it, and sell it i' the town?"

"Lawk a mussy no!" cried Dick in horror. "I canna
abide dogs: niver could. There's that Trust o' yourn,
allays a sniffin' and mouthin' at me, if he be by when I
come. Think o' some ither way, my lass. Look 'ee—
ye ha' got dimonds as a princess bersel' 'ud be proud to
weer. Ye'll niver part wi' 'em, now ye ha' once pit 'em on,
Avice?"

Mephistopheles, of whom I have subsequently heard much
and often, was at his old work with women in the person of
the pedlar of the Peak. Only here Mephistopheles thought
the jewels enough without adding the temptation of passion,
and substituted Self-love for Love; the first is the more po-
tent seducer of the two with the fair sex, which enrols a hundred Avices to one Gretchen.

Dick o' tha Wynnats knew well that, having once put the
things on, the girl would never bear to let them go out of her
sight again unpurchased.

Avice stood with them clasped about her neck and arms,
ruffling her hair in her perplexity, and with the great tears
beginning to brim over in her eyes, because she saw no means
whereby she could make herself mistress of these splendid
gems.

Suddenly she grew very pale; the blood forsook her
cheeks and lips; a sudden thought—hope and fear both in

one—seemed to leap into her eyes, and burn the tears in them dry.

"Is it a matter o' five shillin'?" she asked, and her voice was hoarse and lower than usual as she spoke.

Five shillings were in Reuben's cottage as five thousand sovereigns are in the great world.

"Five shillin'," averred the pedlar, "and I would na sell 'em for that to ony else than ye, my dearie—real dimonds as they be, and wored by a great lady."

"Wait a bit," murmured Avice. "Now I think on it, m'appen I can do it. Just 'bide a bit, will 'ee?"

And still with her face very pale, and a steadfast, reckless, yet scared look upon it, she went out of the door, the sunlight catching the "dimonds" and playing on them, till the poor glass trumpery flashed and glowed, as though it really were some gem of Asia.

Where she went I did not see; she had closed the door behind her. Old Dick tarried patiently, putting the contents of his pack in order again, and did not even look through the lattice.

Dick, I suppose, was a worldly-wise man; and thought that so long as the money was forthcoming for his merchandise, he had nothing to do with whence it came. Pretty girls might not care that he should know.

Presently Avice returned: her face was very flushed now, and she spoke with eager, tremulous excitement.

"I ha' gotten it, Dick," she cried. "Here it be. It's a swarm of siller, sure, to pay all at onst—but the jew'ls are worth it. Here—one, two, three, four, five. All good money. All good!"

The peculiar haste and excitement of her manner struck the shrewd old man, for he rung and bit every coin in succession with care, as though suspecting bad money amongst them from the very volubility of her asseverations. They were all good, however; and he put them by in a leather pouch, chuckling contentedly as he did so.

"I knew 'ee got the money somewhere," he cried. "But

ye wimmen allays want so much pressin' and coaxin' to make 'ee do what ye're dyin' to do! Sure, and ye have the bravest dimonds i' country-side, Avice. Nell at the Dell Farm will be main and mad when I tells her. She's allus rare and jealous o' ye, wench. M'appen ye've got a coin or two more lay by, that ye could gie us for this lot of blue ribbin?"

"No, I ha'n't got a penny!" said Avice fiercely, covering her eyes with her hands to shut out the sight of the coveted ribbon. Already her diamonds scarcely contented her.

"Well, well, don't 'ee fret. Ye got enow on yer neck to make 'em all crazed-like wi' jealousy," said the benevolent Dick in consolation. "And look 'ee, I'll put in this lot of pictur' papers, all for good will; they'll wile ye a bit when ye're dull. They're all about lords and ladies; uncommon pretty readin', and a power o' murders in 'em, too. Them quality seems allus a-cuttin' each other's throats, if one may b'lieve them there pennies."

With which he deposited two or three of the penny numbers of fiction on the little table, and regarded himself, it was evident, as a person of princely liberality.

"I hate readin'," said Avice ungraciously, looking, nevertheless, at the illustrations. "I dew spell these here out sometimes, 'cause I like to see how folk live in great houses. How fine it must be to hev gentry a-killin' theirselves for ye, and a-wearin' o' masks to trap ye, and a-carryin' ye off to palaces i' the dead o' tha night. Do 'ee say as all's true what they tells?"

"All's gospel truth i' tha pennies," said Dick promptly, forgetting his previous scepticism. "It's all dukes what writes in them, and they must know what they does theirselves."

"And does they wear masks, and swords, and drive in gowden chariots, and carry off live princesses?" asked Avice eagerly, the dulness of her imagination stirred.

Dick scratched his head thoughtfully.

"Well—I seed a duke in these parts onst, long ago," he said meditatively, "and he was a little old rum-lookin' chap,

I thought, wi' gray hair and yaller gaiters. And he rid a fat black cob, and he said thank 'ee when I oped tha gate for un. And I could na see as he was anythink diff'rent to Tim Radly the stockin'-higgler, as was amazing like him. But them pennies is gospel-true, lass; niver ye go to doubt it. And now I'll bid 'ee good-day, my wench; for I must get over moor-side afore the strike o'twelve."

And throwing his pack over his shoulder, and taking his staff, the old man left us, and went out by the rear of the house, and began to climb the steep wooded hill that rose between the cottage and the moorlands that lay beyond.

Avice scarcely noticed his departure.' She was absorbed in thinking of the dukes and in gazing at her jewels, with her elbow resting on the table and her eyes fixed on the glass. Suddenly, however, she darted out and called to the pedlar, as he slowly crept up the lower slope of the hill. I could hear his voice reply from above:

"What is't, lass? Ha' ye found siller enow for the blue ribbin?"

"No!" she cried to him. "Ony—ony—I forgot to tell 'ee —if ye see Ben any time don't 'ee say nothin' to him o' tha dimonds. Mind that!"

"O' course not," he sung out in answer. "Wheniver does I say anythin'?"

"Thank 'ee," she called back. "Ye know he dusna like my laying out o' money on rattletraps and bits o' brass, as he calls 'em."

"Ben's a fule," retorted the old man from above, amongst the firs.

CHAPTER III.

Under the Apple-tree.

SHE came into the house again and ran to her mirror at once: she was feverish and little at ease, it seemed, but her "dimonds" still afforded her rapturous delight. The gold was so yellow, and the stones were so big!

3*

She seemed never to tire of clasping them on and off, and changing their resting-place, and picturing to herself, doubtless, the admiration she would draw on her at the wakes, and the bitterness of soul which she would cause to Nell o' the Moor Farm. Hour after hour she spent, gazing at these things and at herself in them, and thinking, idly and purposelessly, yet with a curious mixture of anxiety and savagery, to judge by the shadows that flitted one after another across her face—the shadows of desire and of dissatisfaction.

"If I could ony be where them things be wored all day, and dukes be a-swearin' o' love till they kills theirselves!" she muttered half aloud, over her precious gems.

She had led the simplest and most innocent life possible; she had been no more touched by whispers of evil than the little blue cuckoo's-eye flowering without; she had been brought up with the birds and the beasts, the noble moors and the radiant waters, and had had no more to acquaint her with the guilt of the world than the young lambs at play in the dales. But yet these longings were in her; these senses were inborn and importunate.

Vision she had not, imagination she had not, ambition she knew naught of, and intelligence was dead in her; but these she had—vanity, and greed, and sensuality, the true tempters of thousands of women.

After a while she took her treasures up the stairs, to hide them away, no doubt, in some box in her bedchamber, and there she remained till the day had almost waned, when she came down again and put on the potatoes to boil. She threw them into the pot with their skins scarcely washed, and sat down to peruse one of the "pennies," reading it slowly and painfully, spelling each word out, and tracing it with her forefinger.

She started a little as Trust entered with the setting of the sun, and after him his master. Ungracious at all times to her brother, her manner changed this evening; she welcomed him with more cordial warmth than usual, chattered with a flow of words very rare with her, and busied herself in getting his supper with much more willingness than she had shown on any night previous.

Ben himself looked very pleased with the alteration in her, and responded to it with a caressing tenderness that was infinitely gentle and touching.

"I'd a run o' luck to-day, my pretty," he said, sitting over his potatoes and oatmeal. "There was a lady as had lost her track i' the big pine wood, and I pit her right, and she gi'ed me a shillin' for 't. And soon arter, whiles I was a-workin', there kem a man—a-trampin', you know, as those paintin' chaps and tha fellows as break up the stones wi' a little hammer allays do. They *ses* they's gennlemen, but I niver b'lieve as gennlemen born 'ud go about wi' nasty oil-pots or bags o' bits o' gritstone. Howe'er, that's neither here nor there. This un, he spoke uncommon kind, and I picked him out a atom of cawke and a mossel or two of Blue-John, as seemed to please him, and he gi'ed me a shillin' tew. So I was rare i' luck tha morn. And 'Trust, tew; for he got a lot o' san'-widges out o' this here gennleman's pack. How's ta pup? He look rare an' brave. Eh, my little un, ye'll pull through safe enow, won't 'ee? 'Tis a pretty crittur, sure."

This was the first praise that I ever heard of my beauty, which has all my life been remarkable: it has been lauded by many lips, but by none more honest and kindly than poor Ben's.

Avice received his news with unwonted sympathy, and seemed to desire to atone for the general badness of her careless cookery, by an assiduity that should leave him nothing to desire in his present meal and induce him to linger over it longer than usual. In this, however, she failed. He cared little what he ate, and he had a design he was eager to execute.

The supper, and the thanksgiving for it, ended, he rose and took his gardening tools.

"Ye wunna go and garden tha night, Ben?" asked Avice rapidly. "Do 'ee look: tha sun's down."

"There's a lot o' light, lass," he laughed in answer. "I

allus garden arter 'tis down or afore 'tis riz. Ye knows that well cnow."

"But it's so cold, Ben, and so damp," she urged, with a curious feverishness. "Ye'll get the rewmatiz, sure as ye live, if ye garden this time o' night."

He laughed aloud at this.

"Why, Avice, d'ee think I's an old un of sixty year? D'ee iver know me ailin' of aught? Stay 'ee in if ye feel the damp; but the weather's no been bred yet as can daunt or damage o' me."

And he went.

Trust whispered over my box:

"He is going to bury that two shillings with the rest under the apple-tree. She does not dream he has saved money there, you know."

I said nothing.

"And it's all for her," added Trust; "all for that ugly red gown that she cried for last Candlemas."

Avice stayed by the hearth, with her hands clasped and her head bent, and the ruddy light of the cobble fire playing on her bowed head.

A brief space later there came on the night air a great cry, followed by a sudden silence. Trust rushed headlong out; Avice remained unmovable.

A little later her brother appeared on the threshold. His face was very pale, and he looked dazed and appalled.

"Avice, there's bin a thief here!" he said tremulously, though his grave voice was very low.

"A thief!" she echoed, without lifting her head. "What, hev the fowls bin stole?"

"No; they's in their coops," he answered, with the tremor still in his voice; "but there's bin somebody a-robbin' me, for all that;—a-robbin' you, my little lass, a-robbin' you!"

"Me!"

"Ah, my dearie, ye didna know," said Ben softly and sadly. "I was wrong, maybe, not to tell 'ee; ye'd ha' been more heedful o' tramps about. But ye see, lassie, ye was so

wishful for thnt gownd, and I thoct as how I'd surprise ye.
And, d'ye see, I says to myself, says I, I'll pit every stiver I
can git in a hole under tha old apple-tree, and store it up till
Barnaby Bright, and thin tak her o'er to Ashbourne and gie
her the thing she's a-longin' for. That was wot I thoct, ye
see, and now it's every shillin' gone. The moss hev bin
pulled up, and the hole's clean empty as empty can be. If
I'd ony telled ye, my pretty! And now ye'll have to wait
for yer gownd."

Avice stood, still unmoved, waving to and fro in the glow
of the fire; then at length she spoke, very huskily.

"Lord, how good o' ye, Ben! Who can it be as ha'
took it?"

He ruffled his fair hair in sorrowful perplexity.

"Some tramps, a coorse, my dear. Didna ye hear any
steps about?"

"Niver a one. But 'tis true I went up moor-side—just to
look as whether the gorse's in bloom. It might ha' bin done
whiles I was there."

"I dessay, I dessay! But who could tell as I'd money
there!"

"They might ha' seed ye o'er tha fence."

"Dick o' tha Wynnats ha'n't bin by, hev he? I'm allus
mistrustful o' th' old man."

"I ain't seed Dick come Wednesday was a month. It
must ha' bin a tramp."

"Tramps don't kim much o' these parts," said Ben with a
sigh. "It must sure hev bin one, though. They might look
ower the fence, as ye say. I'm ony sorry for ye, my lassie;
it 'ud ha' bin such a joy t' ye to ha' had that gownd."

Avice went up to him, and threw her white arms round
his neck and kissed him.

"Niver mind, Ben, I'll think as how ye hev gi'en it to
me; that 'ull do jist as well."

He returned her caresses fondly, stroking her hair with a
tender pitying touch.

"Theer's a brave wench! 'Tis rare and good o' ye to bear

't so well, Avice. It dew cut a bit,'cause ye see I was so set up like wi' content, a-bringin' them tew shillin' home jist now; and they'd ha' made sivin, and ther'd a bin but twice that agin to git afore ta simmer-time for ye to ha' tha gownd. And now 't 's all to begin o'er agin; and I canna surprise ye thin, 'cause I've telled ye o' it now—"

His voice fell suddenly. It was a blow to him to have been robbed of this innocent kindly pleasure; and five shillings are not made every day of a quarryman's life.

Avice kissed him yet again.

"Niver ye mind," she murmured, with a certain emotion trembling even in her hard changeless voice: "m'appen the hins will tak to layin' sune—'tis springtide; and if they dew, we'll pit the money by to make up this'n."

"That's a good lass," he said tenderly. "But it wunna be the same to me. The hins' money is allus your'n, my dear; but wot I thoct on was to gie ye somethin' that ye suld niver dream was a-comin'. Howe'er, I'll try and make tha pund up wi'out takin' from yer poultry-purse. Come out and look at tha apple-tree; ye'll see as how it must have been thieved this day, for theer's all the moss pulled-up like, and the marks is as clear as spade could mak' 'em. No dew's fell since 'twas done. Well, we'll leave them as did it wi' God. Sure they wunna be th' happier for 't."

Ben lived between wood and moor, far from the cities of men; and he still held the golden belief that stolen bread must be bitter in the unrighteous mouth.

"Come and look, my dearie," he urged again; and Avice went.

CHAPTER IV.

Trust's Tale.

THAT night, when all was still, I told what I had heard to Trust.

He growled so long and so loud that he awoke Reuben,

who threw open the lattice and called out aloud on the night-silence that he had a fowling-piece ready loaded for thieves.

"'There's no thief save the one as he wears in his heart," muttered Trust. "Ah, it's in times like this that dogs wish they had human tongues."

"Why have we not?" I asked him. I was a young weo thing, and I did not know.

"Have you not heard?" said Trust. "To be sure, you are still in the cradle; but it is a thing you ought to hear, so listen, I will tell you a story.

"In the early youth of the world, in the time when men were not weary with the endless roll of the ages, as they are weary now, there reigned in the East a king. All people dwelt then in the east; the west that is now so great was only a vast dark wilderness, where the lands were all locked in ice, and there only lived the strange and nameless things that we find to-day entombed in the stones and the mines. The east had all the sunlight and all the glory and all the races of men. Do I speak too deep for your baby-age? I tell this thing as my fathers told it.

"Well, this king was victorious, and young, and of beauty and stature exceeding. He had great content in his life, and his dominion was the fairest of any that lay under the orient suns. He had many ministers and friends and lovers; but the one of them all that he loved and trusted the best was his dog—the great Ilderim. In those days dogs were the comrades and the counsellors of men. Men knew then how much wiser than they were the dogs, and sought to take profit of their wisdom; and throughout the breadth of the land all dogs were held in high honour. They were guardians of gold, and took no bribes; they were warriors, and asked no star or spoil; they were public servants, and made no private purse; they were counsellors of kings, and trafficked in no nation's liber-ties. They were strangely unlike men in all things.

"Now Ilderim was the noblest of his race: black, lion-shaped, fleet as the deer, strong as the bear, keen as the eagle, faithful as—ah! what other thing is ever as faithful as

a dog? And he was ever by the side of the king as trustiest
counsellor and truest friend. The king loved Ilderim, and
Ilderim loved the king. Their hours were all spent together.
Together they chased the tiger and elephant; together they
warred with the savage chiefs who ravaged the neighbouring
countries; together they roamed in the balmy rose-gardens
and slept under the pleasant palm-groves.

"The services that Ilderim had done to the monarch were
as countless as the dates on the trees; and when the heralds
shouted forth the great deeds of the great people of the
nation, first of all they proclaimed the acts and the prowess
of Ilderim. And seven times he had saved the life of the
king: once from water, once from steel, once from a leopard,
once from a poisoner, once from an earthquake, once from
an armed foe at midnight. For all these things the king felt
that no gifts the dog could ask would be too great to bestow;
but Ilderim never asked aught. He wore a collar of gold indeed, because the ornament pleasured the king; but he made
no account of the bauble, and if ever he preferred a request
for anything, it was never for himself, but only for some poor
and starving mongrel whom he had met in the streets. All
his own race worshipped Ilderim, and the smallest and
meanest dog amongst them had only to tell his woes and his
wrongs to the palace favourite to have them aided and re-
dressed at once.

"So Ilderim lived with the king a score years and more,
and saved him from evil many a time. Now at the end of
that period the king took a new wife to his harem, and made
her queen and adored her accordingly. She was young and
of exquisite beauty, and she made a slave and a fool of her
lord. With her words she caressed Ilderim; but he knew
well that she bore him no love; and once when she set food
before him he smelt poison, and did not eat thereof. But he
knew that the king loved her, and therefore he said naught
of this wickedness; for Ilderim was wise, and knew well that
a man freshly in love is more blind than the bats at noonday.

"In time it came to pass, and this also full soon, that palace and people all saw that the queen was a wanton, and faithless. Her paramour was a slave at her court. And all the nation knew their king's dishonour; only he himself was still blind. The people murmured, and mocked him, and all the honour in which they held him ceased; and his very throne was in jeopardy because he was fooled by a traitorous wife. And still his eyes did not open; still he swore by the pure faith of his queen.

"None dared to tell him of his own disgrace; for all said, whoever tells it will die. Then Ilderim spake and said, 'Though I die, yet will I tell him; for his shame will turn his people against him, and they will arise and slay him, not choosing to have a fool for their ruler.' 'He will kill even you,' they urged to him; 'hold your peace, and let the end come.' Ilderim made answer, 'Whoso holds his peace when it is for his friend's welfare that he speaks, is a coward. He shall no more be the toy of a wanton.'

"Then he went straightway to the presence-chamber; and he spoke in the speech of men; and he told his lord of that frail wife's dishonour, and said, 'Arise! cast her off, and be strong as thou ever hast been.' But the king, mad with rage, would not hearken; he leapt down from his ivory throne, and drew his dagger out from his girdle, and thrust it into the heart of Ilderim. 'So serve I the foes of my angel!' he cried; and Ilderim fell at his feet. 'I forgive,' he said simply, and died.

"Then when the king saw that indeed he had slaughtered the noblest friend that he had upon earth, he was as one distraught, and rent his robes, and bewailed bitterly all the day through, and called unceasingly on Ilderim's name. But Ilderim lay dead in the audience-chamber, and heard no more the voice of his grief.

"And that night the king himself was slain by his queen's paramour.

"So from that hour all Ilderim's race declared that never more would they utter the human speech of men, since he had perished thus, through man's blindness and woman's sin. The oath was sworn by generation after generation, and gradually the knowledge of this tongue that never passed their lips died out, and has never been learnt again. We still know the meaning of men when they speak, but we never speak their phrases in answer; since death by the hand of a fool and an ingrate was the only recompense that fealty and truth brought to the great Ilderim, or have brought to his race to this day. For men are still what they were in the days of that king; and dogs still are the same, only now we are silent."

CHAPTER V.

Ambrose of the Forge.

THE spring soon deepened into that lovely flush of the early year which is beyond all other seasons in sweetness and in hope. By the time they allowed me to leave my bed and patter about in the sunshine, and wet my little white feathered feet in the burn, it was quite mid-spring, and infinitely beautiful in those north-country woods.

A delicious living sunshine streamed all day through the wide doorway. The rose-thorn on the walls and roof was moved all day by the wings and the songs of the nesting birds that made their homes in it. Primroses bloomed in great tufts under every moss-grown trunk, and were followed later on by the wild blue hyacinths and the lilies of the valley. The tender green fronds of the ferns uncurled to new life, and the waters, freshly snow-fed, brimmed over in every rivulet's channel, and bubbled under every knot of dock-leaves.

Now and then, when I have been nestled on a satin robe at an opera-supper, surfeited with macaroons, almond-wafers, and truffles, I have remembered that pleasant spring-time when I was so well contented, playing with a fir-cone, rolling over the kitten, leaving my coat on a wild briery bough, and dappling my feet in the shallow freshets; and I have felt that I have never been so happy as in that deep old pine wood in the Peak.

This was thoroughly irrational in me, of course. The happiness of our very early years is quite unconscious; and derives its peace from that very unconsciousness. If a child, or a puppy, knew he were happy, he would be analytical; and with the first moment of self-analysis the first shadow of discomfort would fall.

When I had reached the years at which I ate my truffles and macaroons, the pine wood would not have contented me.

When you wonder why you have not the enjoyment of childhood, your wonder is very idle, and the answer is simple; you have not the sublime supreme selfishness of childhood, which just enjoys, and takes no sort of heed of any woes whatever that go on around it. Childhood is an intense egotist, but an egotist whom every one conspires to gratify and caress, so that it need not take heed for itself. If the world showed the same complacent indulgence to the egotism of maturity, the mature egotist would enjoy himself as much as the new-born one.

I, being in the season of that serene infantine indifference to any and every sorrow near me, enjoyed myself in that little woodland cottage; happy, and taking no thought.

I grew extremely fond of Trust and of Reuben Dare: Avice, and I, and the cat, never liked one another. Ben always fed me before taking food himself, kept me warm with moss and wool, lighted the peat on purpose for me if I shivered, and was indeed incessantly troubled for my wants, and good to me. Avice only pulled my curls, or set the cat on me, or threw things at me for teasing her.

On the whole, that brilliant and acute social philosopher, Whyte Melville (whom I am proud to call my friend, for he has a soul that appreciates *us*), is very correct in his judgment when he avers that men have much more genuine kindness in them than women. There is a well-spring of kindliness in the hearts of many men, to which that of women is as a little shallow rivulet, noisy indeed, but of no depth or duration.

"O, why did you beat him, Fred!" cried a peeress I knew once, to her lord, referring to a street-boy who had tried to steal his purse. "Poor little thing, so worn, so wretched! And I dare say no mother at home. You cannot think how my heart bleeds for him!"

"Gammon!" retorted his lordship. "I gave him a thrashing because he deserved it."

The wife with tears in her pretty eyes got out of her carriage at a great shop for French bonbons, and over the sweetmeats forgot her street Arab, then and thenceforward.

My lord—a crack shot at the pigeons, and a gay man of the world—drove down to a club where he generally went for high gaming; wrote a note there that set his people to trace the child home, paid twenty pounds a-year for him for seven years at a school where they taught beggar boys trades, and was thanked a dozen seasons later for a kindness he had utterly forgotten, by a steady and rising young shipwright, in whom he recognised with infinite difficulty the little wretched thief he had succoured.

There is an illustration of men and women as I have found them.

Women's tears flow freely it is true; but they can so easily be diverted from their course by bonbons.

Men always say "gammon" to sentiment, but while they say it, they feel in their pockets, and ponder what's the best thing to do.

"What sall we call ta pup, lassie?" Ben asked one day, when I had grown to a tolerable size, that is to say, about as big as a moderate rat, and when the sweet sunshine of young April was beaming through the woods, and the ground was lovely with the "rathe primrose," and the air radiant with the yellow butterflies, that seemed as though they were the primroses themselves which had taken wing upon the balmy winds.

"Call't? What's matter to call't aught?" said Avice

sullenly, "A beast's a beast. Bapizin' of 'em is sich gammon—"

"Nay, nay," said Ben softly. "'Tis allus well to know a crittur as 'ee do love by some name of his'n as sounds homelike and cheery on tha ear. I mind whin I was a lad, a keepin' o' Melchisedec Stone's cows, there was three on 'em, and the dun she was Bell, and the red 'un she was Cowslip, and the black she was Meadow-Sweets. Well, thim cows they knew their names like three childer, and they'd come for 'em right across the lees; and one day whin I was na wi' 'em, but had been give holiday an' gone a bilberry huntin' up o' tha Tor side, I clomb, an' clomb, an' clomb, till I was that high I got dazed like, and lost my feetin' upo' tha rocks, and came a hustlin' down and snapped my ankle, so I ne'er could move. Ye'll no mind o' tha time; yo was but a babe just bared.

"It were very lonesome theer, and it seemed to me as it were hours that I had laid theer hitched like among tha bracken, with a great white gleamin' limestone a' above, and the water a purlin' and a moanin' iver so far down below. I thought as how night 'ud come, and nobody'd not niver know as wheer I was; and I couldna stir for the perishin' anguish in my feet, and it were na good to holloa out, for theer were naught i' sight save tha crows an' daws a skirlin' agen tha Tor side. An' sure my heart it were fit to break, for I were but a lad, and mither and a' lookit to me for bread, and I thought as how I'd niver see home no more.

"Weel, after awhiles, whin tha sun were gettin' very low, an' tha mists was a' creepin' up, I spied a cow beneath, a grazin' on a slip o' turf just atween a rift i' tha Tor. She were a goodish long way below, but I knew her; she were Cowslip. I dunno why, but that sight o' that crittur pit soul i' me; and I shouted all I could, Cowslip, Cowslip, Cowslip! It seemed as if tha poor beastie could ne'er ha' knowed me sae long, and leave me a' alone theer to dee. And she didna.

"Cowslip, when she heared her name, she left off grazin'

and listened; I called agen and agen. What did she dew?
She just kem a toilin' up, an' up, an' up—they is rare
climbers our hill cattle. She slipt, and stumbled, and fell
about sore; but up an' up she kem, and at last wi' a rare
scramble and hurtin' o' herself badly wi' brambles she
reached me, and made sich a to-do o'er me, an' licked me
with her rough warm tongue, and was as pleased an' as pitiful as though I were her own bairn. Thin, like a Christian,
she set up a voice an' mourned; mourned sae long and sae
loud that they heered her down i' the vale below.

"To hear a cow mournin' like that, they knew as she were
in trouble. Me they'd na ha' lookit for mebbe, even an' they'd
heered me; but Cowslip were worth a deal. So they kem a
searchin' an' a seekin'; an' they could see her white and red
body though they could na see me; and sae they lit on me,
and carried me down, an' 'twere Cowslip as saved my life.
An' iver after that I hev said 'tis allus well to name tha
critturs an' love 'em."

Avice said nothing; she was plucking a dead chicken for
the market, and tore the plumage off, lazily yet savagely,
with a curiously characteristic turn of the hand.

"What'll I call him?" pursued Ben, watching me where
I played with the kitten. "For sure he's just like them pucks
an' pixies as they dew say still live i' tha green wood, and as
I were that longin' ta see whin I were a boy, as I took ivery
white rabbit an' ivery flushed widgeon for 'em. I'll call him
arter 'em I think; theer's no fear as they'll be franzy,* think
'ee?"

"It doan't matter an' they be," muttered Avice. "Wheer's
use i' 'em? They ne'er show na gowd, na no treasure, as
they dew say as a' fairies should; I've seed the rings where
they dances, mysel'; but they're a bad lot, as lives for theer-
selves an' dunno dew tho least lettle o' good."

Ben smiled a little dreamily.

"I dun' know why theer sud na be fairies; for sure theer's
a many o' God's works as wonderful—ony look at a little

* Angry, irritated.

green beetle! Weel—an' the wee people'll na mind—we'll
call ta pup Pixie or Puck."

"Puck's the short 'un," said Avice curtly, "an' Puck he's
allus i' mischief they say, just like that there vermin."

"Puck, thin," consented her brother. "But as for mischief, my lass, there canna be a more mischievous bairn than
ye were i' a' the Peak. It's no a fault i' young things; it's
jist the new-born life as works i' 'em like sac much girdin'
yeast; and the more it dew work, the better ale we gits, they
say, i' arter times, so it dunna dew to pit spike i' bunghole
tew soon."

Which was one of Ben's metaphorical flights which passed
as high over Avice's head as the flight of northward sweeping
swallows that flew by in the still April noon: and thus in the
deep nest of those old green pine woods I was named after
the cheery and tricksy sprite who dwelt once by the hearths,
as he dwells now in the hearts, of the people of Shakespeare's
England.

As soon as he had named me he took me over, one Saturday afternoon, across the wood, to a little cottage that stood
near the quarry. It was a blacksmith's forge to which the
cart-horses used at all the little farms, round about upon the
moorlands, used to be taken when they wanted shoeing.

The work must have been of the scantiest; for the farms
were widely scattered and for the most part poor in cattle;
but the big brawny smith looked strong enough to shoe all
the wild horses of the prairies had they been brought to him.
He was leaning over the half-door of his forge as Ben drew
near; the ruddy glow of the fire behind him, and before all
the budding green woodland depth in which his workshop
was embowered.

"Gie ye godden, Ambrose," said Ben, with that gentle
archaism in greeting that lingers in the pages of your old
dramatists, and the mouths of your north-country peasantry;
you never wish heaven's benison to your friends on night or
morning now, when you meet with them; you only say "how

do you *do?*" how do you thrive—how do you prosper—how
do you employ yourself?*

O terrible age of prose, of hurry, of avarice, and of
officious occupation, which colours with its spirit even your
careless casual salutation!

"Ye're rare and welcome, Ben," said the Samson of the
anvil, his broad face lighting up with a sunny wistful smile.
"Be pickaxe snappit, mebbe?"

"Na," said Ben. "Wark's us dune i' this'n here smithy
that snap i' a score o' year. I kem to ax if so be as ye'd the
leelest mossel o' mittal as 'ud mak a ring fo' tha pup's
throssle? I knaw ye'll gie it an' ye hev?"

"Sure un I will," said the good-natured smith, whom I
had seen once or twice down at our place. "Kem in while I
looks for him; and tak a thoct o' brid and cheese. I'll be
glad to hae a crack wi' ye."

"I'll set a bit," answered Ben, seating himself as he spoke
on a seat in the porch through whose ivied lattice-work the
setting sun was streaming, while a red and green woodpecker
flashed by us in its light. "But I'll na hev victuals na drink,
thank 'ee. I arena' hungered na dry."

When I reached in after years the world of afternoon
teas, of seltzers and sherries, of flower fête ices, of ladies'
luncheons, of coffee and chasses, of Siraudin's bonbons, and
of Fortnum and Mason's hampers, I remembered this reason
of his as one of the most curious I had ever heard given;—
one entirely unrecognisable in the land of his betters.

"We'll mak him a brave un," pursued the blacksmith,
catching me by the throat for measurement, and setting to
work at once on a little circlet of white metal which I in my
innocence thought was silver. "Tha spring she be a comin'
on finely, aren't she, Ben? Tha kirrant-bushes theer be all
set for fruit a'ready, and tha old apple-trees be all on the
bloom. Mebbe y'll take a lettuce, and a bit o' cress like, ta
Avice?"

* I think some one has said this before Puck!—or something to the
same effect at least.—ED.

"Thank 'ee kindly," said Ben, not noticing that with the
name there came a glow on his friend's face that was not from
the smithy-fire behind him. " Ye niver kem anigh us now—
how be that?"

"Weel," said Ambrose, striking so hard at the little bit of
metal that I thought he would shatter it, "1 were wishful to
spik to 'ee o' that, Ben. Ye see—I'd come, and willin', ivery
gloamin' an' that was all; but it wunna dew—it wunna dew—
I canna fritten my heart out for the wench; it 'ull mek a silly
o' me, it will, and so I stays awa' like, and m'appen 'tis all I
ken dew."

Ben stared at him with a stupid amazement, a wondering
emotion in his own gray thoughtful eyes.

"Lord's sake!" he said slowly. "1 niver thoct o' naethin'
o' *that* sort, old chap! Sure an' I couldna wish a better lot for
the little lass. Why sud it mek a fool o' ye?"

" Why it *dew*," muttered Ambrose, sturdily drawing his
hand across his heated forehead and then hammering with
redoubled force. "An that's all about it, Ben. A man's sure
a fule i' sitch things as them. Look'ee—yest'reen was a week
tha wench she were up a' Good Rest farm—ye'll mind?—a
junkettin' a' St. Mark's Eve. An I've iver been soft on her—
tho' I warn't free wi' yew as to't—and I got a chance like, i'
that big close o' theirs wheer tha sickies* grow sae thick;
and said a word or tew. I hadna tha gift of the gab—them
wenches they mak yew sae silly—an sae I jist axed her to
wed wi' me, short like; for I hae luved her, it seem ta me,
iver sin she were a little un i' tha cradle—"

He stopped, and his strong hearty voice had a curious
tremble in it, as you will see in the big sinewy frame of a
bullock when they lead him out to the slaughter.

"And what did tha lass say tew 'ee?" asked Ben softly;
the homely weather-beaten face of him growing infinitely
tender and mournful with sympathy.

"She mocked o' me," said Ambrose humbly. "Well—

* Sycamores. The Derbyshire tongues have an Italian-like love for
easy and soft abbreviations.—ED.

m'appen she were right, A big, hulking, black-visaged lout,
like o' me, bean't unco fit ta tak tha fanciful thoct of a friskin'
bit o' beauty like o' her."

"She made a mock o' yew!" cried Ben, his calm gentle
face lighting up with wrath even against his best beloved.

. "Na, na," murmured the blacksmith hurriedly, unwilling,
it seemed, to stir feud betwixt Ben and his one ewe-lamb even
in the pain of his own passions. "Ony as wimmin will, o' a
man that canna tak their fancies. She mint naught o' malice
i' that; she laughed, but tew a bit o' a lass like her it dew
allus seem queer to see a big un like me afeard o' her—"

"Yew see as how she'd heer naught o't?"

Ben's face was very darkened and troubled, and from
where he sat in the ivied porch his eyes turned on to the face
of his friend with a very pathetic, wistful questioning. The
giant Ambrose shook his head: shaping and fashioning all
the while my little piece of metal.

"Naught o't," he said simply, while his rough bronzed
face grew a little white. "Don't 'ee go for ta plague her for't,
Ben. A lass canna luve ye an' she canna. I'd ha' done my
best handiwork by her—ye're awares o' that,—but I'm tew
old, and tew big, and tew gruesom, to pleasure a gay young
sparrahawk jest loose-like on tha wind."

Ben sat silent awhile, ruffling his hair in sorrowful perplexity; though he had been used to speak of the "little lass"
being "safe to wed," it had always, I think, been a very dim
and distant possibility to him, and Avice was still a child in
his sight.

"I'm dumb-foundered," he said slowly with a sigh. "Clean
dumb-foundered. I niver drimt as ye'd a' thoct of tha wench
—niver! Lack-a-day! It dew seem queer—'twarn't a day
agone as 'twere that she were a little, toddlin', bare-footed
bairn, allus at pranks and play!"

"Na—that's trew," assented Ambrose, who was something
even older than his friend. "Dunna be fashed wi' her, Ben,
for this'n; she canna git tha better jist o' whiles o' a' her
craze for fine claes an' gossips an' rompin', and sich like.

But she is a bonny thing; she'll kem round sure enow—sure
enow!"

But though he spoke generously, he spoke sadly; and did
not, I fancy, believe in his own prophecy over-much.

"It's strange as she niver telled me," murmured Ben;
"an' yo an' me sich neighbours tew!"

"M'appen she did na like?" suggested the tender-hearted
smith. "I looked but a poor fule tew her, ye know—"

"Wheerfor?" said Ben suddenly and almost sternly.

"Wheerfor? A honest maiden wouldna tell ye that: if she
med a mock o' ye—"

The blacksmith rested his huge hammer on the iron.

"She didna, Ben," he said gently, telling doubtless one of
those falsehoods which here and there are even nobler than
truth. "Don't 'ee ga for ta think it. But I *were* a fule, sure
now, to ga dreamin' that a rosy, buxom, gay-hearted, lissom
young lass like that 'ud iver care to settle quiet-like aside
such a hearthstone as this'n, wi' nothin' to tempt her o' gowd,
o' pleasurin', or o' fineries. Dunna ye think more o't, Ben—
I ony telled ye 'cause I thoct ye should know why i hanna
kem o' Moorside o' late."

"Ye've a rare good heart o' yourn, Ambrose," said Ben,
with all his own heart in his voice; and he stretched out his
hand to his old friend's grasp. The other took it, and wrung
it hard;—and by common consent there was silence between
them on this one subject then and thenceforward.

The smith pursued his work and finished, in what seemed
to me an incredibly brief space, a little dainty shining ring
of metal, light as a bent stalk of spear-grass, on whose circlet
he had cut deftly with a little tool my newly-bestowed name
of Puck.

How could his great massive hands, used to deal such
ponderous blows, shape such a trifling toy as this? I cannot
tell; I only know that a man who has the strength of the lion
very often has also the tender touch of the dove.

I fancy, too, that though he was perhaps unconscious of
it, the generosity moving in his heart made this herculean

blacksmith of the Peak more heedful that he should pleasure
his old friend now than he had ever been at any other time.

They said no more words on the themo of his rejected
love; only as Ben rose to go, with a brief hearty phrase
of thanks for the toy in which the smith had so willingly
humoured his fancy, Ambrose pressed on him the lettuce and
cress. Such vegetables grew far better in the little garden
of the forge, which was sunny and of good soil, than they did
in ours, where the great rose-thorn took all nourishment.

But Ben stayed his arm as he bent to cut them from the
ground.

"Let be, Ambrose," he said firmly, "ye shanna gie o' yer
substance to a lass as dunna knaw the wuth o' yer heart."

And he was resolute to refuse them; it had gone sore with
him that the "little lass" should have dealt a stroke of pain
to an honest soul, and should have withheld a secret from
himself.

Ambrose went with him a little way into the wood, so far
as he could without losing sight of his cottage and forge.

"Dunno ye fash her for't," were his last words as they
parted company under a great oak. "She's sae young and
mirthfu', yer know; she dunna tell th' harm that she dew."

And then he turned away and strode with long strides to
his lonely smithy, where the red light was streaming through
its mass of twilit green, as an owl's eyes glow, at even, through
an ivy bush.

It was passing strange, I thought, that these two grave
strong men should be so gentle over a creature who never
cared how she wounded, mocked, flouted, or harmed either
of them, to please her sport or charm her vanity!

When we reached home, the sun had set; Avice was nowhere to be seen; the house door stood open, and all was
silent about the little place.

All day long the fowls kept it alive with sound and movement; for of all mercurial and fussy things there is nothing
on the face of the earth to equal cocks and hens. They have
such an utterly exaggerated sense too of their own importance;

they make such a clacking and clucking over every egg, such
a scratching and trumpeting over every morsel of treasure-
trove, and such a striding and stamping over every bit of
well-worn ground. On the whole, I think poultry have more
humanity in them than any other race, footed or feathered;
and cocks certainly must have been the first creatures that
ever hit on the great art of advertising. Myself I always
fancy that the souls of this feathered tribe pass into the bodies
of journalists; but this may be a mere baseless association of
kindred ideas in my mind.

The cottage was deserted and silent; the fowls being at
roost. Ben, a little alarmed, strode a few yards 'up the hill
behind his house and shouted his sister's name lustily. Ere
long her voice came faintly down from amongst]the bracken
and firs above.

"I'm a comin'! I'm a comin'!"

And in ten minutes or so she did come, rushing hurriedly
down the tangled slope; her eyes were very excited, and her
face was very flushed, and her dress was in a careless disarray.

"Dinna ye hurry, lass," cried Ben, kindly. "Why, lawk-
a-day!—how mauled and muddled ye look. What's a matter?"

"Naethin'!" said Avice, pettishly, as she reached the bottom in safety, and twisted her disordered dress into some
neater shape. "But that beastly bracken, it dew tear ye so;
an' tha blackberry bushes is all prickles."

"Why was 'ee awa'?" asked Ben, wonderingly. "It's ta
late ta leave tha place by itsell."

"I was ony a gossipen a bit, wi' Nell o' Moor Farm," she
answered sullenly. "'Tain't so lively a life, is this'n, that
'ee may na hae a bit o' a crack wi' a neighbour in tha
haverin."

"Na, 'tis a goodish bit dull, I know," said Ben with a sigh,
content with her explanation, though I knew by the growl
which Trust gave, that he at least did not believe in the truth
of it; and that he smelt some male "gossiper" afar on the
evening air. "But, my lass, I want a word wi' ye—why didna

ye tell me as Ambrose o' tha Forge were wishful to wed wi' ye?"

Avice coloured, perhaps at the simple directness of the question.

"Wheer was odds o' tellin' ye?" she muttered. "If 'ee wanna a gaby, he'd ha' kepit his counsel himsell—"

"But look'ee here, lassie," said Ben very gravely. "Ye might be right or na niver ta till me: I wunna say which; winmin be allus queer ta tackle i' such matters. But theer's one thing ye're no right in—an' that be i' yer makin' gume o' him. Ye're pierced him i' tha quick wi' yer feckless sayins. Ye mayna hae mint harm, my dear; I'm na wishfu' to lay blame ta ye; but ye may be sure o' this, Avice, that tha wench as do mak sport o' a honest man 'ull surely live ta be the sport o' rogues."

A hot dusky anger beamed over Avice's bent face as she heard.

"D'ye think," she muttered in sullen wrath, "d'ye think as how cause Ambrose dunna please me, theer wunna be a braver man than him whin I want ta chuse fra' 'em?"

"I dun' know that," said Ben very gravely. "Ye're a poor wench, my bairn, wi' a' yer bonny looks; an' ye canna tak yer spouse a store o' granddam's siller, and a press fu' o' home-spun linen, as Nell o' Moor Farm 'ull do: an' ye've a' the wimmin's bad word a'ready, my dearie, cause ye're sae well-favoured, an' sae saucy, an' sae slow at your chores an' yer distaff—"

Avice burst into a loud passion of sobs and tears, as her manner was when argument told against her.

"Sae ye'd ha' me wed wi' tha fust lout as ax me, jist ta be rid o' my keep, and ta still tha old mithers' blisterin' tongues," she cried furiously. "Weel! I wunna thin. I'll na ga bury mysell i' that wretched hole o' a smithy for ye na a' tha min o' Peak-side! I wunna! I would na gie one straw ta wed, gif tha brid-groom could na set a gowd ring o' my finger, an' a silken gownd o' my back, an' tak me to Lunnun for my moonin, and spend his siller right and left like a man!

Ambrose!—he'll niver stir out o' this here beast o' a wood a'
his days; I'm as weel wi' ye as wi' him."

Ben stood with his head a little drooped upon his breast;
pale under his sunny warm bronze, and hurt exceedingly by
the bitter ingratitude of the raging, selfish, unfeeling words.
Yet they did not break down the gentle patience of his temper;
she was "the mither's bairn," and so sacred to him.

"Ye're verra wrong; and ye know't, my lass," he said
slowly and very gravely; "ye know weel that tha day as 'ud
tak 'ee ta anither home 'ud be tha sairest day i' a' my reckon-
in'; and ye know, tew, that whin I wish ye to be wife t' Ambrose, 'tis 'cause he's good, core through, an' 'ud hev care o'
ye a' yer days if tha stones fa' upo' me, as they may surely
dew ony hour o' my work i' tha quarry. Ye're fractious and
fancifu', and ye quarrel, as childer will, wi' a' tha best friends
ye hae gotten. Weel—ye wunna see yer fault now! Ye're a
woman. But ony tak heed, Avice, that the day dew niver
dawn whin, wi' yer beauty, an' yer fancies, an' yer fearfu'
craze for riches, ye dunna wish, an' wish in vain, lassie, that
ye'd stayed safe i' my heart an' i' Ambrose's!"

And then, as though he dared not trust himself to say
more, lest his voice should break down into a woman's weakness, Ben passed slowly within, across his threshold, with the
saddest shadow on his honest face that I had ever seen there.

Their evening meal was eaten in total silence that night;
but there was a deeper and a sweeter tone than ever in the
murmured words of thanksgiving and prayer with which he
commended his little household to the care of God.

CHAPTER VI.

The Sabbath-breaker.

BEN was infinitely kind to me. When I got a little older,
as the primroses were supplanted by the hyacinths, he used
to take me with him to the quarry, Trust carrying me in his
mouth if I tired. I think they both knew that, when they
were absent, Avice and the cat were too much for me.

, I grew to feel a great deal of respect and affection for Ben in those days by the quarry. To look at him he was like any other labouring man, strong, rough, with his back a little bent, and his hands all over muscle from the daily use of the weighty pickaxe. He was very quiet too, and some of his fellows called him stupid. But he was not that; he had a quaint gentle wisdom of his own, though he was utterly un-lettered, and so simple in trustfulness that a child could easily deceive him.

Trust was right, as, looking back on that time, I know now, in thinking that Ben had some touch in him of the poet. Not of the poet's utterance surely; I do not think he could have strung a line of words together to save his existence; but of the poet's temperament, of the poet's feeling.

He would spend long moments gazing into a little tuft of wood-anemones or of bluebells, with just the same look that your Burns must have had when he gazed at the "wee crim-son-tippit flower." If a bird were wounded by some scattered stone that flew from under his hammer, he took it up and tended it with the same thought in his face that your Cole-ridge must have felt when he wrote.

His fellow-workmen always complained that Ben in his leisure went mooning about; but his mooning afforded him more pleasure than their ale and pitch-and-toss lent to them. He would go wandering about in the wood or on the moor-land whenever he had any spare time, with no knowledge whatsoever, but with a curious comprehension and sympathy in him for all living things that were; from the tiniest spray of the moss under his feet, to the large-eyed oxen that came to rub against his shoulders in homely caress.

Sunday was a well-beloved day with Ben; there was no church within four miles, and he did not care to go to it. Now and then its pastor found his way to the cottage, and rated Ben as a heathen.

"M'appen I be, sir," Ben would say sorrowfully, not sure in his mind whether he were wicked or not.

"I canna go to the church," he said once when much
goaded on the subject. "Look'ee, they's allus a readin' o'
cusses, and damnin, and hell fire, and the like; and I canna
stomach it. What for shall they go and say as all the poor
old wimmin i' tha parish is gone to the deil 'cause they picks
up a stick or tew i' hedge, or likes to mumble a charm or tew
o'er their churnin'? Them old wimmen bo rare an' good i'
ither things. When I broke my ankle three year agone, old
Dame Stuckley kem o'er, i' tha hail and the snaw, a matter
of five milo and morc, and she turned o' eighty,; and she
nursed me, and tidied the place, and did all as was wanted to
be done 'cause Avice was away, waking somewheres; and
she'd never let me gic her aught for it. And I heard ta Passon tell her as she were sold to hell, 'cause the old soul have
a bit of belief like in witch-stones, and allus sets one aside
her spinnen'-jenny so that the thrid shanna knot nor break.
Ta Passon he said as how God cud mak tha thrid run smooth,
or knot it, just as He chose, and 'twas wicked to think she
could cross His will; and tha old dame, she said, 'Weel, sir,
I dinna b'lieve tha Almighty would ever spite a poor old crittur like me, don't 'ce think it. But if we're no to help our-
sells i' this world, what for have He gied us the trouble o'
tha thrid to spin? And why no han't He made tha shirts and
tha sheets an' tha hose grow theersells?' And ta Passon
niver answered her that, be only said she was fractious and
blas-*phe*-mous. Now she warn't, she spoke i' all innocence,
and she mint what she said—she mint it. Passons niver can
answer ye plain, right-down natural questions like this'n, and
that's why I wuona ga ta tha church."

He did not go; Avice did, arrayed in all her glory of ear-
rings and of beads, journeying thither in the donkey-cart of
their only near neighbour. An old woman, who drove about
the country with ferns and greenery of all kinds, and took
her poor worn beast eight miles on its only day of rest, for
the very good and notable reason that "ta Passon were a rare
un for ferns and tha like; and if I warna to be seed i' my
seat o' Sabbath day, he'd niver buy no more on me. It's

main and particular is ta Passou; he cauna abide Sabbath-breakers."

And she always beat the tired ass violently and often, that she might reach the church whilst yet the chimes were ringing. She was a woman who had taken heed to the "passon's" counsel.

Meanwhile the Sabbath-breaker spent his Sabbath mornings out of doors, amongst the things of which he was fondest —the birds and the beasts, and the trees and the heather.

It was in a very unlearned, desultory, dreamy fashion, of course, that he studied them: all the divinity that lies in books was hidden from poor Ben; but he did study them in his own way, and he found many curious things of their lives, and their natures, and their habits, which, if he had only known how to tell his discoveries again, might have ranked him with Audubon and Stanley.

"I just am fond o' tha things, ye see, and so they lets me know about 'em," he would say; unconscious that he was the exponent of the great doctrine of sympathy.

The teal in the brake-hidden ponds; the hen-harrier amongst the sedges; the timid hare under the ferns; the pretty redstart on the boughs; the small dark stoat wading amongst the huge leaves of the burdock; the corn-crake in the scarce patches of wheat that grew, here and there, on the bleak brown moors; the tiny chiffchaff flitting under the gorze all golden with legend-loved bloom; the field-mouse sitting, squirrel-like, by her little home in the ground, where the sweet shady plumes of the meadow-sweet hid her in safety from the eyes of the kite: all these were his friends and familiars; and he would wander amongst them all through the hours of the quiet day, when not even the far-off sounds of the quarry, or of the husbandmen above on the moor farms, broke the sweet, restful, morning silence.

Avice, sitting at church, glancing under her arching brows at the youths beside her, arrayed in her, beads and her earrings, and gazing with envious eyes at the manor pew, where

the great folks were sequestered, received many praises from
the pastor for her assiduity in attending the service.

Ben he called hard names, of which a heathen was not the
least.

Now Avice on her homeward-way beat the donkey with
fury and might, because her soul was sore to think of the
great ladies up in the Squire's red-canopied pew. But Ben,
going to the fern-seller's cottage to meet his sister, went first
to the stable and shook down a fresh bed of bracken, and
filled a pail with water from the spring, and threw a great
arm-load of sweet grasses and juicy thistles into the rusty
rack.

Which of the two would the poor tired beast—if he could
have given an opinion*—have thought the most faithful fol-
lower of the teaching of One who walked in the fields on the
Sabbath day, and rode on an ass to Jerusalem?

These Sundays with Ben were my greatest delight. To
scamper over the boundless moorland; to roll in the short
scented thyme; to watch with wondering eyes the squirrels
leap from branch to branch; then, lying tired, to sleep and
dream, and wake in the pleasant drowsy sunlight: all this
made a paradise of that old silent pinewood to me, and, in a
sense too, to my master himself.

His eyes used to have a curiously-contented look, half
brightness, half sadness, but great contentment for all that, as
he strode through the yielding spear-grass, or lay at length
under the shade of the branches.

He did not speak often; but now and then he did, to Trust
or to me, or to the cushat in the boughs, or to the rabbit beneath the brushwood, or to some other timid moving thing.
And at such times his voice was so gentle, so pitiful, so serious,
that it had a sound in it, to my fancy, like that of the evening
bells when they rung faintly in from the distance across the
broad moors.

* I find our friend Puck is not much more liberal after all than the rest
of creation; and conceives that no race save his own possesses any intelligence!—ED.

Whatever good I have kept in me—and in the world it is very hard to keep any—I owe it to Ben on those still Sunday mornings, in those deep old quiet green woods.

There was one spot I specially loved: it was a dell formed by huge boulders of granite and gritstone fallen one on another; grown all over by ferns and by moss, and by all manner of foliage; and always full of shade even in the hottest. noontide.

There Ben would lie for hours, looking up at the blue dreamful sky, or at the birds moving in the thick leafage.

"And to think," he murmured once, "as the same Hand as shattered down tha mighty stones here, till they lays crushed and o'ergrowed wi' the grasses, yit fashioned them wee blue wing-feathers of tha atomy of a tomtit i' his nest theer. It is wonderfu'! Shanna we niver know how't was done? niver see the sun a bit nearer? Lord's sake! I canna but wish that He'd ha thoct of some ither way o' food for keepin' the varsal world fu' o' his critturs, than tha way o' 'em murderin' one anither, preying on one anither, from tha man on tha ox tew tha sparrow on tha worm. It don't seem right like; as how Him who'd tha power o' makin' that sun move i' tha heavens, shouldna' ha bin able to hit a' some better means for keepin' tha life He giv i' us wi'out pittin' tha lusts in our souls to kill tha weakest things aside o' us. It's uncommon queer—an' sad tew, as ta seem—that tha should na be ony way o' livin' save by dith."

And so the dim, wise, tender, untutored mind perplexed itself in sorrowful pondering; and Ben, who could scarce tell one letter from another, puzzled over problems that the sages and the scholars of the world cannot solve.

If Ben had had education, I think he would have been a man of whom the world would have heard somewhat; for he had all the strange mingling of acuteness and childlikeness, of fine perception and foolish faithfulness, that are so often characteristic of genius. As it was, never having even learned to read, and having from the seventh year of his age been obliged to get up in the gray of the mornings, and go forth to hard, incessant, bodily labour that killed the brain in him, as it were—so that when he returned at night he had no sense to do more than creep up to his truckle-bed and sleep the heavy dreamless sleep of over-toil and of over-fatigue—he had never had any culture of the powers within him. None could tell what ever they might, under another existence, have proved; and it was only through the fairness of nature around him, and the insight he had by instinct into its beauties and mysteries, that he kept alive at all those tender thoughts which, so sweet to the scholar, or the artist, or the noble, are perhaps only full of a dim bewildered pain to the poor man in whom they exist.

I did not discern all this myself, of course; but Trust did, and through Trust I came to see it.

Ben Dare's love for his sister was wonderful; he seemed to see none of her faults, save that ever-craving of gold, of which now and then he so gently warned her. But even his perception of this blemish in her never brought the fact, or the suspicion thereof, to his mind that she had indeed taken his coins from under the apple-tree. No vague fancy of the truth ever occurred to him; he trusted Avice with all his heart and soul, and though many times one could observe that she was an anxiety and a disappointment to him, and that her sullen, ungrateful words not seldom wounded him sorely, he never spoke a harsh phrase to her, and only thought her guilty of "pettishness" such as often besets a spoilt child.

She was not contented, he knew; but then, as he was wont to say if he spoke to any fellow-workman on the matter, "'tis ony tha gaiety-like o' girlhood, look you; they're often like that i' their fust years. 'T 'ill wear off sure-ly wi' time; and m'appen she'll get wed, you know—she's sae pretty—and thin wi' tha childer com', an' that, a nursin' 'em and a pratin' tew 'em, an' a tidyin' o' 'em, she'll forgit a' these little maggits o' fancies an' fineries, and sittle down good an' quiet; I'm sure o' it."

But he was not quite sure in his own heart; and he was disquieted oftentimes for Avice; and took blame to himself because he did not make the house "alive" enough to amuse a young girl; and worked extra hours, early and late, that he might earn more money to replace that stolen from him, and give her some gift or some treat with it—some fairing, some daintier food, or some new bit of apparelling.

"I allays feel, ye know, as if tha mither was a watchin' o' me," he said once to his only friend, after Ambrose of the Forge, a man like himself, in the quarry. "She axed me a' dyin', poor soul, to hae a care o' that little un; and I dew think if anythin' went wrong wi' Avice, 't 'ud vex mither sore, where'er she be,—for tho' they may gae to heav'n, I'll niver b'lieve as they forgits all us down here, or gits hard as stones to what happen till us."

"Maybe no, Ben," retorted his brother-in-labour poking his hands ruefully among his tumbled yellow hair, all white with the powder of the shattered limestone. "I often wonders as how them as is a singin' wi' tha angels—as they *says* they be—can sing i' tune an' time like, whin they knows all as is a happenin' to their friends and their childer below. I suppose they dinna fash theirselves about it; but 'ee hev to git main an' hard like, afore 'ee can be a angel."

Thereon he finished his noonday bit of bacon and bread, and sent his pickaxe with ringing strokes into the stone: he lived on the other side of the wood, three miles nearer the village church, at which he was a leader in the quire.

"I s'uld niver do for a angel," he muttered, as he lifted the axe. "Why—t'other Sunday when my old tirrier, Bee, as you'll well mind un, died o' that lump i' her throat o' Sunday mornin', I couldna git my voice at all for thinkin' o' tha good old crittur; and I had to gie o'er afore the 'Glory be,' and go outside aneath tha yew, and I was a cryin' like a child there—'cause t' old Bee was stiff an' cold. If you'd seen her look, Ben—her look at me till tha verra last!"

Ben was too much a pagan to rebuke his friend; or to insist that the "Glory be" should have been too solemn and awful in its nature for any thought of the dead terrier to have intruded on it, and spoilt the mellow notes of its best bass singer.

In this simple, healthful, open-air life I throve apace, and became exceedingly beautiful and graceful, as I could tell by looking at myself in the clear mirror of the bright running water. If my forefathers and brethren had all died at the Hall, I can only imagine that their lamentable decease must have been caused by velvet cushions and meat-surfeitings. I have often witnessed the melancholy results of epicureanism on members of my noble race.

I throve certainly, and grew to my full size; which never exceeded that of a small rabbit; nor ought indeed to have exceeded it, for the virtue and worth of my people lie in their diminutiveness, as do those of Elzevirs and of Parliamentary consciences.

Even old Dick, the pedlar, who "could na abide dogs," observed me when he came again in Ben's absence one day in the summer; and remarked that I was "a rare nice un surely, an' wurth a sight o' siller," he guessed. Ever after that unhappy speech, Avice regarded me with more favour, but with a glance excessively like to that with which a hawk surveys a lark.

Once she asked her brother,

"Wunna ye niver sell ta pup, Ben? 'Tis pretty, and sae glossy an' white, I believe ye'd get a pund for't, an' 'twere well chaffered for—"

Ben glanced at her with a grave look in his eyes, under which she was silent and restless.

"I shall niver sell ta pup, lass," he said. "I dinna mak a thing fond o' me, and rear it wi' trouble, jist to barter it awa' to strangers, who might tormint it for aught I might tell."

Avice said no more; she knew that there were things on which her gentle and patient brother was inflexible, and even obstinate, however yielding he might be usually to her varied caprices.

I myself heard his decision with infinite gladness, for I

knew nothing then of the great world, and I loved the pine-wood and the moor. I had my liberty, I had kindness, and I had sunshine; a young thing would be very envious indeed that asked, or desired, more.

So the whole, long, golden summer passed, the drowsy bees humming over the countless flowers; the white and rose heaths covering the turf with a maze of soft colour; the lime-stone rock flushing under the red glowing rays of the sunsets; the water-birds floating all day long in the amber light over the beds of the waving sword-reeds; the trout darting by in the clear shallow water, and hiding their pretty bright backs under stones.

The summer was delightful to me; and to Ben it had a dim divine charm, that made the mere sense of living sweet to him, despite all his toil.

Even Avice loved the "summer-time," as your German singers call it fondly; it broke the monotony of her life; it brought stray wanderers over the moors; it sent an artist or two in to the heart of this old dusky fragrant wood; it was the season of harvest homes, and of several wakes in the villages that lay nearest. And Avice, although so idle with her "chores" (*i. e.* housework), and so indifferent to exertion, would walk ten miles any day on the chance of a dance at night, and a supper in some little outlying farm, or some village alehouse where, Ben not being by, she wore her "dimonds," and eclipsed every girl who might foot it there. Whenever she returned from one of these pleasurings she was trebly sullen, and ill at ease always afterwards. But we were the sufferers from that, not she; and so the consideration of the "hard stone in the sweet date" no more deterred her from seizing and devouring her date, than it deterred her sex in the early days of the East.

Ben used now and then to offer some gentle remonstrance against this absolute devotion to gaiety, when its god was worshipped under the questionable roofs of pot-houses; but Avice always made out that she was going with some good old dame whose presence would have sanctioned the very

revels of Bacchus or of Priapus themselves, and he had not
the heart to restrain her from the few enjoyments that broke
the monotony of her years.

A well-dressing, a wake, a dance, a wedding feast, were
such delight to "the lass" he reckoned; it would have been
"unked" to have begrudged her those little mirthful frivolities of a girl's earliest youth. To go with her himself was
impossible; he had to be at his labour by sunrise, and did not
leave it till sunset, whether he were at the quarry, or, when
stone work was slack, at the farms. He could only trust her;
and he did trust her, with that entire faith which all loyal
natures give until—they are paid with the coin of deceit.

"I fear as how the wench is a goin' wrong," said the man
who had lamented the loss of Bee once, at the quarry, to his
wife when she brought him the noonday "bit and sup."
"She's allays a junkettin' somewheres,—or if she bean't
junkettin' she's a mopin'; which is m'appen worser of the tew.
And they do say as how she's a gay 'un; and as how young
Isaac up a tha flour mill and she be arter no good. But I
doubt'n of fashen Ben about it. I might dew more harm na
good?"

"Dinna ye meddle, Tam," said his wife, who was a shrewd
woman. "It's niver no good a threshin' other folks' corn; ye
allays gits the flail agin i' yer own eye somehow."

"Mebbe," said her lord, "I would na mind gettin' hit if I
saved ta corn by threshin' it; but I dinna see as how I suld
rightly. The lass ud say na, and Isaac ud say na, o' course,
and Ben ud niver change a word wi' me agin."

So not even Friendship dared to tear the band off Ben's
eyes.

Friendship, when it is not a bully, is very commonly a
coward.

When the summer had passed, and it was the first warm
mellow touch of autumn that flushed the leaves, and made the
waters flow faster, and shook the brown cones off the fir-
trees, one of Avice's beloved days of junketting came round
with unusual honours.

It was "wake-week" at a little town some twelve miles away, and in addition to the wakes' singing and dancing and feasting, there were a fair and a circus and various other wonders. So at least old Dick o' tha Wynnats, making his quarterly visit with Michaelmas, informed her with much unction and imaginative description in reward for the money she laid out with him—three whole shillings veritably her own from her poultry-yard; the hens being the only things of which she took any real care, because they brought her in some silver with the outlay of which Ben never interfered.

Ben dearly liked a smoke of his pipe, out-of-doors in the still twilight in summer, or by his hearth in the winter. But of late he had not smoked at all, because it "pit wings to the siller, my lass," as he told her; because, as Trust told me, he was trying hard to make up by Michaelmas that sovereign's worth which the thief's appropriation had prevented his possessing at Midsummer.

"It's all in a hole in the timber under his bed," said Trust; "he don't put faith in the apple-tree money-box any more. And even she does not know of this, or it would not be long quiet in his old stocking in that wood cranny."

For whichever purpose it was, however, that he saved his tobacco money, he went without his one enjoyment all through the soft hot summer. Avice knew it, and saw him cast now and then a wistful glance at the unfilled pipe. There was abundance of tobacco in old Dick's pouch; but she did not purchase three-penny worth of it out of her egg-money. She only bought some yards of bright scarlet ribbon, some yards of common lace, some mock amber beads for her throat, and a very small jaunty straw hat.

"Ye'll come ower, sure?" pressed old Dick. "Why, lawk a mercy, 't'ill be sich a sight as hanna be seed i' the country sin th' old King o' the Peak wint to glory hunderds of years agone. There is a lot o' play-actors a comin'—and ye niver seed a play?"

"Nay!" assented Avice with a sigh, "I niver did; what does they dew?"

"Lord sake, my dearie, I could na tell 'ee," said Dick, with much solemnity. "It's all lyin'—all lyin', iviry bit,—most butiful! There's fallers a cryin' their hearts out as was laughin' fit to kill theirsells a minit afore. There's kings wi' crowns o' gowd on as was jist common men, wi' pipes i' their mouths, tew seconds agone. There's ugly trapeezin' mawthers o' gals, as one would na ha' picked out o' street, all smilin' and rosy, and jew'lled and lovely-like, wi' the people a clappin' an' a cheerin' on 'em like mad. 'Tis all lyin', ye knaw; theer's tha beauty on it; and tha folks they goes and take on so as niver was, and b'lieve it like Scriptur they do. Why, I've seed un a kickin' a woman as laid on doorstep i' tha open street (a' least the constable he got a kickin' o' her, and tha crittur moaned, and tha folk about laughed at it as a rare good joke; she'd a been clemmed by the way, she could na get a bit o' bread nohow); weel! and I seed 'em that self-same night, tha self-same folks i' tha playhouse, a cryin' and a clamourin', and a rockin' theer-sells to an' fro wi' grief a'cause a queen on the stage had pisoned herself out o' rage and jealousy. O, tha lyin's uncommon good, 'tis sure to move 'em a deal more'n ony tha fac' itsell."

Avice listened intently.

"But 'ee sed," she began eagerly, "as how ugly mawthers were took i' tha play and med beautiful. Weel-favoured wimmin thim must be—must be—"

"Dazzlin' like tha sun, my wench!" said Dick emphatically. "O' course tha beauties allus looks tha best. Lawk-a-deary me, why if a pretty gell git o' tha stage, she'll go wed a duke afore Christmas!"

"But how does 'ee git theer?" asked Avice, with panting breast.

Dick looked very thoughtful, but he winked his eye with dull unction.

"Eh, ma dear, I dun' know. I is na a pretty gell. But I think as how if I was un I'd jist go wheer a playhouse were; and I'd walk in and I'd ax to see the gintleman as kips it; and I'd show him ma bonny face and ma bonny fute, and a' tha gowd o' ma hair, and I would na doubt much as he'd pit me on tha boords."

Avice listened breathlessly.

"A'out money?" she asked.

"Well," said Dick, "there *is* some as pays money to git theer, I know; but a handsome wench—she ha' got her siller i' her eyes and her lips. If I were ye, Avice, I'd hev a try, that I 'ud, i' tha wake-week. He could na but say ye nay."

She listened thirstily, and with longing, wondering gaze.

"But I is na bright?" she said, sullenly. "Clever, ye knaw—I canna-read but a bit or tew."

Dick snapped his fingers.

"Wimmen as good-lookin' as ye, lassie, need na larn theer A B C! But m'appen ye would na like to leave Isaac," he added slily. "He's a strappin' lad, sure-ly."

"I'd leave *him* this minnit!" she said savagely, twisting to and fro her yards of new scarlet ribbon.

"Ye'r wispin' tha ribbon, ma dear," said Dick calmly; then he bent towards her and whispered in her ear: "Ben dinna know o't?"

She coloured scarlet as her ribbons over her face and bosom, as she murmured back a faint negative.

"Thin, my wench, git awa' soon, ta playhouse o' somewheres if ye're wise," muttered Dick, still in her ear, with a chuckle and a grin. Avice, still with the hot flush on her face and tingeing still her swelling breast, shook him off and went within. The old man, still chuckling to himself, climbed slowly up the hill to the Moorside.

"She'll go ta playhouse," I heard him mutter. "And tha dukes will rin mad ower Isaac's cast-off! Lawk-a-day! the lords' light-o'-loves is allus a honest man's leavin's!"

CHAPTER VII.

His First Betrayal.

It was autumn-time; and work being slack at the quarry, Ben went "a ploughin'," to the various farmsteads lying around;—little clusters of white or gray buildings, with roofs of thatch or red tile, that broke here and there the dark blue of the distant pine woods, the purple of the hills, or the green of the woods and meadows.

Mounting the slope behind our cottage to its highest point, where it became moorland, and shelved down again on the other side, you could see for thirty miles about on every side, and many of these little homesteads caught your sight, nestled in the dip of a valley, caught in the cleft of a rock, or perched on the brow of a hill. Some few of these were far too distant to allow him to go and come to them in the day, and he slept where his work chanced to be. At such times I missed him greatly; and Trust sat with a grave anxious countenance on the doorsill, every now and then awaking the echoes with a short woe-begone howl.

He was going for six days' agricultural work to a farm near Ashford-in-the-Water on the same week that the "wakes," so strongly eulogised by the pedlar, were to take place; and Avice, on the Sunday night before his departure, pleaded hard with him for permission to go thither for the great day of all. Old Dame Smedly, the fern-seller, was going, she urged, and would take her.

"It's tew far for tha donkey to kem and go 'i twelve hours, my lass," he objected, "and I dunna like for ye to sleep fra' hame. Least o' all, tew, i' that town where I dunna knaw a soul."

"But Dame Smedly dew, Ben," persisted his sister. "She hev a half-cousin, an unco' decent man, as own a Public theer; and we culd sleep i' his house tha night, and thin back agen wi' marn. Ye knaw ye've axed her to be wi' me here whiles ye're on tha tramp."

"I'm no' goin' on tramp, lass," said Ben, a trifle annoyed. "I'm a goin' tew Ashford i' tha Water; ye mind it right on well. A Public bean't tha sort o' place for ye, my dearie; there's allus a lot of men a' skittles, and bad wimmin a trolloping about."

"It's a very 'spectable house, Ben!" moaned Avice. "And I think it shame to cast foul words agin the old dame's folks, as is a main deal better off than us aren't."

"I dinna cast no words at 'em," said Ben patiently. "I ony ees, as I allays ees, that a Public ain't a place for sich a wench as yew."

"It's tha ony roof I can sleep under, Ben!—and to lose this wakin' will kill me, it will! There's a fair, and merry-go-rounds, and play-actin', and conjurin' and lots o' dancin'; —an' I didna think ye'd be so cruel as to do me out o't! Whin I sees nothin' in this lonely hole fra one year's end to t'other!"

And Avice burst into tears; using the great weapon of her sex without stint or scruple.

Of course Ben gave in, and let her have her way; the more quickly, though not the more readily, because he knew well that if he did not let her have it, she would take it,—the moment his back was turned.

"Gie me a kiss, my lass," he said sadly, when the storm had passed, and she consented to smile through her tears. "Mebbe ye wunna be up afore I'm off to-morro'."

She kissed him willingly; with pretty caressing ways and words.

Surely Judas must have been a woman—disguised?

With the first gray streak of the morning, he went on his way, over the hills to the Wye-watered dales, where his labour lay, among the golden-brown woods of the autumn.

He signed Trust gently back with his hand, and bid him stay and mind the place; my head he touched lightly and fondly.

"Good-bye, little un," he murmured kindly; "I'll soon be wi' ye agin."

Then he went; through the gray, damp, vaporous air, that was like clouds of steam over all the hills, and whitened as snow all the valleys. There had been no one up to set his breakfast, or to bid him God speed.

As he drew the door after him, and left us alone in the feeble, sickly light of the solitary rush-candle by which he had groped his way to the poor meal he had eaten, Trust threw up his head and gave his long wailing agonised howl.

"That won't bring him back?" I hazarded, for the noise made me feel so miserable.

"I know that!" said Trust sharply. "Howling won't bring a dead sheep to life, but many are the dead sheep I have howled over; where they lay stiff and frozen, down in a snow-drift, poor fools. Though we can't help things, we grieve for them. If you never do that when you are grown up, you will be as hard as a stone—or a woman!"

After which answer, he recommenced his lamentations, with much seeming relief to himself; until Avice opened her door, and called to him to be quiet, or "she'd bang his head off his shoulders."

His reply to this was another howl, only louder, shriller, and more prolonged than ever. She sent a piece of heavy wood flying at him, down the stairs.

Trust watched it coming, got out of its way, and with much contentment saw it shiver the little angle of looking-glass on the wall. Then, satisfied with his vengeance, he composed himself into a ball, and was silent.

Trust and I had a bad life for the next three days with Avice, and the old woman, Smedly; we should have had a worse, only that they were fearful of him when he growled, and this he did, very nearly unceasingly, from morning till night.

On the third day, the husbandman on the Moor Farm borrowed Trust to help him bring in some sheep from a distant part of the moor on which they had been turned out for the late summer graze, and I saw my only friend leave me, with a sinking at my heart—a foreboding of what ill I could not tell.

The fourth morning was that on which Avice and the dame were going to the wakes; and the donkey-cart was at the door by six o'clock of the dawn.

I had understood that "Nell o' the Moor Farm" had promised to look after me, in recompense for the loan of Trust at the sheep-fetching. So I was amazed and frightened when Avice—wondrous to behold in the diamonds, and the lace, and a very bright blue print dress, and the morsel of a hat, all aglow with the scarlet ribbons— jammed me into one of those quaint brown willow-baskets, peculiar to that district, shut the lid with only a peep-hole for air, and set me up on the cart with her bundles and the old woman's red cloak.

I moaned, I whined, I yelped, I made all the uproar I knew how; but it was of no avail; they did not heed me; the cart went jogging on its way.

Through the chinks of the basket I looked at the little cottage, like a robin's-nest in a ivy bush, with the white morning mists hovering above it on the great hill slope, and the bright brown brook running by its door.

Alas! I never saw it again.

The road which the cart took was not up the hill and across the moors; it penetrated the whole width of the wood, and then went through a shallow "sough"* of water, which was in winter too swollen to allow of any thoroughfare that way; and then passed over the brow of a steep stony slope, and so got at last into a high road, called, like a score of others in the country, the Derby road.

My heart died utterly, as we were dragged this weary length, in a progress only interrupted by the dead pauses of the donkey, and the loud blows rained upon his back. I thought of Trust, running, leaping, barking, so joyously, so excitedly, so full of eagerness and of importance, on the far-away purple moor bringing home the sheep—if only he had known!

* A small lagoon, such as is called in Norfolk a "broad."

For I had no sort of doubt or hope left in me; I knew that she was going to sell "tha pup," as well as though I had heard her proclaim aloud her wicked intent.

The journey seemed endless to me; we jogged at last into a little clean, old-fashioned, stone-built town, shady with many trees, and with a noble ancient church in the centre of its market-place. I should think it was usually as quiet as its own grave-yard; but now in wake week it was thronged with men and women and children from all the outlying villages. Its church bells were ringing merrily and madly; its market-place was thronged with booths, and shows, and sports, and flags; and outside a wooden building, on a platform, there were the play-actors of the pedlar's legend, strutting to and fro in all the glory of gold, and silver, and velvet robes, and waving plumes, while one gorgeous creature in scarlet and amber blew his trumpet loudly, and proclaimed the performance of the night.

"Lawk a mussy, look!" I heard Avice cry out; "O, ain't it beautiful? What I 'ud give to ony be that girl wi' the short pink skirt, and the silver shoon, and that crown upo' her head!"

I could have told her that she had looked a thousand times prettier herself, washing in the burn, with her linen kirtle tucked up to her knees, and her white arms and bosom coming forth from the brown leathern bodice like white moss roses out of russet autumn leaves.

But if I could have spoken, what use would it have been to have told such a truth as that to a woman? With all their egregious vanity—voracious of flattery as a fish of food—they are always distrustful of themselves when arrayed in the garment of simplicity.

At another time I should have thought the market-place a gay scene enough, in its way, with its colour, movement, noise, and mirth; and that rich blue sky of the dying summer over all the quaint peaked roofs.

As it was, I was wretched.

We stopped at a dirty tumble-down little ale-house, which

a gaudy sign proclaimed as the Miners' Joy; there were lead
mines the other side of the town in the heart of a luxuriant
woodland, once a royal chase. Here Avice and her companion
were noisily welcomed; and she, for that matter, embraced
by a knot of men before the "Public's" door, of whom one
was her host.

She laughed a little with them; drank a draught of spiced
ale, then took me up-stairs in my basket to her room. When
she had put the finishing touches of finery to herself, she went
out of the attic with a loud slam to the rickety door, and left
me to my meditations, which were none of the brightest.

It was now near the hour of sunset.

Through the thin wattled walls of the "Public," and
through the open lattice, I could hear the various voices—now
of a man and a woman who seemed husband and wife, and
were in the adjoining garret—now of the persons gathered
drinking in the wide thatched porch below.

"Thar go the wench," said one of the former, the wife I
think by her voice, by which I suppose Avice was meant.
"She hev trim limbs o' hern, she hev—kiver ground like a
Polly-wash-the-dish-up."*

"Esau bean't a losin' time," said the man, with a grin in
his voice. "'Theer's his arm about her a'ready."

"She's a willin' un," sighed his wife sadly. "She dunno
let grass grow a'neath her shoon i' courtin."

"She's abuve Esau, tew," said the husband. "She axed
jist now how many dukes theer was i' England—"

"What did tell her?"

"Sed as theer warn'a but one. An' theer is na. Ony our
duke, old woman."

"No, for sure. But what could gell want wi' dukes?"

"She's franzy wi' her bit o' oat-cake; an' mad for a plum
un," answered the other allegorically. "It's thim chip news-
sheets as dew mischief ta gells and lads; makin' 'em quar'l wi'
their lot, and git sae cock-a-whoop an' fulish as theer's nae
standiu 'em."

* A water-wagtail.

"And that's trew. But un mun knaw how world wags?"

"Why mun ye?" grumbled the man. "'Taint naught t'ye.
Ye mind yer kittle biles, and yir hins lay, an yer cabbage
dunna yet worums, and yer childer dunna tell lies to 'ee—
that's wot ye've gotten ta dew. World dunna want 'ee, 'tis
big enow to take care o' itsell—"

"Sure I'm allus slavin' for childer," said his wife, with
something like a sob.

"Ye lets 'em lie," growled the other. "Littlest un, he
told me a wopper yest'reen. I gie him a rare crack o' pate for
't. Reddin' news-sheets an' pratin' o' world, whiles worums
gits at yer greens, an' lies comes pat ta yer bairns—that's
just screeching at neighbour's chimbley-smoke, an' lettin' yer
ain place burn ta ashes."

Here the conjugal discussion was drowned by the tones of
the men in the porch, who were talking political economies
—after their light.

"Times is bad i' Suffeck?" said one voice with an inquir-
ing accent in it.

"Main bad," concurred another which had not the north-
country speech that is Chaucer-like and full of a curious unconscious poetry, but had instead the whine of East Anglia
that is as like the New England whine as the call of one
chaffinch is like to another. "Six shillin' a week is a'most
all as iver ye git. Theer won't be no corn growed soon, if
pipple starve-like a farmin' as we does."

"Six shillin' a week!" ejaculated the miner. "Women
git as much at mill!"

"Hey?" said the Suffolk man. "And a shillin' or tenpence
every week out o' that for landlord. We niver gits a taste o'
meat, year's end t' year's end. And when flour's riz, it's all
as ye can dew to kip body and soul tegither."

"Where's Suffeck?" asked some other person. "I' Americay?"

"Americay! Ye're a born nat'ral. It's somewheres i' tha
south, ain't it, George?"

"Iss," assented the Suffolk George. "'Tis all butifull and

flat as yor hand theer, none o't broke up into these nasty
mounds o' yourn as is ony made to lame man and beast.   Ye
may walk hunderds o' miles i' Suffeck, and hev it all at smooth
and as nice as a mawther's ap'on wi' the starch in."

"But ye dunna get good wage?" said the miner with practical wisdom.

"We doan't," confessed the East Anglian, "we doan't.
And that theer botherin' machinery as do the threshin,' and
the reapin', and the sawin', and the mowin', hev a ruined us.
See!—in old time, when ground was frost-bit or water-soaked,
the min threshed in-doors, in barns, and kep in work so. But
now the machine, he dew all theer is to dew, and dew it up
so quick.   Theer's a many more min than theer be things to
dew.   In winter-time measter he doan't want half o' us; and
we're just out o' labour; and we fall sick, cos o' naethin' to
eat; and goes tew parish—able-bodied min strong as steers."

"Machine's o' use i' mill-work," suggested one of the
northerners.

"O' use! ay o'coorse 'tis o' use—tew tha measters," growled
the East Anglian. "But if ye warn't needed at yer mill cos
the iron beast was a weavin' and a reelin' and a dewin of it
all, how'd yer feel? Wi' six children, mebbe, biggest ony
seven or eight, a crazin' ye for bread. And ye mayn't send
'em out, cos o' labour-laws, to pick up a halfpenny for theer-
selves; and tha passon be all agin yer, cos ye warn't thrifty
and didn't gev a penny for the forrin blacks out o' the six
shillin' a week? Would yer think iron beast wor o' use thin?
or would yer damn him hard?"

"He speak up well," hallooed one of the miners, with a
thump upon the table.

"I'll speak agin *him* any day," said the Suffolker with
fierce emphasis. "Why, look'ee, I'm better off nor most.
I'd some schoolin' when I was a brat; and I scraped and
scraped till I got a cow, and I can make ends meet a bit, wi'
the butter in summer-time. But there's a swarm of men in
the parish as dunno more'n tha beasts in stye. Dunno their
God; dunno their letters; never heard o' tha Queen; never

put a mossel o' mutton in their mouths—dunno nothin'. Field-work is sickly-like, 'cos o' tha wind and weather; and when yer comes to trampin' six mile out, and six in, and ditchin' or ploughin' all day i' tha wet, it stan' to reason as how tha rheumatic come hot and heavy arter a bit, wi' min and wim-min tew. Farmers, they kip theer greyhounds t' run for cups and that loike; and kill sheep for 'em 'gainst their coursin-meetens; but their min they dew starve mostly; and tha cup-board he's empty and the churchyard he's full. You see the lands is too small and min they're too many. That's wheer it be."

"Gentry take up sa much o't wi' woods for shootin'," grumbled the miner in answer. "If ye was ta till a' the grown' wheer's wood—"

"Nay, nay," objected the Suffolker. "That woan't dew. Woods is health to land; in field-work ye maun' gie an' take, as wi' yer fellows. If ye doan't gie timber elbow-room, yer soil 'll be parchin' wi' dry loike a duck in a bayloft. If ye fell yer wood ivery wheers tha land she'll gape wi' cracks, loike a trollop's gound wi' holes—"

"Thin theer's nowt for't but t'immigrate?"

"To dew wot?"

"To gae beyant seas, ta new countries."

"Never heerd on 'em."

"Lord sake! Why, my brither he's theer—in Australy—and he ses as how tha land's jest bustin' like wi' plenty, an' ye can bae mutton for a farthin' a poun', an' ye can get a fat ewe for sixpence, and ye don't never see naebody chilled, nor clemmed, nor tatter'd."

"Lawk-'a-mussy! Well—'t 'ud come cheaper to Parish to sind us all theer, I'm thinkin', than to kip so many on us all starvin' and rottin' at whoam?"

"They dew send a many."

"Mebbe. Never heard o't in our parts. They s'uld come and spik about it; and shove us a bit and git us off right away: ye know we're rare and like the blow-flowers in pots. We'd stick in pots for iver, a'out blowin' nor naethin'; and jist gie up tha ghost along o' theer bein' no mould, and no room, and our roots a clingin', and a clingin', a' out nought to feed 'em. But pit plant in bigger pot—pot him out o' doors, whether he like 't or not—and he'll git strikin' agin, and blowin' like mad. He will; and so 'ud we. I'd loike to hear more o' these new lands?"

"I'll git Sue to read tha letter to ye if 'ee come o'er to my place," rejoined the Peak miner. "She read rare. She don't hev to spell out not more'n ivery ither word or so. Be 'ee long in these parts?"

"I kem 'scursion. First time I was iver out o' Suffeck. But my aunt she hev done well, a marryin' this Public; and I tho't I'd see her for onst. Ye're main and queer, wi' yer land all muddled like into these up and downs. Ye must ha' rare big moles to throw up sich sky-high mouns?"

This was uttered with no sense of humour, but in a very grave spirit of wonder and of inquiry.

I did not catch the miner's reply, as the men moved within, no doubt to get fresh tobacco and more beer; and instead of their conversation I heard again the grave, grumbling tones of the husband and the more plaintive ones of the wife in the attic near me, whose lower voices had been drowned by the loud arguments of the East Anglian.

"Ben will ha' trouble i' that gell," I heard the voice of the man say. "She's off trapezin about a'ready; crazed-like to gape at ta play-actors."

"Well-a-day! that's ony nat'ral," said the softer female voice, with the tender exclamation that has lingered in those parts since the days of your Shakespeare. "Gells sud bide by hearth, I know that right on well; but when they're young, and hanna na mother like, they gits dazed wi' lookin' i' tha glass, and hearin' tha lads crack o' theer gude looks. And for sure 'tis a bit dullish for Avice, all along o' hersilf i' tha quarry-wood, and she's just a bonny, feckless thing, wi' na mind in her."

"She hev as good a home as ony jade can want," growled the man; "Ben's that douce tew her, and that fearfu' o' crossin' her, that she live, she dew, like a mouse i' a corn-bin. But theer it is—pit mice i' corn-bin, pit 'em i' a barn wheer theer's a score o' coombs i' sack, and a score o' coombs a' lyin' loose,—why, ye know, Jess, as I know, mice they'll niver go eat tha loose corn, they'll jist gnaw holes i' tha sackin', for sheer sake o' thievin' and reivin'.* And wimmen they's just like mice; giv' 'em their pleasure easy to come by, they'll nashen and fritten theirselves till they can run aside and gnaw tha sackin' of some joy as God and men hev forbid to 'em. It's queer—it's awfu' queer. But m'appen tha A'mighty knew Himself what He med tha vermin and tha gells for—it's more nor we dew, I reckon."

And with that sorrowful reflection, sadly uttered, his voice ceased, and his heavy nailed boots clanged slowly down the wooden stairs. I never knew who it was that spoke, but I conclude it must have been some miner, or quarry cutter, or ploughman, who thus addressed his wife; in that utter oblivion that she must have been once a 'gell' herself, which seems a natural result of the bonds of marriage.

I was left alone all the day, evening, and night; and whimpered and sobbed myself to sleep as best I could, with the big autumnal moon glowing through the little leaded lattice, and the shouts of the township's revelry coming faintly on the soft night wind.

It was dawn when Avice Dare returned: full dawn. Her face was deeply flushed; her hair dishevelled; her dress disordered; she laughed vacantly as she moved about, and she threw herself half undressed upon the bed, and slept soundly, without a single movement, several hours through, lying face downward with the air blowing in upon her.

I had once seen a man drunk at the quarry; it seemed to

* I also have heard farmers say this of mice in a barn; but in justice to the maligned rodents I must say that I have had two mice in my rooms for the last six months, which, being well fed, never have touched food not given them, even when left alone for hours. The theft of all animals comes from hunger. I do not believe any of them care to steal for stealing's sake—except perhaps monkeys, to whom theft is charming because it is mischief.—ED.

me that she laughed, and moved, and slept very much as he had done, under the potency of liquor.

Yet when at noon she awoke, and bathed herself in the cold, clear water, and shook out all her tresses, and dressed herself in a white bodice and a scarlet kirtle, she looked so charmingly, thanks to her youth, and her health, and her wonderfully perfect beauty, that I felt as if my suspicion was hateful and full of shame.

She stopped in her attiring once; and leaned her head on her hand; and stared at her face and form in the piece of mirror, which was much larger than her little bit of glass at home.

She seemed to survey herself quite mercilessly, with all her love for herself; and to be taking stock, as it were, of her capital of physical loveliness. The scarlet lips, the glowing brown eyes, the round white arms, the bosom that rose above the edge of the bodice that only rivalled it in whiteness; the tender tints and the soft curves of her limbs—she studied them all with a curious mingling of vain worship, and of mercantile foresight, fused in one.

Then she dressed herself in haste, clasping about her a quantity of fresh tawdry trinkets—new gifts, no doubt, from the fair—and turned her attention to me, whom she seized with a sharp and feverish force; as though I were in some manner the talisman whereby she would summon the magic of Fortune.

It was a lovely morning; through the open window the autumn air blew strong and sweet; the sun shone; the rooks in the high trees cawed; the bells of the churches chimed merrily;—but Avice heeded none of these.

She consigned me afresh to my basket; and as this time I was permitted no peep-hole at all, I could only surmise that I was carried downstairs into the little dirty porch of the house. This porch, with oak settles fixed against it, was a favourite drinking-place of the miners, I believe; and more spiced ale, and toast, and mulled elder wine with crab apples bobbing in it, and possets of various kinds made with honey

and milk, and cloves and apples, and all the old Elizabethan
drinks that are still brewed in the North, were being eagerly
called for, with the sweet circular wake-cake always in vogue
on such occasions.

To all these, Avice, it seemed ,rendered full justice; as the
men kept crying to her, "Well drained, my lass." "Take a
sup o' this." "That's a good un to drink, aren't she?" "Ye
suld kip a public, my wench; ye're jist tha one for't." But
if she drank much she did not tell what was in her basket,
and she went, at length, forth, decorously enough with the
old woman Smedly, into the streets and the market-place.

For myself—I was too terrified to do anything, even to
moan; and the close confinement of the basket made me feel
very faint.

I suppose she met some one by appointment, for she
stopped in a lonely by-street, and a man's voice addressed
her—a small, thin, wiry voice, that I hated.

"Am I right, ma'am? I think I must be; Dick told me
to look for the prettiest lady in all the town."

Avice laughed; a laugh of pleasure, at the coarse stupid
compliment.

"Are ye the gentleman as wants a dog?" she said; "leastways a pup?"

"I am, ma'am. I always want pups; I deal in 'em."

"Well, thin—I hae brought 'ee un. Brither Ben he dunna
know; he'll be mad like:—I'll hev to tell him as how I took
ta pup wi' me, 'cause I feared as how Nell o' Moorside 'ud
forgit to gie it its meals, and i' the press o' market-place I
lost it. I sall hev to tell him some gammon like, surely,—for
he's rare and fond o' ta pup—"

"Ah', I see! But you, ma'am, naturally do not like dogs
about the house?"

"O, I dunna care for that. 'Tis a teasin' little wretch, for
sure; but they dew say as how 'tis a deal o' valew, and I
want tha gowd, as Dick told ye, and so—"

"I see! Allow me—"

"Allow me," meant opening my basket, and taking me

6*

out by the skin of my neck; a barbarous custom too prevalent.

They were standing, quite alone, under an archway that connected a malting-house and a meeting-chapel—a droll metaphor in stone, of the Church leaning on the World.

This part of the town was entirely deserted; the noise and merriment were but dimly heard; no one was near.

He examined me with the most minute and detestable attention, and looked very shrewd and avaricious as he did so. Finally he replaced me in the basket.

"Your price is high, ma'am: very high. I doubt if I shall ever see it back again. The pup is not of the value you suppose: nothing like it, still—as I promised Dick; and as you need the gold; and as the dog is certainly pretty, to say nothing of its mistress's beauty; I will purchase it for what you asked."

"Three pun'," said Avice thirstily.

"Three pounds—including basket?"

"O, ye may have the basket!" said Avice, with feverish haste. "Hand o'er the gowd, theer's a good crittur!"

He counted three sovereigns slowly into her hand; it clutched and closed on them, and without even a word of thanks or farewell, she drew her skirts up about her, and flew off down the street like a lapwing.

The man stood and gazed after her, bewildered at her sudden flight.

"She's a queer one," he muttered. "No good, I fear, for all her handsome face. But the dog's worth twice his money, anyhow."

With that he heaved up my basket, and bore me away to his lodgings.

I was his henceforward.

CHAPTER VIII.

In the Market-place.

It is of no use now, to recount all the misery I suffered.

I can recall it as though it were yesterday; and I cried my very heart out like a baby as I was. The man was not at the first unkind to me, though he struck me some few times sharply with a riding switch when I would not cease from my moaning and sobbing. He was rough too, and hurt me in handling, but he did not starve me. He chained me, indeed, by my light collar to the leg of a chair, and kept me prisoner in his little sitting-room upstairs that looked out on the market-place; but he was out a great deal, and I was left chiefly alone. I might be there but a day, I might be there for a week; I cannot recollect. I only know I was miserable. The first thing that recalled me to consciousness was the sharp sting of a whip across my back. I shrieked with the pain; in Ben's house even Avice had never dared to beat me. The only response to my cry was a sharper blow than the first; and this was repeated till I was literally blind and stupefied, and was quiet because numbed with anguish.

Then evil woke in me under my torments, and I bit and foamed, and flew like a mad thing—ah, how often your "mad dog" is only a dog goaded by torture till he is beside himself, like a soldier delirious from shot-wounds!

The perfection of your scientific training is to make us either cravens or furies: what a fine result!

For this defence of myself, I was thrust in a dark closet, and locked in there for the rest of the day and the night.

Over that time of misery I will pass; I hardly care even now to recall it.

With the next morning my new owner called me out, and gave me some bread-and-milk. He did not beat me this time; I believe he was afraid he might kill me, as I was very delicate, and thus he might never realise his lost three sovereigns.

After I had eaten this, he left me, chaining me again to the leg of a chair under the window, and locked the door of the little parlour upon me.

Once again alone, my grief was unrestrained; so much so that the woman of the house came and hammered at the door and swore at me for a "dratted yelping beast," which only made my cries the louder. As several hours went on, however, and my solitude remained unbroken, I cried myself so hoarse that I was unable to emit any sort of sound at last, and thought I might as well vary my imprisonment by looking out of the casement.

It was a deep old lattice-window, shut; but by jumping on the chair I could see perfectly down into the market-place, and, in spite of all my woe, I derived a certain amusement from watching the varied life and mirth that were to be seen below. There was one little pane open, too, for air; and as the window was low down, like the upper windows of all country dwellings, I both saw and heard with ease.

It was now fully past noon by the height of the sun, and the fun of the wakes was mounting high also—its perihelion of course was not till the dances and the "play-actin'" of the night.

There were numerous tawny-coloured booths filled with cheap toys, and sweetmeats, and spar-ornaments, and wearing-apparel, and all manner of tawdry little fineries. There were the roundabouts, in which men and women and children went gravely circling on wooden horses till they were giddy. There were all sorts of quacks, vending everything from medicines that cured every disease in the pharmacopœia to knives with a hundred blades for twopence.

There were Cheap Jacks screeching themselves deaf over delf-plates from Staffordshire, and earthenware pans, and copper-saucepans, and pewter-pots, and shiny black kettles; all these valuable articles being literally given away, they averred, for a song. But when a lusty ploughman took one of them at their word, and carolling forth a stave off "Gaffer Grey," claimed one of the black kettles for his "missus" as the recompense of his musical performance, the Cheap Jack loudly protested against such literal interpretation of his figurative language, and a very pretty bout with fisticuffs was the result, the innocent kettle ultimately being battered to pieces in the fray.

Such is men's justice; in all their quarrels there is always some poor luckless kettle which, sinless itself, gets the blows from each side!

Besides all these amusements, there were itinerant musicians playing in and out of tune; there were wandering organ-boys with monkeys, who had strayed out of the cities with the ending of summer; there were red-cheeked country lasses, staring open-mouthed at all the wonders, and their sturdy lovers from mine and farm and quarry and marble-works, treating them to all these sights with broad jokes and uproarious laughter. And lastly, there was the crowning glory of the whole—the mimes outside the wooden theatre, who were strutting again to and fro, in all the spangle and silver-lace, and cotton velvet, and pink calico, of their royal adornment. And over all the scene there arose one loud and continuous hum and rage of every noise ever heard under the sun—from braying trumpets, penny whistles, screaming infants, brawling men, shouting vendors, untuneful brass bands, and screeching women's shrill incessant laughter.

For the spiced ales, and the mulled wines, and the sweet possets, were driving a brisk sale; and even at this time of the day the larger half of the crowd, male and female, had already taken far more than was altogether good for it.

I looked everywhere in the tumult of the market-place for the scarlet ribbons of my cruel tyrant and traitress; but Avice was nowhere to be seen.

I recognised Isaac of the flour-mill—a tall, well-favoured, flaxen-headed fellow of twenty-two or so—but she was not with him. I thought he seemed wholly devoted to a pretty little brown modest-looking maiden, whom I thought I had once seen in the wood, and heard of as the blacksmith's sister. Was Avice inside the theatre, I wondered?—had she joined herself to the "play-actors" in pursuit of the peddler's counsel?

The afternoon sped fast, even in my captivity, with all this throng below me to watch, in its coming and going, its ebbing and flowing. The deep warm glow of the late day spread itself over earth and sky, making mellow the grays of the old stone buildings, and tingeing with a richer purple the line of the circling pine-clad hills.

Suddenly—near on sunset—I heard a voice that made my heart leap. It was asking,

"Hev ony o' ye seed my Avice?"

It was the voice of my dear old gentle Ben!

I stretched out as far as ever I could, but my head would not go through the tiny aperture alone left unclosed. I could see him standing almost under my casement, but he could not see me. I yelped, and barked, and screeched, in the longing to attract his attention; but my voice was feeble, and he never heard.

"Hev ony o' ye seed my wench?" he asked again. "She's i' the town, I know, wi' tha owd woman Smedly?"

"I seed Avice somewhere about," said one of the women, rather hurriedly: the others were silent.

Ben looked very happy; he had a little rose in his bosom, and was dressed in his best fustian suit.

"I got ower work quick at ta Ashford Farms," he said, with a ringing and cheerful voice to the woman who had spoken; a poultry-seller by trade, bright-eyed, and with a pleasant elderly face, an old friend of his, and of his mother's before him. "I know'd tha little wench 'ud be here, and I kem ower to gie her a treat like. I've pit by a pund's wuth o' siller as she dunna guess aught about; and she can ha' what she likes wi' it—a gownd, or a shawl, or a lot o' fairins, or jist whativer she fancies. She telled me as how tha public tha dame was to tek her tew was called tha 'Wheatsheaf;' but I canna find 'Wheatsheaf' nohow."

"Theer's no 'Wheatsheaf' i' tha town nowheres," said the poultry-woman, in a very low voice.

"Nowheres?" said Ben, astonished. "For sure thin tha lass is so careless, she'll ha forgat the right name. But, how-e'er sall I find her if I dunna know tha public? I' such a throng as this'n, 'tis like lookin' for a needle i' a bottle o' hay. Ha' ony o' ye seed her? Ye sed ye had."

"We seed her yisternight," muttered a man in the group about him.

"Well! wheer was that, thin? Canna ye say?"

"I' tha porch o' 'Miners' Joy.' "

"Ta 'Miners' Joy?' Is't that the public? Wheer dew it stand? I'll go straight tew it. It'll git tew dusky for tha lass to see to git her fairins, and I hev to gae back wi' tha marn."

The poultry dame laid her hand gently on his arm.

"Dinna gae to 'Miners' Joy,' Ben."

"Why na?" he asked quickly. "Why na?"

None of them spoke. He looked swiftly and fiercely from one to the other.

"What is't ye kip fra me?" he said, in a very low voice, while his fair, ruddy face grew white. "Is tha little lass dead?"

"Na, na, Ben!" cried a score of voices. "She's well enow —trust her, tha minx. It's ony——"

"Ony what? And how dares ye to call her names?"

His mouth was set, his face white as death, his gray sad eyes flashed fire.

The old poultry-woman still kept her firm, pitying hold on his arm.

"Dunna ye tak on, Ben. I'd na say a harsh word o' yer mither's child; but tha lass is no worthy o' a that. She's a bad un!"

Ben flung off her hand with a fierce oath.

"If 'ee was ony a man as sed that! Wheer's my lass? Wheer's Avice? I'll hev tha truth out o' ye, sin I wring a' yer throttles for it!"

They were frightened at his gesture and his tone: they called out as with one voice:

"She sold ta pup tew days agone, Ben; an she's gaed wi' tha gowd she got to Lunnon town; and she's telled tha play-actors she's meanin' to be one o' 'em i' that great city; and ye suldna tak on so; for everybody knowed 'cept yoursell that she's been a gay un iver sin she cud cock her eye at a man. Theer stan' Isaac o' tha corn-mill as was her sweetheart this summer-time through;—ax him—he'll tell ye what a light-o'-love she was; and wi' more'n na him for sure if 'ee ony know'd all."

Ben stood still and rigid, with his face like a dead man's, and his teeth clenched on his lower lip till the blood gushed from it.

Isaac was loitering near.

He flashed his gray eyes over the youth.

"Isaac Cliffe, be this'n tha truth?" he said slowly.

Isaac grinned—a half-sheepish—a half-victorious laugh.

"'Tis trew," he muttered. "And I'd ha' wed her, and med a honest woman o' her, I would, Ben;—ony ye sees she was bad, core through."

The words were scarcely uttered ere Ben had sprung on him and seized him, and flung him up in the air. The lad was strong, and a famous wrestler; he struggled, and fought, and dealt back blow for blow; but he had no force against the violence of passion and of agony.

The people shrieked aloud that they were killing one another, and tried to tear them asunder, and threw themselves on the wrestling arms and heaving forms; and at length by sheer conquest of numbers dragged Ben away off his prey, and held him motionless amongst them, while others who had come to the rescue, hurried the youth, swooning, and bruised, and bleeding from every limb, into the shelter of the nearest ale-house in the market square.

All the hearts of the dense throng were with the dishonoured and forsaken man; they closed around him and craved his pardon, and cried out rough tender words of sympathy and sorrow; while the women, with tears coarsing down their cheeks, left booth, and mart, and show, and came about him and sought to comfort him.

"Dinna take on so," they murmured, "sure tha wench is no wurth it. An' she ha' gone to play-actin' and sin; and ye'll see her na more i' this life; and we knows as ye ha' done a' yer duty by her; and wimmin ha' got tha deil in 'em some-times; and theer's na man strong enow to cope wi' tha deil an' a wench together. Dinna ye tak' on so; ye've amaist killed tha poor lad, as was na so much to blame whin a's been said."

But he heard no word that they spoke. He stood upright, rigid as a stone; gazing straight before him like a bull wounded unto death, but with the power to slay still in him.

Then he threw his arms above his head with one loud cry: "Tha little lass!—tha little lass!"

And he fell forward like one dead; his face striking the stones of the street.

The people closed around him as mourners close around a grave.

They hid him from my sight: I knew no more.

CHAPTER IX.

Jacobs' Church.

I can but dimly recall the nights and days of misery that followed on my betrayal by Avice Dare.

They are all in a blurred mass of blows, and oaths, and dark closets, and starvation, and brutal teaching of antics that were styled pretty tricks, and nothing stands out clearly to me save the one remembrance of how utterly wretched I was.

I think nothing in the world is so intensely unhappy as an unhappy dog. We are of such vivid natures, of such lively imaginations, of such constant affection; and as we can never tell our woes, but are almost sure to receive a cuff or a kick if we only murmur at our weary lot, we are beyond all other creatures miserable.

I wonder now that I did not die;—but if everything died that is full of wretchedness, your world would soon have but a sparse peopling.

If the brutal treatment my purchaser looked on as "training," had long endured, I dare say my young and tender frame would have given way beneath it; my spirit certainly would have been broken. Happily for my safety he soon received an offer of a few guineas for me, in a month's time from his purchase of me, which he immediately accepted. This offer transferred me to a new home, in which, at least, I found peace and repose, although these were accompanied by a rider which too often goes with them—*i. e.* dulness.

It was in a dower-house, amist the flatness and unloveliness of that "fen country," whither the man who had bought me of Avice had taken me when he had sped by night out of the little Derbyshire town, fearful no doubt of Ben's vengeance if he should be discovered. Here I became the property of an old and rich woman, who was the owner of this melancholy though peaceful hermitage.

She was good to me in a general way, though often precise and severe, and I suffered but little whilst with her. But there was nothing there to call my affections into play, and nothing that was of sufficient interest to mark out those years in my remembrance; nothing that could make me forget the loss of my dear friends, Ben and Trust.

No doubt this period was beneficial to me, for they were two years in which I was well fed, well cared for, and taught all those gracious and highly-bred manners which have ever since always distinguished me. They were good years for me, morally and physically, I am well aware; but they were dull ones, nevertheless, and bear to my mind all the haziness and dreariness that your earliest school days commonly wear to yours. They were quite uneventful, as life in the house of an aged, wealthy, and eccentric recluse usually is; and beyond the hours I spent in the trim, high-walled, damp gardens, or in the big, yellow carriage, like a state cabin on wheels, I had absolutely no diversion except listening to the interminable readings with which my old mistress had her hours occupied.

She had been a woman of the world, in her time, I believe, though I know not what trouble had made her now solitary in her dull jointure-house; and she was very liberal in her range of literature. All languages being equally intelligible to us (though we can never comprehend why you have not all one and the same, as we superior animals have), I derived considerable entertainment from hearing the innumerable works, in various tongues, which her companion read aloud to her almost from morning to night.

To my thinking, it seems as dreary work for any person close on her grave to stuff her brains with new knowledge, as for an artist to elaborately fashion a piece of pottery that he knows will be broken on the morrow; but she appeared not to feel it so. Besides, she was very fond of French memoirs, and of all sorts of fiction, on the principle, I fancy, on which an actress, no longer upon the stage, likes to read over the old comedies that she once played in, when flowers were showered at her feet, and all the gay gladness of triumph was around her.

And thus my own mind, as I listened week after week, month after month, to these continuous and versatile readings, became stored with a vast and varied human knowledge. The depth and width of it will, no doubt, astonish you as you peruse my autobiography, though I endeavour to suppress all evidence of my scholarship as much as I can, since I am aware that to ask one's reader, or one's spectator, to think, is the direst offence that either author or actor can ever commit.

Perhaps also, if you find any touch of egotism, as of vanity, in these pages, you will kindly remember that in these early days of my education I heard a great number of religious autobiographies. It is remotely possible that their influence may still colour my style; though I had excellent counter-infusions of all kinds, ranging from Martial to Montespan, and trust that the latter sway is the stronger.

No doubt these two years were salutary for me, in body and in mind; and the wondrous tales that I heard read, filled me with all the rash, eager, longing of youth for a closer sight of this marvellous great world. Alas! it came in a manner I had little looked for: I chanced one day to accidentally break a very fine Vernis Martin vase, of which my old mistress was extravagantly fond; and as I had been often before denounced as a mischievous, tiresome, frivolous little creature, because my animal spirits and childish joyousness would ill-tone down to the gray monotone of an aged invalid's desires, I was forthwith sentenced to exile. A green and red parrot—as monosyllabic a creature as a mechanical toy, and as greedy as a Director, or the Liquidator that invariably comes after him—was purchased in my stead; and I was consigned to the butler, to be sold wherever, and for whatever he chose.

I need not say that in this place I had never ceased to passionately regret my dear old master in the noble pine woods of the Peak. Indeed, I had sometimes lamented for him aloud in a grief that brought on me angry words, and even angry strokes; so little sympathy have men or women ever with *our* woes, although for theirs we feel so keenly, and fret ourselves so ceaselessly. Twenty times at least had I endeavoured to run away, with the full intent of trying to find my road back alone to the well-beloved little cottage under the rose-thorn. But I had been always thwarted, overtaken, and punished for what they called "straying," though it was but the simplest and most natural exercise of fidelity.

My anxiety, therefore, was tenfold increased at the prospect of a new removal, which seemed to consign me still farther from him, and might plunge me into still greater wretchedness. Yet, like all youth, hope mingled with my fear, and I vaguely trusted that if the coming change did not take me back to my first beloved home, it would, perchance, lead to some brighter, gladder, more sympathetic existence than that which I had spent in the old, dull, moated dower-

house amongst the marches. My little brain was teeming
with a myriad of visions—dogs have very vivid fancies, as
you may tell by the excitement of our dreams. I scarcely
knew whether I hoped most, or dreaded most, from the new
adventures into which I should be cast, when, sold to a metropolitan dealer, the butler bore me forth, for the last time,
from the gloomy gates of the place where, if I had not known
joy, I had at least been safe, and well, and innocent.

It was midwinter.

The fens were half-covered with ice. The water-fowls
were dying of cold and of starvation by the thousands. The
bitter winds were rushing in from the northern ocean across
all those desolate marshlands and reedy still lagoons. Farther
towards the east the sea was washing over the dykes and
piers, and the salt water was flooding coppice and meadow,
killing the river fish, and drowning the river birds, till fisher
and farmer were dumb with despair.

It was a very cold, cheerless season. It was a very long
and terribly weary journey in such weather up to the Great
City: a journey on which I verily think I should have died,
had it not been for the goodness of the railway-guard, who
took me with him in his van, and wrapped me in a bit of
rug.

We arrived late at night, and there was no one to meet
me at the station. The guard was off duty till the next
morning came round; he pitied me, and tucked me under his
arm, and carried me away.

"I'll take you round, myself," he said to me, looking at
the parchment label on my collar. I like men who speak to
me as to a creature of reason and of feeling. "You're going
to a rare rum bad lot, you are."

The din, the tumult, the gas-glare, the wild uproar of the
London streets drove me almost mad with fright; and, but
for the strong detaining hand of my guard, I should have
flung myself under the wheels in sheer terror and been
crushed to atoms.

O, how could people live and breathe and endure existence

in such holes as this, I wondered! Hundreds of small houses crowding on one another; story on story mounting to the murky smoke-veiled heaven; the stench of candle and soap and bone-boiling and manure factories, steaming over all the place; the only light the flare of the yellow gas, through the leaden fog, on faces haggard with misery, hideous with debauch, vile with crime, or death-like with starvation! My very blood curdled in me as I saw and heard, and turned blind and sick with the fetid odours of this Gehenna.

Once I had heard my dear friend Ben talk to the workmen at the quarry of the cities and their foulness.

"I went to Lunnun once, Tam," he said, "you'll mind the time; I was a fule, and the 'scursion he was so cheap-like; I was tempted. Well, I'm glad I went. I niver know'd till I did how much I had ta thank God for i' bein' country-born and bred. They're stifled, Tam—just stifled. Th' air's all smoke and reek; an' the winds is all pison; and whin ye look up'ards there's a great black hand like a divil's wing a' stretchin' far o'er atween ye and tha sun. There bean't a mossel of grass as *is* grass; there bean't a leaf as don't look sick and swounded; there bean't a bird as dew sing; not a child as dew laugh; the birds fight and the childer screech. They're all jammed togither, like turf-sods when ye pack 'em close; theer's allus a horrible noise i' their ears; and a horrible stench i' their nostrils. Now how should un grow up decent, and God-fearin' like, whin they niver see the blue sky, nor smell a flower as blows, nor feels tha sou'-wester sweep agin their faces? Ta Passon he talk a deal of divils and sich like: weel!—if theer be 'em anywheres, for sure it was they as fust drew min into cities, that they might forgit their God i' tha stenching drouth, and be ready to be swept i' ta hell, all o' one muck an' one heap!"

I remembered Ben's words when I also entered that abomination of desolation—the eastern half of the City of Labour.

In the little cottage in the pine-wood, even in the dreariness of winter and under the drag of poverty, there had been beauty—beauty in the white, smooth, glittering snow; in the branches all silvered with the hoar-frost; in the leaping flame on the hearth that played on the lattice panes; in the beautiful clear steely skies with the northerly stars burning through them.

But here!—I shuddered as I saw the gray, dust-strewn, mouldy tenements; the tawdry frightfulness of the few attempts at ornament, the ghastly tumult of the choked street —choked with thieves and beggars, and tally men, and ballad-sellers, and prostitutes, and costermongers, and wretched horses starving in the last years of age, and ghoul-like children quarrelling with the poor stray dogs for offal. Poverty is bitter in the country: but it is heaven beside hell compared with poverty in the city.

The way seemed to me interminable through these most hideous streets. Where the guard stopped was before a little low row of filthy crowded houses, all alike, and all hemmed in on one another, with gas flaring about on either side, and stalls of horrible-scented fish, of coffee, and of oranges, standing down the narrow way with little oil-lamps flaring above them under shades, and miserable children gathering round.

My protector knocked at one of the low doors.

"Bill Jacobs?" he asked.

"Bill Jacobs, yer are," growled a beer-thickened voice as the door unclosed.

A hand clutched me savagely by my throat.

"O-ah, this 'ere little beast!" he muttered. "Anythin' to pay?"

"Nothin' to pay," answered the guard. "'Tis a pretty critter you've got there. I wouldn't mind standin' ten bob for him."

The other man, still holding me by the neck, growled out a sardonic laughter.

"I dessay yer wouldn't. Ten sovs, my lad, or nothin'."

And with that he slammed the door in the guard's face; and I felt, with a fearful sinking of the heart, that my only chance was gone for ever.

This new home of mine was in a hideous little house, and

consisted of only one room, with the cellar immediately below.

The room was black with dirt and smoke; there were two cupboards in it, one occupied by two badgers, the other by two small dogs. The cellar beneath appeared full of dogs, to judge by the howling and moaning that proceeded from it. There was a miserable bed in the chamber; a rickety table; a few cages filled with miserable choking throstles and larks, half dead with stench and captivity; and there was beyond, seen through a little window in the back wall, a yard of which I knew the purpose ere I had been many hours there.

Such was the abode of Bill Jacobs and his wife; the latter a wan, gentle, broken-spirited creature, whom he kept black and blue with bruises, and who sought, I found, to do all the little she was able to mitigate for us the horrors of this Black Hole.

The first thing that Bill Jacobs did with me was to fling me at the woman with a curse; the next was to turn all smiles to two youths who were waiting his advent. They were slender gentleman-like boys, about seventeen, and, as I imagine now, must have been public school lads. They had come for some pleasant pastime, it seemed by their looks and words: it proved to be the baiting of a badger.

I will not sicken my readers with the narrative. They probably know all the details of how the poor, brave, stout-hearted animal holds his own against the terrible odds, till, foe on foe being sent against him, the agony of his wounds and the loss of his blood cow even his fearless spirit, and he submits to be dragged forth; a mass of torn fur and ragged flesh, helpless, blind, and shivering.

In this instance the sport was doubly horrible, because neither badger nor bull-dogs had any heart or zest for the fight; they both shrank back, and had to be scourged and pricked and dragged to the encounter; and when it was all over, the limping, bleeding dogs were kicked back to their cellars, and the badger was thrown in his hole to recover from his injuries, only to again go through the same ordeal of torture.

And the slender-limbed boys, with their pleasant voices, were charmed, and left two sovereigns with the exhibitor of the spectacle, and went out in glee and gaiety, having enjoyed a favourite sport of Young England.

It made me very ill and sick at heart; it was the first bloodshed I had ever seen, and the sight had been very hideous to me, and had made me shudder greatly.

How could I tell myself that I might not be torn in pieces next?

It seemed hell itself, this place to which they had consigned me.

The man's horrible curses; the howls of the dogs in the cellar; the wailing of the puppies in cages; the sight of the blood and the torture; the shrieks of the animal that he kicked or beat, or forced into some wretched hole too small for it to turn in; the sad filmy eyes of the poor birds sitting moping with their feathers all in disarray; the piteous terrors of the woman every time her husband's savage glance lit on her, as though with every look she feared a blow: all this was more dreadful to me than I can ever describe.

Almost all day long I was shut up in a cage lest I should roam away—a cage of wire about a foot square, in which my limbs became so cramped, and my sight so stupefied from being set away on a dark shelf, that I almost ceased to keep any account of the passage of the days, and hardly knew when night fell and dawn began.

Now and then, by urging that such confinement would be my death, his wife Jenny got permission from him to let me run loose a little in the yard; but even then I was so terrified lest evil should happen to me, that I hardly dared to go from underneath the folds of her cotton gown.

I was sorry for her too; she had such an utterly wretched, colourless, woe-begone life, that it seemed frightful that any one of God's creatures ever should be condemned to live such.

She never stirred out; she was the butt and scapegoat of her brutal husband, and she had nothing to do from morning

7*

until evening, save to dress the wounds of the torn and baited creatures, and revive enough vitality in them to enable them to go forth again to meet the torture.

She was a tender-hearted woman too, which made her lot an agony scarce less than that of the martyred beasts. I have known her stretch her arm between a dog and her husband's whip, though the cruel lash cut into her flesh like a knife; and I have seen her seize his hand, and scream for pity, when he was thrusting a red-hot needle into a canary's eye to blind it (on the fancy that it sang better in blindness), though with the next moment his huge fist surely levelled her with the boards.

I daresay many such problems have puzzled bigger heads than mine; but I often marvelled whatever compensation could ever be found or given for that long, unrewarded, stricken life, which was spent unseen of men, subject to the brutalities of a drunkard, and racked by the witness of cruelties that it was absolutely powerless to prevent?

An old dog, Punch by name, who had been there many years (and to whom this tyrant was alone not cruel, because he had once seen Punch strangle a man that strove to beat him), told me that in a bygone time she had had a little child, and that, though the child had only lived two years, it had lived long enough for its blue eyes to grow pale and dilated with fear at its father's steps—long enough for its mother to say that she thanked God when she laid it down at rest within its little quiet grave.

This ruffian was indeed one of the greatest brutes that the world ever held.

Dog-fancier was in his case, as in most others, a delicate synonym for dog-stealer; and the society that met in his den was composed of some of the very worst blackguards in London. These men smoked and drank, and swore and gambled, in the lowest and coarsest fashion that they could; and were especially hilarious when one of them had brought in a valuable animal, for whom its master would be certain to offer fabulous rewards, or a priceless little pet dog, that could be slipped in a pocket and carried out of the country before its owner had scarcely discovered its loss.

The big dogs they drugged, lest their bark might be heard and recognised, until such time as a reward high enough to satisfy their own cupidity was advertised; when they would put on a clean shirt and a virtuous face, and take the captive home, with many declarations of their own tenderness towards him, when they had found him astray "right away by Barnes Bridge, sir—'alf starved—as I'm a livin' man." Which fable, if the dog had a mistress and not a master, usually brought about an extra sovereign to the good Samaritan.

The small ones they generally sent on to the Continent; and one little fellow, only four years old, told me he had been stolen fourteen times by Bill Jacobs' emissaries, on each of which occasions they had never sold him for less than twenty guineas, sometimes for more, and always in different cities of Europe.

He was called "Cosmo," "short for cosmopolitan," he explained to me. "You know that means a citizen of the world —one who has seen many countries and many minds. But myself—I hate the title. It means, as far as my experience goes, that you have a smattering of everything, and a knowledge of nothing; a bill at every inn, and a home in no country; everybody claims you, and you can claim nobody; your standing-point is on a see-saw, and you are a tennis-ball for all rackets."

And he was certainly extravagantly bitter on the subject of his cosmopolitanism. To have been sold and bought a dozen times always sours a dog; though I have known men who have been sold and bought a hundred times, who have only got very fat and very comfortable in the process of exchange.

But, then, you see the men pocket the money; and the dogs don't.

Anything more utterly degraded, wretched, and desolate than I was at this prison of Bill Jacobs', I could not suppose ever had the unhappiness to exist. If it had not been for Jenny Jacobs, I should not have lived a week. ·

She did all she could to better my condition, and to comfort me in my misery, and whilst I was with her she in a measure succeeded. But she used to be sent out by her husband "charing," and was half the day away; and in her absence I was consigned to the cellars, where all the hapless animals which Jacobs had stolen, or purchased cheaply, were immured with scarce any light, foul water, clanking chains, and the scantiest food that would suffice to keep breath in their bodies.

You think you have no slaves in England! Why, half the races in creation moan, and strive, and suffer, daily and hourly, under your merciless tyrannies! No slaves! Ask the ox, with his blood-shot agonised eyes, mutilated for the drovers' gain ere he is driven to his end in the slaughter-house. Ask the sheep, with their timid woe-begone faces, scourged into the place of their doom, bruised and bleeding and tortured. Ask the racer, spent ere he reaches his prime, by unnatural strains on strength and speed, that he may fill the pockets of your biggest blackguards with mis-begotten gold; old whilst yet he is young, poisoned in the hours of his victory, caressed by princes in the moment that he ministers to their greed, cast off to street hire and hourly misery in the worthless years of his weary age. Ask the cart-horse, doomed, through a long life of labour, to strive and stagger under burdens, to bear heat and cold, and hunger, and stripes, without resistance; fed grudgingly, paid for willing toil by merciless blows, killed by doing the work of men as the Egyptian slave died in the lifting of the last stone to the King's Temple, or consigned, as the only recompense for years of usefulness and patience, to the brutalities of the dissecting-room or of the knacker's yard. Ask us!

What! You tell me this is but the issue of an inevitable law? Ay, so it is; of the law of the stronger over the weaker. But whilst you thus follow out that law on millions of chained and beaten and tortured creatures, have conscience

enough, I pray you, not to brag aloud that you keep no
slaves, not to bawl from the housetops of your reverence
for freedom.

When will you give a Ten Hours' Bill for horses—a Pro-
hibitive Act against the racing of one- and two-year-olds?—
a Protection Order for cattle?—and an Emancipation Movement for chained dogs? Nay—when will you do so much as
remember that the coward who tortures an animal would
murder a human being if he were not afraid of the gallows?
When will you see that to teach the hand of a child to
stretch out and smother the butterfly, is to teach that hand,
when a man's, to steal out and strangle an enemy?

The time passed, as I have said, very monotonously, very
miserably, the chief part spent in the cage upon the shelf, or
in the cellar I have named. I believe that Jacobs failed in
his efforts to get a purchaser for me; for sometimes he would
wash me and comb me, and carry me forth, through many
streets and past grand white mansions, and into green
carriage-crowded parks. He would offer me now to one,
now to another of people passing by; and when we reached
home again he would curse me and pinch my flesh and forbid
his wife to give me any supper, alleging that I ate my head
off—as indeed I almost could have done, so devoured with
hunger was I oftentimes.

The only day that Bill Jacobs was at all in decently
human temper was upon the Sundays of each week.

At this lodging of his there was a back-yard; and in the
back-yard was a rat-pit. On Sunday mornings there used to
be grand spectacles of rat-slaughter. And there were
numbers of young men—very gentleman-like men, some of
them—who would pay half-a-guinea for admission, and a
seat to see the rats being killed, and the rat-dogs torn and
worried in the conflict; and the prices ranged as high as a
sovereign a seat when, in addition to its ennobling sport,
there was one of the badgers brought out from the cupboard
to be drawn.

"Jacobs' Church" was a byword amongst a certain sporting community; and I have seen men whom I subsequently saw in the House of Commons, and at the celebrated Clubs, come thither on a Sunday morn after a late breakfast, to assist at the precious spectacle of dogs and rats fighting, tearing, and slaughtering one another, till the pit was red with blood.

What did the police do?

O, nothing. Jacobs paid them well to be quiet. They took up an old man for selling periwinkles during divine service, and they locked up a little beggar child for sitting sobbing on a door-sill, both just outside Bill's house; but they knew better than to come to lords and gentlemen, and members of parliament, and disturb the Sabbath circle round the rat-pit.

Most of our race, kept here thus, of course were beagles, rat-catchers, bull terriers, and the like; and, by the way, how sharp, how hard, how full of concentrated cunning and ferocity combined, become the countenances of your rat-catching dogs! They are exactly like the faces of your men on the turf: of a surety debasing pursuits mould the features as the hand of the sculptor moulds the mask from clay; or else why should your bull-dog, who is for ever drawing badgers or chevying vermin, get that look for all the world like that on the face of your prize-fighters? And why should your young lordling, who spends all his patrimony on "yearlings," and all his time on the "flat," approximate so closely in tone and aspect and countenance to the bookmakers, and blacklegs, and trainers, and jockeys, who between them contrive to rob and to ruin him?

It is needless to say that I was very frightened and miserable in such society. They made dreadful mockery of me and my white silky curls; and they were perpetually fighting and swearing amongst one another. Their conduct was fearful; their language I happily did not comprehend.

There was one old bull-dog, who looked the most savage yet the most honest of them all, who protected me from their violence, and was, in his own hard, rough way, kind to me.

He was by name Tussler, and was, I found, the hero of a hundred fights. He deigned to talk to me a good deal, and tried to enlighten my ignorance; but I did not understand much that he said; I only felt that life seemed, by his showing, a constant rough-and-tumble affray in which the weakest always went to the wall.

Tussler told me he had belonged to a bruiser who had but recently departed from the scene of his earthly combat.

"They made me chief mourner with a bit of crape on," he continued. "I don't know why they thought crape necessary, for I was really very sorry that he died. The world thought Jemmy Brown—he was called the Game-Cock always: you must have heard of him? Never!—damn it, where have you lived?

"Well, the world always thought that the Cock was a brutal bloodthirsty fellow. You know he had a very neat way of pounding his man's face into a jelly; and when he got him doubled up at the ropes he always went into him—awful. He killed Old Swipes that way—an Irish bruiser Swipes was, and only twenty when the Cock smashed him as dead as a door-nail—but it was only in the way of business. It was a job, and he liked to go through with it.

"Outside the Ring Jemmy was the best-natured creature going. When a badger half-murdered me, the Cock nursed me like a woman. And there never was a man that stuck as the Cock did to a friend. There was one in particular he was fond of—one he'd been with at school as a child, and one he had never lost sight of; a poor devil that never came to any good because he was such a soft-hearted thing, and ended at last as a super—a man you know that goes on the stage to carry a flag, or a torch, or a sword, and say nothing.

"Well, one day Jemmy was engaged for a private match in a gentleman's rooms at Oxford; and if he failed to be there punctually, he'd agreed to pay the bruiser whom he was to meet forfeit stakes of twenty-five pounds;—and you must know that the money was a deal to the Cock, for he lived fast and was often out at elbows. Just as he was starting for the fight there came a letter by morning mail: it was only a line or two scrawled by this super, to say he had been taken bad in his lungs as he was acting as standard-bearer down in Cornwall, and the doctors had told him he'd die; and he begged to see Jemmy before he went to his grave.

"What did the Cock do? never paused a second, just tossed the forfeit stakes to his friend, and started that minute for Penzance. The poor super died an hour after Jemmy got there; but he begged of the Cock to take care of his son, a little un with no mother, and a pretty puny five-year-older.

"The Cock took that lad, and he sent him to a good school; and he laid him up in lavender, as it were, and never let him hear a harsh word. He never let him see the Ring, because he thought as the dead wouldn't like it; but he had him trained up for a glass-stainer, and the boy is at it now: very quick at his art, and quite steady. Now I call the Cock a good man—what do you say? And yet the world called him a precious villain: and they were very near swinging him on a gallows when he pummelled the breath out of Swipes."

I could say nothing: all moral and mental perception were too utterly confused in me with this combination of virtue and murder.

"There's a deal of goodness that the world never sees," said Tussler in conclusion, "as there's a deal of viciousness it never guesses. Now, myself, I love worrying rats, and cats, and badgers—I am never so happy as when I lay a dozen dead all round me—but I should scorn to hurt a lame dog, I wouldn't kill a cat that fought for her kittens, and I would have let the Cock beat me to death if he'd wished just because he was my master and I cared for him."

I ventured to hint that, with so much natural goodness of character, it might be as well to be merciful even to rats and to badgers.

"O, damn it, no!" he replied with considerable acerbity. "They are one's foes by nature. A badger would kill me if I didn't kill him. I choose as men choose,—I just nip his neck. Don't get preachee-preachee! Did you ever hear of a rum lot called Quakers across the Atlantic that were always prating of peace?—well, my dear, they burnt everybody that didn't agree with them. That is what the peace-makers always do."

I was silent out of deference: conscious that he could nip me in the neck if I differed.

Much the same motive lies at the bottom of most of the reverence that this age sees rendered to kings and queens, creeds and codes.

Such conversations as this did not make me less miserable, less terrified, at the prospect of this world into which I was plunged; or less regretful of that happy, innocent, playful life that I had led in the little cottage under the pines.

Old Trust would have felt every hair on his head stand on end at the enormities I heard and witnessed; and that humane creature, who had sorrowed over a frozen lamb, would have howled in disgust at the conversation of this sporting community,—conversation exclusively of the number slaughtered, and of the prowess of the slaughterers.

Subsequently, I have often been present at hot luncheons in manorial woods after battue-shooting, and once also at an Imperial hunt in the forest of Compiègne; and the talk at both has borne the closest possible resemblance to that heard in the bull-dogs' cellar at Bill Jacobs'. But I did not know this then; and I was only immeasurably frightened and horror-stricken.

CHAPTER X.

He is launched on Life.

I REMAINED some little time at this wretched place; the only things that solaced me being the poor woman's great care, and the rough kindness of Tussler, whose conduct was far better than his language, which, I must say, was awful. The winter was merging into spring, and I had been there about three months, when Tussler was sold to a sporting baronet, and I became aware that some change was about to take place in my own affairs.

I had been washed, combed, made smart, and dressed in a little scarlet jacket that Jacobs, in his good humour, was wont to aver made me look just like an Ascot post-boy; I still wore the little bit of a white metal chain collar, graven with my name, which had been forged for poor Ben by the burly smith at the forest-forge in the pine-woods, who though his chief labour lay in shoeing the huge cart-horses, yet had shown so light and facile a touch at little pieces of metal work, that could pleasure a maiden in her fancy, or a child at his play.

When I was thus dressed, Jacobs bore me out with him, he chuckled, and seemed content; I was thrust into a small dark wicker den, that was tied down over my head; and I knew no more. "Hold yer jaw, yer beast," he said once with a shake of my cage, "what are yer yelping at?"

I was yelping because, as he carried me into the street, and I thrust my head a little forth from my basket, in the damp, chill March morning, a girl went by us with a basket full of little penny-bunches of country-born violets, blue and white; and the sweet familiar fragrance of them brought back to me, so vividly, the clusters that purpled all the moss-grown ground under the trees of my lost but unforgotten home.

When your dog, lying near you, gives a sudden cry, as though of pain, you kick him;—ah! my good sirs, it is only because he is troubled with too much memory; a disease which you, who are of the world, worldly, you who forget with such pleasant ease all disagreeable trifles, from your marriage vows to your unlimited liabilities, are little likely to catch from him by contagion.

Bill Jacobs carried me swiftly through his own hideous quarter of the town towards open squares and spacious streets, and masses of what looked to me like palaces;—and palaces they were, as I knew later on, castles of Indolence wherein the Kings of Clubs reigned supreme.

He turned up one of the by-streets leading out of the chief of these great thoroughfares; and after some little delay was admitted into a building bearing the inscription of "chambers," and passed up the staircase to a room on the second floor of this, to me, mysterious domicile.

It was a very pretty little room, all rose-hued and gilded, and bright with gay chintz, and with manifold ornaments, not in the very best taste. I thought it must be the apartment of some fair feminine thing; but there was no one in it, save a man of about thirty years; small, handsome, and bearing about him somewhat the air of that class which I have later on heard characterised as the "would-be swells" of society.

He was exquisitely attired in a morning dress of mulberry velvet; and had coffee and brandy beside him on the daintiest of inlaid stands; and he was glancing through a yellow-covered novel, which he slashed idly with a pretty paper-knife, as he looked up and spoke.

"Brought the beast, Jacobs? Let's have a look at him."

"A perfect animal for a lady—quite perfect, sir," my owner responded, handing me over as roughly as though I were a bit of wood, for inspection. "You want him for a Russian princess, sir, I believe you said?"

The young man nodded assent; and asked if I should stand the climate, to which of course Bill Jacobs gave an un-qualified affirmative; and the next fifteen minutes was em-ployed in one of those minute and merciless analyses of me,

which dogs hear made in their presence, and human beings
only behold in their critics' newspaper articles.

But it comes to very much the same thing with both—
and whether it be a dog-fancier inspecting a terrier, a dog-
buyer staring at a mastiff, a leader-writer dissecting a statesman not of his party, or a reviewer passing judgment on a
poet not of his clique, the whole quartette equally ignore all
the excellences that stare them in the face, and only dwell on
the one fault they can find in breeding or training,—in strain
or in style.

The moments seemed centuries to me, nor was I in the
least reassured at the prospect of being bought for a woman.
Little Cosmo, at Jacobs', had told me that parasol handles
could rap fearfully hard, and small, high-heeled, embroidered
boots kick with exceeding asperity and severity.

Ah! you people never guess the infinite woe we dogs suffer
in new homes, under strange tyrannies; you never heed how
we shrink from unfamiliar hands, and shudder at unfamiliar
voices, how lonely we feel in unknown places, how acutely
we dread harshness, novelty, and scornful treatment. Dogs
die oftentimes of severance from their masters; there is Grey
Friar's Bobby now in Edinboro' town who never has been
persuaded to leave his dead owner's grave all these many
years through. You see such things, but you are indifferent
to them. "It is only a dog," you say; "what matter if the
brute fret to death?"

You don't understand it of course; you who so soon forget
all your own dead, the mother that bore you, the mistress
that loved you, the friend that fought with you shoulder to
shoulder; and of course, also, you care nothing for the mea-
sureless blind pains, the mute helpless sorrows, the vague
lonely terrors, that ache in our little dumb hearts.

I am a dog of the world now,—O yes,—just as your best
men are men of the world. But I think to most of us cynics
the world is only a shield of bronze,—held before us to hide
the breast-wound. What do you say?—the sentiment is not
new I am well aware; but it is emphatically the truth.

I have seen so many of these shields, so brilliant and polished, and proven, which rang so hard and so keen, repelling the sharpest spearheads; but the hearts that beat under them throbbed;—throbbed in pain till they were quiet in death. If you have not,—where have you lived?

Well,—my barter this morning in the little rose-coloured room was soon effected, and the purchaser paid for me in four crisp five-pound notes, Jacobs of course protesting that I was worth quite treble the amount.

I was thankful when he was gone; no fate could be worse than the durance I had undergone in his cellars.

The young man soon after passed into his bed-chamber adjoining; and I was left alone with a very big dog, whom I had noticed asleep in the window.

He reared himself up, and surveyed me; I liked his look; he was a kingly creature, called indeed King Arthur, and I thought he would fight my battles for me whilst I was there.

I am brave enough in my way; but I have necessarily far more mind than matter; and a little Maltese dog can no more find courage of use against a hound's fangs or a brute's boot, than your chivalrous soldier, with all the blood of the cavaliers in him, can find his avail him aught against your dainty, devilish, thirty-inch shell, with its pretty steel dominoes of slaughter.

He stared at me, and growled a little:

"Humph! so you are for *her!*"

"The Russian Princess?" I asked timidly, feeling that he growled at her, and not at me.

"Russian Princess!" he echoed. "Fiddlesticks!"

"Shall I stay here, then?" I inquired.

"No, I know who you are bought for;—but I don't want to say. I have lived long enough to learn discretion."

I found King Arthur, when I knew him better, the frankest, blindest, most easily cheated creature in creation; but it is always this sort of character that shakes its head most sapiently, and believes most implicitly in its own politic reserve!

"Who is that gentleman that buys me?" I ventured to ask him.

"His name? Leopold Lance."

"And is he your owner too?"

"Goodness no!—I belong to Derry Denzil; he only left me here while he went to Paris. He'll be back to-night. Belong to little Lance?—no, thank you! I hate this room; one can't turn in it without knocking something down. You should see Denzil's rooms, big as barns, with nothing less solid than oak, and bronze, and marble in them. This place is for all the world like a woman's stall at a fancy-fair. Women do send him some of the nicknacks—actresses do when they want a puff in the *Mouse*, and would-be fashionable ladies do when they want a line as a leader of society—but for the most part he buys them himself; and then hints with a smile or a word that they come from the Countess of somewhere, or pretty Mrs. Thingamy. Leo's weakness is *bonnes fortunes;* and when he don't get any, he makes them to his fancy; metamorphosing how d'ye does into appointments, and dinner cards into letters of intrigue, just as your costumiers turn a girl out of the streets into a superb Anonyma, till a man spends his whole fortune on the very same creature he gave a penny to twelve months before at a crossing."

Of this peroration I did not comprehend one word; but it sufficed to make me the reverse of comfortable as to my own future prospects. The good-natured, gallant King perceived my perplexed dismay, and hastened to comfort me.

"You will be well enough where you are going," he said. "If you were a man she would pluck you as bare as the back of her hand; being a dog a kick of her boot—thirty guineas a pair her boots are, real silver-gilt heels that go click-clack like a cavalry-man's!—or a mouthful of cayenne pepper instead of biscuit, or some little trifle of that sort, will be the worst she will do for you. And Fanfreluche is there; Fanfreluche is a good little soul, good at the core you know! though she's a little devil with her teeth at times, and the

vainest creature living, she is as staunch as steel, and as game
as a bantam-cock, and can be a very good friend when she
likes. Besides I will have a care of you myself; I sometimes
come there with Denzil. And Pearl can never look me
straight in the face, isn't it odd? An honest dog's eyes always daunt those women. They seem to think that we scent
them out as thieves; though their crowbars may only be cast
from the metal of barefaced greed; and their skeleton keys
made of men's broken honour—"

"Pearl? who is Pearl?" I interrupted him.

"You will know soon enough," he said curtly; at that
moment my purchaser returned from the inner room, caught
me up, and fastened with great care on my collar a pair of
exquisite filigree ear-rings, slipped me and them into a
basket, and gave it to a man in waiting, who departed with
me without a word.

Of course of where we went I had no knowledge: I was in
almost total darkness. The ear-rings I would have scratched
to pieces willingly; but the exceedingly narrow space in which
I was confined prevented my cramped limbs from any indulgence in such vengeance.

The journey seemed endless to me.

At length, by the sounds I heard, I concluded my tem-
porary abode had been carried into a house and into a room.
I thought I had been hours in that wicker-work dungeon;
and when, on the lid being thrown sharply open, I sprang
out on a piece of blue velvet, I gave a sharp prolonged howl
of misery.

For that I got a sharp box on the ear from the hand of a
woman, and, looking up, I saw that I was on the lap of one of
the most magnificent persons it has ever been my fate to behold.

But O!—how hard her hand had slapped me!

She read a note that lay beside me with some effort, as
though reading were unfamiliar to her, laughing a little
grimly as she did so; then, tossing it aside, clutched eagerly
at the ear-rings to which I suppose it had drawn her atten-

tion, and tore them off, utterly regardless of the curls of my hair that she plucked away with them.

The ornaments were very elegant, and their Genoese filigree was all enriched with jewels. She examined them with the keen intentness of a testing jeweller; then put them aside in a mosaic box on a table near.

The apartment was a small octagon chamber, all blue and silver, and exceedingly luxurious in its appointments—genuine luxury moreover, and not the affectation of it that had been visible in the meretricious rooms of the man who had sent me hither. She herself was simply superb—attired in blue velvet that harmonised with her chamber, and was relieved by rich old lace at her bosom and elbows, and a single large diamond at her throat.

The tearing out of my hair had hurt me inexpressibly; and I shrieked aloud with the pain, hiding under a couch.

She gave a gesture of intolerant anger; pulled me from my hiding-place, shook and slapped me till I had no senses left, and then flung me aside with a brutal violence so that I fell heavily on the sharp edge of the ormolu fender.

Then without even a glance at me, she swept out of the dainty boudoir with the mosaic box in her hand, leaving me half-stunned to recover as I might.

I was roused from my stupor by the touch of a very slender cold nose; and looking up timidly, I saw a tiny fairy-like form, clad in blue, with a gold circlet of bells round its throat:—a "toy terrier" in point of fact, who ranks in our species much as your *petits crevés* and your pretty *cocodettes* rank in yours. This was evidently the little worldling of whom King Arthur had spoken.

"I am called Fanfreluche," said the small creature, who had very bright eyes, and a very keen, coquettish, sharp little face. "I shall be sure to go now you are come. She changes us almost as often as she changes *them*."

"Whom?"

"Never mind, my dear. You are a child! She hurt you, I am afraid? She can be very violent if you rouse her—"

"Indeed, she can," said I with a shudder. "Who is she pray? Can you tell me?"

Fanfreluche grinned significantly.

"My dear—I know as much about her as most people, but I can only tell you what she calls herself, and that is Laura Pearl."

"And what does she do?"

Fanfreluche showed again her little sharp white teeth.

"Everything, my dear, that was ever invented by the devil and improved on by women."

I shuddered again; even in that little market town in the Peak the people had seemed to take it so uncomfortably for granted that the devil and the fair sex always were in partnership and good accord!

"Is she a lady?" I inquired timidly.

"My precious innocent—she has some of the finest jewels in the world. That makes a lady, don't it? She has fine horses; fine servants; fine wines; the best cook, the best laces, the best everything. A lady?—O yes!—the girl that sells cigars, the ballerina that dances in gauze, the housemaids that sweep the steps, they are all ladies now, thanks to jargon and the penny press."

I did not understand, but Fanfreluche evidently considered she had said something very witty.

"Are you worth much? I doubt not: you come from a very bad lot," she continued a little superciliously. "I wonder what Beltran will think of you. Anything he praises is *chic* directly. He said my shape was exquisite one morning; and I went up instantly from twenty to fifty-five guineas."

The little wicked thing looked so immeasurably vain and self-conscious, as she twisted her head askance to get a sight of her tiny coral collar with its row of gold bells, that she disgusted me; pretty and worldly-wise though she was.

"You cannot be so very much more *chic* than I," I growled sulkily, "since you confess you are to be sent away now that I have come."

8*

Fanfreluche sneered a little; with an indulgent good nature however.

"Bless the baby!" she cried, as though she had been a matron and a mastiff at the least. "What an ignoramus it is! Why, my dear, she will sell you as soon as she shall have had you a month or two. She sells us all; and the more we are worth the quicker we go:—provided she can do it decently. *They* don't know that, you see. O no!—we are always 'stolen' or 'lost' she tells them. And they are such out-and-out fools—they believe it! And then they send her others to replace us; and the game goes on again; and altogether she makes a very pretty annual perquisite out of her 'pets!'"

"She must be a very wicked woman!" I said indignantly, in my hurry.

"Not much good!" said the little creature carelessly. "I don't know that she's worse than scores of others though. There was Frédégonde, that I lived with last year in Paris— why Frédégonde would eat up a hundred men a quarter, and all the youngest and the brightest and the best too; and no end of them boys, well nigh young enough to be her own sons!—"

"Are they cannibals, these women?" I cried utterly bewildered.

Fanfreluche grinned sardonically.

"Yes, my dear; all cannibals. And they eat bones and all; crunch—crunch—crunch;—and get rich, and laugh, and fare gaily over the brainless skulls they have sucked dry, and the hearts they have torn out and devoured!"

I had a dim perception that Fanfreluche was speaking metaphorically, but I was not sure; and her words made me very ill at ease. It was horrible to be in the possession of a man-eater.

"There comes Lizzie. I have to go out with her, but I will see you again," said the little lady, as a pleasant-visaged maid appeared at the doorway.

"Why are you going out?"

"To be 'lost,' I daresay. But I don't intend to be lost to-day; I want to see more of you. You amuse me; you are such an innocent! You will soon lose all that, to be sure. This is a capital place for learning the world and its tricks. Does my blue jacket sit right? I can't bear it to wrinkle. Beltran admires my figure so much."

"The jacket's all right," said I peevishly, scarcely looking at the little tight-fitting azure silk coat that she wore. "And who's Beltran?"

"I'll tell you when I come back. Ta-ta, little one," cried Fanfreluche, hastening away to the chime of her tiny golden bells.

I was very sorry she was gone; there seemed a certain kindliness in her despite her assumption of cynicism, and her unfeminine chatter; and though she scoffed at a good deal, I thought she sorrowed also for some things.

Left alone, I glanced timidly around the room where I lay curled under a sofa: I was looking everywhere for the bleaching skulls, and the broken bones, of all the poor wretches whom she declared had been devoured here. I saw nothing of the kind, and I began to think that she must have been fooling me when she talked of this elegant boudoir as a slaughterhouse.

I saw, indeed, golden tazze, costly china, exquisite pictures, oriental stuffs, silks and satins, and furs, a malachite vase, a jasper table, a little ivory prayer-book, with the twisted monogram in turquoises and pearls upon the cover. Were these what the skeletons and the skulls had been transmuted into by the modern crucible of venial passion and unscrupulous greed?

This solution of her mystery did not occur to me then; but now I know well that it was the right one.

For several hours Fanfreluche never returned. I was left wholly to solitude. I became fearfully hungry, but no one brought me anything to eat; and in the end, like a child, as I still was, I sobbed myself to sleep, thinking that I would

give all the world to exchange the broidered-satin cushion
into which I sank, for a bed of moss under Ben's old pines.

It was nearly dark when I was awoke by a dainty chime
of fairy-like bells, and beheld Fanfreluche by my couch.

"Well, my dear!" she began in her pert patronising way.
"How have you been? Dull enough, poor little wretch. I
have had no end of fun. I have been out driving with *her*
in the carriage, shopping and flirting all this time. I love to
go to the shops; we are first-rate customers, you know; we
always pay our bills, we do indeed. You see we can afford
to be honest; it's always one of *them* that writes the cheques!
And how splendidly the silk-mercers, and the jewellers, and
the milliners, and the florists, and the fruiterers serve us: you
see we pay very much better than the great ladies do; we've
got the great men's money, and their wives have not. That's
how it is. Why! when I go into the bonbon-seller's, they
stuff my mouth full with sweetmeats and macaroons: they
wouldn't pay all that attention to a mere Duchess's dog!"

"Is it such a great thing to be a—Pearl?" I asked, hesi-
tatingly.

"A magnificent thing!" said Fanfreluche, with a smack
of her lips. "All the fat of the land, my dear. And all the
cream of the milk. There was a time, you know,—I've heard
my grandmother talk of it,—when it was a great thing to be
a great lady; one of the heads of the nobility, you know.
You set the fashion; you ruled the tone; you shaped the society; you could ban with a frown, or elevate with a smile;
you were besieged for your ball tickets, and you were the
cynosure of all eyes in your dress. But now—bless your
heart!—if you are a *grande dame*, you are just nowhere.
Nowhere at all, except for wretched little puddling political
purposes, if you belong to a 'Party.' As for all the rest,—
Pearl and that lot have it. If you, the great lady, bore men
with exclusivism, they levant and go off to Pearl et Cie; if
you want to rule them with a light hand, they kick over the
traces, and laugh at you with Pearl et Cie; if you won't be a
dowdy, out of the fashion, you must follow the modes that

Pearl et Cie set; if you buy a fan, if you go to an opera, if you drive a new-fashioned equipage, if you adopt a costly costume, whether you like it or not, whether you know it or not, you are merely obeying the lead of Pearl et Cie. I have heard old Lord Brune talk of the rules and regulations of Almack's when he was a youth—gracious! the men of our day wouldn't stand one of them. They'd leave the Patronesses to dance a minuette in solitude, and come and make chaff of the old women over Pearl et Cie's claret and chicken!"

And Fanfreluche stopped to take breath, having fairly preached herself out of it.

I was very much bewildered, and not at all clear as to what she might mean.

"Then these Pearls are the real sovereigns of the world?" I ventured to suggest, glancing at the turquoise-studded prayer-book, which looked made for a Chapel Royal.

Fanfreluche followed my glance, and grinned, till what with her red lips, her white teeth, and her coal-black eyes, she looked for all the world very much like a very small devil.

"O yes! We go to church, my dear; we are very religious, I assure you! Sovereigns, did you ask?—to be sure; and sovereigns you know always did have a nice knack of pillaging everybody right and left, and then dying in the full odour of sanctity. We, now and then, die in a hovel, it's true, after all our brilliancy, if we lose our beauty very early; but then so do the sovereigns by the way, if they happen to lose their crowns. So the parallel fits both ways. Yes!—they rule, do Pearl et Cie. If they only saved their money oftener and lost their tempers less often; if they only didn't dissolve their diamonds in vinegar as it were, and fly into passions with their very best friends and paymasters, they might rule the world. They do rule the bigger half of it as it is."

"But why do men—?"

Fanfreluche interrupted me, turning up her small thin nose.

"My dear! Men like to be cheated and pillaged, and

sworn at, and made fools of, and ruined;—they do positively
relish it.. Or if they don't, how should Pearl et Cie possess
the power men let them possess? A fact is a fact, you know.
No good being blind to it. The sun will stay in the heavens
however you may blink at him—"

"'Then you think—?'"

"'That the devil himself drilled women; and capital for-
agers he made of them!" snapped Fanfreluche. "They don't
stand steady fire, they won't fight on the square, and they
never can carry out a campaign logically; but for sharp-
shooting, and pillaging, and skirmishing, there are no guer-
rillas like them. Hungry are you? Poor little fellow! Well
—they will be dining in a couple of hours; then I'll take you
downstairs. We live very well here; very well indeed. I
never touch a bone—on principle; we give them all away
to the poor of the parish. Ah, my dear! you don't dream
how religious we are!"

And the tiny creature—she was very much smaller than I
—grinned again so diabolically that it positively frightened
me to be in her presence.

"When I say we live well," she resumed, seeming dearly
to love her own chatter, "of course I speak with a reservation.
Men and women spoil all they eat with their barbarous fashion
of cooking it. Hams boiled in Madeira, pigeons stewed with
champignons, chickens smashed up with tomatoes, ducks *bi-
gorrés* with Seville oranges, lobsters drowned in oil and sauces,
oysters crowded with truffles and mushrooms—bah! it makes
you mad to think of it. Every dog knows better than to spoil
two good things with one another; we like the simple favour,
each rich in itself. Who ever saw a dog put two things in
his mouth at one time? But these barbarians put a hundred
—the flavours of a hundred at the least. And then they call
that Babel of contradicting essences and anomalous tastes
'good cookery,' and the concocter of it is dubbed a 'chef.'
Bah! I long to bite the legs of every one of the cordons
bleus!"

I answered nothing: of course milk and bread and a trifle

of cold meat had been my only food, and I knew no more of
what she meant than of the flavours of the dishes she men-
tioned.

But, like everybody who cannot tell a truffle from a
tomato, I kept a discreet silence, and determined to show
myself a thorough gourmet by liking nothing when I tasted it.

"Of course," continued the Lilliputian lady, with intense
spite. "Laura Pearl never, I will be bound, having eaten
anything except cabbages and black bread in her early days,
will never now be content with anything except the brands
that are a guinea the bottle, and eatables that are six months
at least before their due season. Her dinners and suppers
have every vice of the fashionable school stuffed into them.
That fellow in the kitchen gets a hundred and fifty a-year;
and all he does is to turn good food into claptrap *compôtes*,
while his gravies are all glaze and his *pâtés* all pepper. But,
goodness! you know nothing about all this; you are a baby.
Hold your tongue and let me lie quiet, or Beltran will tell me
my eyes are red, and say I mustn't have any chicken." .

"Is Beltran omnipotent here?"

Fanfreluche showed her teeth.

"Just now, my dear—yes."

"Who is he? You said you would tell me."

"Beltran? O you little ass! I thought everybody from
Paris to Patagonia knew Vere Beltran. There aren't a creature better known. Where on earth have you lived?"

"Not in the world," I said humbly, feeling fearfully
ashamed, like the little coward I was, of my dear old Ben
and his little cottage.

"One can guess that, innocent, without your telling one.
Well, since you don't know anything, expect to be pretty con-
siderably astonished. We're enough to take the hair off the
head of any uneducated being."

"Are you so *very* wicked, then?"

"Wicked! what a silly old-fashioned word. My dear
child, we're only a trifle fast and very intensely fashionable.
Wicked!—good gracious, no! And if scandal-mongers say

that we play a trifle too high, why it is very malicious of them; and our roulette-wheel is only a pretty toy that any-body may buy for a guinea."

And Fanfreluche grinned afresh.

"But who is Beltran?" I pursued.

"You'll see him," said Fanfreluche pettishly. "He's a very good fellow, though the world don't think so. He owns the Coronet, you know—"

"The public-house?" I asked; for opposite Bill Jacobs' there was an inn with that sign, very much frequented by thieves and dog-fanciers and blackguards of all sorts.

"Public-house? Good heavens, no! Our theatre!"

"A theatre! Does he dress in green and spangles and carry a long white whip?" I demanded breathlessly, thinking of the magnificent persons I had beheld outside the booth at the wakes in the Peak, and believing that I should show that I also knew the world.

Fanfreluche screamed till she choked herself.

"O you dear little simpleton!—you're as good as a play yourself. Why Beltran is a Viscount, you little fool; and he only keeps the Coronet as he keeps his horse and his valet and his cigar-case. His name don't show, you know. Old Aaron is the only man the public ever hears of—the acting manager, you know. Villanous old screw!"

"Lord Beltran is very rich, then?"

"He ought to be!"—and she gazed into the fire with an expression that was plaintive and very serious for this cynical, worldly-wise, frivolous young lady.

"But he is not?" I ventured to infer.

"Who says so? It's no business of yours or of mine if he isn't!" retorted Fanfreluche quite fiercely.

I perceived that, with all her wickedness, she was a loyal little thing to her friends, amongst whom this Beltran seemed to stand foremost.

"Was it he who bought me and sent me here?" I in-quired, to change the subject.

Whereon Fanfreluche became her own sardonic and scoff-
ing self once more.

"Pooh! no. He's an awful fool; but he's not quite such
a fool as to purchase a thing of Bill Jacobs. Any dog Bill
sells he steals again in a month or two. Don't look so frightened. Laura will sell you herself most likely before Bill gets
a chance. Set a thief to foil a thief you know."

"A thief!" I murmured, unable to reconcile such language
with a lady of whom I had just heard as one of the sovereigns
of the world. "But who is that man, then, who sent me
here?"

"Leo Lance, my dear. Only an author."

"But he gave twenty pounds for *me*."

"Did he? O!—and the ear-rings were two hundred the
pair. Yes, I know; that's just the price he got—Beltran gave
it him—for that new little thing they are going to play. And
he spends Beltran's money so!—*Chut!*"

And the small dame clicked her little white teeth like the
teeth of a trap. I saw something was wrong, but I was not
aware what it might be.

"Beltran's such an awful fool, you know," she explained.
"He's one of the cleverest men on earth, and keen as an
eagle in some things; but where there's a question of money,
or women, or play, or kindliness, pooh!—he's a downright
blind bat, an idiot! He pays Leo Lance for a burlesque he
didn't want out of pure good-nature—do you suppose he
dreams that the Mouse lays the gold out in trying to steal his
mistress?"

"I don't know, I am sure," I muttered vaguely, not having
an idea what she meant. "The Mouse—what have mice to
do with burlesques, and what may burlesques be, pray?"

"A burlesque, my sweet little daisy," explained my
patroness, "is an epitome of the tendency of this age to
reduce everything of heroic stature to pigmy proportions, and
to render ridiculous all that other ages have venerated. A
burlesque is the resource of writers without wit; the grinning
mask whereby they conceal their inability to laugh the laugh

of humour; the juggling of words and phrases with which they counterfeit the Hudibrastic strength and the Rabelaisian mirth that is not in them nor in their times. There!—that is not mine; I heard Derry Denzil say it; so take it for what it is worth. As for the Mice—that is a name we give Leo Lance, and Derry, and a few others. They've a paper they call the *Mouse*,—a sort of burlesque itself, only Denzil pours real acid into it,—and they are all Mice that write for it; and there's nothing they don't nibble at; and the trap's not set yet that can catch them. But for mercy's sake, do hold your tongue, and let me be quiet and get some sleep. Wake me when the clock strikes eight, and don't say a syllable earlier."

And she curled herself up and slept, and no efforts of mine could arouse her. As for me, I sat the whole time bolt upright, quivering all over with excitement;—mice, actors, thieves, sovereigns, cheese-baited traps, and ivory prayer-books, chasing each other in wild confusion and discord through my brain.

Into what a world I had alighted!

CHAPTER XI.

He sees Society.

Precisely as the timepiece chimed eight hours, Fanfreluche awoke and shook herself.

"Come down," she said. "They will be soon at dinner. It's an off-week at the Coronet, Easter you know. You see we're so pious; we keep the feasts and the fasts of the Church! Now don't you mind if she raps you hard with her fan-handle, or if the Mice hit champagne corks at you; if you make an atom of noise you'll be turned out of the room."

"Are the Mice always here?" I inquired, dreading these untrapable rodents.

"You silly! of course not. But they come pretty often— with the others. Beltran's wines are excellent—"

"But is it Beltran's house, then."

"O you little donkey! of course not," cried my chaperone, exasperated. "Of course it's not his house—only he pays for it and for everything in it. Can't you put two and two together? Come along! You will find the dishes burn your mouth; that cook, though they think so much of him, has only one idea of seasoning—and that one lies in the pepper-pot!"

With this she trotted through the half-opened door, and down the pretty staircase with its gilded balustrade and its bright-hued carpets, and into the dainty hall, mosaic paven, and filled with hothouse flowers and small orange-trees.

She led the way into a room that literally dazzled me as I entered it; it seemed one sheet of light; a miniature sun in the blue arc of the ceiling shed down its rays, the atmosphere was heavily scented with pastilles and flowers, the table seemed a-blaze with gold and silver, and the hangings of the walls were azure satin, silver-starred.

There were seven or eight people round the table; and a voice called Fanfreluche. She obeyed its call, and I crept timidly after her, and gazed around from a safe position under a chair.

There, taking courage, I glanced round the room. I recognised my purchaser, and I recognised my mistress. The latter dazzled my eyes like the sun-chandelier above head.

She seemed literally on fire with the superb rubies that glittered all over her, and shone like sparks of flame upon the exquisite whiteness of her skin. Flame-coloured robes gleamed under the black shower of her laces; her scarlet pomegranate-like lips, the rich flush on her cheeks, the lustre of her great brown eyes—all were full of colour glowing like the hues in a stained-glass picture when a red autumn sun streams through it. It was a perfect beauty of its kind.

The splendid lips had a cruel sensuality; the splendid eyes had a hard rapacity; the splendid ruddy-tinted hair shaded a brow that had the low brutal ignorance of the savage act on it. But—with all that youth, that colour, that magnificence of loveliness, who remembered that?

Not they, certes, who sat around her board.

Ah, fools! when you gaze on the "flower-like face" of a woman, do you ever pause to notice where the animalism speaks through it?—the greed, the cruelty, the lust, the ignorance?

"Animalism," do I say? I have lived now so long in your world and its cant, that I have caught up all its jargon. "Animalism," forsooth! A more unfair word don't exist. When we animals never drink only just enough to satisfy thirst, never eat except when we have genuine appetites, never indulge in any sort of debauch, and never strain excess till we sink into the slough of satiety, shall "animalism" be a word to designate all that men and women dare to do?

"Animalism!" You ought to blush for such a libel on our innocent and reasonable lives when you regard your own. You men who scorch your throats with alcohols, and kill your livers with absinthe, and squander your gold in the Kursaal, and the Circle, and the Arlington, and have thirty services at your dinner betwixt soup and the "chasse," and cannot spend a summer afternoon in comfort unless you be drinking deep the intoxication of hazard in your debts and your bets on the Heath, or the Downs, at Hurlingham, or at Tattersall's Rooms. You women who sell your souls for bits of stones dug from the bowels of the earth; who stake your honour for a length of lace two centuries old; who replace the bloom your passions have banished with the red of poisoned pigments; who wreathe your aching heads with purchased tresses torn from prisons, madhouses, and coffins; who spend your lives in one incessant struggle, first the rivalry of vanity and then the rivalry of ambition; who deck out greed, and selfishness, and worship of station or of gold as "love," and then wonder that your hapless dupes, seizing the idol that you offer them as worthy of their worship, fling it from them with a curse, finding it dumb, and deaf, and merciless, a thing of wood and stone.

"Animalism," forsooth! God knows it would be well for you here and hereafter, men and women both, were you only patient, continent, and single-minded; only faithful, gentle, and long-suffering, as are the brutes that you mock, and misuse, and vilify in the supreme blindness of your egregious vanity!

From beneath my chair I surveyed with some interest and with more trepidation the society around the banqueting-table of Laura Pearl, while Fanfreluche, kindly squatting near me, drew my attention to each personage in turn.

"Look yonder, at that tall slender man farthest from Pearl," she murmured to me in that language which, like the utterances of the fairies, cannot be heard by the gross ears of human creatures. By the way, with all your vaunted superiority, a fly can eclipse you in sight, a bird in volitation, a wasp in architecture, a bee in political economy and geometry, a water spider in aquatic science and subtlety, a—good heavens! one could spread the list over ten pages!

"Do you see that tall fair man with the white flower in his coat?" pursued Fanfreluche; "the one with the handsome, contemptuous, weary face, the gray eyes, and the dark straight eyebrows, who looks 'aristocrat' all over him, and has made his face as expressionless as a colourless piece of repoussé work—that's Beltran. You're afraid of him? So are most people at first sight, and a good many of them ever afterwards for that matter. I don't know why; it's only manner with him. The fools toady him so; he's obliged to give them a good sound kick with the boot-heel of insolence as it were."

"Why does he keep the society of fools?"

"Little donkey! He lives in the world, don't he?" cried Fanfreluche with immeasurable sarcasm. "It's very easy to get into ditch-water, but not so easy to get out. Besides, a man as rich as Beltran has been—pshaw! *is*, I mean—can't find a world quit' of a flood of parasites, any more than a salmon can swim in rivers free of minnows. Look there, that little fellow with the brilliant eyes, and the full lips, and the

crisp brown hair—isn't that he who bought you? Yes? I
knew it. Well, that's the Mouse, Leo Lance. He was the
son of a tobacconist, they do say, somewhere down south;
but had a classic education, and uncommonly sharp wits. He
writes well and he talks well—in his own way; cribs right
and left; but wears his stolen clothes so that they look like
his own skin. Anyhow, he is in society to a good extent,
and lives with the 'swells,' whom he copies and worships,
because they're of use to him; and damns and detests, because they only admit him on sufferance, and don't take him
amongst their own women."

"He did buy me," I murmured; "why does he not notice
me now?"

"Pooh! he's never seen you before, my dear," said Fanfreluche, with her peculiar grin of significance—"never!
Don't be so indiscreet as to recognise him. The great art in
society is to be able to stare our oldest friends in the face as
if we'd never met them in all our lives before. It's an art
that's always handy; for nine times out of ten you do really
want to cut them; and if you don't, it only looks good style
to have forgotten people, and makes them feel themselves of
no consequence in such a great world as yours—"

"But with real friends?" I began, my mind reverting to
my dear old Ben.

"Pshaw! my little daisy," scoffed Fanfreluche. "There
are no 'friends' now-a-days; there are only acquaintances.
Beltran is 'friends' with ever so many men, whom yet he
pills with black balls every time they're put up for his
clubs."

"That bright, fair-faced, curly-haired boy, is the little
Marquis of Montferrat," she resumed. "He has been of age
a year, and is half-ruined already. What by? O, yearlings,
and women, and big *coups* at the tables—the old story!
Yonder's Evrecombe, his well-beloved Mentor, who, with the
women as his assistants, decoys him into what nets he
pleases."

"A swindler?" I inquired tremblingly.

"A swindler? Good gracious, no!" cried the little lady. "Evrecombe is a perfectly well-born gentleman. Did you ever see a more elegant person? And the day little Monti shoots himself, or rushes out of Europe with worse dishonour than death at his heels, his Mentor will sip an ice drink in his club, and murmur serenely, 'I warned him!'

"Do you see Deringham Denzil, there?" she pursued after a brief pause. "Derry, as they call him; a big fellow, awfully handsome; bearded and bronzed like an Asiatic? Looks like a guerilla chief, doesn't he? with his reckless, devil-may-care, picturesque face, and those great sinewy limbs of his?—well, he is one of the Mice too; and for a caustic piece of incisive irony, or a wistful tender touch of thought, there is nobody equal to that stalwart debonair brigand. He has a story too, but I'll tell you that some other time. That man, with the superb golden-haired head there, is the painter Marmion Eagle (he's a colossus in the studio, and mad as a March hare out of it; all great artists are); and the delicate handsome creature next him, with a face like some pretty brunette's is a cavalry-soldier, St. John Milton. He has been cut all to pieces a hundred times, and has seen more service, and killed more men to his own hand, than any man of his years in the army. Hear him tell how he set the skulls of all the Asiatics he had ever killed in a row on the top of the flat roof of his house, one illuminating night, in Calcutta, with the skulls all filled up with clay, and a candle stuck into each, and lighting up the fleshless jaws, and shining through the orbless eyes!—it will make your very blood run cold. But he never does talk of himself hardly—your great soldiers are always very modest over their own bits of derring-do. There, I don't see any one else to tell you about;—of the other two, one is a guardsman, and the other a member of parliament; both pleasant fellows, gentle as women, and wild as the grouse in November. But listen! there's Beltran calling me."

She trotted up to her hero, who stroked her and gave her a sweetmeat from the gold bonbon-stands on the table; doing this he caught sight of myself, and asked whence that new white dog had come.

"I bought him," said Laura Pearl carelessly; and I wondered her voice did not break the spell of her beauty for all of them, it was so harsh, so coarse in fibre, so metal-like in its resonance. "A man offered him to me to-day in the Park for a guinea, collar and all, as you see him."

"Stole him, then?"

"Well, that warn't my affair if he did."

She distinctly said "warn't."

"Yes, it was. What do you buy dogs for? You can have dozens given you."

"It's a pretty beast, Beltran?"

"O! pretty enough. Looks awfully miserable too. Hungry —eh?"

He addressed the last phrase to me, and in the anguish of my feelings I could not restrain a piteous howl. He laughed, and set me down some croquettes of chicken on his own plate.

"I hate the dogs messing and feeding in the rooms," muttered the Pearl sullenly.

"Better take care they're fed out of it, then," said Beltran, in his negligent, indifferent fashion: she looked angered, and struck Fanfreluche a sharp blow with the ivory sticks of her fan.

I wondered if these gentle amenities were the custom between lovers in the fashionable world of Pearl et Cie.

"Worth twenty sovereigns, if he be worth one," murmured Beltran, surveying me as I ate. "Pure Lion-dog, eh, Lance?"

"Looks so," responded the Mouse, putting up his eyeglass to study me.

"Would you know the man that you had him from, Laura?" asked Beltran.

"Good gracious, no! I'm sure I shouldn't!"

"And why on earth did you buy him?"

"'Cause he seemed dirt cheap at a guinea. What a heap

of fuss and nonsense, Vere, you make about that little wretch!"

I turned hot and cold, and trembled over my croquettes: I had only been up at the table one minute and a half, and already I had heard four gigantic, and apparently utterly meaningless, falsehoods! Was this inevitable in "high society?"

Beltran laughed a little; it seemed to amuse him to be accused of making a fuss about anything, as it did, indeed, appear utterly irreconcilable with the extreme quietism, and half cynical, half languid weariness of his habitual tone and manner.

The moments that followed were not sweet to me; for they passed in my being handed about from one to another until I had run the gauntlet of the whole circle. Happily their verdict was favourable; and all of them, Leo Lance the most emphatically, congratulated the Pearl on having so cheaply obtained such a thorough-bred. All, indeed, save Beltran, who having affirmed again that, if she got me for a guinea, the man had stolen me, shut his lips, and vouchsafed no more on the subject.

The Mouse and those loudest in my praises offered me nothing to eat; Beltran, to whom my presence seemed scarcely satisfactorily accounted for, remembered me, and gave me a slice of a duckling and a handful of almond-cakes. After this they forgot me; except when Laura Pearl, with Lance and the little Marquis, amused themselves in frightening me out of my wits by letting off rose-water crackers in my eyes, and pelting me with crystallised chestnuts, till I was both deaf and blind.

"Monkeyish malice, my dear," murmured Fanfreluche, as an enormous hard bonbon hit me sharply on the eye. "Boys, and cads, and women have it. Go under Beltran's chair."

I was so confused, and indeed so hurt, though their missiles were only rose-water and chestnuts, that I heard little of all that passed at the table.

Pearl laughed very often, laughed long, and laughed

9*

loudly, showing the most magnificent teeth in the world; and some stories were told, which, if not over-decorous, were to a surety wittily, if wickedly imagined. Beyond these the proprieties were in no way violated; and if it was all laughable chatter enough, mere gossip of the day lightly told, there were none of those brilliant scintillations which outsiders are given to imagining as coruscating perpetually in such spheres as this.

Men, as I know now, do not take the trouble to be amusing in the society of Pearl's sisterhood; they pay, and think the purse-strings quite enough to draw, without being wearied to draw also on their mental capital.

What good things there were said, came from the merry mouth of Lance.

"If that Mouse hadn't sung, and didn't sing, he wouldn't feast in this cheese," Fanfreluche metaphorically explained to me; and when I asked further explanation, added:

"Little goose! Beltran gives him dinners; and he is to amuse Beltran. It's a fair exchange. Do you suppose our Stuart princes don't keep their Will Somers to jest for them? In old times, you know, the noblemen's fools wore motley, and jingled bells atop of their caps; now they wear dress-coats, and half-guinea rosebuds in their button-holes. But the class hasn't changed a bit. And their lord's whip is an insolent word; and their lord's wage is paid out to them in dinners and suppers, and water parties, and race-weeks, and mayhap, if they're very presentable fools indeed, in a club ballot and an autumn shooting."

"The poor fools!" I murmured, for fellow-feeling makes us wondrous kind, and I had just been the butt of crackers and marrons-glacés.

"Poor indeed!" sneered Fanfreluche. "It's the poor princes, I think! paying all they do for dull wit that they could eclipse in a second themselves if they only weren't too indolent to talk! The fools make pretty perquisites, I can assure you, and run up all the rungs of the ladder in no time. I've seen a fool—in the end—sift aloft, looking sanctity and

decorum itself, and gripping his money-bags tight, while the
Prince sank below in a bottomless sea of ruin, with the sharks
of Debt and the vultures of Venality tearing him asunder
between them!"

"It is his own fault?" I suggested..

"Not at all!" snapped Fanfreluche. "He has been ten
to one too heedless to watch, and too generous to distrust,
like—but you know nothing about it, you are so young; and
youth is always as obstinate as it is ignorant, and as illiberal
as it is illiterate. I hate youth!"

"But you are not old yourself, surely?" I demanded.

"Pooh!" scoffed Fanfreluche, "I am feminine! And into
every feminine thing, my dear, the Devil, before it is born,
instils the knowledge of evil: for he still keeps the apples by
him with which he tempted poor Eve; only there is but the
juice of evil left beneath the rosy velvet skin, for the golden
side that held the knowledge of good is all shrivelled up,
withered by the winds of sin that blow for ever through the
universe."

And having said this she would say no more, but sat
watching with her black and brilliant eyes; and looking so
fearfully like a very little but very terrible devil herself, that
I trembled, and thought that indeed through the warm
fragrant air of the banqueting-chamber I heard and felt the
passing breath of that sirocco of guilt which, daily and
nightly, sweeps over the sick and weary world, and burns it
with consuming fever, and will not let it lie in peace, and
rest.

The dinner lasted long; there were some thirteen services
—I counted them in amaze; at its close there was the scent
of variously-scented smoke, and the laugh of Laura Pearl
rang louder.

From the table they passed to the drawing-room up-stairs;
which glowed with ten times more light, ten times more
colour, ten times more brilliancy than the other apartment,
and was indeed one mass of scintillating gold, and silver,

and amber; not a large room, everything in the house was small and *bijou*, but intensely luxurious and very costly.

They had not been there many moments before they gathered round a table on which stood a pretty little apparatus, made of rosewood and ebony and ormolu; a sort of plate, it seemed to me, in which her hand, with its rings blazing forth bright rays, was for ever carelessly tossing a little ivory ball.

What they were doing I could not tell; it engrossed them entirely. Some grew very pale, some very flushed; all were intent, silent, breathlessly eager; and they rarely moved, save when one or other of them went to a marble stand, on which claret-cup, and cognac, and effervescing waters were placed, kept cool amongst great glittering rock-crystals of square cut ice.

Their faces wore a curious look, I thought. I have seen it often enough since then at half the gaming-tables of Europe.

I had gazed at them, amazed and entranced, for half-an-hour or thereabout when Fanfreluche approached me.

"Come away, child," she whispered. "It's midnight, come to bed."

"I want to stay here!" I remonstrated. "I want to see them—"

"O, do you? They're not attractive to see. Some of them must lose, you know; and some will be drunk when the morning finds them. Beltran won't, but three or four of the others will. There is no drinking now-a-days we're told—O no!— and no gaming-houses either. What a precious clever thing is Legislation; it bars men out from doing a thing in public, and so they go and do it ten times more in private! But then nobody guesses it, you see, and that's all Legislation cares. They've shut up the silver hells, and the gentlemen lose an estate in a night at the Cocodés' Club, and stake hundreds on the Red in their mistresses' drawing-rooms. So Law means to shut up the public-house; and the working men will soak themselves in gin and rum in their own cellars all Sunday

long, and pay twenty per cent. more for the liquor because it
will be supplied at a risk. O, Law is wondrous clever! But
do come away, little one; you're only a baby, and this house
isn't edifying after midnight."

"Your Beltran can't be so very good, then, since he is so
fond of it!" I retorted, angry to be treated so childishly.

"Pooh, my dear! Beltran seeks what he scorns; and
caresses his own ruin. He's not uncommon there. I tell you
he's an awful fool, and I never said anything at all about his
morals. The world thinks very badly of him; and so may
you if you like. Come away—that's all."

And by dint of threats and persuasions she half drove and
half coaxed me out of the room, and into the little, dark, deserted boudoir we had previously occupied.

"Go to sleep, child!" she cried, pushing me on to a soft
silk mat; and I was too sleepy in truth to disobey.

Once I awoke myself in my vivid dreams to ask her a
question.

"Is that woman *really* a sovereign, Fanfreluche?"

I could see even in the moonlit darkness the grin of her
little white teeth.

"O yes, my dear—honour bright. If you doubt it, just
go and look in at the fashionable photographic shops: you'll
see her between Queen Victoria and the Archbishop of
Canterbury; and she sells better, they say, than either the
ermine or the lawn. Good-night, and for gracious' sake don't
chatter!"

CHAPTER XII.

At the Coronet Theatre.

WHEN I awoke the next morning, I certainly found myself
in a blue velvet-hung apartment; I stared at myself repeated
a dozen times in as many mirrors; I wore on my collar a beautiful azuresatin rosette nearly the size of my head; and the
man who brought us our breakfast served us minced chicken
on a very exquisitely painted china plate; but I had been

more joyous by far on the rough red bricks of Ben's cottage kitchen.

"These fine things don't make one's happiness," I murmured pensively to Fanfreluche.

"No, my dear, they don't;" the little worldling admitted. "They do to women; they're so material, you see. They are angels—O yes, of course!—but they're uncommonly sharp angels where money and good living are concerned. Just watch them—watch the tail of their eye—when a cheque is being written or an *éprouvette* being brought to table. And after all, you know, minced chicken is a good deal nicer than dry bread. Of course we can easily be sentimental and above this sort of thing, when the chicken *is* in our mouths where we sit by the fire; but if we were gnawing wretched bones, out in the cold of the streets, I doubt if we should feed in such a sublime mood. All the praises of poverty are sung by the minstrel who has got a golden harp to chant them on; and all the encomiums on renunciation come from your *bon viveur* who never denied himself aught in his life!"

"Then everybody is a hypocrite?"

"Not a bit, child. We always like what we haven't got; and people are quite honest very often in their professions, though they give the lie direct to them in their practice. People can talk themselves into believing that they believe anything. When the preacher discourses on the excellence of holiness he may have been a thorough-going scamp all his life; but it don't follow he's dishonest, because he's so accustomed to talk goody-goody talk that it runs off his lips as the thread off a reel—"

"But he must know he's a scamp?"

"Good gracious me, why should he? I have met a thousand scamps; but I never met one who considered himself so. Self-knowledge isn't so common. Bless you, my dear, a man no more sees himself, as others see him, in a moral looking-glass than he does in a mirror out of his dressing-box. I know a man who has forged bills, run off with his neighbour's wife, and left sixty thousand pounds odd in debts behind him; but he only thinks himself "a victim of circumstances" —honestly thinks it too. A man never is so honest as when he speaks well of himself. Men are always optimists when they look inwards, and pessimists when they look round them."

I yawned a little: nothing is so pleasant, as I have known later, as to display your worldly wisdom in epigram and dissertation, but it is a trifle tedious to hear another person display theirs.

When you talk yourself, you think how witty, how original, how acute you are; but when another does so, you are very apt to think only—What a crib from Rochefoucauld!

However, of course I did not think this then; I only thought that I wished Fanfreluche was not quite so much given over to the love of her own chatter, and inquired of her how we were to spend the morning.

"It's a chance, my dear," she responded. "She's always amusing herself; but she'll leave me to split my very throat with yawning all day long sometimes. They're awfully egotistical, those women—specially *this* class. You see, all their girlhood through, they lived hardly; and were beaten and worked, and half-starved; and thought a scrap of bacon or a scrag of mutton a feast for the gods; and could hardly pin their rags together enough to look decent, or keep the wind and the rain from their shivering bodies. Well!—when they come into this world, and are dressed like empresses, and stuff sweetmeats all day long, and drive hither and thither, and eat and drink of the best the earth gives, why naturally they can't have enough of it. And their necklace stones are as big as walnuts; and their wines are poured out in floods; and their dishes are all over-seasoned; and their horses all step up to their very noses; and their houses are gilded from the area gate to the attic. They over-do it all in fact, just because they are in love with it; and in the same way they are in love with pleasure, and exaggerate the pretty prancing creature till her laugh is a roar, and her dance is a breakdown, and her smile is a grimace, and her rosebud is a peony, and her bright frolic is a frenzy."

And Fanfreluche snapped her teeth together, with the air she always wore when she thought she had said something that was especially clever.

I listened bewildered and awed.

"But *she* never came out of hard life and starvation?" I breathed scarcely audibly.

"I don't know where she came from, child," returned Fanfreluche pettishly. "I declare you spoil all generalities by dragging them down to personalities—you are almost as bad as a woman. As for starvation—may be not. That was a figure of speech. But she came from obscurity, my dear, —she can hardly read; she can hardly write; she don't speak common grammar even now! She'll get awfully drunk on her Jules Mumm and her Poméry; and she's as common and vulgar a creature, in all save her beauty, as any Irish fishwoman that ever swore at old Billingsgate. You know she was playing in burlesques at a horrid little East-end theatre, when *we* first heard of her (I lived with Frédégonde then); Freddie is dead now; killed herself with absinthe, and too many truffles. Old Lord George picked Pearl out of the East; and first set her going in this sort of style, in a little villa, with a pair of cream ponies, and all the rest of it. Lord George died, in less than three months, of apoplexy, in at White's one night; and Laura had two or three adventures, picking up no end of jewellery, and gold, and nicknacks on the road as it were. Finally she threw herself at Beltran's head; and he took her to Baden; then brought her out here in the burlesque of Corinne and the Crowner, last Christmas. Act! No, she can't act a bit. She has no talent. But she can look amazingly striking; and she poses wonderfully well; and as at our house we have chiefly those burlesque or extravaganza pieces, good looks and attitudes are perhaps the chief things that we want. Besides, she don't depend on that: if Beltran broke with her, which he's scarcely likely to do, and if she didn't take another engagement, she'd have her handsome face and that dear little innocent roulette wheel! Pearl, so long as she is only the fashion, can make her thousands as fast as she pleases—"

"But had she really nothing then, two years ago?"

"Pshaw! Those—Pearls—never do have anything while they live in their oyster-shells. That is, till they've broken a man or two. When Lord George—he was an old virtuoso, you know, my dear, and poked about in very queer places after his bric-à-brac!—first lit on her in Houndsditch, or Shoreditch, or some ditch or another, she was drinking gin and eating tripe in a little kennel of a room off her music hall, where she showed for two shillings a night, and lived in an attic with a low comedy man. He took a ten-pound note for giving her up, and said he'd never sold a bit of trash half so profitably in all the days of his life—"

"What was her real name?" I pursued, haunted by this vague fancy, which yet seemed to me utterly incredible and insensate.

"I'm sure, my dear, I don't know," scoffed Fanfreluche. "They never have any real names. There may be women who have no alias; but there are no women who have only one! She called herself 'Laura Pearl' when she came amongst us. If a mare win the Blue Ribbon of the Turf, what on earth does it matter whether she has been christened Venus Anadyomene, or Sally, in the stable where she was foaled? She has won the Derby; and nobody cares a straw what her name is. They pile their money on her—"

"But they do care what her race was?" I hinted with an acuteness that surprised myself.

"Ah, to be sure they do," assented the little lady. "But then, my dear, men are much wiser about their horses than they are about their women. They look for vice in their racer's eye, but they never heed it in their mistress's; and though they wouldn't bet a single shilling on a screw, they'll squander tens of thousands on a vixen!—"

"Since she was this vile low creature, why did you tell me she was a sovereign?" I grumbled in reproachful wonder.

"Because she is one, you daisy," said Fanfreluche, with curt acerbity. "The good people are afraid of 'mob-rule' in Europe just now,—the fools!—the very dregs of the mob rule already; the Mob Feminine raised on high from the gutter, with its hands clutching gold, and its lips breathing poison, and its vices mimicked in palaces, and its lusts murdering the brains, and the souls, and the bodies of men!"

I made no reply; I was a little impatient of her exordium, and I was pursued with this strange thought which had risen in me, and which I rejected as madness.

I remembered the girl in her russet bodice with her yellow glass beads round her throat, chaffering in the ivy-hung porch over the open pack of the little withered old pedlar;— I remembered the woman who had blazed in her rubies, and her flame-hued radiance of colour, under the fiery glow of light in her supper chamber; it was not possible that these twain could be one?

I felt blind and giddy, and sick at heart.

"You are ill, you little simpleton," said the sharp yet kindly voice of my monitress. "If you can't stand the sight of evil in this world, lick up some arsenic at once, my dear! Ah! there's Lizzie come for us for a walk. She is a good creature;—yes—though she serves a Pearl. A woman may be virtuous in any atmosphere if she like. Lizzie hates evil with all her soul—to be sure she is ugly, poor thing, which makes innocence come easier!—but she was once brought by accident into the service of the Pearls, and now nobody of another class would take her, and she must work and get her wages, or her old mother would starve. So she stays. There is good to be found everywhere, my dear, if you only look for it—and excellence in nothing."

With which she trotted out of doors into the Park, which was nigh at hand; and I followed her, very sad at heart still.

For no young thing can be consoled by the negative comfort that good only barely balances evil on earth; and the assurance that excellence is as unattainable as the four-leaved

shamrock. When we are very young we could better bear
evil in extremes if thereby we could only obtain good in extremes likewise.

It is the certainty that vice and virtue are so fearfully
even; so perfectly weighted and measured in the same scales;
so entirely impotent one against each other; which makes
their drawn-battle through all the ages,—for which no end is
perceivable in the future,—so dreary, so depressing, so hopelessly melancholy to all creatures that possess the chivalries
of an innocent youth.

In the latter half of the day we went out again: and this
time I was promoted to the dignity of the front cushion in the
dainty little equipage which Laura Pearl drove herself, with
a tiny groom standing behind her, and two of the handsomest
gray ponies on the town in her silver-plated and red-ribboned
harness.

She did not drive with any sort of skill, and she used the
whip unsparingly; but she drove with fury, and without any
fear whatever, so that her science appeared considerable and
her narrow escapes were many and startling.

It was raw chilly spring weather, the Easter week falling
early that year, and there were not many people in the Ladies'
Mile; but she never stopped under the leafless trees without
being surrounded by a bevy of good-looking, well-bred men;
and she did not sweep round the turning at full trot without
all the eyes that were there following her in admiration. Indeed, so great was the homage she received—for even some
women in splendid carriages gazed at her with intent interest
—that I began once more to think that she must be a crowned
queen of some kind, and that Fanfreluche had only been
laughing at me when she talked of two shillings a night, and
the Argyle Rooms, and the Low Comedy lover who took ten
pounds.

"Look, how they stare after her, and how the men bow?"
I whispered to Fanfreluche. "She must be very eminent and
powerful in some way?"

"Never said she wasn't, my dear," returned that cynic

with a grin. "She's one of the best chaff-cutting machines
for chopping up men's fortunes and souls in double quick
time that has ever been wound up and set going on earth!"

"But they can't worship wickedness?" I expostulated.

She grinned again.

"Can't they, my dear? Will you tell me what they do
worship then? The greed of the capitalist, the fraud of the
diplomatist, the time-serving of the statesman, the lies of the
journalist, the cants of the author, the chicaneries of the mer-
chant,—they are all worshipped if only successful. And why
then object to the successful vice of a woman? You know the
Ark of Israel, and the calf of Belial, were both made of gold;
—Religion has never since changed the metal of her one
adoration."

I did not understand, and kept silence, watching the scene
that to me was so strange and beguiling; though Fanfreluche
turned up her nose at it, because, being Easter week, there
was nobody in London, as she said with much scorn:—
even her beloved Beltran having gone with that noonday to
Paris.

After the Park, we drove to the shops; and my impression that our charioteer was a regal ruler, and that the chatter
of Fanfreluche was untrue, was deepened by the excessive
deference with which the bowing shopmen treated her.

They came out, and stood bareheaded in the sharp east
wind, listening reverentially to her commands; or when she
descended, and entered their establishments, welcomed her
with that hideous subserviency of the snob-mercantile to a
good customer, which can only be equalled by his equally
hideous brutality to a penniless debtor. We followed her,
Fanfreluche taking the initiative, and nothing could exceed
the civility of the business people: in one place they gave
me a ball, in another they fed me with macaroons, in a third
they let my little dusty feet trample a new amber satin dress
unchastised, in a fourth they kissed me.

I became quite puffed-up with pride.

"You little idiot!" sneered Fanfreluche. "You think it's

for yourself? My dear, if Laura Pearl liked to go through the town with a boa-constrictor, every shopkeeper would fondle the reptile, and stuff him with rabbits. She pays better than anybody going—you see she's so astonishingly honest! If *they* get arrested she'll only shrug her shoulders; but she'll always keep well to windward of Whitecross-street herself!"

I did not answer. My mouth was full of my red-leather ball, and I thought some jealousy lurked in the cynic, because when they gave me a macaroon they only offered her a very plain biscuit.

I did her wrong in this. But whenever yet did any living creature not prefer to imagine ill-natured envy in a friend, than to suppose a compliment to himself insincere?

By the time we had been through half-a-dozen of these establishments, the pony-carriage was piled high, with scores of tempting packages, covered with the crimson-lined tiger-skin.

"What can she do with them all?" I asked, getting over my anger.

"She don't want one of them," said Fanfreluche curtly, as though the plain biscuit still rankled in her mind. "But she likes to get them, and strew them round her, and break them, or burn them, or toss them to her maid. Ah, my dear, you little dream the ecstatic delight that exists in Waste, for the vulgarity of a mind that has never enjoyed Possession, till it comes to riot at one blow in Spoliation!"

"I do wish you would answer me plainly," I said sulkily, "without—without—"

"Epigrams?" she added sharply; "I daresay you do, my dear. Epigrams are the salts of life; but they wither up the grasses of foolishness, and naturally the grasses hate to be sprinkled therewith."

At that moment we had reached our home, which was an elegant little bijou house, near the Park; and Laura Pearl, as she was about to put her jewelled whip in the rest, hit me a sharp crack with the long white lash as I jumped out eagerly to the ground; I shrieked, and she laughed:—I felt sure *then* that she was no sovereign, but only a very vile woman.

"What had I done?" I asked piteously of Fanfreluche; wishing now that I had given her the macaroon.

"Nothing in life, my dear," she replied. "She hits you as she ruins them—because she finds fun in the sport. But you see she never hits me—why? Because the first time she did I bit her. To show your teeth, and make them felt too, is the only way with women like her. She whips you, and you crinch to her—she'll hit you a dozen times in a day. She flies at them, and they give her a cheque, or a diamond, or a carriage-horse;—she'll have her furies a dozen times in a week. If you treated her to your teeth, and they to a few sound curses, she would trouble neither you nor them any more—"

"Is Beltran even afraid of her?" I whispered.

"Well, he is!" said Fanfreluche, with a sigh. "He's as bold as a lion with men; hard as nails in the hunting-field; fought two duels abroad in his young days; and saved five sailors from a sinking ship last autumn. But he is afraid of the Pearl. Not afraid of *her*—you know, but afraid of a scene, which he hates; afraid of her temper, which is the devil's; afraid of her vengeance, if ever he left her. Afraid—well! afraid, as the boldest men are of a woman whom they know is bad to the core, yet whom they love for her beauty, and fancy is faithful to them, and have trusted with more secrets of their lives than they care to remember. Why do these connections often last all the years that they do? Love? —Pooh! Very little of that; but very much of the force of habit, and very much of the dread of annoyance."

"But why put themselves in the power—"

"Tut, my dear! Why does a lad climb a walnut-tree when he knows a spring-gun is underneath? He only thinks of eating the walnuts; and always trusts that this one particular spring-gun is unloaded."

"Well, some guns are rusty and will not do harm?" I had

heard Ben Dare say that the guns in the preserves were thus
sometimes after heavy rains; and I thought the allegorical
allusion came in neat and pat.

"Possibly, my dear," said my lady, who did not like other
people to be epigrammatic. "But if a gun ever rusts enough
to prevent explosion, no woman ever lets her power of evil
rust long enough to get out of use! And now scamper up-
stairs to Lizzie; I want my dinner. There'll be no fun to-
night; Pearl goes to dine with a Whig Duke (the Privy Seal),
at one of the big inns."

"Why does a Duke have to dine at an inn?" I asked in
wonder; my only notion of an inn being derived from the little
public of the Miner's Joy in Derbyshire.

"Why, you simpleton, he don't invite Laura to dine with
his Duchess at home, does he? Besides, these huge hotels
are charming. Last season I belonged to the Guards; and I
went every Sunday with them to their crack dinners at the
Leviathan."

"I thought the Guards had a mess?"—I had heard the
bull-dogs talk of these things.

"You goose, so they have. But they can't take Pearl et
Cie to it; and they like Pearls on a Sunday. Pearls are their
way of keeping the seventh day holy; so they dine at the
Leviathan, or Richmond, or Greenwich. Get upstairs!"

We spent a quiet evening, when the mistress of our des-
tinies had swept down to her brougham at nine o'clock, gloriously apparelled in a marvellous glimmer of hues, and foun-
tain spray of laces. Fanfreluche looked after her with a grin.

"If she only never drew off her gloves and never opened
her lips, who on earth could tell her from the proudest *grande
dame* of them all? She'll come home in good humour. Privy
Seal has a very grand, gracious fashion of doing things. She'll
be sure to find a big sapphire drop in her bonbon-cracker,
and a jewelled holder with a rare flower or two by her plate,
and very likely a mechanical humming-bird to fly out of the
épergne, and nestle in her bosom with a choice ring in his
mouth. His Grace has very pretty inventive ways. But he's

cut down all the woods round his noble old castle; and he won't pay one of his son's debts at Ch. Ch."

"Does he pay his own?"

"My dear!—a Duke and a Privy Seal never is asked to condescend to such a commonplace!"

"Is Beltran jealous of him?"

"Pooh! Jealousy isn't his form at all. He's the most indifferent of mortals, though he is in love with her in his way. Besides, he *thinks* she's faithful to him. He couldn't do more if he were a husband; and she a Griselda and an Arria Pætus!"

And Fanfreluche grinned again with the look which always made my blood run cold, and made me believe that after all this good-natured, bitter-tongued little black thing might prove in the end a limb of Satanus. Which was an uncomfortable thought of the only friend that I now possessed in the width of the world.

"The Coronet's open to-night," said Fanfreluche to me a few evenings later. "There's the new extravaganza coming on. When she goes do you follow me, and nip into her brougham, and hide yourself as I do under the silk mat. She won't notice, ten to one, or if she do notice she won't care, so long as we make no noise. I often go myself; it's awful fun. They quarrel fit to kill themselves."

And with much trepidation of soul I prepared to follow my daring leader. At a little before eight Laura Pearl passed out to her neat night-brougham; and with rare good luck we eluded all vigilance, and were concealed among the curls of the friendly mat and covered by the flow of her velvet skirts without any one being aware of it, or at least attempting to eject us.

I shivered and trembled; of where I was going I had no sort of conception. And from what I had seen of the stage at the Wake-feast I was firmly persuaded that "play-actors" were chiefly armed with whips and swords; and that there was always first and foremost amongst them one red-and-white devil, in a motley-painted skin, with a mouth grinning from ear to ear, who thumped everybody right and left, and sat down upon babies till they were flattened to pancakes.

If there should be a clown here?—and if he should sit upon me?

However, curiosity is, generally speaking, a stronger passion than even cowardice, and it proved to be so with myself.

The Coronet, as I learned subsequently, was a very fashionable theatre. It had ruined everybody that had ever had anything to do with it; and had therefore made good its title to fashion as strongly as Pearl had made hers.

It had been erected some dozen years; and in that space of time had brought to grief no less than fourteen various proprietors. The veritable owner of it was, oddly enough, a country clergyman, to whom it had been left by his father, a metropolitan contractor, who had first built it, and then claimed it for debt. His Reverence was a strictly Evangelical person, and, as I have heard, denounced the autumnal fair held in his south-country village with fearful anathema. But he did not sell the theatre; and every half-year his lawyers transmitted him six hundred pounds, the biannual rental of those hapless mortals who had been severally trapped into becoming lessee. The good lessor drew the money, but always ignored the source, and spoke vaguely thereof to his agents as "my late father's properties in the west-end of town."

I have heard also that the defunct contractor left him two gin-palaces; but of this I am not sure: at any rate, this reverend person had so many thousands a-year in addition to his piety, that his bishop presented him with a living of very high value, feeling it apostolically incumbent upon himself to obey the precept of "to those who have much shall much be given."

The first lessee of the Coronet had been a man in the Guards, whom it had ruined in one winter season. It brought him so deeply into the Jews' hands, that he had to sell at a ridiculous loss.

The person who succeeded him, being an actor himself with some capital, should have known something of what he

10*

was about. He was fool enough, however, to attempt high
art, and was smashed utterly in a twelvemonth; exquisite
scenery, for which he had paid 700*l*., going at auction for
20*l*., and genuine buhl cabinets, purchased in Paris for 200*l*.
apiece, being knocked down for a 5*l*. note. I believe he died
very miserably in a wretched estaminet in the north of France,
as a man deserved to do who insulted the London public by
offering to improve its taste.

It would fill pages to recount the various adventures of the
various proprietors of the theatre, which I heard by degrees
from the omniscient little Fanfreluche. Few escaped with
only a scorch from its furnace that smelted their gold so fast:
none escaped with entire impunity; many cursed it loudly and
deeply. One pretty boy (although so young, already in your
parliament, and of great promise there), the younger son of a
great peer, took it for an actress whom he adored—a beautiful brown foreign singer, for whom on his little stage he
brought out the delicate, delicious Venetian *bouffe* opera, that
was caviare to the English musical world. In two short
seasons, the boy-politician spent so much over this miniature
opera and over her, and plunged so hopelessly into the abyss
which money-lenders dig for the young and the rash, that on
a stilly June midnight, just at the hour the House was closing
to the public and opening to its privileged few, a shot was
heard in his own little brilliant supper-chamber; and when the
people flocked thither, they found him stretched across its
threshold—dead.

Some said that a scene he had by chance witnessed between his dark lady and one of his own comrades in her re-
tiring-room had more to do with it than even his losses in
money. It might be so; at any rate, the Israelites put in
claims for thirty thousand pounds, spent in those two seasons
when he had kept the Coronet open. They said also that
when the beautiful brunette found him lifeless, with his own
bullet through a heart that had scarcely beaten three-and-
twenty years, she shrieked and wept, and tore her hair in
agonising grief; but all the same she drew the big onyx ring

off his left hand, and unhooked from his watch-chain the jewelled locket that held her portrait.

All these things, of course, I heard later. At the moment we drove up to the stage-door, the Coronet was leased by our friend, Vere Essendine, Viscount Beltran, who had owned it for the last two years or so, and who (as it was whispered) had lost as much as any of his predecessors, even in that brief space, only that he would probably choose to show longer fight, and would not so quickly prevail on himself to relinquish a favourite amusement.

"Keep close to me," whispered Fanfreluche. "Close!— or else you'll get stolen."

As we descended, the glow of the countless gas-lamps, the pressure of the waiting crowds, the huge letters on the glaring posters, the noise and the confusion, and the glitter of the cross-lights so dazed and terrified me, that I was in danger of forgetting her injunction, and being trampled to death in the street. However, by some miracle, I escaped destruction, and followed my patroness through what appeared to me the most hideous dark passages I had ever beheld.

"She goes to dress. I will show you over the house," said Fanfreluche in her pertest manner, as she trotted along through this seemingly interminable maze.

I heard loud gay bursts of music; I was blinded by alternations of sooty darkness and of blazing light; huge walls of canvas trembled like the shaking walls of an undermined house; vast barriers of timber and of iron loomed above-head and around; loud shocks of sound reverberated through the melody-filled air, as men in paper caps pushed to and fro, in grooves, enormous masses of wood and metal. I was surrounded by devils, imps, fairies, butterflies, peasants in white muslin, shepherds with ribboned crooks; woolly lambs standing on two legs and sucking their thumbs; green and white water-lilies with their arms akimbo, and their tongues thrust in their cheeks at a joke; a winged sylph drinking from a pot of porter, and a golden-haired wood-elf smoking a cigarette.

In a word, I was in that mystic region commonly known as "behind the scenes."

My first impression was, that it was a Pandemonium amidst an earthquake of canvas and timber; my second, that it was extraordinarily commonplace with all its bizarrerie, and intensely vulgar and dreary with all its glitter.

The time was an entr'acte; the previous piece was ended; the burlesque not begun. From the body of the house, of which I caught an oblique glimpse, there came at intervals, above the music, hideous shrieks, hisses, and stamping noises.

"The gods are impatient for a break-down," said Fanfreluche to me; though why gods were there at all, and why they desired any. one to break down in their performances, was not within my comprehension.

She hurried me hither and thither with breathless rapidity. I could only catch flying speeches, and passing glimpses.

"My old man's in front. He'll be good for a necklace when he sees me in this here," said a Water-lily, twisting herself round in the shortest and most transparent of gauze tunics.

"A necklace of brass farthins, then!" sneered the gold-haired Wood-elf. "A ugly old cove like that, as is a filthy Jew-pawnbroker, by the looks on him!—"

"He ain't!" screeched the Lily. "He's a real live lord, and you knows it. He's Lord Algernon Vereker—he is! It's only yer spite, 'cause the stalls don't care a dam for yer cellar-flip-flap! Did ever you get a boo-kay, Miss, in all yer born days! Leastways, since yer mother sent yer out to sell yer pennorths o' tripe and greens?"

What the injured Wood-elf might reply, and what fearful and veiled sarcasm might lie in the tripe-and-greens allusion, I never knew, for I was hurried away to a little dirty bare room, where three Fairy Princes were eating hot kidneys and drinking bottled porter.

The three Fairy Princes were gorgeous in bright satins and gold lace, and showed elegant legs in white silk stockings; and would have been all three really very pretty girls, but for the terrible red paint round the mouth, and black paint under the eyes, and greased white powder on their foreheads and arms.

"Who's in front?" asked Prince Azor, with her mouth full of kidney.

"O, all *her* swells," said Prince Silvertongue savagely, "and all the Press lot. First nights is always just alike. Packed!"

"I see your little chap in the stalls, Mary Ann," said Prince Charming. "You oughter do business with him. Uncommon soft; good for a bracelet a-night; if you keep him well in hand—"

"Better nor that!" said Prince Silvertongue scornfully and mysteriously. "Ain't there no hysters? I hate kidneys, leastways unless I'm at Evans's."

"A cursed bad piece this here," grumbled Prince Charming. "No; there ain't no hysters. A cursed bad piece. The Mouse have spiled it out and out, just to give *her* her dances and attitudes. He's awful spoons on her. I've a good mind to pay forfeit, and go to Alhambra."

"O, lawk! Do take care, you stupid! You've upset all the rouge, and it's a-running among the gravy!"

"Stupid yourself!" retorted Prince Azor, who was the one apostrophised. "You've addled your head along of that gin sling. You've only got two lines to say, and I'll swear you'll say 'em upside down—"

The call-boy's shrill treble was at this instant shouting, "Miss Delany, Miss Visconti, Miss Villiers!" And answering to these patrician names, away the Fairy Princes rushed, leaving the rouge to fraternise with the kidneys, and their quarrel to wait over till the next pause in the performances.

"Curtain's up!" said Fanfreluche curtly, as a storm of applause greeted the appearance of the three Princes, who appeared to be prime favourites with the audience, and who were smiling with radiant sweetness before the "floats."

The shrill treble vociferated afresh:

"Madame de Rohan!—Miss Plantagenet-Courcey!"

I gazed breathless, to behold the representatives of those historic and time-honoured races, so dear to me through my favourite French Memoirs. The two who responded to the call were my friends Water-lily and Wood-elf, as they in their turn sprang on with light pirouettes and fond embraces before the footlights.

Away after them went pell-mell the imps, and the lambs, and the shepherds, in what appeared to me inextricable confusion, though they kept perfect step to the music, and soon formed figure dances out of the chaos.

"What in the world is this?" I asked, in a very agony of amazement.

Fanfreluche turned her little nose in the air.

"The merest business, my dear! The sort of senseless whirligig all these things open with. Give the public twenty pair of good legs a side, and you may treat it to just what hash of puns and balderdash of verse you like. But we *do* do the thing better than most houses. Beltran has all the dresses from Paris; and he sent over the imps themselves from the Folies-Marigny. English children always have too much flesh to make into sprightly demons—and a heavy glum devil's a dreadful thing."

With that she rushed under a white-bearded, ruby-robed king's legs, and darting round at the back of the scenes brought me out on the other side of the stage.

"Look at him!" said my chaperone. "He only comes early first nights. How indifferent he is! And yet there's over a thousand gone clean in this blessed burlesque to-night, not to speak of all the expenses afterwards!"

She referred to Beltran, who leant with his back against an iron girder, and a cigar in his mouth, talking to two other men; with a look of that utter indifference, and of that curious quietude, with which such men as he are pleased to cover the natural restlessness and recklessness of their gamester's temperament.

"Nearly a thousand pounds gone to-night," I cried aghast, "and he can look like that!"

"Pooh, my dear," scoffed Franfreluche. "Last season when I belonged to him, he lost three thousand one night at a certain club where they don't play money down—more's the pity!—and he walked out of it just as calm as he is now, and smoked, and read a new story of Derry Denzil's through before he went to bed."

"He must be enormously rich?"

Fanfreluche grinned.

"My dear, I've seen a millionaire bemoan himself for days over a five-pound note left in a railway-carriage; but if a man bear troubles and losses easily, why, I know he's a gentleman and a beggar!"

"But how can a beggar have thousands to lose?"

"Don't take one so literally! You literal people are the bores of society and the murderers of wit. Look there—that tall big fair man with him is one of his pet friends, Paget Desmond, of the *First Life;* and that other one with the stoop in the shoulders and the red beard is the great *censor morum,* Dudley Moore, proprietor and editor of the *Midas.* All social sins shrink under his scourge;—what a pity they haven't that alliteration in the burlesque;—and all social sinners are mercilessly exposed under his searching lantern. There is no one comparable to him for stoning a man of genius in his virtuous fury; there is no one touches him for moral lessons, conveyed with a scholarly asceticism that utterly ruins the transgressor whom it rebukes—"

"And yet he is here to-night?"   ·

"O yes, to see the forty pair of legs! And has in town a meek-eyed mistress to whom he is moderately faithful because she 'stands being sworn at' so well; and keeps down in the south a charming little abode that bears the closest family likeness to the Parc aux Cerfs. His virtues are nobly printed on fair white paper; his vices are only written on the dusky rags of broken honour."

"He must be a very bad man?"

"Pooh! He is a great man; and wields a great power—in its way. Why, my dear, if the *Midas* condescend (which

is doubtful, for it is æsthetic and highly intellectual) to say
that our forty pair of fine legs have placed us at the very tip-
top of high art and of moral excellence, why the public will
say so after it. Other ages gabbled their paternosters because they were priest-ridden; ours gabbles its platitudes because it is press-ridden."

But I was tired of hearing her chatter, and looked around
me.

Close by was a door that stood a little open; beyond it
was a very comfortless sort of dressing-room; not much better
than that in which the fairy princes had eaten their kidneys;
and out of it, as a butterfly from its dingy chrysalis, emerged
at that moment Laura Pearl.

She was exquisitely arrayed in golden tissues, that floated
about her like sunlit air, and showed all the curves of her
form, all the grace of her limbs, while a girdle of real sapphires flashed fire beneath her breast, and a coronal of the
wondrous blue lilies of the western world glowed above her
brow.

"She's about as much as they'll stand," muttered Dudley
Moore.

I surmise that he alluded to the transparency of her draperies.

Beltran nodded to her, without removing his cigar.

"Knew those blue lilies would tell," he murmured. "You
look very well, Laura."

"Thank you for nothing!" she responded graciously, with
much scorn. "I go on now, don't I?"

"In a minute. Little Courcey is encored in that forest-
song."

The Pearl's brow lowered and darkened; the first scene
had taken about ten minutes; the audience had not yet beheld
herself; and yet they were stopping to encore the Wood-elf
(who was certainly charmingly pretty) in a little snatch of a
ballad of ten bars!

"What a fright that Courcey girl always makes of herself!" she muttered. "Who saw her dress?—she's like a bundle of green twigs and grass!"

"I should be very happy to see her dress," responded Beltran. "Unluckily, she locks her door."

The Pearl flashed a savage glance at him.

"Well, if Paris couldn't give you better nor that in costumes," she laughed viciously, "you might just as well have gone to a tally-shop. What do you say, Mr. Moore?"

"My dear lady! I buy so many second-hand articles when I pay my staff for their written opinions, that of course I stand up for tally-shops with all my heart and soul!"

Beltran laughed; and Laura Pearl glanced rapidly yet stupidly from one to another, as though suspecting them of making fun of her.

At that juncture the Mouse rushed in from the back: tremulous, agitated, flushed, eager.

"You should be on, you should be on!" he cried to her. "For mercy's sake don't keep them waiting!"

"O, gammon! They'll wait as long as I choose!" she retorted: but however she thought better of it, and as the elves and the lambs, and the imps, and the devils rushed off the boards in two opposite armies, she glided herself on to the stage in her character of an enchanted water-queen; with whom the three fairy princes were destined to become wildly enamoured.

From where we stood, an oblique view of the stage, and of a little piece of the stalls, and of the stage-box on the opposite side of the house, was obtainable. The fury of applause was great; even the stalls clapped their delicately gloved hands; and she was received with tumultuous welcome.

To me she looked only a very scantily-dressed woman, going through strange antics in a labyrinth of wooden beams and flapping sails of painted canvas; but I suppose she looked very different from the "front."

That is just the difference that makes everything so curiously altered to different spectators. And your stall-lounger

always thinks your stage-carpenter such a prosaic dolt; and
your stage-carpenter always thinks your stall-lounger such a
consummate fool; and will so think, no doubt, until the end
of time; at least so long as stalls and flies shall have their
being.

All that followed only bewildered me more utterly than
ever.

It seemed one endless succession of wild rushes hither and
thither on the parts of the elves, and lambs, and shepherds,
and devils; and of the most unaccountable conduct in the
fairy princes, who combined the most mediæval of dresses,
and the most chivalrous of heroics, with the broadest of street
slang, and the wildest of casino dances.

There was a romantic minstrel, love-lorn and desolate,
with curls that hung to his waist, who yet bore a banjo and
sung a yelling negro melody. There were river gods, with a
noble old Neptune and a beauteous young Aquarius, who yet
at a certain point discarded all dignity, and abandoned themselves to the Cancan in a manner worthy of students of Paris.
There were charming delicate nymphs who at a signal became living aisles of roses, or blossomed severally into glowing azalea shrubs, yet who after realising all the Greek
dreams of Dryads and Hamadryads, burst all at once into a
comic chorus that made the delighted house literally shriek
aloud with laughter.

Finally, there was the enchanted princess herself, who
looked like a poem and moved like a picture, with the bright
azure lilies, and the blue flashing sapphires; yet who, at the
very moment in which she was rescued from her captivity
and betrothed to Prince Silvertongue, broke forth into a dog-
grel declamation, and danced with all the vigour of a sailor,
and all the license of a *débardeur*, first the hornpipe and then
a breakdown! And—O shade of outraged Thalia!—what
applause she got!

"I think it's a success," said Beltran, quietly, when, the
piece having come to an end, the house shouted for her, and
for the Prince, and for the Wood-elf.

"Not a doubt of it," answered Dudley Moore.

"I'm glad little Courcey's got a call," said Paget Desmond. "She's a jolly little girl."

"She's the best lot amongst 'em," assented Derry Denzil. "That little rat's as honest as the day."

"They seem to take to it, don't they?" asked Leo Lance, pale and breathless.

"Yes; I think you're pretty safe this time, Mouse," assented Beltran. "But for heaven's sake don't make them talk such awful nonsense, next thing you do."

"Nonsense," echoed the Mouse. "Why, that's just what makes it swing smooth. If there'd been ten ounces of sense in it you'd have heard nothing but hisses."

"He's quite right," said Dudley Moore gravely. "The lucky knack of combining the most perfect scenic effect with the most utterly unredeemed vulgarity in speech and gesture is the great essential of dramatic success. Here he has very fittingly wedded *Undine* and the *Belle au Bois Dormante* in his story,—two of the most delicately poetic legends in their different manners that we possess; and he has mixed with them break downs, balderdash, casino dancing, street jargon, countless execrable puns, and occasional indecent allusions. The result is success. The barbarism and *bizarrerie* of the whole thing is undoubtedly rather funny, and precisely hits the popular tastes and desires. I congratulate Mr. Lance immensely myself. The wisest man possible is the man that knows his own age."

The poor Mouse looked dissatisfied and chagrined at this questionable form of felicitation; but he did not dare to complain of the almighty Censor's sarcasm.

Beltran laughed, a little impatiently.

"What a patriotic task, then," he said with a dash of self-contempt, "to supply the sinews of war to those barbarians!"

Dudley Moore shrugged his shoulders.

"My dear Beltran, you must be patriotic, for you amuse the people at a loss, I believe, of some fifty pounds a-night every season. But that isn't your fault. You supply them with what they like best. Our ancestors performed their mysteries and their mummeries, at different seasons and on different stages; but we, who don't believe in the one and are fearfully bored by the other, mix them both together, and take the decoction, indifferently, both in Lent and at Christmas."

"But are we so bad after all?" said Denzil. "I suspect that sort of cry has been raised in each century. Look at those gospel parodies, those religious plays you speak of, in the Middle Ages. Were they really anything so very much better in taste, do you think, than these burlesques and pantomimes of ours?"

"Perhaps not better. But I say they were duly distinct from the fooling; and the fooling too was more genuine than ours, I am convinced. Pantomime was once the genius of gesticulation: the Pulcinella, the Stenterello, the Scaramouch the Arlecchino, required talent of no slight sort in the mimics who represented them. To tell a whole tale solely by the means of gesture and of facial expression—that was ingenious at the least. But what ingenuity is there exhibited by a man's louping about in woman's clothes, spouting bad puns; or in a girl's casting herself into the violent and ungraceful postures of the Cancan? It is simply vulgar, unredeemably vulgar."

"Well, the modern public likes it," hinted the discomfited Mouse.

"Of course. You know the Roman story of the people rating the pantomime plays a thousand times higher than those performed by 'only' the living *personaggi*. Well, your public, Mr. Lance, is much like the Italian populace. They will have the scene-painter, the sensational realism, the Lancashire clog-dance, the pot-house jig,—the wooden puppets, in point of fact, bobbing upon wires,—sooner than they will have the living flesh and blood; pathos, and passion, and genius."

Beltran threw his cigar away, right into a heap of tinfoil and muslin,

"You're quite right; it's awful stuff," he murmured. "But when I tried classic art with that wonderful French woman—you remember?—the gallery was crammed full, but the stalls yawned awfully the first night, and never came afterwards. Now look at the stalls; we've had to add three rows to them And what's done it? Nothing but Laura's breakdowns."

Dudley Moore took snuff out of a tiny box.

"My dear fellow, people don't want to think after dinners of a dozen services. High feeding and comet wines induce a frame of mind in which good ankles and bad puns are far preferable to anything that displays intelligence in the actors, and requires intelligence in its auditors. Pray don't attempt to return to high art while you've those forty pairs of fine legs and the Pearl's cellar-flap dancing."

"Hang you cynics!" said Beltran. "Come and have some supper."

At that moment Laura Pearl came off the boards, she and Prince Silvertongue, literally covered with bouquets; the little Wood-elf had only one, a mere cheap knot of early roses, deftly tied with a blue ribbon, probably the gift of some boy-artist or young musician.

"You did that amazingly well, Laura," said her lover, going up to her; "I'm really very much obliged to you."

"O bother!" she responded graciously. "It's a wretch of a piece, little Mouse; you should have given *me* all the breakdowns, and I've only that beggarly one at the end. Vere, do send me something to drink into my room. I'm dead-tired and as thirsty as pigs on a market-day."

"So you had a call at last?" said Beltran kindly to the little Courcey, as the Pearl disappeared in her dressing-room. "And some flowers too, I see."

The Wood-elf's blue eyes sparkled.

"It was that little song, my lord, as Mr. Denzil put in for me. Mayn't I sing it every night? Do let me!"

"Of course you may. It is in your part."

"But—but," whispered the Wood-elf, who seemed shyer than any other of this astonishingly voluble and dare-devil sisterhood, "if you won't be angry, *she* said as how she'd have it cut out. She couldn't abide me being called along of her; and if I don't have the song they'll hiss me."

"Confound her!" muttered Beltran, as the poor little Wood-elf turned hot and cold at her own temerity in adventuring a remonstrance against the person who was omnipotent with the lordly owner of the Coronet. "You shall have the song, never fear. I'll speak to Wynch myself about it."

Wynch was the acting and ostensible manager; and the Wood-elf's soul was comforted.

"What he says he'll do, he'll do," she murmured, cherishing fondly her knot of roses, while the costly bouquets showered at Pearl were first stripped of any bracelet, note, or other article they might contain, and were then cast aside to wither as best they might.

At this instant Prince Silvertongue, passing me hastily to get across to the room on the other side where the porter and kidneys had been indulged in, kicked me sharply with her scarlet boot, and tore some of my hair out with her gilt spur. Naturally I shrieked loudly with the pain, which for the time was very severe.

Beltran heard and took me up under his arm as he went, followed by Fanfreluche, to his own supper-room; a very pretty apartment, hung with amber, and uniting in it the elegance of a boudoir, the luxuriousness of a smoking-room, and the artistic disorder of a studio. The same room, I heard afterwards, where the boy-politician had shot himself six years before.

"Why will you bring these dogs here, Laura?—they are always getting kicked, or snubbed, or stamped on by some one or other," he asked her impatiently, as she appeared in this chamber, having changed her attire with marvellous celerity, to the velvet and lace of her home dinner-dress.

"I bring 'em because I choose to bring 'em," she answered him sullenly. "That big brute of Denzil's is often enough in the place."

Now, she had not known that we had been with her, and, as Fanfreluche had averred, might have kicked us out of her brougham had she done so. What then could be her motive for this speech? simply, I imagine, to disagree with him, which was a form of amusement that seemed to afford her never-failing refreshment.

"Denzil's dog can take care of himself. These little things can't," he answered her. "By the way, Derry, that's a charming little song you put in for that Courcey girl. Lance is awfully in your debt for it, and so am I."

Laura Pearl's arched eyebrows lowered, and her eyes beneath them grew full of flame and gloom.

"Little Courcey has a pretty voice," Denzil answered. "If she were well taught she'd come out wonderfully. The girl's a game little thing too—keeps straighter than any one of them."

This last phrase he muttered *sotto voce.*

"She squeaks like a penny trumpet," the Pearl observed with savage scorn. "And what you stuck in them ten bars for, Denzil, beats me. I'll have 'em out to-morrow."

"No you won't," said Beltran quietly.

"Won't I?" she cried furiously. "Then all I says is, Beltran, you may find who you can for my part, for I'll never go on your stage no more to have calls and bouquets and thingumbobs flung at that little minx aside of me."

"Very well," said Beltran carelessly. "There are lots of people can do the breakdowns; and you know that's all you *do* do, Laura."

"I'll write a song for you too," added Denzil, with wicked intent. "That's easy enough; and the Mouse can make room, I daresay—"

"When you know I can't sing!" she shrieked in a gust of passion. "And as for you, Lord Beltran, if you *could* get people so easy out of casinoes to fill your hole of a theatre, why wasn't you successful with 'em before I come? Answer me that! And as to insulting of me for that wretched little toad of a Courcey, I'll see her and you—"

But I had better not record the foul language with which she polluted her handsome quivering lips, and transformed one of the most beautiful women Nature ever created into a hissing, mouthing, furious virago.

Beltran sat quite unmoved under the tempest, employing himself in concocting a continental drink with ice, forced strawberries, and a little chambertin wine. Indeed, for aught any one could have told, he might have been as deaf as a stone.

"I wouldn't agitate myself if I were you," he said very quietly, when the hurricane of her words was exhausted. "There's your favourite *ris de veau en demi-deuil*, hadn't you better eat it?"

And she did eat it. The men round the table, of whom there were some eight or ten, could not help smiling at this anti-climax.

Beltran still devoted himself to his ice with the gravest face possible. But I fancied that Laura Pearl knew, somehow or other, that she would not be permitted to carry her point about the Wood-elf's ten bars of song.

"He cares nothing about little Courcey, my dear," Fanfreluche explained to me under the table. "But he cares a deal about keeping his word. Won't she make him pay a price for it,—just!"

Apparently her good-humour was restored by the *ris de veau;* at any rate her murmurs were drowned by Derry Denzil, who had one of the mellowest and most flexible of voices, and who, sitting down to the piano that occupied a nook in this pretty supper-room, chanted, with gay music of his own, some camp-songs of the Austrian army, in which he once had served.

The Mouse came in, radiant because the carriages were standing thick in two ranks down the street, and because the doorkeeper had averred that every one had gone away delighted with the entertainment. He was genuinely hungry also, from anxiety and suspense, and could in verity eat the dainty things provided, which the other men who had hurriedly left their dinner-tables to be present were not. In consequence they had only trifled with claret, or drunk brandy and seltzer, whereas he really was thoroughly ready for the larded game and the mayonaise and the oysters; and he managed to devour very nearly as much as Laura Pearl herself, chattering with voluble mirth all the time, and bringing an element into the society which was very much wanting there; since the conversation, having commenced in disputes, had declined into ennui.

After a little time they all began to smoke—the Pearl included, though she threw away much more of her cigar than she consumed. While the Coronet's lights were out in every other part of the house, the players gone home, and the great doors shut to the street and locked, laughter reigned in the bright amber-hung room; and the chimes of a neighbouring clock were tolling two in the morning when they all sauntered forth by the stage-exit and went into the cool white moonlight to their waiting cabs.

"It's a success—an out-and-out success!" I heard the Mouse mutter to Denzil as they lounged out to the air.

"For you,—yes!"

"Well! Why not for him?"

"Why?" replied Denzil slowly, with a big cheroot in his teeth that resisted all attempts to light it. "Why? O, because it never makes any difference to him whether the Coronet pays or loses. Old Wynch will tot up *your* half of the profits correctly, because you've very bright eyes, my dear Mouse; but Beltran—well, Beltran may be permitted.to see that his gallery brings him in a surplus of something like eighteenpence halfpenny a week. That will be about it, I fancy."

"He's a confounded ass!" muttered the Mouse.

"Yes, he is. He trusts Wynch and you."

And Denzil, with a short good-night to them all, strode away in the moonlight alone, while Leo Lance waited to murmur farewell to the Pearl and to close the door of her brougham.

11 *

"Are you coming, Vere?" she asked sharply of Beltran.
"No, thanks. I'll go and see what they're doing at the
Cocodés."

And he turned away to get into a hansom and drive
rapidly to that fashionable night-club, where the highest of
high play was to be obtained all through the early hours of
the dawn.

The Mouse had his rejected seat in the brougham.

"A lift" was the least she could give, I suppose, in return
for my ear-rings and me.

CHAPTER XIII.

Bronze.

In attempting to jump into the brougham my feet slipped,
and I fell heavily to the ground. No one perceived my accident, and the carriage moved on quickly, while a shrill little
yell from within it told me that my faithful little chaperone
and cicerone alone had witnessed, and was powerless to help,
my misfortune. I was stunned for a moment or two by the
sharp concussion, and lay panting and scarcely sensible on
the hard stones of the deserted street.

A good Samaritan, who was the only passenger past the
loneliness of the darkened and melancholy theatre, saw my
plight and paused by me. He was a rather large, rough,
brown dog; his coat was very shabby and tangled, as if worn
by wind and weather; and he had a very sad tender face,
that made me think of old Trust's.

He stopped and sniffed me, and drew me gently out of
the roadway with his teeth. I was, or fancied myself, too
much hurt to move, and lay right in the way of all passing
carriages, indifferent to all danger from their wheels.

"You are a poor tiny thing to be all alone at this time of
night," he said to me kindly. "What are you doing? Have
you lost yourself?"

I told him my adventures.

He was not a dog of the world evidently, for he knew nothing of Pearl, or Fanfreluche, or even the name of the
theatre under whose porch he had drawn me; consequently
it was not in his power to lead me aright, or indeed to help
me in any way, save to shelter me with his bigger body from
the wind, which he did with much care and tenderness.

"Will you take me home with you?" I ventured to ask,
emboldened by his honest kind eyes.

"I have no home," he said mournfully, "otherwise I
would. I sleep under bridge-arches, or doorways, or anywhere I can; where I am not hunted away—"

"But that must be very miserable?"

"Yes, it is miserable. But there are tens of thousands of
human creatures that do the same. I must not complain.
Sometimes I am allowed to lie in an empty basket, in that
great market where they sell vegetables and flowers; there
it is very warm and safe, and the sweet scents of the thyme
and the lavender, and all the cool wet leaves, make me dream
I am in the country once more."

"You came from the country?"

"Yes,"—his eyes grew unutterably sad.

"Why did you leave it?"

"Well—I followed my master. He was but a lad, barely
twenty; his people were poor, and he was restless at home,
and he had dreams of wondrous things that he could do in
the great world, if only his steps should once wend thither.
It was a sweet, happy, fragrant place—that little farm where
we lived; all in the heart of the green fresh pasture-lands,
and the apple-orchards, and the blossoming high hedges,
with the little brooks singing beneath them. But Harold
was ill content there. He had music in his eyes, and fever
in his voice; do you know what it is that I mean? Well, he
would leave them—the father, and the mother, and the little
girl Gladys—and would go forth on his own path to some
greatness. I do not think he ever knew what; but dreamt of
all impossible beautiful things. They wept sorely; but he—
he came smiling away. I followed him. I had been his in

his childhood, and he had always been good and gentle to
me; my heart nearly broke at quitting that fair green place
of my birth, but what could I do? I could not let him wander
alone."

He paused; there was no sound save of the night winds
stealing sadly through the empty portico of the deserted
theatre.

"Well—he came straight hither; came out of the pure
free country, and from the sight of the sun, into this furnace,
where men's souls are for ever consuming, and the smoke of
their passions and woes is spread, like a veil of darkness,
between them and heaven's light. The lad had dreamed
divine dreams, that I know; I have seen the look on his face
when he walked under the summer stars, or saw the moon
burn through a night of frost. And he came here—here!—
to squalor, and vice, and manifold miseries, and ceaseless
greed, and a fathomless gulf of unmeasured iniquity!

"What he really strove to do I cannot tell. He strove
hard, whatsoever it was. He wrote all the day long in that
little, dusky, blackened attic, in the roof under the smoke-
cloud, which he had chosen instead of the bright, broad,
wooden chamber, under the great oak boughs, with the
birds singing against the lattice, that had been his at his
home. He wrote—wrote—wrote, all day and all night too,
till all the colour died out of his face, and all the light out of
his eyes.

"At times he would go abroad, and wander amongst
strange crooked streets, and enter first one house and then
another. And in one he was met with derision; and in a
second with coldness; and in a third with a rebuff; and so on
in every one of them; so that he left each with his bundle of
papers clenched in his hand, and the broken bent look of an
old man on his lithe young form. Yet he never seemed
wholly to lose courage. He would write, and write, and write
again; and go again to these houses, or to fresh ones, with
his eyes all aglow with hope; and again come forth from
them with the glow quenched, and his steps dragging slowly

over the stones. And all this time he had but little money; and it grew less and less; and soon we all but starved.

"Many tender letters came to him from the little farm in the orchard-country, but I do not fancy he ever answered them. If he did he was too proud to tell them that all their fears were true, and all his dreams were dead. For if he had only once hinted to them of his want, I know that they would have stripped themselves to the last coin to send him help, and the child Gladys would have worked in the fields as a reaper rather than ever have let him need unaided.

"Well—each day grew worse than the last; and his cheeks grew hollow, and his eyes wild, and his hand, when it touched me, burned like flame. He still wrote—O yes—but he wrote at night only, and all the other hours through he wandered to and fro, to and fro, in the endless maze of streets. It is sad to be young, and alone, and utterly miserable, in a great city that has no time to think of you, no glance to give you, no ear to lend to your sighs!

"And at last one evening he would go out alone; he would not have me with him. He stooped and kissed me on the forehead, and I felt great hot tears fall on me as he did so; but though I begged, and prayed, and moaned, and entreated all I could to go with him, he put me back into the room, and closed the door on me, and I heard his steps going swiftly down the staircase, and out into the street. Well—from that hour he has never returned."

"He is dead, then?" I asked, awe-stricken.

"Ah! that I cannot tell. I am looking for him always, dead or alive. After a little while the people of the house drove me away with blows, when they found that he did not come back. I used to lie in the street before the door day after day, night after night; they would throw wood and stones at me; they wounded me sorely often, but they could not make me leave the spot while there was a chance of his coming there. It is so horrible—to lose a creature you love, into darkness like that. Men can speak and explain, and other men pity and aid them. But we—we can only suffer, and wonder, and be wretched, and dumb!"

I listened, awed and full of sorrow—this loyal, faithful, tender-souled creature, Humanity in its besotted arrogance called a lower beast than Laura Pearl!

"Have you never seen him again?" I asked softly at length.

"Never again. But I look for him still. I must find him at last. One man was good to me and would have given me a home, and fed and caressed me; but I could not stay with him; I could not go to comfort and rest whilst the boy was unfound. I seek him everywhere. Sooner or later I shall know where he is—"

"But you must suffer greatly?"

"Suffer? Yes. But so did he. I have hunger and thirst continually; a drop of muddy water, a scrap of offal, is all I can get without stealing, and I never will steal. The people beat me and kick me, and the boys stone and hoot me—you see, I am nothing but a stupid stray dog to them. And they are cruel."

"But could you not find your way home to that country place that you love?"

"O yes. It is fifty or sixty miles from this city, but I could find my way well; I should know the road, and I could walk it in less than a week. But how can I go home whilst I leave him here? How can I see them all again without him? If I knew he were dead indeed I might go; they love me, and perhaps in some sense I could comfort them; but until I do—whilst there still is a chance that he lives and may want me —I have no right to turn my face homeward. If I went and forsook him, do you think I could sleep one moment in peace, though I were to lie in my old nest among the sweet hay in the apple-loft under the oak-boughs?"

I was silent. The greatness of this unselfish elevation appalled me. This rough country dog could feel such fidelity and nobility as these, whilst the men and women I had quitted—

"Forgive me, little one," he said kindly, imagining that he had wearied me. "In babbling of myself I have forgotten your troubles. What can I do for you? I have nothing in the world, and not even a kennel to share with you."

"What was your master called?" I asked, still haunted by the story, to the exclusion of my own woes.

"Harold. His people's name was Gerant, but we always called him and his little sister Harold and Gladys. But do not let us speak more of them. I want to aid you if I can."

I could not tell him how, for I saw no possible issue to the dilemma; but I begged and prayed of him not to leave me. I had such a dread of Bill Jacobs' finding and seizing me.

"Ah, you are afraid of the thieves?" he said gently. "They never touch me. See what a protection it is to be worth nothing! A valuable dog, and a rich man, have no true liberty in their lives, for they are for ever being hunted and trapped by the spoilers. I will not leave you; and I can still keep a rabble at bay, though I am old, and my teeth are not strong. We are as well here as anywhere; the portico keeps the wind off a little."

So we sat there while the quarters and hours were several times tolled from the neighbouring church; and he warmed me with his rough, curly body, and tried to his uttermost to shelter me from the unaccustomed exposure of the night. Carriages flashed past; now and then a foot-passenger went by; but no one took any notice of us.

Now and then there came by us a man of distinguished appearance, walking slowly, with his hat over his eyebrows, and his face very pale. When I saw such a one I guessed that he had been playing at the Cocodés, or at some other of the night card-clubs of this fashionable quarter, and had lost. Now and then such a one would be accosted and pestered, and cursed horribly when he put her aside, by some wretched, haggard, painted phantom of a woman that made one's blood run cold by even a look at her wolfish, leering, hungry eyes.

"Poor creature!" I said involuntarily, as one of these—the worst of any I had ever seen—came by us.

"Poor indeed!" said my good Samaritan. "And yet, after all, this is rather a sham sentiment that we are guilty of when we pity these women so profoundly. For they call our brothers, the lions, beasts of prey; but how holy are their ways, how continent, how innocent, how merciful even the worst that they do, beside these women! These women murder the young of their own kind. What lion, what animal, ever did that?"

"But they have been tempted?"

"Well—yes," he said thoughtfully. "And how? Look you here. A few nights ago, as I was seeking Harold in all likely and unlikely places, I strayed into a Casino not very far from here. It was one where gay, rich, foolish youngsters go to see dancing women, and specially to see one now who is a sort of empress there—they call her Lillian Lee. She 'shows herself nightly to the populace for gold'—that was a line I heard Harold quote so often.

"I took a long look at this Lillian of theirs before they saw and turned me out. I knew her then. The last time I had seen her she had been hop-picking in our fields some five years ago at harvest-time.

"That girl had as good a mother as ever breathed; a widow-woman, but full of thrift and cheerfulness and virtue. They lived in a pretty little cottage, hard by the water-mill; the mother bred poultry, and took the fowls and ducks to market, with herbs and a few vegetables that she grew, and she washed linen for the old vicar and two or three other people. She was always a contented woman, and loved her daughter—well, as only mothers can love. If the girl had been but like her, they might have been very happy. But you know it is of no use to sow wheat upon stone and sand.

"Letty—that was her name—Letty had nothing of her mother's temper in her. She was for ever sulking, and fretting, and refusing to work, and squandering her pence on finery, and mooning away her days in the sun. The only thing she would do was a little hop-picking in the season, because there were many men about, and idle play, and license that was worse than play, in the hop-grounds, where all the wild Irish and the labourers on tramp came, and wasted far more than they worked for most of the time they were there. One day at the middle of the hop-getting, when Gerant came in to the noonday dinner, his face was very grave. He was a quiet God-fearing man, and it was but seldom that he allowed anger to stir in him. 'Lettice Dean must never darken these doors again,' he said to his wife— the children were not as yet in from the fields. 'She is vicious and vile; she turns to sin as bees to sugar. Have a care that she comes no more nigh to Gladys.'

"The mistress asked trembling what the girl had done, and he answered her that Letty had wanton ways, and he had surprised her love-making with one of the drunken Irishmen, where they stood under a hedge. A little while after that the poor woman Dean came weeping sorely to Gerant and his wife, and told them how the child had left her without a word, taking all she owned with her. She had stolen even her dead father's old pinchbeck watch from under her mother's pillow whilst the old woman slept, and had carried off even the few little bits of silver spoons, and salt-pots, and suchlike, that had belonged to her great grand-parents, and were the pride and treasure of the cottage. Well, they traced her to London, I believe, and there they altogether lost her. I only found her the other night—as Lillian Lee at this Casino."

"And you think her temptations were—?"

"Greed, and vanity, and discontent. No others. She loved wickedness and pleasure; she robbed her mother whilst sleeping; and she went to vice because she desired its wages.

"By the way, the old woman died; lost all heart and strength, and could no longer labour for her own support, and would have gone to the workhouse but for Harold's father and mother, who, in the press of their own poverty, tended

and succoured her to the end, which indeed was not long in
coming. Now, wherefore should we pity this creature—Letty
Dean or Lillian Lee?

"'The flowers hang in the sunshine and blow in the breeze
free to the wasp as to the bee. The bee chooses to make his
store of honey, that is sweet and fragrant and life-giving; the
wasp chooses to make his from the same blossoms, but of a
matter hard and bitter and useless. Shall we pity the wasp,
because of his selfish passions he selects the portion that
shall be luscious only to his own lips, and spends his hours
only in the thrusting-in of his sting? Is not such pity—
wasted upon the wasp—an insult to the bee who toils so
wearily to gather in for others, and who, because he stings
not man, is by man maltreated? Now, it seems to me, if I
read them aright, that vicious women, and women that are
of honesty and honour, are much akin to the wasp and to the
bee."

I was silent. His grave gentle speech recalled to me my
old familiar friend Trust, and seemed so strange—and yet so
simply-wise—after the satiric sharpness and the acidulated
worldliness of Fanfreluche. The one was so tenderly thoughtful, probing to the core of all things; the other was so contemptuously indifferent, skimming the surface of all truths.
And yet—when all was said—the Samaritan and the Satirist
alike pointed to the same deduction! These words of his,
moreover, recalled to me the vague fancy that had moved me
as to the past of Laura Pearl.

Ah! these women may well be rough to us, and shrink
from our eyes, when we remember so many things that they
have consigned to the grave of oblivion, and which they believe they have sealed down for ever, because they have
rolled to the door of the sepulchre a burial-stone of gold!

"It is very cold for you," said Bronze kindly, waking me
from my half-sleepy reverie. "Bitterly cold for spring. I do
not mind it; I have been houseless all the winter, which
was a hundred times worse than this; but you—how you
shiver!"

"It is nothing," I tried to say valorously; "you have lost Harold long, then?"

"All the winter, and all the autumn; and he lived in wretchedness here—about a quarter of a year—rather more. That makes eight, or ten, months. Gladys will soon be getting into womanhood."

"Is she a pretty girl?" I asked him, wondering if she also would ever be transformed into a Pearl or a Lillian Lee.

"More than pretty. Letty Dean was pretty. Gladys has a beautiful little face, like a white crocus of the spring. She was a strange child too—so silent, so gentle, so dreamy, and some said not very wise. But her eyes would blaze like stars when Harold read poetry to her, and I fancy myself that she thought over-much for her years; and that she had—what do they call it?—genius; and that it was only because she was silent that people fancied her simple. It was odd: those two children led such quiet, ordinary lives: rising with the sun; eating food of the plainest; always in the open air; rained on by summer showers; blown on by autumn winds; seeing nothing except the animals and the birds on the farms, and having no books except their Bible and their *Pilgrim's Progress*, and the plays of a man they called Shakespeare:—and yet there was something noble and uncommon about them; and they seemed always to be hearing such wonderful things, when they lay on the grass, or wandered under the trees."

I understood what he meant. I had seen something of the same thing in poor Ben.

But by this time I was so tired that I ceased to hear him speak, and I fell sound asleep, and forgot that my cushion was only the stone step of the Coronet theatre. The wind and the rain did not come upon me, for Bronze lay down by me in such fashion that his brown curly body was a firm barrier between myself and the elements. There is a wondrous deal of kindness in men and in dogs—women, I do not think, have much of it.

"O woman! In our hours of ease
So smiling, soft, and glad to please,
And steadfast-rooted as the oak,
And patient-tempered as the moke,
Let only cash and still be falling,
An awful tongue hast thou for railing!"

This elegant parody had been sung by the three fairy
princes in the Mouse's burlesque, and had been received
with exceeding applause; and it was wandering still through
my brain as I sank to sleep under the portico of the Coronet.

When I awoke it was dawn—one of those cheerless gray
dawns that early spring brings in cities.

In the Peak these mornings had been beautiful; by reason
of the seas of white cloud-like mist, the sweet damp dewy
scents, the water-drops that glistened on every leaf and
blade, the purple glimpses of the half-hidden hills, the soft
unearthly hush that reigned over all things till the low
twittering of the little nest-birds broke its silence. But
here—here it was only cold, ugly, impressibly dreary and
dispiriting. I woke in consequence sorely frightened and
sorrowful; and the tender-hearted Brouse had much ado to
console me.

"I am so cold!" I moaned. "And so hungry too!"

"How long is it since you had food?" he asked.

"Ever since six last night!"

"Ah! And I have been two days without picking up
anything, save a piece of mouldy bread that lay outside an
area-gate! But then I am old, and very hardy, and you are
helpless and young; that makes a great difference. Well, I
suppose if we wait long enough, the theatre people will come,
and they will know you—will they not?"

At that moment, through the dim light in which the day
and the gas feebly struggled for dominance, there approached
the form of a man, looming large through the dusky and
yellow steam of the fog.

It was Lord Beltran.

He was walking slowly, with his great-coat thrown back
as though he sought the chilly air; his head was bent, his

face was pale, and the stephanotis in his button-hole drooped
—dead.

I sprang out on him, and managed to arrest him. He
paused, and raised me.

"Is it you, you little atom?" he said kindly. "Has she
left you here on purpose? Not likely though, as you're of
value!"

And with that he took me, thrust me kindly and carelessly into his pocket, and moved onward. I struggled, and
whined, and contrived to draw his attention to Bronze, who
was looking on with wistful and patient endurance of oblivion.

He whistled Bronze to him.

"You look stray and starved, my friend. Come along too
if you like."

Bronze understood; and came timidly near, and touched
his hand with a grateful motion of his own rough tongue; but
he did not move after us, and the last thing I saw of him were
his two sad, kind eyes, gleaming with their soft hazel light
from out of the portico darkness.

My heart was full at leaving him thus. But what could I
do?

I was horribly cold and hungry; and this is a combination
which kills sentiment in bigger people than myself. The
emotions, like a hot-house flower, or the sea-dianthus, wither
curiously when aired in an east wind, or kept some hours
waiting for dinner.

CHAPTER XIV.

Sunday Morning.

In ten minutes or less I was comfortably installed in Beltran's chambers, which were but at two or three streets' distance from the theatre. They were the two prettiest rooms I
have ever seen in my life, connected with an archway, and
decorated with imperial blue; they were the abode of a refined

gentleman, of a connoisseur too moreover; things of great
antiquity and much beauty were scattered about; ivory,
bronze, marble, china, enamel, metalwork, gleamed out of
the prevailing hue of deep azure; and here and there nestled
a mirror, and here and there hung a picture.

Beltran set me down on the hearth-rug, and cast himself
into an easy-chair, having changed his dress for a velvet
smoking garb that his man brought to him.

"Give the little beggar something to eat, Ferrors," he said
of me to his servant; and then composed himself to read and
to smoke.

I liked his face better than I had hitherto done. It was
very delicate and thoroughbred, with that handsome profile
which seems to mark like a brotherhood your English aristocrats. It was cold and contemptuous indeed in expression,
but by the kindliness that came, when he smiled, into his
calm languid eyes, I thought that much of this cynical in-
differentism was only surface deep, and much of this serene
insolence was only a trick of manner.

When I came to know him well I found, indeed, that Vere
Essendine, Lord Beltran, was one of those persons very hard
for men, and very easy for dogs, to read. There were, to
mislead his own kind, the slighting languor of habit, the contemptuous serenity of manner, the listless fatigue of tone, the
continual suppression of all feeling beneath phrases of half-
sardonic and half-ridiculing brevity, that are common amongst
those of his order. He was not a little reckless, moreover;
was given to seeking his own amusement, without reckoning
its cost either to himself or others; and although no one ever
remembered to have seen him out of temper, he could be
very merciless with his quiet indolent speech on occasion.

But dogs saw much more than these: dogs noticed that he
was never ungentle to them; that he never forgot them; that
he smiled with his eyes as well as with his mouth; and that
he, like themselves, took punishment without complaint, not
from insensibility, but from the courage of breed, and the
endurance of training. And the stray ones of our kind would

know this, by that peculiar prescience of our own which you
are pleased to call "instinct" because you cannot in the least
comprehend it; and they would follow him home, and trust
themselves to his pity and shelter: will you have anywhere a
surer witness to character?

I imagined that he had some punishment to bear just now;
the novel dropped on his knee as he sat, and his eyes were
fastened on the fire that burned brightly within his pretty
porcelain-panelled stove.

Once he took from his waistcoat pocket an old letter,
with some figures jotted on it in pencil; studied them, and
thrust them back with a muttered word that sounded like a
curse.

The figures, I doubt not, were those of his play losses that
night at the Cocodés.

Soon after that he drank some soda-water, and went to
bed. I did so too, and I shame to confess slept soundly, un-
haunted by so much as a dream of the poor patient Bronze,
whom we had left in the chilly bleak dawn, alone with his
hunger and sorrow.

We hear a very great chatter of "sympathy" in this
world: is there aught of it, I wonder, that is anything beyond
fellow-feeling?

When I fairly awoke on the morrow it was noon; and
there were four or five men in the inner room, where a table
was laid out with breakfast.

It was Sunday, I knew, by the clanging of the dissonant
bells with which you herald your periodical fits of devotion;
and Sunday breakfasts, as I learnt later, are a favourite
form of distraction with such men as these amongst whom I
had fallen.

The guests were waiting for their host; and the silver
dishes were still covered.

They were talking of the previous night at the Coronet.

"Safe to run," said one, in whom I recognised Paget Desmond. "Ought to make money by it?"

Pack. I. 12

"Humph!" said Derry Denzil, who was there without his big dog.

"What do you mean by that, Derry?" asked another, a slender, fair languid man, whom they all called Ned, and whom I found was, in rank, Earl of Guilliadene.

"Paper!" returned Denzil briefly, with much scorn.

"Paper? O, hang it, no! Stalls were full of fellows one knows; and the private-box women were all in good form."

Denzil laughed grimly.

"Well—don't you know how she does it, Ned?"

"She? Not an idea!" replied the Earl.

"I'll tell you, then. Nine-tenths of those men get her pass—get it all through the season, and, when she takes her benefit, what charming big cheques the lovely Laura receives as a quid pro quo! House is full: she explains to her friend that it's all orders; he believes her; so it is in a sense; only the money that should have gone in at his box-office goes instead at the end of the season to her. Thing is perfectly simple. You see?"

"I can't say I do exactly," muttered the fair earl. "Old Wynch must know?"

"Of course old Wynch knows. But when it suits his own book to net gains in like manner, of course it don't pay him to check here. Besides, they understand one another; and Wynch is a wise man in his generation. He knows that she'll be worth her ten thousand a-year for a very much longer spell than Beltran will."

"She don't do anything except those breakdowns," murmured Lord Guilliadene. "I'd get a score just as good as she out of the Holborn Casino any night."

"That's nonsense," said Denzil calmly. "She's the handsomest creature about the town. I hate her, but I must admit that. Besides, you know old George made her the fashion."

"O, she's *chic;* if the clubs saying so can make her so—"

"As of course they can," cried Paget Desmond. "No woman can hold her own against the clubs for any length of time. You remember Mrs. D'Eyncourt? Well, that woman was superb; and a wonderfully fine actress too; but you know she was confoundedly honest, and had awfully queer notions; and when old Beaujolais enclosed her a set of diamonds she sent them back—sent them back, by Jove! as if he'd been a pot-boy offering her a pennyworth of periwinkles. Beau, you know, never forgave it, and he got her talked down in the clubs and other places till she hadn't a ghost of a chance. She was a very plucky woman, fearfully plucky woman; and thought she was strong enough to beat him. But of course she wasn't; of course she went to the wall. She was fairly driven off the London stage, you remember?"

"Yes," added Mark Mountmorris, a man in the 9th Lancers, "and I saw her stitching shirts as hard as ever she could sew, in a little garret window, in a beggarly German town. That's always the way women come to grief if they defy clubs—"

"And diamonds!" concluded Derry Denzil, with that laugh which was too grim for his handsome sun-browned features.

"Well—Pearl will never sin that way," said the narrator of Mrs. D'Eyncourt's misfortunes and mistakes. "Day before yesterday she came to muffin-worry in Fred Orford's rooms—you know he always has a lot of women in at five o'clock—well, he'd just been getting things at the Brialmont sale; china chiefly, and some queer old Moyen-age jewelry; and it had all come in from Christie's, and was lying about there loose. He didn't offer her a thing, on my soul he didn't, for I was there and heard every word he said; but—the deuce!—if she didn't ask for all the Saxe and Sèvres that took her fancy, and carried the best of 'em off with her before Fred had got a word in edgeways! He was awfully savage; the best of it was, too, that he'd promised all the Saxe cups and saucers to the Duchess de Vistaherilla, and he has had to write Lord knows what lies to account to her for 'em as broken!"

"I wish she'd come to my rooms, and ask me for my

12*

bronzes," said Denzil, with a curt significance that suggested the reception which the freebooter would receive among his Antiques and Barbédiennes. "Don't you think you were dreaming, Mount, when you fancied you saw Mrs. D'Eyncourt in Germany? Germany too! Such an indefinite word; you forget we've left one Teutonic Empire behind, and haven't yet come up with another."

"I *did* see her," said Mountmorris decidedly. "Saw her in a beastly little place off Homburg. One knows *that* woman in a second just by the way her head's set on her shoulders. If she hadn't been a fool and sent back old Beau's diamonds, she'd have been—"

"When was it you saw her?"

"Deuce! I don't remember," answered Lord Mark. "Yes —stop—last autumn surely. I recollect now, because I'd lost over a monkey at Homburg, and was dead lame for want of remittances, and had nothing to do except go mooning about. I wonder *you* don't know what's become of her. You admired her awfully when she first came out. Always were about with her too."

"She was a very good actress," said Denzil briefly; and said no more.

"Yes, she was," said Beltran, at that moment entering from his bedroom. "What did that woman disappear for, Derry? It was a mystery to me at the time."

"No mystery at all. Beaujolais had her run down, I believe."

"O, nonsense! That wasn't it all. Beau can do a good deal, and kill an actress with a sneer as well as anybody; but he couldn't drive a woman away out of the world, and make her vanish into space as she vanished. I always thought *you* were at the bottom of that?"

"Did you? It's four years at least since Gertrude D'Eyncourt left the stage: how should one remember anything about her? It's time enough to welcome and bury twenty Rachels; and she wasn't a Rachel by a very long way."

"Perhaps not. But she was in thorough-bred form always, and a very good actress too. Where's that brute, by the way?"

"Her husband? I don't know."

"You *used* to know all about them, Derry?"

"Of course I did. But I've lost sight of them both long ago. You hear what Mount says, he saw her stitching shirts near Frankfort. That's later news than any of mine."

He spoke indifferently, but his face grew a little paler under its bronzed tinting, and he dashed a good stoup of brandy into his breakfast-glass of seltzer.

"She was a very good actress. I wish the Coronet had her," said Beltran meditatively, tossing me a plover's wing. The attention drew all eyes on me; and they recognised me with one voice.

"Yes, it's Laura's dog," he answered them. "I picked him up in the street last night. I've half a fancy to keep him."

"She'll weep her eyes out for him," said Denzil curtly. "Unless you find him worth thirty guineas!"

"O, we'll square it, of course," said Beltran, with a touch of annoyance. "I'll send her that pink Dresden tea-set there that she's longing for; it's worth twice as much as the dog. I don't think she'll mind the exchange; it'll be a good one for her, as the little beggar only cost her a sovereign."

"How did Jacobs let him go for that?"

"She didn't get him of Jacobs."

"O, didn't she? Well, I saw the very model of him there a month ago, only with a sooty coat instead of a snowy one."

But Beltran was not attending, and missed the hint conveyed to him.

For myself I nearly wagged my tail off with gladness at the prospect of escape from the Pearl's brodequin-kicks and parasol blows.

Emotions are quite as detrimental to a dog's tail as they are to a lady's complexion. Joseph Buonaparte's American wife said to an American gentleman, whom I heard quote her words, that she "never laughed because it made wrinkles:"

there is a good deal of wisdom in that cachinnatory abstinence. There is nothing in the world that wears people (or dogs) so much as feeling of any kind, tender, bitter, humoristic, or emotional.

How often you commend a fresh-coloured matron with her daughters, and a rosy-cheeked hunting squire in his saddle, who, with their half-century of years, yet look so comely, so blooming, so clear-browed, and so smooth-skinned. How often you distrust the weary delicate creature, with the hectic flush of her rouge, in society; and the worn, tired, colourless face of the man of the world who takes her down to dinner. Well, to my fancy, you may be utterly wrong. An easy egotism, a contented sensualism, may have carried the first comfortably and serenely through their bank-note-lined paradise of common-place existence. How shall you know what heart-sickness in their youth, what aching desires for joys never found, what sorrowful power of sympathy, what fatal keenness of vision, have blanched the faded cheek, and lined the weary mouth, of the other twain?

The breakfast was a long but by no means tedious affair. There were curious old wines and quite new dishes to be tried; and with the due leisure taken over these, and some pauses betwixt them, filled up by music from Denzil and a magnificent buffo singer of the Blues, who amused their minds with trying over a new score of an unpublished comic-opera lent them by its French composer, the hours from noon till four o'clock sped away with sufficient rapidity; in a dusky atmosphere of aromatic smoke, through which the singers' clear full notes came oddly, like a carillon ringing through a misty Flemish dawn.

"'That's a capital opera," said Beltran musingly, as Denzil's hand crashed out a lusty riotous chorus from the big Kirkmann. "Who'll do it?"

"O, its written for Schentach, of course," said the player, naming a famous French songstress. "They are keeping it for next New Year."

"What if one had it at the Coronet?—bringing Schentach over of course."

"Good gracious! aren't you near enough ruin already? Schentach refused half-a-million francs a-month from the Sultan last week."

"And she's an ugly woman," said Beltran, contentedly resigning his idea in its birth. "But we must do something; an everlasting breakdown, and an eternity of negro melodies is not a very lively prospect."

"Pays," said Denzil curtly, with a crash of the chords.

"Does it? Ask old Wynch."

"Ask an auditor at the year's end," responded the other with brief significance.

Beltran blew away a ring of smoke.

"Couldn't do that. Wynch would think one suspected him."

"The best thing he could think."

"I don't fancy so. Trust people wholly or not at all."

"An excellent rule. But why do you never practise but the first half of it?"

"Go on playing, Derry, that chorus is charming; but it seems to me that I've heard something very like it before. It's the same measure as the old *Rataplan*."

"Of course it is. It's borrowed body and soul. The originality of men and monkeys is only variations upon imitations."

"Don't get epigrammatic in the daytime. There's a season for all things; and you're not writing musical critiques for the *Mouse*."

"By the way, did you see that poem in this week's number? It's out of the *Mouse's* line, utterly."

"A poem! Never read one."

"Well, read that. It has a kind of grandeur in it, and is worth something."

"Do you mean 'Demeter'?"

"Yes. It's only a fragment."

Beltran stretched his hand for the paper, glanced through

it while Denzil and the guardsman recommenced their duo from the sparkling Frenchman's score.

Beltran began to read indifferently, but with more gravity and interest as he proceeded. The verse occupied about a column and a half of the *Mouse's* thick toned paper. He threw it aside a little wearily when he had ended.

"Is your sixpenny sheet going to make us think? I claim back my subscription."

"Don't you like the thing?"

"Like it? Pooh! One likes a burlesque, a pigeon-match, an American oyster, a number of the *Mouse*. One doesn't like *Samson Agonistes* or *Prometheus Unbound*."

"You class that bit with the latter?"

"Pretty nearly. It is crude, indeed, and overwrought; but it has the conflict of strength and suffering in it that they have. The idea of putting such a poem as that pell-mell in your pot-pourri of nonsense verses, club-scandals, whipped-cream wit, sublime self-sufficiency, and fashionable philistinism! It is to place a chained god in a smoking-room—a fallen Titan at an Arlington whist-table. For heaven's sake, since you must be court-jesters, don't fetter a desert-chief beside you to make your motley fouler. Be consistent, even in your foolery."

Denzil laughed, leaning over the piano.

"Come, the poem's done something. It's made you say actually what you think for once! Don't you want to know who wrote it?"

"No, indeed. When I was a boy—strong on such matters —I traced so many philosophers into snuffy back parlours, and discovered so many philomels in curl-papers, that I never feel the faintest tinge of curiosity in literally personalities."

"Who did write it, Derry?" asked the guardsman, looking over the verse with a mixture of good-natured wonder and contempt, just touched into a vague admiration.

"Well," answered Denzil slowly, striking some wistful, solemn, minor chords with his left hand as he spoke. "You see the name there, Harold Gerant. It's not a feigned name, as you're thinking. The manuscript came to little Lance just twelve months ago; was put aside and forgotten. A week or two since I lit on it, in looking over old copy that was to be burnt. I thought I saw stuff in it, and told him to put it in type. The address on the page was a street in Whitefriars. I wrote there, and had no answer. I asked some publishers if they knew the name; one of them told me it belonged to a boy who was always pestering them to accept his rubbish. They had a consummate scorn for him: he asked them for no money, only begged they would print what he wrote. I found out the place yesterday, quite by chance. The people of the house said a lad of that name had lived with them three or four weeks, but had gone out one day and had never returned. Some dozen days after his disappearance a body had been found in the Thames, at low water, just beneath Westminster-bridge. They had gone to see it, and had recognised it by the long fair curling hair. The features had been disfigured beyond all knowledge by striking on the piles of the bridge. That is the history of the poet of 'Demeter.' He will not make us think any more."

There was a long silence as the deep soft tones of his voice died down; not one of those present spoke.

At last Beltran raised himself, and looked at the Dresden clock.

"Five, as I live! Stay here as long as you like. I must go and see half-a-dozen women over their tea. Remember, we dine at Richmond. I will call for you, Derry, at your rooms, before I drive round to take up Laura."

And he went to change his velvet attire, that he might carry no odour of Turkish tobacco into the dainty patrician boudoirs, where they were never at home on the seventh day to anything over a dozen.

I thought how heartless he was.

Denzil remained alone after the rest of the Sunday breakfast-party had departed.

He did not rise from the deep-seated chair in which he had sat as he played through the last bars of the opera; he

did not relight his cigar, which had gradually died out from
his inattention; his face was very grave, very dark, very
melancholy, now that he deemed himself in solitude.

"Working—starving, perhaps—in a foreign land. My
God!" he muttered once, unconsciously aloud. And then he
started up, and paced to and fro the two chambers with swift
uneven steps, and with his head bent on his chest in depth of
thought.

Once he went to a portfolio of photographs that leaned
against the wall, and drew one of the great sheets out, and
placed it upright, and gazed at it; his eyes shaded with his
hand.

It was only the head of a woman; a very noble head,
standing out like a cameo from a black background of
shadow.

He looked at it long; so long that in the wavering light
of a London sunset, that glowed through the misty close of
the day, the great soft eyes seemed to gleam and change,
and the curling proud lips to move and breathe. It seemed
a living thing to me; and I think it did so to him also.

Then he flung it back with nervous force amongst the rest
in the portfolio; and throwing himself again into the chair,
buried his face in his hands, and sat immovable; while the
quarters chimed again and again from the clock on the
mantelpiece and the church belfry in the street without.

The opening of the inner door, as the servants, supposing
all the gentlemen had left, entered to clear away the breakfast service, aroused him; and he rose and went:—if his eyes
had not been wet with tears I never saw human tears on
earth. And, having lived but a short life, I yet have seen
them often.

An hour or two later, when Beltran had again entered and
again gone forth, as I looked from one of the windows to
divert my loneliness, I saw him dash past in his mail-phaeton
driving two sorrels tandem, with two grooms riding after him.
Beside him sat Laura Pearl, in all the splendour that gold
broidered cashmeres and genuine ermine could give; and be-

hind them, leaning over and laughing with a cigar in his mouth, was Deringham Denzil.

I began to suspect that men were very different in society and in privacy.

CHAPTER XV.

His First Season.

THE transfer of the pink Dresden for myself was, I believe, satisfactorily effected; for that particular act of china disappeared, and I remained undisturbed in Beltran's possession, and speedily became a favourite with him.

I had a very agreeable life. His two servants, being devoted to him, were very good to me. There was no one to teaze me; and, as there were a great many people always coming and going in his rooms, I seldom was without amusement. There were men breakfasts and men dinners often in these pretty costly chambers of his, that had as many treasures in them as Christie's itself on a view-day.

In the mornings, artists, and authors, and guardsmen, and diplomatists, and pretty actresses, and witty dramatic adapters, and all sorts and kinds of people would get together in the rooms, whether Beltran were there or not—some looking in for two minutes, some staying two hours. In the late afternoon, not rarely there would come some fair friends or relatives of his own caste; dainty haughty women, who would have their five-o'clock tea out of his egg-shell china, and talk scandal with the most charming air in the world, and feast me on muffins and sugar; his servant being always at the doorway on guard, so that no member of the Pearl order, or female aspirant to the boards of the Coronet, should be admitted whilst these noble dames and delicate damsels drank their orange-pekoe, glanced over the bric-à-brac, and talked the last news of the day.

He very often, also, as I say, gave dinners in his rooms; for they were large, and the cook downstairs was one of the finest in London. And whenever men did dine with him

there was sure to follow gold-crown whist, with heavy betting
on the tricks, or, more generally still, some game of quick
hot hazard.

Taken as a whole, the mode of life was bewilderingly
brilliant to me; and, with a week or two of it—being sugar-
plummed by the actresses, praised and patted by the great
ladies, and highly favoured by my noble owner—I utterly
forgot the episode of poor Bronze, and had—alas! I shame
to write it—very nearly ceased to regret Reuben Dare.

I soon, indeed, became really attached to my new master
and all his friends. They were "thorough-bred" to the
core.

You object to that word? You think I am wedded to an
order? *Fi-donc!*—how you always misappreciate your greatest
instructors!

Have I not shown you how I could love and honour a
simple unlettered north-country quarryman?

He was a gentleman in his own way, my poor gentle-
hearted Ben; for he was loyal, and incapable of a lie, and
tender of soul to women, and without one shadow of false-
hood, or of pretension, on his honest life. And he had in a
manner a right to be so by race as well; for Trust (who was
an antiquary in his fashion) used often to tell me that, in the
old old times, when there were yeomen in England, and the
stout handbow was the terror of all her foreign foes, the
Dares were stalwart and sturdy northmen, who rode out with
the Peverills, and with the Vernons after them, and struck
many a fair blow, and sped many a straight arrow, and tilled
many a broad acre, in that old dim time; though, during
the long passage of the centuries, their sons' sons had fallen
to a low estate, and become one with the hinds who sowed
for other men's reaping, and garnered for other men's
feasts.

In truth, too, despite all the fine chances that you certainly
give your peasants to make thorough beasts of themselves,
they and your real aristocrats have the only really good
manners in your country. In an old north-country dame,

who lives on five shillings a week, in a cottage like a dream of 'Teniers' or Van Tol's, I have seen a fine courtesy, a simple desire to lay her best at her guests' disposal, a perfect composure, and a freedom from all effort, that were in their way the perfection of breeding. I have seen these often in the peasantry—in the poor. It is your middle classes, with their incessant flutter, and bluster, and twitter, and twaddle; with their perpetual strain after effect; with their deathless desire to get one rung of the ladder higher than they ever can get; with their preposterous affectations, their pedantic unrealities, their morbid dread of remark, their everlasting imitations, their superficial education, their monotonous common-places, and their nervous deference to opinion. It is your middle classes that have utterly destroyed good manners, and have made the prevalent mode of the day a union of boorishness and servility, of effervescence and of apathy—a court suit, as it were, worn with muddy boots and a hempen shirt.

And I am terribly afraid that this will only get worse and worse. The elegance of the aristocracy, and the simplicity of the peasantry, are alike being swept away; and there looms in the distance of your future only one awful mass of hurry, ignorance, ostentation, frivolity, and barbarous rudeness which, styling itself Society, shall only be—a Mob.

. If I am too discursive, pardon me; I have lived a good deal amongst women, and may have caught up their habit of leading a discussion on the Neo-Platonics round to Valenciennes edging, and branching off from the New Comtist doctrines to the crack in their old Worcester card-bowl.

All women talk discursively; in your stupid ones it is an awful bore, but in your really clever women it is charming; —that bird-like flitting over the deepest of waters may be done with an infinite grace, and sometimes your bird will bring you a pearl that all the deep divers have missed. The "felicitous surprise" is, I believe, one of the greatest charms in your laws of rhetoric; and no one deals in this more than does the woman of quick talent and of facile tongue, in her gay vagaries which will in their most erratic moments still keep some method in their madness.

I liked my new owner, as I have said, very quickly; and I liked all his friends and companions—the "swells," as your snobs *will* call them; the men with the pale handsome faces, borne by crusaders and cavaliers before them; the men with the gentle quiet ways and the contemptuous ring in their voices, and the easy indolent insolence to all forms of pretension; and the frank, kindly, generous hearts for those that know them well; and the manner that is so natural to them, yet which no outsider can imitate—the manner that varies so little in love or in fury, in pleasure or pain.

It is the fashion to rail at them nowadays; but that invective has a good deal of cant and a good deal of envy in it —ay, even envy of such slight things as the accent of their voices!—and, like all cant and all envy, it is a true child of the Father of Lies.

I who write, have I not been purchased by their money and made captive to their power? And is there any crucial test to tell you a man of breeding like the manner in which he will treat a thing that lies in his power? Well—I, who thus have opportunity of examination and judgment passing the common rule, do affirm that in all which makes a man loyal, brave, patient, and of high honour, frank of speech, honest of thought, faithful in word to friend or foe, without self-consciousness in distinction, and without complaint or self-pity in adversity, I have never known the equal of your English gentlemen.

And I have been with them in their dark hours and their gay hours; I have seen them in their weal and their woe. Ah! those men amongst you whom you only behold staking their money on their cards, lounging down their club steps, smoking their cigars in all the capitals, and swearing good-humouredly in all the languages, of Europe; those men with their dainty blossoms in their button-holes, and their careless fashionable jargon on their lips, and their pleasant indifferent laugh at all created things, and their easy languid philosophy that holds as its first thesis that nothing on earth ever matters, I know them better than you—I know what tempests of tragedy have broken over their heads, what deathbeds they have watched with agony in their souls, what whirlwinds of passion have shaken them for women fair and false, what capacities of quick and true sympathy lie in them to start to life at the tone of a voice that they love.

I know; you do not. But you may believe me—the knightly soul is no more dead than in the old days of Holy Grail; the wild reiver still grows reverent to true innocence as in the years of Astolat; the gallant heart still beats to passion and remorse, still thrills with pity and with pardon, even as in the time of Lancelot and of Arthur.

You judge these men from the externals of their lives; they in the fashion of the day like well that you should deem the worst of them; they wear the habit of a negligent indifference, as their fathers wore the helm and the hauberk of steel: what do you know of them in their best hours? In the moments when their voice trembles on a woman's ear with a word, spoken amidst a crowd, that is for ever a farewell; when their heads are low bent to take a dying mother's blessing; when their eyelids are wet as they look at the green grave of an old dead comrade; when their very souls are riven, as the oak in storm, as they sit in the still gray dawn, and think—and think—and think—of the woman whom they have learned to speak of as a jest, yet who lay for a while in their bosom, only to flee from them in cruel craven treachery, and leave, as legacy in her stead, bitter despair and utter unbelief.

Allons! You will say I cannot be a dog of the world if I allow serious thought, or sad memories, to steal over me. Let me hark back to my recollection of the happy time that followed my discovery by Vere Essendine under the portico of his theatre.

Beltran was not a very good man, as the world counts goodness. He was indolent; he was contemptuous; he had very little respect for women, which indeed was, I think, their

own fault; he had the half-sad, half-slighting scepticism of
his period; and he held that there was nothing on earth in
the least worth making a fuss about. But he was always
kind of heart; sincere in an unusual degree; just in action
whenever he troubled himself to act; and of a very great deli-
cacy and generosity towards those who needed his assist-
ance. In truth, he gave away far more than most ostenta-
tious benefactors of their species expend, only that he did all
his gentler and better deeds in darkness, and was more irritated if a charity was traced to him than if a hundred vices
were laid at his doors.

And the world did indeed abuse him very badly. To be
sure, he had been rich when he had succeeded to his title,
and had managed by this time to throw away almost everything he had ever possessed; and this is a sin of which society is always very intolerant. To jeopardise your power to
give it good dinners is always an eighth cardinal sin in its
sight.

Besides, Beltran was a man whom the world feminine had
always found it impossible to marry; and there were many
bitter things said of him in the boudoir and drawing-room.
For this he cared very little; he went his own ways; spent
much time in travelling and yachting; preferred the *demi-
monde* to any other female world; and having some half-
dozen friends passionately devoted to him, was disliked,
though deferred to, by most others who knew him.

"Lord! if that's a lord, I wish the land was chuck full of
lords," said a brute of a bargeman once on a dark misty
night. There had been a collision on the Thames between
his coal barge and a naphtha-laden brig, and one man, coming down from a yacht lying at anchor in safety, had plunged
amongst the crashing timbers and the blazing waters, and
fought with the hideousness of that double death, until he
brought out from the crushed and smoking cabin of the barge
two little drowning children whom the river was choking,
and the flames were straining to devour, in their sleep—

brought them unhurt, golden and white and rosy, amidst all that wreck and deluge.

Their father, the coal bargee, had been a virulent agitator amongst his own kind—a fierce sullen demagogue of pot-houses and coaling-stations, inveighing against the cursed aristocrats with savage fury. But when he saw those two little curly heads raised in safety through the blinding water and the hissing fires, he shook like a shot-struck elephant, and groaned aloud.

As for Beltran, he only laughed a little—very quietly, they say, though his loins were scorched and blackened by the smoke, and his left arm had been dislocated by a blow from the shivering timbers.

"That sort of thing's easy enough," was all he answered to the wild plaudits round him. "Don't worry, please. Nothing's worth a fuss."

The bargee from that hour adored him, and narrated the tale in all those places wherein he had been previously wont to thunder forth his foul invective against the "nobles." The history bridged class hatred, as that poisonous gulf could not have been bridged by sentimental socialism cast as a sop to Cerberus.

Beltran had done better for his order in this demagogue's sight than if he had gone up on the wings of a bribed-for, lied-for, and truckled-for "people's confidence," into the lath-and-plaster temples of "office."

Dogs never have any difficulty in remembering the slightest event or the lightest word that has ever occurred or was ever spoken in their presence. Our power of memory is something marvellous. It is to the human mind as the inscriptions on the Pyramids, that never wear out, are to the lines in your modern tombstones, that a few years efface.

No doubt the shortness of your memories is a very convenient thing for you; for without it I really don't know how you could have the conscience to repudiate your debts, swear in your witness-boxes, take your marriage vows, traverse your divorce petitions, or do half the things that you *do* do.

But, owing to the perfection of *our* remembrance, I can recall every trifle of the life that I then enjoyed with my new master. He generally took me with him in his pocket, and I saw a great deal of life in that manner. You think a pocket is a circumscribed sphere of observation? Nay, not more so than a club window.

Besides, we get out of the pocket, and run about hither and thither. But you, how few of you ever move out of the circle of thought in your club!

It was a pleasant, idle, artistic, amusing season that had commenced with me in Beltran's ownership. Noons spent at Christie's, or Philips', where one could hear a prime minister set his soul on a small bit of old Chelsea, and see a cabinet of Marie Antoinette's knocked down to a Jew appraiser; could behold the collections of a lifetime sentenced to the hammer by a thankless heir, and a courtesan's priceless jewels be received by and bought in for duchesses, is as complete and caustic a satire upon Life as one can want to enjoy on a sunny spring morning.

Half-hours passed in the odorous cedar-lined studios of fashionable artists, with the smoke of choice cigars curling round antiques and bric-à-brac, and the sherry and seltzer hissing in long fairy-like glasses of Venice; where art critics fondly conceded that the luxury of a Rubens must mean the genius of a Rubens likewise, and gave the R. A.'s ill-scumbled and over-glazed portrait of some patrician beauty credit for a "depth" and a "tone" that existed alone in the hue and the taste of his clarets.

Sunday afternoons idled agreeably away under the limes and acacias on the smooth sunny lawn of some fair singer's or actress's toy villa by the Thames, with chit-chat and ices, pretty women and tea, the newest of flowers, and the flower of news. Sunday dinners at some dame's of the high world, with six or eight guests at the utmost, of people perfectly suited; and with the *chasse* lightly followed by some few bits of music or song, of an exquisite choice and of a faultless execution—some exhumed glee of Arne, some unknown morsel of Schubert, some plaintive passionate love-lay of Gounod.

Mornings passing to and fro in the Ride with a cigar in his mouth, and a rosebud in his coat, and a glossy sorrel neck curved delicately under the light caress of his whip. Minutes checking the hack under the trees, and casting the cigar to the winds of heaven, to hold in soft murmured converse some patrician coquette with proud blue Plantagenet eyes, or some witching head of a foreign legation with a name out of the Libro d'Oro of mediæval Europe.

Hours, still termed "morning" though at sunset, taking his drag down the Mile, with his wild chestnut team fretting and flinging as though curb had never galled, nor ribbon ever controlled them; while aloft upon the box some duchess of *demi-monde* avenged with reckless reign the *lèse-majesté* to her order of the noontide intrigue in Rotten-row.

Suppers where nothing was eaten, but five pounds a head was paid for looking at some flowers and hearing some champagne corks drawn, and tasting some half-a-dozen grapes or a slice of water-melon. Suppers where, after opera or theatre, great ladies in their paint and pearls would insist on being taken into grated galleries in forbidden places, to make a fast of feasting on stout and cheese and pickles; or suppers where, after opera or theatre, casino celebrities, late maids-of-all-work, would insist on being taken into gilded chambers in grand hotels to make a farce of scorning comet wines and hothouse pine-apples.

In all these I was often his companion, going into a very small compass, being swift of foot after his horse, though so small, and being a favourite with all women, save one, for my beauty, my curls, and my tricks.

Nay, he being influential and I infinitesimal, I even went into the clubs with him; and I learned to look out of the windows in Pall-mall and St. James's-street with quite as sapient and supercilious an air as any club *habitué* could desire. I was very quick to hear, and observe too, the remarks that they made there, and the contempt or interest, as it might

13*

hap, with which they lifted their eye-glasses at the women passing without.

Indeed, I became so accomplished in discernment that I turned up my nose at a hired brougham and job horse, though the prettiest creature sat behind the shabby panels; and cocked my ears and wagged my tail at a well-appointed equipage, though rouged and brazen audacity lolled on its cushions; doing these with a power of selection that proved me to have become, in a month or two, a consummate dog of the world.

As for my first initiator, Fanfreluche, I soon began to feel the polite disdain for her as "only a woman," that your youngster, who has been three months in the Guards, feels for the kindly coquette and "frisky matron" who took him up on his first introduction into society, and put him in the right set, and got him into the right clubs, and gave him a nook in her opera-box, and a word at her parties, when nobody else noticed the fledgling.

My days and nights passed in a perpetual round of sweetmeats, antics, ladies' kisses, mischief, mirth, and dainty dishes. When I thought of poor Ben's cottage, and old Trust's dinner of crusts and oatmeal, I shame to say I thought of them with wondering scorn. There were people and dogs who lived like that, and never knew the taste of a truffle or the look of whitebait. Of course I entirely forgot that the time had been—a few weeks before—when to myself also truffles and whitebait had been names unknown; but persuaded myself, till I ended in believing, that I had fed on nothing else all the days of my life.

What hypocrites you call them, those pretty "outsiders," who, brought from obscurity into riches and pleasure, will talk as if they had been great ladies all their lives long!

Now, judging them by myself, I have little doubt they are partially sincere. When we like a climate we get acclimatised very soon, and when we detest our birth-place we cannot have any pangs of nostalgia. Now, they do both of these; and when they try to talk you into the idea that they

were born in the purples, believe me they have first induced
themselves to believe the thing they wish.

"And ye shall walk in silken tire," seems to every woman
so inevitable a law of her being, that she will forget that the
time ever existed when she transgressed it in homespun.

Fanfreluche I saw occasionally, meeting her in a walk,
or at such times as Beltran took me with him to the Pearl's
house. But there was a coolness between us, owing to her
supposing that I had fallen out of the brougham on purpose,
and planned to be picked up as I had been; a mean imagination, consequent on the intrigues and deceptions that were
her daily atmosphere, which I resented too much to explain
away.

Bigger creatures than I have sulked a true friendship into
its death by torpor, from being too obstinate and full of pride
to clear aside a wrongful supposition. Ah, good people, take
my advice: be as careful in choosing your friendship as in
choosing new blood for your hound kennels; but when once
your choice has been made, slay the hydra of your *amour
propre* seventy times seven over, rather than let it live and
grow and stand like a monster of darkness, between you and
your chosen friend.

The fact was, too, that Fanfreluche loved Beltran with
all that curious force which your cynical, worldly-wise co-
quettes can sometimes throw into an attachment; and the
poor little satirist was jealous of my place in those pleasant
chambers. I saw this, but I did not pity it. It was very
sweet to my feelings that I, the baby and little fool as she
called me, should have thus prospered and distinguished myself at a bound, while this Rochefoucauld on four legs, this
female Juvenal, in a blue jacket, had been left to the caprices
of a dancer of breakdowns. This feeling was a small one; I
know it, but I think I have seen something like it in
humanity.

She laughed grimly when she heard the tale.

"So Beltran purchases a burlesque in good faith for two-
fifty; and the Mouse spends the money in trying to divert

Laura's fealty; and Beltran gives a thirty-pound bit of china for a puppy his traitor bought for a song; and the Mouse daren't say anything because he knows he was guilty; and Laura nets sheer profits from both sides, and cheats them both in the long run. Well, it is neat certainly."

But though she thus grimaced and jeered at it, it was evidently very bitter and unwelcome to her that this singular turn of good fortune should have befallen myself and not her, and that the pink tea-set should have bought me back in her place.

On Mrs. D'Eyncourt accordingly she would at first vouchsafe me no information; "the D'Eyncourt was before her time," she averred, though I believe on my soul she knew all about the affair, whatever it might have been.

"She was an actress, wasn't she?" I asked.

"O yes; an actress of genius, I have heard."

"And has disappeared?"

"My dear, everybody has 'disappeared' who isn't starring and staring before the world's footlights. We are uncommonly fond of our celebrities,—O yes,—we buy their photographs and steal their characters with the greatest ardour imaginable. We are always flinging flowers before them, and throwing stones after them, with the most affectionate energy possible. But it's only while they're in the range of our eyesight. If they retire, or pause, or only get sick for a little, we've done with them. Your statesman may have overworked his brain in your service; your painter may have paralysis; your author may have gone to his *otium cum dignitate;* and your actress may have married or be a-dying;—it's all the same; they have disappeared, and the world thinks no more about them."

"But this woman—"

"This woman was a great fool, I believe. She had no money; she had a blackguard for a husband; she had nothing but her talents; and she gave herself the air of a duchess."

"She was a gentlewoman, perhaps?"

"What has that to do with it? She had no money, I tell

you. Birth without gold is a fine-feathered bird, with both his pinions cropped off close at the point. Much use his plumage is! and fine fat worms he'll pick up in the morning!"

"But she was surely right to send back that old nobleman's diamonds?"

"O yes—and so wise, my dear! You see; here is Laura with one little green beetle for her hair worth its two thousand guineas, and this D'Eyncourt woman stitching shirts in an attic in Germany as you tell me."

"A woman should not sell her soul for a—"

"Beetle? As good as anything else if it's in fashion. A scarabeus at two thousand guineas, and a shirt at seven brass groschen,—I'm much obliged to you for that pat illustration."

And I could not get any more out of her, for she trotted off with her nose in the air to where Laura Pearl's pony carriage stood by the rails in the bright noon of the now budding spring season.

I was only being aired by the valet whilst Beltran himself was attending a private view of some foreign pictures.

By the way, *apropos* of valets, let me say a word on your servants.

Beltran's man was an excellent fellow; but, as a rule, I do think the class of body servants is the most detestable class in the universe. How you allow their snobbism, their affectations, their impudence, their ignorance, and their general offensiveness, as you do, is one of those things that no dog can understand.

You go and laugh at Charles Surface's valet on the stage, as though his ridiculous impertinence had no parallel in your own attendants, and as though in appearance, at least, the "gentleman's gentleman" of that generation were not a million times better than the wretched cad in his cut-away coat and chimney-pot hat, whom you call "servant." Jeames, in his powder and plush, may be bad enough; but I vow that your "own man" is ten thousand times worse. The former does, at least, by his garb and often by his manners, show what

station he fills; but the latter looks only like some member
of the swell-mob, and very often scarce behaves any better.

I suppose he has virtues in your eyes. I suppose he can
be trusted to compound honey-and-ink boot-varnish; he can
be trusted never to put an evening flower in your morning-
coat, or *vice versâ;* he can be trusted to make a brandy-
smash, perhaps, not half-badly; he can be trusted, when he
takes four notes of appointments to four different ladies, not
to beget eternal confusion by leaving them variously in the
wrong places; he can also, maybe, be trusted not to tell the
maid attendant on that patrician dame with whom you play
at platonics so pleasantly, of that small villa amongst the
Kingston woods, where you pursue another form of worship.

He may have all these virtues—or you think he has them
—but what others he has you would be puzzled indeed to
say. On my word, I hardly know which is the worst "form"
out—your familiar friendship with the blackguards of the
turf when you want them to give you a "straight tip;" or
your familiar association with the over-dressed, moustached
impudent, pretentious cads who pocket your fifty or sixty
sovereigns a-year for the trouble they take in smoking your
cigars, reading your letters, riding your horses, assisting your
intrigues, and imitating your vices.

You are given, very continually, to denouncing or lament-
ing the gradual encroachment of mob-rule. But, alas! whose
fault, pray, is it that bill-discounters dwell as lords in ancient
castles; that money-lenders reign over old, time-honoured
lands; that low-born hirelings dare to address their master
with a grin and sneer, strong in the knowledge of his shameful
secrets; and that the vile daughters of the populace are
throned in public places, made gorgeous with the jewels
which, from the heirlooms of a great patriciate, have fallen to
be the gew-gaws of a fashionable infamy?

Ah, believe me, an aristocracy is a feudal fortress which,
though it has merciless beleaguers in the Jacquerie of
plebeian Envy, has yet no foe so deadly as its own internal
traitor of Lost Dignity!

CHAPTER XVI.

Romances of the Row.

ONE of my greatest pleasures were these mornings in the Row, especially when Beltran used to walk there in lieu of his usual noontide canter. At such times I would mount the chair beside him; and, sitting upright on that green iron throne, I passed the peripatetics in review with a countenance that I was satisfied presented the most complete copy of the superciliousness, serenity, and sarcasm, which I saw on the faces of those around me.

If there be a Republic on earth it is the Ride from twelve to two on a May morning.

O, I know it is the most fashionable lounge you have, but it is a Republic for all that! There could Bill Jacobs lean against a rail, with a clay-pipe in his mouth, and a terrier under his arm, close beside the Earl of Guilliadene, with his cigarette and his eye-glass, and his Poole-cut habiliments. There could Laura Pearl, or any other of her order, sit with their priceless old laces, and their skirts of satin or velvet, sweeping against the soft, white, filmy dress of a duke's child-like daughter, in her seventeenth year, and her very first season.

There Marmion Eagle, the handsome painter, who was the Wagner of Art, and had so much genius that no one dared to hang or to purchase his pictures, could place himself by a penny next to his forbidden love the wondrous-eyed Lady Gwendoline; and for one sweet half-hour forget that he was a madman, and she a great noble's betrothed. There Maude Delamere, wearing her gold-laden cashmere as none other did, could flirt away her pleasant morning, side by side with the great Duchess of Astolat; while the duchess, eyeing the shawl, would silently appraise the worth of the marvellous fabric, and honestly admire the beauty of the wearer, being herself the only person in all London who knew not that both

cashmere and Delamere were as much the property of His
Grace of Astolat as was his stud or kennel.

There could the tired shop-girl, escaped for an hour from
the heated show-rooms on some thrice-blessed Belgravian
errand, pause beneath the trees, and receive a fresh incentive
to remain virtuous on ten shillings a-week by the sight of
Lillian Lee, with her glistening chignon, and her velvet habit,
and her jewelled whip, leaning down from her hundred-
guinea hack to laugh with Lord Brune and Freddy Orford.

There also could the weary author, or the generous gentleman, whose brain was being maddened or whose heart was
being broken by the curse of too much honour and too little
gold, behold how great a thing it was to be a cheat; as Fio-
dora, the great usurer, rode by on his black Arab; or the old
withered yellow face of the unwedded capitalist, Baron
Moresco, brought smiles to those fair patrician lips with
which they never greeted mere wit or talent, blood or beauty
in the men who passed beside their chairs.

The Row surely is a Republic; for in it first come, first
served; and a copper coin will throne alike the ambassadress
and the traviata, the aristocrat and the cad, the creditor and
the debtor. But all, still, are not equal, you object? Ah,
bah! if that be your objection to a Republic, you had best
remain a Conservative till the end of time.

On this common ground I met, as I have said King Arthur, and Fanfreluche, and many other dogs of high rank and
breeding who were wont, like myself, to saunter their mornings away in the Park.

Once also I saw Bronze—poor, patient, faithful Bronze.
He was wandering wearily among that gay butterfly crowd,
searching, searching, searching everywhere, on his endless
and hopeless errand. A groom lashed him with his whip; a
policeman kicked him away as a stray cur; Lillian Lee rode
her horse viciously at him; Laura Pearl's page drove him
with a curse from resting a moment under her carriage out of
the scorch of the sun. And I—well!—I have promised you to

be as honest as Jean Jacques—I, throned on my green chair, affected not to see him.

Partly, it was because I dreaded greatly to tell him that the boy Harold was dead, and that his quest was useless. Chiefly, I knew it was because a Countess, Beltran's sister, had spread her gold-broidered burnous for my throne, and the Astolat dog, the most supercilious of poodles, sat beside me; and with my snow-white curls, my gay blue ribbon, and the pretty arrogant air with which I had learned to cock my eye and lift my nose, I shrank from recognition of that dusty, tired, starving, homeless creature.

It was shameful, I knew; our race is scarcely ever tainted by such weaknesses; but, whilst you condemn me, think a moment,—are you eager to bow to a ruined man in the Row? Will you check your horse by the rails to smile on a poor relation? Will you shake hands in the face of the town with a penniless strolling artist in a linen blouse, and with a wooden pipe in his mouth, though you may know he has the genius of a Raphael and the heart of a François d'Assise? No; ninety-nine out of a hundred of you won't. My false shame of poor Bronze has many analogies in your humanity.

Yet none the less did I feel remorse for it; we always do feel acute remorse whenever we descend to your level by wounding a friend, or by fawning on a foe. And I would fain have darted after him, and made full and instant amends for my wickedness, but, at the first motion that I gave, the Countess's little hand caught my collar, and held me motionless down on my seat.

It seemed indeed as though she had divined my intention; and felt that a display of friendship from Prosperity to Poverty would be an unseemly anomaly, unfit for that place of fair fashion.

I confessed my sin that day to Fanfreluche.

"Bless me, my dear!" said that cynic. "You've no business to have learned your lesson so quick; you don't live with a woman!"

She had never recovered, nor was ever likely to recover,

the sharp jealousy which she felt of my selection by her hero; but she had an excellent heart in her way, though such a bitter little thing, and she was often very good-natured indeed.

That day I coaxed out of her at last as much as she knew of that story of Derry Denzil's, which she had once promised, and always afterwards refused, to tell me.

He had just passed us, on his black mare, with his glass in his eye, and his cigarette in his mouth, and the sunshine full on his dark, handsome, reckless face.

"Story, my dear? every one of those men has a story," said Miss Volubility, when I reminded her of her promise. "It makes me mad to hear that wretched Mouse, when he wants to slate a very good novel, declare that there is no romance in real life. Good gracious! Why, no novelist would dare to write half the things that I know have happened; the coincidences are too marvellous, the fates too bizarre, the anomalies too glaring, the skein of circumstances too entangled, in real life, for any novelists to dare to paint exactly all that they see or know.* Do all reviewers live in a nutshell, and absorb themselves in an eternity of knitting and muffins, and three-penny whist, that they persist in declaring there is no romance in real life? Heavens! the unutterable woe, the insane passions, the extraordinary contradictions, the horrible ruin, the wonderful accidents, forming themselves like a kaleidoscope picture, that I have beheld in my season of existence! The wildest novel was never one half so wild as the real fate of many a human life that to superficial eyes looks serene, and placid, and uneventful enough. Life is just the same now, as in the ages of the Œdipus agony, and the Orestes crime. It is only that now—they show nothing."

"But tell me what happened to him," I urged, yawning a little.

"O, you little idiot!" she cried, disgusted. "One would

* I beg thoroughly to corroborate this opinion of Mdlle. Fanfreluche, whom I report faithfully, but with whom I do not always agree.—Ed.

certainly think you were a woman—always staring at one
little whelk on the shore, and always ignoring the whole great
ocean and sky! The whelk is the one narrow personality;
the waves and horizon are the vast expanse of universal cir-
cumstance.

"You are almost as bad as an English girl that I belonged
to once for a few months. She was the wife of the great Bel-
gian painter, Philip Cornaro; she was a pretty creature, with
no brains. One glorious evening, down by the Biscay coast
—they lived there at that time in an exquisite villa—he was
painting out-of-doors; painting a great golden comet that
floated over a purple sky, above a moonlit sea.

"The bells of a campanile rang eight and nine and ten;
he painted on and on and on; and I sat quiet beside him.
For there was a spell in this marvellous night, with that
mystical messenger from the unknown gods to men waiting
there, in the still starlit skies, above the hushed calm waters.

"The girl stole up beside us feverishly twice or thrice.
At length, as the bells rang the tenth hour, she came again
swiftly and shook him by the arm. He started—thus unwel-
comely roused from out of his great mystic dreams.

"'Come at once, Cornaro,' she whispered; 'I have waited
so long—so long!'

"He roused himself with a sigh.

"'I cannot come,' he said patiently, gazing with his whole
soul in his eyes, at the sea and the sky.

"'Cannot! And why?' she cried in vexed wonder.

"'Why!' he echoed, 'look there, love—that splendour will
never revisit the earth for five centuries.'

"She pushed the brush from his hand with a pout on her
ruddy lips.

"'The comet! Who cares for that? you must come in.
The tea is getting cold!'"

"And then people say that incompatibility of character is
not reason enough for a divorce!" the duke's poodle added,
as Fanfreluche paused in her long recital.

"Ah, they say so, Poodle," that cynic responded. "But nobody's ever proved it yet, I think."

"This is not Denzil's story?" I urged, my mind curiously dwelling on Mrs. D'Eyncourt.

"He's fifty stories, my dear," said Fanfreluche. "They all of 'em have. Look there—do you see Peel Vavasour, that little, dry, slender chip of a man who is hardly bigger than his own fusee? Well, he's the hardest rider that ever sent a horse at a six-bar; and the boldest trooper that ever led his men into the jaws of hell. Yet do you know that, for ten whole years, that man has been given over, heart and body and soul, to the wildest, saddest, direst passion that ever possessed a life?

"See yonder too—on that sorrel hunter that is plunging and tearing at its bit—that is Sir George Maude of Effingham. Is he not your beau-idéal of a fair, frank, fearless, sunny-hearted English gentleman, with his golden beard blowing in the wind, and his blue eyes glancing in the light, and his manly laugh ringing out so cheerily? Well, my dear, go home with George, or rather go where he never goes, to that grand old Effingham in the western woods, by the western seas, that looks like Launcelot's ocean-castle; and you will find the picture of a woman there. A woman with Titian's hair and Boucher's velvet eyes, smiling; with a scarlet flower held against her lips, in a pretty unspoken symbolic 'hush!' Well, that woman was George's wife.

"And the picture is locked in a darkened room that never is opened; nor hears the fall of footsteps, nor sees the light of day. She had all his big, brave, kindly heart, and all his loyal undoubting honour. So she broke the one and betrayed the other. To do him the more shame, moreover, she chose her paramour out of his own kith and kin. It was a horrible tale—of worse than passion, of worse than sin. George pursued them to Paris, and would have killed his cousin—strangled him by the sheer force of his hands—if the crowd in the Bois had not torn them asunder.

"He has been freed by the law, and the woman has

wedded her lover. But the old halls of Effingham never see
their master's face; the old forests never hear the ring of his
rifle; no children's gay feet tread the grasses; no woman's
glad voice wakes the echoes. And that man is haunted for
ever, by a ghost that will never be laid."

I answered nothing—these revelations saddened me.

"Look there again," pursued this pseudo-philosopher.
"You see that cold, fair, sardonic-looking creature there, on
a dark bay, wearing a rose in his coat, and riding with Paget
Desmond? Well, that is Vivyan Bruce. He is a colonel of
Guards, and in the Brigades they always call him Mephisto;
while society in general is given to saying that if Satan himself does ever walk abroad in man's guise, he clothes himself
in the fleshly garb of wicked Vy Bruce, who is the deadliest
shot in all Europe, and the wildest gambler that ever shook a
main. Well, do you know that there is a blind woman, still
lovely even in her sightlessness, dwelling in the daintiest
river-home by Cliefden, who could tell you that for tenderness, pitifulness, thoughtfulness, there is not the equal of
'Mephisto' in the world. It was the old, old story, of sweet
forbidden love, and lives that met too late. One terrible
night she, young and beautiful, and weary of heart, for a
love that never could be hers, standing beside her casement
close by the gates of Frascati, was stricken by a sudden
stroke of lightning darting from above Albano, and made
blind then and for ever. Her husband cursed her, and
abandoned her; this man alone cleaved to her, and took her
in her senselessness and sightlessness, deeming her even thus
yet fairer than all fair women. The world calls such love
sin—ah, the world is so very wise! Well, many years have
drifted by since then; but go you and ask of Beatrice Silviera
in her solitude, where to be *his* consoles her for the loss of all
besides, whether that man be indeed a devil, as they say; or
whether his voice be not ever gentlest, his care be not ever
surest, his patience be not ever perfect, his love be not ever
infinite to her, in her darkness and her helplessness, whose
eyes can never again look once into his own."

I was silent—awed by her unwonted gravity. I looked at him; he had a cold, hard, careless face, I thought; and he laughed idly where he rode with other men.

"You poor little brat!" cried Fanfreluche contemptuously. "Are you, who are a dog, as foolish as those poor scribes who, being at their wits' ends for what to say, declare romance is dead in human lives? Pshaw! Do you think that, because our friends there ride with flowers in their coats, and cigars in their mouths, and call the loveliest Helen only 'not bad-looking,' and show their friendship to Patroclus chiefly by 'getting up behind him,'* and lounge in the smoking-room of their clubs as though they had not one care upon earth, that therefore they never search for a four-leaved shamrock? never challenge fight for a brazen shield they deem silver? never wear the sackcloth under the silk, and the iron belt under the velvet? and never hunger vainly for the sight of a Holy Sepulchre that has no place save in their dreams? Chut! —you know nothing of men!"

I was abashed. To me the riders of the Row looked nothing but a fashionable mob of well-dressed, well-mounted, easy-tempered, and somewhat bored gentlemen. But I supposed she knew best; and to be sure Denzil, gazing at the photograph in solitude, had been a very different person to what he looked now, where he had checked his horse beside the rail, and leaned from his saddle to laugh and talk over the Epsom chances with Fred Orford.

"Look at Derry," said Fanfreluche sharply, feminine-like, coming round (now I had ceased to ask her) to the very point on which she had refused information. "Derry is one of the gayest-tempered and most popular men on the town. And yet that man has had a good deal of grief in his life, and one murder. He comes of a great old family, and he went through Eton and Christ Church, and into the Guards, and all the rest of the course; and till he was five-and-twenty thought himself

* Mdlle. Fanfreluche used the fashionable slang she had caught up at the Turf, or the Rag, or the Raleigh. She means backing their friends' bills.—Ed.

rich as Crœsus. At that time his father died, leaving just a
hundred thousand pounds' worth of debt behind him. Derry
didn't say much; but he just sold the estate—a grand old
Cornish place that he loved passionately—paid all the debts,
dowered his two sisters, left the Guards, and went into the
Austrian army.

"There he rose rapidly; he was of the very stuff for a
cuirassier; but when he had got his majority, and had been
there some nine years, and had grown fond of the service, an
unlucky thing happened: he was second in a duel. It fell to
his lot to measure the paces. Now, you know he is a giant in
the land, and his strides are longer than those of most men.
The other second, who was an Austrian of very high rank,
sneered thereat.

" 'You seem determined to place distance enough between
your principal and mine!' he cried scoffingly.

"Denzil took no notice, and the duel was fought. It ended
harmlessly, with a bullet-graze on both sides. When it was
over, Denzil went up to the other second who had jeered him.

" 'You complained a moment ago of my putting too much
distance between the combatants,' he said quietly. 'We will
fight as close as you like now.'

"Then out he drew his handkerchief, and tendered one
end to the Austrian—Highland fashion. So, breast to breast,
with the width of that bit of cambric betwixt them—as many
gallant gentlemen were wont to stand for the death-word in
the old wild Scottish days—they fired. The shots were simul-
taneous, and both fell. Denzil was severely wounded in the
breast-bone; but the Austrian was shot through the heart. *

"His brother cuirassiers concealed our friend's place of
sanctuary until he had recovered sufficiently for them to get
him in safety out of the country; but his career in the army
was over—the high station of the dead Austrian made the
duel an offence beyond pardon. Denzil took this death greatly

* I can bear witness that Fanfreluche describes the duel as it actually
took place, without any exaggeration. So unusual a fact in a female
narrator, that I think it necessary to testify to it.—ED.

to heart also; it was the only duel ending fatally that he had ever fought, and he travelled in many strange eastern lands for some time. Half-a-dozen years ago he came back to the old London life; a thousand a-year or so had been left him by a relative, and on this, with what he makes by these novels of his, that are so gay and so mournful, so weary and so witty, he lives well enough. But—"

"Who is Mrs. D'Eyncourt?" I asked.

"Mrs. D'Eyncourt? Well, Mrs. D'Eyncourt was a very handsome woman, who was all the rage in London when I was just out, and belonged to the Household Brigade. She was an actress, and they made her the fashion—for a time. She was an astonishingly beautiful woman, which helped her wonderfully; and an astonishingly proud woman, which went dead against her. She came of an old race, they said; and she was deeply read, and highly cultured. Her husband was a great scoundrel—a sort of gentleman-swindler, who drove her on to the stage, and spent all she gained there; yes, and would have had no objection to have taken any of her money, howsoever it should have been made. He would have staked his wife at piquet, just as soon as he would have staked a sovereign. Denzil was always about with them. He got Mrs. D'Eyncourt her best engagements. He wrote the best critiques that appeared on her. He was in the stalls or behind the scenes nearly every night that she played. He was very much in love with her—that everybody saw. But then, so were a good many others. She had the ball at her feet when she chose to spurn it away. That is, when she had been the talk of the town for two seasons, and was really making something like fame, she disappeared—nobody knows where. Everybody thought Denzil was in the secret. I can't say whether he was. But at any rate, the same night that she vanished, her husband was thrashed within an inch of his life by somebody; and found black and blue, and scarcely able to speak, with the door of his chamber shut on him. I always thought Derry did *that*."

"And Mrs. D'Eyncourt?"

"How your head runs on that woman! The last night that she appeared was a great triumph for her. A certain cabal—there is always a very strong cabal against a woman who is so unsexed that she won't accept diamonds—had done their best to write her down; had derided her, condemned her, stoned her with injury and insult from the catapults of their criticisms. But the woman was gloriously handsome, resolute too in will, and of singular talent. She was, for once, stronger than the strong clique against her; she carried the public with her; and the curtain fell at length on a shower of flowers, and amidst a storm of applause. But that night was the last that the town ever saw Gertrude D'Eyncourt. Of course, they all said that Derry had hidden her somewhere, especially as he went abroad the day after. He came back six months later, looking ill enough, and he horsewhipped one fellow who had repeated (so that it came to his hearing) what all the town said of this woman. And of course they were all quite sure *then* it was true."

"But was it?"

"How can I tell, child? All I know is, that I have never heard a syllable about her from anybody, till you told me the other day of that news of Lord Mark's. But, good gracious, how you chatter! There are our ponies moving off. I wouldn't miss going with them for worlds. Pearl lunches this morning with some men at the Leviathan, and that hotel is the only place where they do aspic with plovers' eggs so that I can eat it."

And away the little chatterbox and gourmet trotted, ringing her golden bells, and presently jumping into the carriage, was whirled out of sight by the swiftly-trotting feet of Pearl's ponies.

Derry Denzil was talking over the Danebury cracks, by the rails; Peel Vavasour was making some man shriek with laughter, by relating a new *double entendre* of Schentack's; Sir George was discoursing with great animation of the last run of the season with the York and Ainsty; and Vy Bruce

was murmuring idlest nonsense to Lillian Lee, as he lighted
one of his cigarettes for her use.

I sat on my chair bewildered and saddened. You always
are, I think, whenever Belphegor first unroofs the houses for
you.

CHAPTER XVII.

Beltran.

T<small>HE</small> new burlesque throve at the Coronet. It was a success,
as you say in your odd jargon. The reckless breakdowns,
the puns—which it seemed really had some humour in them,
and were therefore quite uncommon—the splendid Parisian
dresses, the lively music, all insured its popularity. And
Laura Pearl shone in her jigs—the number of which was increased, according to her desire, with a rollicking zest that
raised her higher than ever in the stalls' estimation.

She was generally late to arrive, sullen when crossed for
a moment, capricious and ungrateful to an incredible extent
and self-willed with a stubbornness of temper which would
have brought her heavy fines and loud curses from the tyran-
nical "old Wynch" had she been one of those luckless girls
who lived in attics and slaved on twenty shillings a week. As
it was, of course nobody dared say a word to her; and all the
wrath of that Jupiter Tonans, the acting manager, fell on the
oftentimes innocent, and invariably defenceless, heads of
those hapless young players who had holes in their gloves,
and rents in their boots, and a hungry pinched look in their
faces, and who toiled in the rain and the gaslight to and from
the theatre on foot, whilst her brougham drove up or away
with much noise and fury and display, and a dashing roan
mare that stepped up to its nose.

Although Beltran had protested against dogs being taken
there, I often went down to the Coronet with him; and few
things ever amused me much more when I ceased to be bewildered at the strangeness of the life there.

He was not very often there himself, however; except on

such evenings as he had those suppers which were the talk of
the town—little costly dainty repasts, where a certain sort of
wit really did circulate, dead though wit is in your modern
society, and where they sometimes played piquet, or écarté,
or lansquenet till the morning. There were scarcely more
than ten or twelve men, his most intimate companions, that
ever had the entrance to the little gilded amber-hued
chamber; and, of course, as it became to be considered very
chic to get the pass there, and as equally, of course, all the
women of his own world were jealous in their own minds of
what they could not enter into; the many who were excluded
said very fearful things of the few who were admitted; and I
do verily believe that Beltran's suppers were considered by
society to recall Borgia's feasts, or D'Argenson's nunnery.
He knew this very well; but he only laughed at it himself,
and did nothing to uproot the conviction. He knew very
well, also, that he seldom drank anything stronger there than
iced seltzer-water, and never did anything worse there than
lose his hundreds on a quatorze of queens. He could have
made an end to the reports in a week by inviting a score
when he only asked half-a-dozen; but that would not have
been a mode of remedy at all like Vere Essendine.

So he continued to shut his doors against the many; and
the many continued to assert that the Coronet supper-room
was a compound of the Parc aux Cerfs and the Agapemone,
with champagne and piquet in its entr'actes.

All the horrors that were whispered of it, however, never
prevented the chastest dame that ever I heard of, or the
haughtiest Belgravian matron, from accepting with pleasure
and smiles his offer of a box for the season. Indeed, to spend
an hour and a half while the burlesque was on behind those
dainty rose-silk curtains of the *loges*, with little cups of orange
pekoe sent to them in his tiniest and choicest china, was one
of the pet amusements of the great ladies of his own order;
and they would turn their handsome eyes from resting
through their lorgnons on the Pearl to smile with sunny welcome on his entrance to their box.

Of course, they all considered his conduct shocking when
they spoke of it in their own boudoirs; but that was no reason
why they should refuse his fashionable theatre and his
fragrant tea. And they never gave a sign that they knew
Laura Pearl was anything more than a very well-dressed
marionette made of wood and hung upon wires.

In your admirable world there is nothing more easy or
more convenient than to ignore—except, indeed, it be to go
one step further, and forget.

Your unlucky people, who find it difficult to do the first,
break the rules of tact and of good society; your unhappy
people, who cannot do the last, break things of less consequence—their hearts.

In this new world of mine I liked every one save this
Pearl of price; and she, for her part, cordially detested me,
though by me she had gained a pair of ear-rings worth two
hundred sovereigns, and a pink tea-set worth fifty. Whenever she saw me—if Beltran's eye was off her—she slapped,
or shook, or pinched me; and once gave me a fearful fall by
jerking me off the carriage-rug from the footboard of a very
lofty mail phaeton.

"Be so good as to leave that dog alone, Laura," Beltran
said to her one day when she was clutching mercilessly at my
curls till I screamed.

"I sha'n't, then!" she retorted, and therewith struck me
with her fan so hard a blow that the tortoiseshell sticks broke
in shivers.

Beltran smiled, well pleased.

"Women's temper generally ends in their own losses," he
murmured. "You don't look handsome when you get savage."

Which assurance only made her more furious. This sort
of amenities was the usual characteristic of their intercourse;
and I often marvelled why a man so fond of repose, and so
impatient of anything like a scene, could voluntarily subject
himself to it. I remarked this once to Fanfreluche.

That little canine *cocodette* turned her nose in the air with
her wonted gesture of scorn.

"My dear, where's another woman so handsome?"

And this was true.

You people, when you write about love, do not allow enough weight to the influence of purely physical attractions. The town had pronounced Laura Pearl the "handsomest thing out." It is as agreeable to a man's pride and sense of possession to hear this said of his mistress, as it is for him to hear his year-old racer pronounced nearer perfection than all the two hundred and odd horses to be seen in the yard on a Sunday afternoon. This is not a lofty motive for passion, you say? Ah, well, I cannot help that. A great many of your motives are not lofty.

Beltran, moreover, had been bred and born in a sphere where women, after all, are really held in much the same esteem as in any oriental country, though they are treated with more outward forms of deference and courtesy, and cost a very great deal more for their maintenance. In his youth he had been besieged and disgusted by marriage-makers of his own order; and he had now in his manhood got into a congenial habit of only seeking his loves in a world from which the demon of marriage was exorcised.

He did not want mental power in his mistress, nor yet affection; he found the first, in plenty, in other forms of society; and he looked on the latter with a sort of horror as on something that would "bore" him infallibly and unbearably.

Indeed, like many men of his time, he did his very utmost to persuade himself that he was heartless, and everybody else that he was mindless.

Yet a keener intelligence than his few men were born with; and a truer friend than he was never lived. Now, your fine intelligence will always soon or late grow dissatisfied with abasing itself to the senses; and he who can be a sincere friend has also in him the capability of sincere love.

A trifle, too, showed me this temper in him.

[And by the way, permit to add that if you were quicker and wiser at guessing your companions' characters from the

indices of trifles, you would not make those everlasting blun-
ders of foolish trust and idiotic suspicion which so continually
excite in you the contempt and wonder of dogs!]

This happened when I had been about a month in his
possession.

"What a pity that boy was in such a deuce of a hurry to
kill himself," said Denzil, one evening, as they drove down to
a Richmond dinner. I being ensconced in the back-seat, and
there being, for once, no woman in the front.

"What boy?" asked Beltran.

"That poor young wretch who wrote the *Demeter*. I see
they have brought some posthumous poems of his out 'by the
late Harold Gerant,' and they are likely to make a sensation.
There is certainly wonderful stuff in them."

"How do they get out if he's dead? I thought publishers
would have nothing to say to him."

"They would have nothing—whilst he was alive. That is
their way. They have a knack of thinking that genius, like
Ganges grass, only exhales its worth when it's been well
crushed. It seems that there were manuscripts of his lying
about in various places; and after the issue of that fragment
the Trade thought it a decent speculation to collect, and to
issue them."

"More fool the Trade, then. While Massinger, and
Ford, and Marvell lie unread in ninety-nine libraries out of a
hundred, who wants the catchpenny jingle of 19th-century
verse?"

"Come, come; you said yourself that there was great
promise in that fragment."

"So I might. But I take it if the man's dead it don't
matter much what he promised; he can't come up to time
with any of it, whether it's a promissory note or a promissory
poem."

"Don't be a brute, Vere! The poor lad would rest quieter
in his grave, I fancy, for knowing that those thoughts of his
are not all lost."

"Everybody does rest quiet in his grave, I believe, unless

he's scooped up with a spade by an enterprising Railway
Company. You literary men do allow yourselves such poetic
license of expression. Surely, from your own sentimental
point of view, you ought to be awfully glad this young idiot
did kill himself: who would know anything of Chatterton if
it weren't for that lucky dose of prussic acid? and who would
care a hang for Shelley if, in lieu of dying poetically, he had
lived to grow fat, leave off his sailor's jacket, read family
prayers, and turn laureate?"

"If you would only read this book—"

"I! good gracious! When do I ever read anything, unless it be a novel of yours, or of Lawrence's?"

"If you would only read the poems you would see what it
is that I mean. There are a hundred faults in them, of course;
but there is a wonderful glow of imagery and depth of thought
in them for the works of so mere a boy. No pretentiousness
either; no borrowed Catullan images; no mock incestuous rapture; but the strength of passions struggling with their tempters, like young lions in a net; and yet, with all their latent
woe and fire, the purity of a mind that had evidently fed on
the simplicity of some free, open-air, and meditative life—the
only true life for the poet and the painter. If you would for
once read them—"

"But I never shall, my dear Derry. So I will take your
praises on trust; the only way not to be obliged to disagree
with them. Just now, rhapsodies on bisque soup and red
mullets are more to my taste. I wish your dead boy all sorts
of living laurels, but I clearly foresee that he will grow into
a bore. Pray don't let us have too much of him."

Denzil flung himself back in his seat, a little out of
temper.

I, lying coiled in my tiger rug, wondered within myself.

It so chanced that a month or so earlier I had happened
to go out in the forenoon with Beltran, at a different hour to
his usual one. And he had wended his way, walking, with a
cigar in his mouth, to a certain house of business; where with
my own ears I had distinctly heard him, in a somewhat long

business interview, commission the principals of the house to
search for all manuscripts bearing the inscription attached to
the poem of *Demeter;* when found, to have the noblest of such
fragments selected by some scholar competent to make the
choice, and then to have them printed and issued with as
little delay as possible, and at his own cost. I had also heard
the persons he thus commissioned ask if they might, without
offence, inquire the reason for his interest in the young dead
penniless writer? and had heard his answer. "Interest?
None in the least. I never saw him in my life. But the boy
had genius; and it ought not to be buried with his body."
And therewith he left, desiring that his name should not in
any way be associated with the affair, but that the publishers
themselves should appear to be the originators, as well as the
executors, of the matter.

Herein it appeared that he had been thoroughly well obeyed.
The poems had appeared, been discussed, been admired, and
the name of the dead boy was on the lips of many; but not a
soul ever dreamed that he had so much as thought twice of
the story of the suicide that Denzil had told at his Sunday
breakfast.

But why conceal this generous and sympathetic action?—
and conceal it too with this cynical assumption of contemptuous indifference?

Nay, I cannot tell; I can only say it was his way of bely-
ing himself; a way I have known in more men than one of
like temperament.

"They do good by stealth, and blush to find it known;"
or rather swear impatiently to find it known, as their manner is.
I do not say that this masking of all their better acts and
thoughts is of itself commendable; but I think, in view of the
innumerable creatures who crow out aloud their own charities,
and of the abundant hypocrites who only fold their robes to
hide their vice and avarice, such exceptions as his are refresh-
ing, and not to be condemned. If you have not known men
like him, men of this order and of this habit of speech and

act, you will not be likely to comprehend the character of this master of mine.

Presently we dashed over Richmond Hill, and drew up before the old Star and Garter. And here Beltran, with the Duke of Astolat, Ned Guilliadene, a Chargé d'Affaires, and a Guardsman, gave one of those dinners which seemed part and parcel of his duties as lessee of the Coronet. A dinner where all the prettiest of his actresses blossomed forth in the most intensely Parisian of dresses, and many hundred pounds' worth of diamonds and rubies. Where the portly dame, always attached to the house, who would be either Hamlet's mother or Mrs. Candour, the Countess Capulet or Mrs. Bouncer, appeared in velvets of the richest purple, or violet, or ruby, for she played propriety on many scarcely proper occasions, and this is a lucrative office always gratefully acknowledged. Where that charming woman, Mrs. Delamere (who on the stage had something of the sympathetic acting and elegant ease of the French school, yet saw herself almost disregarded by an audience eager for the breakdowns and burlesque of Laura Pearl), brought the superb grace and proud negligence of a duchess, though her forsaken lord was a wine-merchant's clerk, who had wedded her out of a milliner's work-room. Where the male comedians, making in private the same blunder that distinguished them in public, thought coarseness and buffoonery were wit; and took an insane relish in the privilege of the moment, which allowed them to address without prefix as "Beltran," and "Brune," and "Desmond," and "Denzil," men who, meeting them the next day in Pall-mall, barely gave them a nod of the head as good morning. Such a dinner as their host had sat at hundreds of times, bored to death by the drear monotony of the thing, which so exactly reproduced itself one year after another. He knew precisely when Mrs. Delamere would smile, when Mrs. Mac Mundo would frown, what puns his first comedy-man would make, and where he would infallibly make them; what pretty consternation his actresses would show at the first questionable story that came round with the chablis; what flushed amuse-

ment they would receive a much naughtier one with, when
they had come to the chartreuse; what riotous laughter the
Pearl would give to the punsters as she crammed the crystallised sweetmeats into her rosy mouth, and had her armies of
glasses replenished again and again; what exquisite dignity
disdainful Maude Delamere would show as she swept away
on the terrace with her black laces all trailing about her; and
what nonsense he should be expected to murmur in the scent
of the geraniums and heliotropes to these women, every turn
of whose features and every tone of whose voices he knew as
well as the letters of the alphabet. Dinners at which his
actors would drink the rich wines, and the actresses eat the
rare fruits, of his giving; but from which as often as not they
would drive away, the one to curse him as a swell because he
had not laughed at their broadest joke, and the other to
mutter against him as a niggard, because the enamelled or
jewelled present laid with the bread-roll under their napkin
was a shade less costly than what they had desired.

Little Fanfreluche was right.

In other ages the jesters fed on blows and black broth,
yet oftentimes loved their princes, and would have died for
them had only their jingling bauble been a two-edged sword.
But in this age the wagered fools, fed on the fat of the land,
and drenched with the choicest of vintages, have none such
fealty as this, but rise from their master's board to spit forth
venom behind his steps, and ring their bells to chime out his
dishonour.

CHAPTER XVIII.

His Views on Dinners.

Apropos of these Richmond entertainments, I often wondered, by the way, why men, who had their own admirable
cooks, and their own elegant abodes, and their own choice
selected wines, were so addicted to coming out to dinner at the
Star and Garter, or Ship, or any suburban place, that it was
fashionable to dine at in this manner.

I often wondered what peculiar attraction existed for them in spending about five times as much on their dinner as it would have cost at home, only for the sake of getting in return a questionable cuisine, lumpy sauces, cold soups, and fifth-rate champagnes at exorbitant prices.

I never solved the question; and I cannot but think the mode is an extraordinary mistake—a great waste of time and money, without any adequate *quid pro quo*.

If I, instead of being a dog, fed at best on scattered crumbs, were a rich man, and a man of influence enough to be able to command whatever society I chose, I should never dine out of my own house.

But if everybody did that, you object, who would there be for guests? Pooh! my dear friend, men will never be so equal but what there will always be your gay, courtly, silver-tongued, half-bankrupt, though well-born Martial, who will always be charmed to enjoy the magnificence of Lucan's villa. And if I were Lucan, I would always eat my *cœna* at home.

A dinner is not a thing which should be left to chance. The choice of so delicate a combination as the *menu* should never be given over to hazard. And now that I am on this topic, forgive me if I add my mite to all that has been already written on the great science of dining.

I have seen a great many dinners in my time, since that first London season with Beltran. Duchesses', actresses', millionaires', playwrights', nobles', and bohemians' dinners—I have been present at them all, one time and another, and I cannot forbear from a few remarks on the subject. Dining, or rather giving dinners with success, is an art. Epicures have recognised this long ago, but I want it universally recognised.

There is no reason in life why Rus, with only his bottle of old port, and his new-laid eggs, and his plump home-fed pullets, and his sunny apricots fresh from the warm south wall, and his honey drawn from his own cabbage-roses and carnations and white jessamine flowers, and a ruddy-cheeked, clean-handed Phillis, and a shady, leaf-bowered, sweet-scented little chamber, should not study to give an entertainment very charming in its own fashion, quite as well as Urbs, who has his swift, silent, clever men-servants, and his gold plate, and his porcelains costly as gold, and his cook, with the soul of a Carême, and his magnificent pines, and his hothouse-grapes, and his wonders of food brought from all ends of Europe, and his perfect wines all of comet years, and his brilliant guests culled from the Legations and the two Houses, from White's and the Guards' Club, from Brooks' and Boodles'.

The two entertainments will be at the two extremes of the art, of course; but there is no reason why they should not both be true art—like a Meissonnier and a Poussin.

Lookers-on see the most of the game, they say. Perhaps you will bear with me a moment, whilst I tell you one or two things that I think of your dinners.

They are not anything like what they might be. Here, in London, you have every requisite for the very best dinners—dinners to call up Brillat Savarin, in ecstasy, from his grave. You have the best wines, you have the best food, you have handsome women, you have clever men, and you never spare any expense; how is it, then, that in London you reiterate the eternal complaint—all of you—that there is no such thing as Society? It is really very ridiculous; you ought to be ashamed of the confession.

You echo it one after another, and yet night after night you go on elbowing each other at assemblies that resemble a crush on a hustings, and crowding together in fashionable mobs at garden-parties, and you do nothing in the world to remedy the defect.

Now it is a fact—if you don't go to them I can't help that —it is a fact that there are little dinners even in London which are a success, because they are thoroughly enjoyable.

Why are they so?

Well, one can hardly give a recipe for Society any more than for cooking an omelet. It is not a knowledge to be taught; it is a thing that comes by nature; a thing of genius.

They are agreeable, first of all, because they are given out of a genuine design to amuse and be amused, and not merely to "knock off" a social duty, and occupy a space in the "fashionable intelligence."

Also because they are small enough for the ball of conversation to be tossed lightly, and rapidly, from every hand; the talk is not therefore a mere buzzing and cross-fire of a score of voices.

Also because the host or hostess has the supreme talent of selection, and also the supreme talent of leading the conversation, unostentatiously, but skilfully; it is almost as great a talent as that of leading aright at whist. And this also in a manner must come by nature, though it may be increased and polished by study.

If you are people who will persist in giving huge "feeds," as slang very fittingly styles them, of thirty or forty covers, I cannot hope to instruct you. But if you are open to conviction and willing to give little dinners (one every night if you like) of four, six, or at most eight, guests, just listen to me.

Be firm in rejecting an odiously long *menu*. A dozen services are quite enough in all reason; and to risk too great length, is certainly to risk *ennui;* a touch of *ennui* will make your dinner a failure, even though your cook should be a Vatel.

Take heed to have amidst your dishes two or three which, whilst exquisitely prepared, yet shall be perfectly simple and wholesome; remember that your very choicest *bon viveurs* are the very people most grateful for a change in this respect; and remember too the great Savarin's eulogy of a larded fowl which he preferred to all the chickens fricassée'd, suprême'd, marengo'd, singara'd, or bordelaise'd that could be proffered him.

Have a care that your servants are perfectly educated in the science of the wine-book, so that they may be certain to give the proper vintage at the proper time, and neither fill the glasses too fast or too seldom. Have your table elegantly

appointed, and a fair show of gold or silver to brighten it;
but let your flowers be far more conspicuous than your plate,
since they must be far more beautiful, and you do not want
your board to look like a great silversmith's shop-window.
The most delicate porcelains and the exquisite cristalleries
of Clichy or Baccarat may be mingled with advantage;
Majolica or Dresden is too heavy, to my taste, for a dinner-
table.

Pray do not follow the ridiculous mode of thinking it *chic*
to have everything out of its proper season; it is never really
good; if you be a real genius you can well afford to abandon
the flavourless asparagus of mid-winter and strawberries of
Christmas with silent contempt to millionaires and the *demi-
monde*, who have no other thought than to display their ill-
gotten gains.

As regards the number of servants, I think you make a
mistake in fancying it is their quantity and not their quality
that is of importance. When there are too many they only
tread on one another's toes, as they have trod on my tail
many a time. A couple of men perfectly trained will do
more for the comfort of your guests than a dozen powdered
giants behind the chairs, if the giants be secretly intent on
listening for the last new scandal or afraid of injuring their
own dignity by a swift movement.

Unless a servant be as exact as clock-work, and as indifferent to the talk round him as an automaton, he is not worth
the tax you pay for him. A servant that I know well would
not start if a thunderbolt burst at his feet when he was handing the asparagus, nor give a sign that he heard if a score of
Sydney Smiths were doing their best to kill him with laughter
as he changed their plates; now *that* man is worth his weight
in gold. But there are thousands of footmen who will preserve a decorous aspect of earless and eyeless gravity
throughout a dinner, while very many of them are listening
and seeing with all their might for all that—hence they wait
badly.

To the good servant his attendance is his art, and he has

no thought except to obey its rules absolutely. The most beautiful woman should be sexless, and the most eloquent scandal-monger be tongueless, for aught that he should know or should care. Now, you can make your pattern servant as you can make your standard rose—at least, if you be fit to give a good dinner you can.

Of course you will never in future years resort to the hideousness of food set on the table, now that the Russian mode has once taught you how to refine, and, if one may say so, to spiritualise eating. Nor will the grotesque folly of nodding the head over each glass at some neighbour, like a mandarin on a tea-box, in a custom called "taking wine" (of which I have heard, though it was over long before my time), ever be revived, it is to be hoped, for nothing can well be more thoroughly absurd. Yet the present system of pouring the same wines in everybody's glass, without any seeming remembrance of the exceeding difference in men's wine-palates, is not what it ought to be.

There are men who only like two sorts of wine in one evening; men who like a different vintage with each service; men who like all their wines still; men who abominate certain brands; men who like the French order of precedence for their wines; men who like the English order, which is exactly contrary to it; all those various tastes should be more consulted than they are usually by butlers.

Of course my own race are all Rechabites, therefore I treat this question from a purely impersonal point of view. No one, I am happy to say, ever saw a dog drunk; inebriety is one of those "superiorities" which you are so naturally proud to claim over us. Men, pigs, ducks, and geese are the four orders of creatures distinguished by a capacity for drunkenness; perhaps it is for this reason that they all four make more noise over their own small affairs—a rise in gold, a swill-tub, a caddis worm, or a blade of grass—than any other created thing ever is overheard to do.

But all these, after all, are the merest matters of detail compared with the one essential element of prandial success

—*i. e.* the conversation. After all the great account that we make of decoration and of cookery, I have seen two thoroughly enjoyable dinners—one in a little set of chambers where the carte was confined to beef-steaks, oysters, Poméry Gréno and Pichon de Longueville; and the other in a little fishing inn overhanging a picturesque trout-river, where the entire fare consisted of those dainty fish perfectly grilled, and a grand capon, that would have warmed Falstaff's heart, washed down by the sparkling ales of Trent.

But then, those who dined at the first were six of the gayest, cleverest, and happiest-tempered people that ever tilted together in a playful tournament of tongues; and the anglers who laughed over the last were two of the wittiest writers that have ever charmed the world; a soldier whose silver speech is as lightly brilliant as his deeds of daring are of sternest fame, and one woman, frank, bright, full of grace and of beauty, a child in her mirth and a queen in her empire.

N.B. Of these four, none were in love; if only one had "lost his head," the harmony of the dinner would have been most probably at an end; the perfect freedom of it certainly would have been. They were only friends, in that intimate, pleasant, half-romantic friendship, which only men and women of the highest intelligence can know.

The one great element of success at a dinner is the talk; and who shall give a recipe, as I say, for that? It is a thing that goes by nature, like the gift of colour and of song.

It is preposterous to say that your men do not talk well. I have heard talk to the full as brilliant and as epigrammatic as anything the cleverest writer can put into the mouths of his imaginary characters. When I hear people protest that in real life no such witty converse as you find in very witty novels can ever be met, I wonder where these protestants have had the misfortune to live. As I said in my introductory remarks, it is almost as difficult to print the wit one hears as it is to petrify a *soufflée de fécule;* but if you never hear wit in this world—good gracious me!—you must keep very bad company.

I think it is a mistake to think that tremendously clever people are required to obtain radiant conversation. Your very great genius, your very abstruse scholar, is often a very stupid fellow, so far as lingual utterances go. The best men at a dinner are such men as are to be found by the dozen at the best clubs in London; men of quick intelligence, of good culture, of consummate worldly knowledge, and of just that sparkling, mischievous, pleasant, social wit which is to conversation what the truffle is to cookery, or the champagne is amongst wines.

These men are to be found, and better companions need never be sought. True, at some tables they may sit silent, *morne*, and as contemptuous as their politeness permits, but believe me, that is only because at those tables you are boring them. Get them into a congenial atmosphere, their tongues will go, their mirth sparkle, and their laugh be heard as enjoyable as any one can wish. They *can* be the most amusing companions in the world; if they are not so with you, it is your fault: you bore them in some way.

Politics you should banish absolutely—if people are not of one mind about them they are sure to quarrel over them; if they *are* of one mind no subject can be drearier. Some little bit of political news, quite fresh from some Legation or some Secretary of State, before the world has heard it, is all that should be admissible.

Any quite fresh scandal is a great relish; especially if you know something about it that no one else knows. Perhaps you had better take heed that the chief of the actors involved are not present; though, indeed, in this age you are all so entirely free from prejudice on these points that (if you be discussing a divorce, for instance) you need not mind the presence of the relatives in the least, scarcely of the husband now-a-days; the only person whose feelings must not be hurt is the co-respondent. Where this last interesting personage is in the plural you had better not invite two of

15*

them at the same time; they are sure to have either too much
jealousy, or too much compassion, for one another.

Du reste—Don Juan is always a delightful fellow, and the
most amusing guest you can ever obtain, unless indeed it be
weighing on his mind that he will have to marry Julia Ab-
bandonata. In which case of course you cannot reasonably
expect him to be lively.

If you have not the knack of setting the ball of talk
rolling, it is impossible I can impart it to you: one cannot
make a good host any more than one can make a great composer: both are born. Still there are a few things which help
it. In the first place, there is the care needful in the selection
of your guests; they must suit one another; or you will have
discord; a mingling of classes or of opposite political parties
is, I think, a mistake: men are most at ease in their own
caste; if you introduce an "outsider," he or she must be a
very brilliant one.

Let your party be of very small number rather than, for
sheer sake of enlarging it, introduce the wrong element because you cannot get the right. There is a certain unity of
feeling, and common likeness of tone and manner, in an
Order, still more so in each "set" of that "order," which is,
if made use of, an essential aid to harmony in itself. It is
an infinite *ennui* to a man to sit next to another who does not
catch his allusions flying; it ruins conversation when one
person outside the pale fails to understand all that is cause
for mirth or for chat within it.

Likewise, you should be very careful not to let any topic
get worn threadbare; the instant it is getting the least bit of
a bore, sweep it away with the brisk besom of a fresh and
welcome subject.

A little scandal is, as I say, an excellent thing; nobody is
ever brighter or happier of tongue than when he is making
mischief of his neighbour; but it is a two-edged sword that
requires very dainty handling; and all caps of slander unluckily fit so very many heads, that you must be heedful how
you select them.

If it be a party of both sexes, ask people that are *a little* in love with each other, for people a little in love are always eager to shine; but banish all *grandes passions;* they have an eloquence of their own indeed, but they are very stupid society at a dinner-table.

And now, if you be a woman, let me offer you one piece of advice, though I know you will never follow it: DON'T THINK OF YOURSELF. Resign your pet flirtation *pro tempo;* don't care for "making play" even with your favourite lover. Do not indulge your own palate, nor meditate on your own dress; let your heart and soul be with your guests, let your whole mind be given to the guidance and the surveillance of the conversation. Remember that your dinner is your campaign, and that on your skilful direction depends your victory.

But then withal you must be quite at ease, and not in the least pre-occupied, or your influence will be *nil;* you must be always gay, alert, suave, ready to skim over a difficulty, to supply an hiatus, and to prevent a pause; you must lead with radiance and with tact, and yet you must be perfectly willing not to shine, and to let your powers lie *perdu* if your guests are in full career without you, and if your self-assertion would be their interruption.

Do you think this all very hard?

Well, my dear, if it were ten times harder, would you not have your reward when men should declare that your dinners were the most charming in London?

One last word,—leave the table early, and do not grudge the men their half-hour of solitude. Nay, send them cigars and a *chasse* to prolong it. A trial to you, I know—but they like it; don't you believe them if they tell you they don't. They may call it a "barbarous custom;" but it is one that they relish exceedingly, as they do many other "barbarities" —their vices to wit; and you will be all the more successful as a dinner-giver if you have the sense in you to see this.

The most charming woman will be only wise if she take

fully into her mind the conviction that too much even of herself may be a bore.

I don't know what more I can tell you; one cannot make
a dinner-giver as I have said, any more than one can make a
Michael Angelo. I am half afraid, too, that you English,
despite your repute for hospitality, have not the genius of
entertainment in you. You are far too self-conscious and
you are seldom light-hearted enough.

If I were to tell you, also, all that I have heard your
guests, when they have got out in the night air and had their
cigars fairly in their mouths, say of dinners that you had
thought quite perfection, you would not believe me. There
is nowhere such a thorough-going sceptic as a man or woman
who disbelieves in his or her own shortcomings.

So I will not weary you longer on the subject, as I can
hardly hope to improve you, even if you have not skipped
this chapter in my memoirs, which is probable. Let me only
paraphrase a famous saying, and add:

"*Montrez-moi ton menu, je te montrerai ton cœur.*"

CHAPTER XIX.

He studies the Stage.

I LEARNED many wondrous things betwixt Epsom and
Ascot. A brief space, indeed, yet one that to me seemed
longer than the whole of my previous life, so crowded was
its every hour with new and marvellous experiences. Worldly
experiences, I mean. Intellectually, I am not sure that I ac-
quired much.

Indeed, to a little brain teeming with memories of the
Théâtres Beaumarchais, Voltaire, Molière, Feuillet, Sardou,
Sandeau, &c. which I had heard read so continually at the
Dower-house amongst the Fens, the views of dramatic litera-
ture held at the Coronet appeared of the most extraordinary
character. They certainly had one merit—simplicity.

The verb "to steal" was the only one that a successful
dramatic author appeared to be required to conjugate.

For your music steal from the music-halls; for your costumes steal from *Le Follet*; for your ideas steal from anybody that happens to carry such a thing about him; for your play, in its entirety, steal the plot, the characters, the romance, the speeches, and the wit, if it have any, of some attractive novel; and when you have made up your parcel of thefts tie it together with some string of stage directions, herald it as entirely original, give a very good supper to your friends on the press, and bow from your box as the "Author."

You will certainly be successful: and if the novelist ever object, threaten him with an action for interference with *your* property.

These I found were the laws laid down by London dramatists; and they assuredly were so easy to follow and so productive to obey, that if any Ben Jonson, or Beaumarchais, Sheridan, or Marivaux, had arisen and attempted to infringe them, he would have infallibly been regarded as a very evil example, and been extinguished by means of journalistic slating and stall-siflage.

Beltran had indeed now and then imperilled the peace and prosperity of his Coronet by certain forms of opposition to this quiet régime of uninterrupted theft. Once, I heard, he had actually lost some hundred pounds by relinquishing a piece at the day before its production, because he found out that it was a piracy from a novel, and that the novel-writer had an antiquated prejudice against being robbed.

Also, when a piece was taken from the French, he had the weakness not only to pay the Frenchman for doing him the honour to use his creation, but actually had "translated and adapted from the French original" printed in his programmes and advertisements; a ridiculous concession to truth, which kept his house half empty—the English public naturally fearing pollution from so unnaturally unadulterated an article.

But Beltran was quite an exception amongst lessees; and it was no wonder that all the town by the voices of its prophets declared for once unanimously that he must be ruined in a twelvemonth. Indeed, they said it was only the wisdom

of Dudley Moore and little Lance that had saved him from
destruction hitherto.

"What's that new piece you have advertised, Vere?"
asked Paget Albermarle at one of the Sunday breakfasts.

"This," answered Beltran, tossing over to him a paper-
covered book.

"*La Péché de Vivienne*," read Albermarle, "and you call
it *Vivia's Secret*. What sort of a thing is it?"

"O, a glorious piece," said Denzil, lifting his head. "I
saw it in Paris a month ago, with the Desaix in it. A terrible
piece, strong and noble, and full of a curious kind of poetry,
and of a wonderful power. Desaix looks superb in it too.
She is a grand woman. But you never mean to say you are
going to bring it out, Beltran?"

"We are going to turn it into English for the Coronet,"
answered Leo Lance, striking into the conversation. "It is
wonderfully effective, as you say. We shall have to shorten
it—make it three acts; and it will be more of a drama than a
tragedy, of course. There's no time for a long play before
the burlesque."

Denzil shuddered very visibly.

"A drama—three acts—one knows what that means!
Good heavens, Vere! How came you to decide on the thing
before I came back? I could have told you that you haven't
a creature in your company capable of giving the Péché de
Vivienne."

Beltran lifted his brow wearily.

"You were at Nice, and we wanted something; we have
been doing this old legitimate business too long; Lance suggested this play, and thought that it read very well."

"Of course it read very well! It is the finest thing they
have had over there since *Marion Delorme*. It is a tremen-
dous tragedy, I tell you; and you have vulgarised it by this
atrocious title already!"

"Mr. Lance is an excellent adapter," put in the quiet
sonorous voice of the great editor of the *Midas*. "He always

filters so well, that no residuum of the original genius ever appears."

The hapless Mouse coloured and fidgeted where he sat; but he never dared to resent the sharpest thrusts of this great censor.

"I intend to adhere quite closely to the French play," he muttered sullenly. "It will only be slightly shortened; I shall hardly change the text at all."

"Then you may withdraw the piece after its first night, Vere," said Dudley Moore serenely.

"Don't you like it?" asked Beltran.

"Like it!" echoed Dudley Moore. "How is that the question? It is a very clever play; very clever, though I am scarcely so enthusiastic on its merits as Denzil. But it is a play simply unproducible in England."

"O, nonsense!" cried Denzil; "how is it worse than dozens we give? The poor woman never sins but once, and that under such circumstances, and with such agonies of remorse, that the moral is the finest possible. There's not an indecent line in the tragedy; it is only fearfully human and real."

Dudley Moore shrugged his shoulders.

"You write for the English Public, and don't know them better than *that!*"

"Than what?"

The editor closed his cynical mouth, and entirely refused to say.

"Than to suppose that they like what is human and real, he means," said Beltran. "They don't care the least about that; they like a little broad farce, a little rough murder, and a little rosewater sentiment. Anything more bothers them; they can't understand it."

"Then why, in heaven's name, fritter away on them a grand play like this?" cried Denzil.

"Can't be helped now. Lance has begun it, and the announcements are out."

"And who is to play Vivienne?"

"Maude Delamere, of course."

"What? A character almost as awful as Phædre, and quite as desolate as Antigone, represented by a graceful coquette in point lace and pearls, who will take poison as sweetly as if it were a cup of coffee, and will die with elaborate care not to tumble her train? Preposterous!"

"Blaze away, Derry!" said Beltran resignedly. "But the thing's settled. There's only one question: to keep to the story or not. Old Wynch will have it that it won't do."

"Old Wynch knows his world," said Dudley Moore. "Of course you must change the story, in its chief incident. Indeed, I don't see that Mr. Lance need acknowledge any indebtedness to his original; he will only appropriate the main idea, all the characters, as much of the passion as he dare use, and all the wit that he can contrive to translate. *Si peu de chose!*—not worth a reference."

The poor Mouse moved uneasily.

"My intention was," he murmured, "to have given the piece quite as it stands, love and all."

"What! with the susceptibilities of the British Public!" said Dudley Moore. "They never stand any nonsense with the seventh commandment, remember. You must change the illicit love into a decorous bigamy. Indeed, you might try trigamy. They wouldn't at all mind three husbands."

"Bigamy!" sighed the adapter. "They never have enough of *that*."

"No. The English conscience is so intensely mercantile, that it has no notion of a passion that does not result in the cheating of somebody," said Denzil, taking aim at me with a coffee bonbon. "Bigamy is fraud; and the fraud commends it to the public of these very commercial isles. But it will ruin all the symmetry of the piece; it will entirely destroy its purport. It will make it altogether witless, senseless, absurd. It will neither have point nor intention; neither meaning nor object!"

"No sort of objections to it on the stage those," answered

Dudley Moore quietly. "*You* ought to be well aware of this, Mr. Lance; you have had theatrical successes."

Little Lance winced, as he usually did, beneath the great censor's flagellations.

"It is different with this," he muttered, half apologetically. "Denzil is right. You see, it's really very grand in the original. A great sin, and a great repentance, and all that; symmetrical, you know; really artistic; and if one has to change it into bigamy, it will just be vulgarised and brutalised, that's all."

"Precisely," said Dudley Moore, still in the most affable manner. "We want something to attract a London fashionable audience, don't we?"

"Don't go in for a dramatic conscience, Mouse," said Beltran; "it's too late in the day—all that sort of thing."

"You have had one, my dear Vere," said Dudley Moore. "I think, on the whole, you have spent more on it than on your racehorses?"

"The deuce I have!" murmured Beltran. "Take your own way, Lance, if you like—"

"Only," the censor interrupted, "you won't have a week's run if you do. With Lady Frederic just bolted for the third time, and Lady Stevenham coming into the 'D. C. with her amatory four-in-hand, the aristocracy will be infinitely too virtuous to look at a heroine who sins *once*, and then repents."

Beltran laughed a little. The world had added his name to those of Lady Stevenham's favoured quartette, and he knew well enough that he had only waltzed twice with the woman, and scarcely thought about her as often.

"I'd chance that," he made answer. "The thing is, that French part is an awfully strong one, and I've nobody strong enough for it, if we render it as it stands."

"There's always the Delamere."

"Pshaw! Maude Delamere is a very pretty creature, and drapes herself uncommonly well; but she could no more give

the passion of that French play than she could do you Phædre
in the original."

"No," assented Dudley Moore. "Mrs. Delamere acts very
gracefully, and dresses very charmingly, and is one of the
few Englishwomen that can carry a Cashmere; but she is
Mrs. Delamere in every part that she plays, and if I saw her
in Lady Macbeth, I should expect to see her with her fan
and her eye-glass, her black guipure lace, and her afternoon
tea."

"To be sure! The perfection of an actress is to get out of
herself; and none of ours ever do that."

"They're too fond of themselves."

"That's just it. They're a set of nice-looking women
who dress well, and look well, and—never forget it!"

"The greatest actress I ever saw," put in Denzil, "was a
little Jewess of Cordova. She had no sort of beauty; she
was small and yellow; she had nothing in the world but
those wonderful Israel eyes, and a voice like a silver cymbal.
And yet, what a genius that creature was! She was only
playing in a wretched Spanish theatre, just for the populace;
but I went night after night to see her. It was marvellous!
That woman could reach every passion and every pain in
human nature. She was transfigured, metamorphosed, the
moment the fury of art got into her. She would give you
anything: an old man dying of wretchedness, a young girl
wild with first love, a miser gloating over his gold, a homeless child heartsick and lost, a forsaken mistress burning for
vengeance, a discrowned queen daunting a mob, a murderess
stealing to slaughter, a maiden blushing over sweet shame—
that creature *was* them all, one after another, as she would.
You never saw *her* at all. You only saw the thing that she
chose to create."

"Nothing short of that is genius," said Dudley Moore
briefly. "The only great actress is a woman whom you utterly forget in the impersonation that she chooses you to see.
The actresses we are blessed with are always making us
think, how well A looks to-night, how intricate B's coiffure

is, how becoming that tawny satin is to C, and how resplen-
dent are D's diamonds!"

"What did you let that Jewess slip for, Derry?" asked
Beltran.

"Well, I shouldn't have let her slip. It's years ago now;
but I had half a mind to take her over to Paris or London
just on the chance. It seemed atrocious that such transcen-
dent gifts as these should be wasted on muleteers, and water-
carriers, and olive-pickers. But just about three weeks after
I had first seen her act in a comedy of Calderon's she was
killed—killed horribly, gored to death in the streets, by a
circus-bull that had broken loose from his drivers maddened
with the midnight-glare and the tumult of the people. I
didn't see her die, thank God."

He said it so simply, and so touchingly, that there was
silence for a moment in the chamber.

"It is always so!" said Dudley Moore at last, with a plaintive *pitié de soi-même!* "These dear Delameres, who are of no
earthly artistic use, always live on and on, till good dinners
and too much champagne destroy the only symmetry they
possess—that of form. And a creature of genius, like this
Jewess of yours, is always killed by a bull, or a fever, or a
bit of orange peel on the pavement, or something that is
blundering and bizarre!"

"Mrs. D'Eyncourt had some genius, eh?" said Beltran.

"No," Denzil answered rather coldly. "She was a woman
of beauty, and of talent; but she was by no means a genius."

"No," said Dudley Moore. "I remember her very well;
a splendid woman, but she had not genius. I doubt if any
Englishwoman ever has; I cannot call one to mind. Your
great feminine intelligences have all been Italian or French,
and your great feminine actresses all Jewesses. An Englishwoman is never impersonal enough, nor sympathetic enough,
for real genius. With her 'the great I is the measure of the
universe.'"

"There was Mrs. Siddons?" hazarded Denzil.

Dudley Moore took snuff.

"I have grave doubts of Mrs. Siddons. She was a goddess of the age of fret and fume, of stalk and strut, of trilled R's and of nodding 'plumes. If we had Siddons now I fear we should hiss; I am quite sure we should yawn. She must have been Melpomene always; Nature never."

"You are very hard to please!" said Denzil.

"I never am pleased," responded the great censor meekly.

"Well, let us finish about the piece," interposed Beltran. "Is it to be a fine play badly acted, or a bad play decently acted? It must be one or the other."

"O, the bad play, of course," decided Dudley Moore. "Your women always dress well, and build their hair in the latest fashion; so long as you do that, the Public won't mind what words they hear so long as they are not words that fly utterly over their heads. Your people always look good style; and if the play's tolerably silly they'll be strong enough for it."

"I wish they heard you!"

"They have heard me—fifty times. But it don't make any difference. They stare at the stalls, while they talk of the moon, and they keep an eye on the *Times* critic as they writhe in their death agony."

"You wish this thing made irrational and stupid then?" asked Beltran, stirring the leaves of the French play-book.

"I wish you to have a success, my dear fellow—yes."

Beltran laughed a little.

"Well, do as he tells you, Mouse. He knows best. Don't make the stalls yawn, whatever you do, that's all."

"They won't yawn," said Dudley Moore confidently; "not if they find there is going to be bigamy early enough in the first act, and if you transform that grand old priest of the Paris piece into a Yankee elder from the Salt Springs, or a pedagogue of the Busby type."

Denzil ruefully drew caricatures with his pencil on the paper cover of the *Péche de Vivienne*, and heard in silence.

"What does that mean, Derry?" asked his friend, construing the silence into disapproval.

Denzil flung his pen into the fire.

"It means, that I'd either have something like Art in the house, or I'd shut the place up altogether!"

"Art!" echoed Beltran impatiently. "Where's the use of talking about Art? The company won't play it, and the public won't come to it."

"Well, shut the house up then."

"And turn those forty pair of fine legs out of work? For shame, Denzil," said Dudley Moore. "What a churl you must be to put such thoughts in his head! The piece will do admirably. Don't mind his nonsense, Mr. Lance. You change the play, as I say; and if Worth makes for Mrs. Delamere, and somebody puts her in good humour by sending her some new jewels; and Beltran invites a dozen of the right men to dinner on the first night; and if those new scent fountains play in the private boxes and on the staircases; and if the plot is carefully confused so that none of the press-men can make head or tail of it, and thus are driven back in despair to praise the dresses and the drawing-room sets for which your theatre is always distinguished, why, I will undertake to say that you will have a good run all through the season!"

"Yes," laughed Beltran, "and the next week's edition of the *Midas* will take *Vivia's Secret* as an example of the utter degeneracy and absolute foolishness of the English stage in the Victorian era!"

"Ah, that may be!" said the editor placidly. "But, my dear Vere, if my advice fill your house, my staff may well be allowed to cut-up your actors. If you let them murder a fine piece, would you be any the safer from the *Midas?*—even though the emptiness of your theatre made you *look* for once like high Art?"

"That's a fact!" sighed Beltran. "Well—fire away Mouse. As it's to be all dresses and drawing-room sets, it can't tax your brains over-much."

The Mouse obeyed; and three weeks later *Vivia's Secret* was brought out and became the talk of the town. Mrs. Delamere's dresses were pronounced divine; the cabinets in the salon scene were really of marqueterie; one of the scenes was a real luncheon, with real champagne cup and real things to eat; the carpet on the stage was a genuine Aubusson; gallons of perfume danced away every night in the fountains; the plot was profoundly incomprehensible; the action delightfully rapid; and every one had the pleasure of feeling that the heroine was as immoral as possible, yet that by a judicious dual use of the marriage-service she admirably contrived to avoid shocking the most delicate susceptibilities.

Dudley Moore chuckled: and a stinging satire on it duly appeared in the *Midas*. But the satire only sent people more eagerly to the box-office of the Coronet, and had no other appreciable effect.

Indeed, this anglicised version of *La Péché de Vivienne* was so entirely successful that the stalls were filled, even before the burlesque: an unprecedented occurrence which, as Fanfreluche told me, rendered Laura Pearl's temper absolutely unbearable, and caused her to break her ivory hair-brush upon her maid's shoulders.

CHAPTER XX.

La Reine Cocotte.

THE theatre was one of my greatest amusements.

I soon understood the fascination which that peculiar form of ruin possesses for men, and the attraction that draws your nobles and gentry to play the part of impresario.

Your wares are pretty women; your business is amusement; your patronage is extensive; your society is of that easy sort which lets you keep your hat on your head; smoke with your female companions; show you are bored when you feel so; and wear your shooting-coat in the drawing-room both actually and allegorically.

All that is disagreeable in it—all the agreements with male players, all the ill-tempers of female ones, all the debit and credit accounts, all the law difficulties with irate authors, and all the practical worries of the whole thing—you can entirely delegate to your acting-manager, whose name alone appears before the public. To be sure, for this form of diversion you will be likely to lose your entire fortune in something less than three years; but then, as in many of your pursuits —the turf or the cards to wit—it is quite possible to lose it in three days, or even three hours, this objection is hardly to be urged against amateur-lesseeship for a moment. It is true also that you will get tired of it very soon; and then you will find its nets so cleverly woven around you that you will be unable to get out of them. But this, again, is so universal a characteristic of all your pleasures in which women are concerned, that it is scarcely worth while to mention it against theatres in particular.

It is further true that, after amusing the public for several seasons, after benefiting a great number of human beings by your employment of them, after behaving very generously and charitably in hard winters to your poorer employés, after honestly doing your best to bring something like Art on the stage, and after seeing your ancestral acres melted in an actress's diamonds, and your manager and treasurer retire with a villa and an easy competence—you will be within an ace of your entire ruin, and will be condemned by society *in toto* as a *roué*, a brute, and an idiot.

But—if you do not mind these little trifles—to play at being an impresario is perhaps the best fun there is out. You are in all things like the mover of the automaton chess-player hidden beneath the table, and laughing in your sleeve to hear the silly crowds agape with wonder at your marionettes. There is only this difference: the chess automaton is honest and don't take his master's money; *your* automata, when they see that the game is all up, will make a clear sweep of the board before you have touched a brass coin.

'These reflections, however, did not trouble me, nor Beltran

either. There was plenty of money then, whatever there
would be afterwards; and the Coronet, with all that apper-
tained to it, was in its way very amusing.

The *sous les cartes* of everything always is amusing. Pardon this ungrammatical jumble of two languages; in my time
I have associated with so many English adapters of Parisian
plays.

There was plenty of diversion; as for the virtues, I suppose you don't look for them very often in a green-room. Yet
you might sometimes, and find them.

"There goes the biggest fool in all London," said Lord
Brune one morning, as he watched Beltran pass down St.
James's-street.

"Eh?" asked Paget Desmond in amaze; being given to
thinking his friend one of the keenest-witted men on the town,
in which indeed he was right.

"The *very* biggest fool," averred Lord Brune solemnly.
"Do you know the last thing that he's done?"

"Last thing? No."

"Well—just this. Know woman that played mother's
part in *Vivia's Secret* all first month?—ugly beggar, yellow,
gray-haired, and all the rest—woman not worth sixpence?"

"Yes; broke her leg last week in the street. Had to get
substitute."

"Exactly. Well, her boy came crying to Beltran; little
wretch, eight or nine; said his mother'd sent him to say she
must give up the part for good and all; leg was broke above
knee, and she couldn't stir for six months, if ever. Boy made
a beast of a row, bellowing. They'd nothing at all to live on.
What do you think that ass has done? I got it out of old
Wynch. Continued her salary, by Jove! and had her and
the boy sent down to the sea, and all the rest of it, at his
cost. A woman as ugly as sin, too!"

And Lord Brune went out of Brooks's in immeasurable
disgust.

A few hours later, I heard some other men ask Beltran

what had become of the old actress that broke her leg in the
street.

"How should I know?" he answered them. "Nobody ever
does know what becomes of old women. Women oughtn't, by
rights, to live at all after forty; we never look at 'em later
than that."

"They go to workhouses, I suppose?" suggested Fred
Orford, with that sort of vague, pensive curiosity with which
a connoisseur wonders where all the ordinary china that he
only uses for coffee, and does not care to catalogue, goes.

"I suppose they do," said Beltran. "It don't much matter.
We've done with 'em."

And if he had known that old Wynch had betrayed him
to Lord Brune, he would [have been much more seriously
angered than if he had discovered the gravest of that worthy's
secret peculations.

About his faults or his dollies people might chatter till
they were tired, for aught that he cared; but for his better
deeds he had an almost morbid horror and avoidance of
publicity.

"I don't believe you are so bad as people think, Vere,"
said Lady Otho Beaujolais to him one day. She was a pretty
creature with whom he had that sort of pleasant harmless
platonics which are so common to the present period.

He shrugged his shoulders.

"Don't you, dear? Well, pray don't say so."

As for Laura Pearl, of course she always took him at his
word,—being a woman incapable of any sort of insight into
such a character as his,—and I think that his greatest attraction for her lay in the fact that she thought him the incarna-
tion of human heartlessness.

I saw her often.

I never saw her without marvelling by what spells she induced a man of his temper and his taste to endure association
with her own coarse, cruel, and mindless life; by what sorcery
of personal beauty she persuaded him to forget her ignorance,
her brutality, and her avarice.

16*

From the first moment that the blaze of her splendid
auburn eyes had flashed over me I had been pursued by
vague memories to which I hardly dared give shape and
name; from the first hour in which I had beheld her covered
with rubies at the head of her banqueting-table I had been
ceaselessly haunted by a fancy that took entire possession
of me.

For the accent of the moors and the dales rang in her
voice; the scent of the old pinewoods seemed to come to me
as she flung her perfumed hair upon the wind; when she
gazed on the shining stones of priceless girdles, carbuncle-
studded, there was in her eyes the look I had seen given at
the "dimonds" of Dick o' the Wynnats' pack; and when
there floated in the gaslights the golden and gossamer tissues
of her stage attire, they half veiled and half revealed the
same form that I had used to behold imprisoned in the
russet garb of a ragged linsey, as the whiteness and the
softness of the almond are shut in by their brown fibrous
shell.

I felt sure, and yet I doubted.

The conjurer Gold can baffle even a dog's keen scent and
faultless memory.

At last one day I knew.

There was a theatrical question that had brought them
all down to the house in the forenoon—a question of whether
they should or should not accept Mrs. Delamere's *ultimatum*,
which was to have her salary doubled at once or to withdraw
from the company altogether. She was entirely wrong le-
gally; but as *Vivia* was then at the height of its first success,
and as *Vivia* without Mrs. Delamere would have been in racing
parlance nowhere, and as that lady, if coerced into keeping
her engagement to the letter, was perfectly capable of breaking it in the spirit by acting so sullenly and so badly that the
audience would have been driven away in ennui and disgust,
she obtained her own terms in full triumph.

The cabinet council had broken up; a note had been
dispatched to Maude Delamere couched in terms to satisfy

the utmost exactions of that capricious beauty; Beltran, Denzil, and the rest had gone their own ways; and I, by a stroke of ill-fortune, had got accidentally locked up in that famous supper-room, which served also as council-chamber.

I knew there was no chance of escape till they came again in the evening, which one or other of them was certain to do; and I composed myself dolefully to slumber away the dulness of the intervening time. An hour might have elapsed when, to my pleasure, I heard a key turn in the door. I thought it might be some servant whom Beltran, missing, had sent for me.

Instead, I saw Laura Pearl.

How had she entered? He believed that he alone could open that room, as he had had affixed to the door a steel lock of very complicated Italian workmanship, of which he possessed the sole key. I presume she must have had a skeleton key made, and that his antique fastener was not of such mysterious manufacture as he supposed.

She entered, admitted old Wynch after her, and closed the door with her key.

"Get to business," she said curtly, seating herself by the table.

He seated himself opposite, and obeyed.

Unperceived, where I was curled up on one of the couches, I listened in horror.

The wicked old man, with as dry and simple a commercial exactitude as though he dealt of groceries or calicoes, detailed to her the various matters in which he was her pander, accomplice, and financier.

Appointments, intrigues, gifts of jewelry, letters of flattery or of folly, careful audits of how much gold such and such poor fools would yield before their final ruin, elaborate estimates as to the probable value of so much gilded youth caught in the toils—all these he laid before her in what seemed a sort of custom of periodical auditory, received her instructions, and proffered his advice, having in all between

them but two simple objects—to make money and to cheat
men.

She listened attentively, answered with that curious
shrewdness which often accompanies complete intellectual
ignorance, thrust the presents and the letters into her car-
riage-bag to be examined at leisure, and began and ended
the conference with that good humour and brevity which
perfect harmony between two confederates alone can bring
about.

As Avice Dare had conspired with the Pedlar of the
Peak, so did Laura Pearl conspire with the Pandarus of the
town.

As her solitary object then had been the amassing of silver
and the betrayal of her brother, so her solitary object now
was the amassing of gold and the betrayal of her lover.

It is a terrible thing to corrupt a woman—ay, so it is; but
it is a more terrible thing when Nature has made a woman so
corrupt that no fiend, if there were one, could teach her aught
of evil.

She dismissed him at last carelessly, but good-humouredly,
as a clever workman lays down a clever tool.

"I forgot one thing," said the old man, returning a pace
or two. "The old woman in Shoreditch wants ten shillings a
week for the boy. She says now he is over three years she
cannot afford to keep him for six."

She listened with an angry gloom on her face.

"Ten shillings is a deal for the keep of a brat," she
muttered, turning round and round on her finger a sapphire
ring, worth a king's ransom in the old days when kings were
deemed things of worth.

"So it is," said old Wynch dryly, with a gleam of humour
in him. "It is almost as much as the keep of a parrot."

The sarcasm passed by her unfelt.

"He's sure to go on living, I suppose?" she asked
sullenly.

"Well—yes," said the old man with a smile. "Some
children will, you know. I suppose bad air, and sour milk,

and mouldy bread, and bruised flesh, and the stench of those bone-boiling places agree with 'em. Seems as if they did."

"What do you mean? I'm sure the woman's good enough to him," she answered sharply, as if a momentary touch of conscience smote her.

"O, very good," said the old treasurer, with his queer smile. "She's so fond of children: she's got thirty all in one attic to take care of; she's a true Christian, that woman. Shall I say she shall have the ten shillings a week? If a child dies when it is out to nurse, it is always a nasty business. There are inquiries, and a great deal of nonsense talked about 'neglect' and 'abandonment' and all that."

"Very well; she shall have the ten," she said reluctantly; "but not a farthing more, mind—not never."

"I'll tell her so," said Wynch; and he went out with a pleasant-spoken farewell.

Laura Pearl remained behind him, locking herself in, and spelling through some of the notes, and testing some of the gems she had received through the good offices of this unlovely Mercury of sixty years.

She had made at least a score of rendezvous—one at her milliner's, one at her florist's, one in Kensington Gardens, one in Richmond Park, one in the coffee-room of the Leviathan, one in this very room of the Coronet. And to preserve them all from collision or misadventure, and above all, to time and arrange them so that none of them should be known to Beltran, required as much ingenuity and precision as your betting-book requires from you.

It is true, she had one great thing to help her; she knew all his ways and hours and habits, and through her spies and his servants knew quite well all his movements when he was away from her.

Men object to the surveillance of a wife, and most justly; but they seem to forget that it is nothing compared to the unscrupulous espionage of a courtesan.

She was some little time occupied in arranging her book of engagements; for though she seemed to have a system of

marks and crosses that she herself understood, all usage of
pen or pencil appeared strange and awkward to her.

This business at length completed, she shut up her
morocco bag, and took her burnous from the chair to depart;
doing this she saw me for the first time, and caught me up
with a quick gesture of dislike; no doubt to torment me in
my master's absence.

. The sun was shining strongly through the window by
which my couch stood, and, as she seized me, the light
gleamed on that little ring of white metal that Ambrose of
the Forge had graven with my name, and which I still wore
about my throat.

It caught her sight for the first time.

She grew suddenly pale—for she had no need of rouge
upon her rich and ruddy skin—and the blood came and went
strangely in her face. She stared intensely at me, spelt the
letters on my collar slowly, over and over and over, then flung
me from her, as though I were an asp.

"It's the pup!" she muttered, as she sank down into the
great curved chair. "It's the beast of a pup! I might have
known it!"

Lying where she had thrown me, I grew deadly cold; I
also knew her now.

For a second, in her hard splendid eyes there was a look
of craven fear, of troubled memories. No living creature is
without some conscience; and the fangs of recollection bit
now into hers so sharply, that they aroused it for an instant
from its gold-drugged sleep.

"Poor Ben! poor Ben!" she muttered. "Be he alive, I
wonder?"

Perhaps she had never thought of him from the time that
she had betrayed him until now. It seemed so.

For the instant remembrance held her in its thrall. Beholding the little creature whom she had sold into bondage
that she herself might escape to the liberty of sin, she saw
again the sheltering rosethorn, the dark mournful yews, the
open cottage door, with the brown brook running on its way,

the soft peaceful purple hills, the blue kingfisher perched beside the pool, the deep green wood with all the sunlight quivering through, the tender homely face of the man she had betrayed.

The dead time had no beauty for her—O no. These women are but ashamed that ever they were innocent; they are but fevered and enraged to know that the days ever were when they were poor, and lowly, and of no account. It had been abhorred by her when it had been her present; it was loathed by her now that it had become her past.

Yet in a sense it smote her; for a brief space her conscience thrilled with life. Yet not strongly, nor for long.

She shook her hand in the light till it flashed in every facet of her gleaming rings; she looked at her reflection in the old silver mirror of Venice that was opposite her; she cast down her eyes, and gazed upon the diamond locket that rested upon her breast under the soft silks and laces of her dress:—and she laughed. The same laugh with which, tossing her arms above her head, she had beheld herself the mistress of the mock jewels of the old pedlar of the Peak.

"I ha' done well," she cried aloud in the silence, her native accent strong in her voice in that moment of excitement. "I ha' done well! If ony Nell o' Moor Farm could see me now!"

Then she thrust her foot against me, and spurned me to the farther end of the chamber, and passed out and away to her carriage.

I heard the shiver of her silk robes on the stairs of the theatre; I heard the chime of her ponies' sleigh-bells through the open window; I heard the rush and roll of the wheels as she dashed down the stone-paved street; and I knew now whence it came, that instinct of terror and aversion which had possessed me; I knew now whence they rose, those memories wherewith her voice, and her eyes, and her cruel beauty had been so strangely weighted for me.

For this woman was indeed Avice Dare.

Perchance it might be urged she would have never found

her way to gilded wickedness, had not the old pedlar of the Wynnats first thrown open the door of temptation.

Well, perhaps not; she would only have wedded Ambrose of the Forge, or some other honest-hearted toiler of the woods and moors; and merely dishonoured a name that was of no account, in the brutal orgies of drunken miners and herdsmen; and only have dwelt, in sullen discontent and savage repining, in a little lowly cottage, that her passions, and her sloth, and her violence should have made a hell to her husband and children. She would have done less injury indeed, because her sphere would have been the village on the moorland, instead of the cities of the world. She would only have broken a poor labourer's peace instead of a score of rich men's fortunes. She would only have been a ragged tipsy virago at an alehouse instead of a splendid cocotte, who swept nobles and gentlemen at will into her net. She would only have been the curse of one unhappy man, about whose neck her sin and shame would have been hung for ever like a millstone, instead of being as now the Circe, into whose fell power there were gathered high names, and proud titles, and fair lands, and lordly honours, to be devoured, or destroyed or levelled with the swine, or stripped and made a mock of as she would.

O no; there would have only been the common tale of a wretched cottage home, and a female drunkard, and children who quoted "mother" as authority and example for all evil doing, and a woman losing all likeness of her sex through sullen hatred and through dull debauch. Only that.

Imprisoned in the cage of obscurity and poverty, this kite could only have struck gloomily and hungrily at such poor feeble worthless mice, and larks, and night-moths, and other home-bred things to which her native moor had given life. Loosed to full flight, she could pursue all birds of rarest plumage that spread their golden wings out to the sunlight of a glad fair fate; could tear the breast-feathers of the proudest falcon that ever flew; and could dip her thirsty beak into the heart's blood of a score wild, happy, thoughtless, heedless pigeons, slaughtered on a summer's day to yield her sport an hour.

But would she herself have been more innocent? Not one whit.

If you want a truth (which is not very likely, for it is a ware that is never saleable), take this truth: a woman guilty for the sake of gold would be guilty without gold for sheer love of guilt. When Mephistopheles finds that he can tempt Gretchen with jewels, he is a fool for his pains; he might know that he has wasted his money; she would have been sure to have come to his realm of her own accord—unasked.

CHAPTER XXI.

The Wood-Elf.

ONE evening towards the close of the season a misfortune chanced to me. I was lost.

Beltran went down to speak at the Lords—a thing that he scarce ever troubled himself to do—and I, following him without his knowledge, got divided from him in the maze of streets about those legislative houses of yours whose architecture will last just about as long as the laws passed in them will endure—perhaps even a little longer, gimcrack though the architecture be.

I was sorely grieved and frightened, of course, and ran, and ran, and ran, wildly hither and thither; not knowing any better, and getting under the feet of the horses, and losing all my senses in the din and press.

It was quite late also, and night, although a midsummer night, was coming on apace. I could have found my right road if left to myself; but you always put as many obstacles in the way of a dog's return to his home as in the way of a man's or woman's return to honesty and virtue.

Boys hooted at me; cabmen swore at me; girls chased me; and cats spit at me; and terrified, blinded, and deafened with the noise and the pursuit, I had no other thought than to rush away and away at my topmost speed, eluding every grasp, until at length, fairly exhausted, I was caught by the gentle hand of a girl. It stopped me, and stroked me tenderly, so that my terrors were stilled.

"Poor little thing," she said in a very soft voice that had in it the sound of extreme youth, almost of childhood. "Poor little thing. Stay with me."

It was so dark in the little narrow street into which I had unconsciously darted, that I could not see her features; but her touch and her tone reassured me, and I let her lift me in her arms and caress me.

"We are both stray," she murmured. "You seem like a little friend."

Then I felt her tears fall on my forehead, and by dusky moonlight I saw that she bore in her other arm a sheaf of sweet country flowers—bluebells and moss-roses, and other tender homely blossoms that crown the cottage-walls and meadow-hedges with their beauty.

I suppose she strove to sell them, for standing there she offered them timidly to some passers-by; a few of these thrust them roughly aside; most hurried on without reply; none took them. I wondered how they could refuse that touching mute appeal.

Finding all effort useless, she turned, with a heavy tired sigh, and went up the little street into another more narrow and poorer still, and opening the little door of one of its desolate houses, entered and passed up its stairway, dark and steep, and smelling foully, to a very small, bare, comfortless garret. She put me down upon the floor, and struck a match alight. By the gleam of the little lamp she trimmed, I saw for the first time the face of this flower-girl.

It was excessively lovely—very pale, very sad, but of infinite beauty. It looked wan, as though for want of nourishment; the bow-like mouth had little colour; and the large eyes, of that gray which burns dark as night, had heavy circles under them. Her weighty yellow hair was coiled simply about her head, and her black dress was russet-hued

from age and well-nigh threadbare. She was very poor, it
was easy to see, and by the thinness of her transparent cheeks
it seemed as though she had not tasted good food for many a
day; but she was very young, sixteen years at most, and
was lovely despite all the cruel antagonism of poverty and
sorrow.

Who could she be? All alone, thus, in the heart of
London.

I, who had seen life in the green-room of the Coronet
and the chambers of Vere Beltran, knew at a glance that
this girl was proud by instinct and most pure in innocence.

Yes; though she had been out in the gas-lit streets at ten
of the night, and only sold poor drooping thirsty flowers that
no one cared to buy.

She poured some water from the broken pitcher for her
faded harebells and moss-rosebuds; and laid me on a
corner of her bed; and put out her lamp, for economy's
sake, no doubt, and undressed herself and knelt down to her
prayers.

I do not know why it was; but as I saw the linen fall off
her delicate slender shoulders, and the yellow rippling hair
fall down almost to her feet—as I saw her kneel there with
her hands folded on her bosom, and that look upon her face
which Sant has given to the prophetic child of Israel—I
thought, curiously enough, of Avice Darc as I had once seen
her when she had sought her couch, with that wicked triumph
in her own bared charms, and that wicked discontent within
her soul, flinging herself upon her bed without a thought of
prayer, with only a muttered savage word because her beauty
was unseen of men, and her sleep was taken on a rude flock-
pallet.

This child's eyes filled with tears, and her chest rose and
fell with sobs as she knelt; the moonlight, the one unstained
thing that a city could not pollute, came streaming in upon
her, and seeking this creature who also was incorrupt amidst
corruption; the quarters tolled often whilst she prayed there,

and yet I do not think her prayers were for herself, for I
heard ofttimes the murmur, "Harold, Harold, Harold." After
a while she came and stretched her young limbs on the hard
narrow canvas bed; her eyes closed with a long breath that
still was a sob; and—so merciful is even sorrow to all youth
—that before long she slept, and, by the look upon her face,
dreamed peacefully.

She awoke early, at sunrise, and caressed me with a gentle
little hand that was very white and very thin. When she was
dressing she looked sadly at her flowers. Despite all her care
of them, they were dead. Bluebells are the shortest lived of
all flowers, once gathered; they are little gipsies, though such
modest ones; they must have the freedom of their green
wood and their hedgerow; bring them beneath roofs, they
perish.

Cage robins and gather bluebells, they both surely die;
they are the innocent bohemians of the forest and the lane.

"I have nothing to give you unless you will eat dry
bread?" she said to me, breaking off for me a piece of a stale
loaf that seemed the sole contents of the little cupboard in
her attic. Now, I had dined late, and was not yet hungry,
and I abhorred dry bread; but lest she should deem me ungrateful or dainty, I scratched my throat with a few of the
rough morsels. If you have not seen a dog force himself to
eat something he dislikes because he fears to vex the feelings
of the giver by refusal, you are a very poor observer.*

Whilst I was eating it, the door was thrown violently
open, and on its threshold stood a stout, red-visaged, untidy
woman of fifty or thereabouts.

"Where's my rent?" she demanded fiercely.

The girl's pale cheeks grew paler still, but she looked
calmly and fully in the infuriated face that was turned upon
her, though her voice trembled a little as she answered.

"I am so sorry. No one would buy anything of me yesterday. And, as I told you, I have not a penny left. But if you
will kindly have patience—"

* I have seen it.—Ed.

"Patience!" echoed the virago. "I've had a deal too much patience with such muck as you. A comin' into honest folks houses without a shillin' to bless yerself—a sellin' nasty weeds in make believe to look a trade—a takin' bed and board like a thief a knowin' ye can't pay for it! Patience! I'll hev patience! Giv' me what yer owe, or I'll send for the police this minnit!"

The child grew ashen pale now, and her limbs shook; but her eyes did not lose their resolute frank clearness, and she answered firmly still.

"Indeed—indeed—I paid you every farthing till this week. You know I did. And if I could only find my brother—"

"Yer brother! Gammon o' yer brother!" yelled the woman, coming farther into the chamber. "Stow that trash. I've had enow of it. Go and tell that rubbish where yer please, yer poor pitiful white-faced mawther, but don't think to come over me no more with it. It's a pack of lies—"

"It is true!" The colour flashed back into the girl's face, and her eyes gathered a sudden deep fiery glow.

"Lies or no lies, it ain't nothin' to me. I ain't to be done no more by it. Out ye shall pack, with the constables to look after yer, if ye can't give me my money. Give me my money! Give me my money!—"

"I cannot give you what I have not."

She spoke with a strange dignity in one so young, and the passion of the vixen had not power to break her self-command.

"Then yer'll hev to make it," yelled the woman. "Will yer go on the streets and make it? Yer well favoured enow, if yo waren't so shabby dressed and so white i' the gills!"

"I will go in the streets if you will let me," answered the child, not comprehending the base question. "But I have no money to buy fresh flowers; and, only look—who will buy those? They are quite dead!"

"And I wish you was dead along of 'em!" shrieked the fury, made more violent by the innocence of the answer. "I'd have the shower o' hair off yer head anyhow, then, and make

a penny by that. Th' idee o' comin' and using o' honest
victuals, and honest folk's beds, and cheers, and tables, without so much as a bit o' linin to leave behind yer as yer payment. Ye'd a box when ye come, and it's dratted empty now,
for I looked in't last night, and there wasn't nothin' but a
nasty mouse a' gnawin' at the lid."

"I have sold what I had, to pay you for the last three
weeks," the girl replied to her, quietly still, and with a certain
pathetic pride.

"O, yer have?" retorted her tormentor; "and ye hain't got
a mossel o' nothin' then, let alone the rags on yer back? Well,
then, to jail ye'll go, my lass, and that as sure as you're a im-
pident, lyin', white-livered hussy as ever crep into a honest
house to—"

"This will bring you your due," the girl said coldly, and
from where it was hidden in the bosom of her dress she drew
out a little old-fashioned round gold locket, and tendered it
silently to her torturer. It was given in silence, given with a
singular firmness and reticence of all emotion; yet there was
that in her face which made me fancy that to part with the
little locket was worse to her than to part with her life.

The woman clutched it thirstily, with the ruthless greed of
her cormorant class.

"A bit o' pinchbeck!" she muttered, biting it, smelling it,
testing it as best she knew how; it was genuine gold, however,
and she was compelled to admit thus much to herself.

"It ain't worth half you've had this week," she said
sullenly. "But it 'ull dew. I'll no send yer to jail if ye'll
trape off this minnit; and here—here's tuppence to get yerself
a loaf with; nobody sha'n't say as I deals hard with yer,
though ye've took me in shameful, and I a poor lone woman."

The girl took up her little straw hat with one hand, and
myself with the other.

"The locket is worth twenty shillings, and what I owe you
is but six. God forgive you if you were ever so wicked to my
brother as you have been to me."

Then without even glancing at the copper coins which the

subdued virago, in a sort of stupid shame and gloomy wrath, held out to her, she went away down the narrow dusky staircase, and through the low door, into the street.

It was a beautiful summer morning; the sun was radiant even in that dreary place, making indeed its squalor, and its unloveliness, and its grimy outline, more hideous and more desolate.

Sunrise is beautiful in the country; but in the by-ways of a filthy city it is only sad—ay, and even fearful. Night pityingly covers, with its cool gray shade, that scrofula of brick, and mud, and dirt, and vileness, with which men have defaced the sweet fair face of nature; but the sunrise only shows in their uttermost nakedness those throbbing festers of the earth which your mad humanity exalts as triumphs of the tribe of Enoch.

The child went slowly out, and down the narrow road; it was too early yet for any of the closely-pent population to be stirring. A footworn cat moved here and there, the sparrows twittered in the gutters, a tired homeless starving dog slunk, shivering, through the warmth of dawn. She, moving like a creature in a dream, walked mechanically where chance took her.

A woman-child alone in a great city—there is nothing more pitiful on earth.

She went on and on, slowly and dreamily gazing straight before her. Her hands were very cold, and her lips were as white as marble.

Suddenly she paused, with a quick gasping breath; her frame shook with a feverish shudder; her eyes closed, and she reeled against the stone wall by which she stood. The next moment she sank senseless on the flags.

She fell in a half-sitting posture against the old steps of a deserted house; so that, to any passer-by, it would have looked as though she only rested there and slept.

I, sorely frightened and sorrowful for this young desolate creature, could only cower helpless near her; I knew not my

*Puck. I.*17

way home, and if I had done so, should not have had the heart to leave her.

She appalled me in her awful stillness. I had never seen death, but it seemed to me that surely I saw it now.

I moaned aloud, thinking to summon aid. I did no good.

From a house farther down a woman threw open her lattice, and shouted to me to be quiet, or she would brain me with a bit of wood. A young slender man, with his hands folded upon a book that bore a red cross on its cover, passed by on the other side; he paid no heed to my sad cries; doubtless he was on his way to early matins, and was too absorbed in thinking of his own salvation to have an ear for me.

Presently there came into the street a cheery, ruddy, stout-built woman with shining brass pails on either side of her, whose metal clang resounded through the silence, and brought the cats out from the area rails, eyeing her expectantly. There was no one up to receive her in any one of the quiet little houses of the street; and she filled, from her milk-pails, each one of the jugs, or pots, or tin-cans, which were set out on the doorstep, against her coming, in that curious trustfulness of each other which the poor so often show, in such marked contrast with their acrid suspicions of the rich.

These pots and cans were, for the chief part, covered, but in one or two the cats, dipping their noses, had a feast; and one unlucky puss, being unable to withdraw her head, set forth full gallop in her prison, raising a loud clatter with the pitcher on the pavement, and banging it to and fro till she released herself.

Even at that moment I could not but think how like she was to a human being caught by the neck in the jug of his poverty, after drinking up all the cream of pleasure; but from about the cat's head the earthen jug did at length break, falling away in a thousand pieces: who amongst you ever releases himself from the iron pot of debt?

As the woman drew nearer to us, I gathered hope that she would stop and take some pity, for her face was a broad, and

homely, and pleasant one; and she had the tan of the Berkshire sun still on her skin, and the accent of the Berkshire
people still in her voice. But I was disappointed.

She glanced at the recumbent figure, indeed, but she only
turned aside so as not to step on it.

"More muck o' bad gells!" muttered this comely-looking,
sun-bronzed Pharisee, with her pails—thus passing on with
judgment.

Her cry soon echoed down a distant street.

I awaited with a trembling heart, powerless and very sad.

After a little while I heard a suddenly swift pattering of
feet, the rush of a large breathless body, the panting of an
eager creature, and round a corner in full speed came the
form of a big brown dog.

Emaciated, dust-covered, footsore, I recognised him in a
moment:—it was Bronze.

He threw himself on the girl's form; he kissed her fran-
tically, he moaned over her, he lashed her with his tail in a
paroxysm of idolatry and joy: he never saw me, but I did not
need one glance from him to tell me who his darling was.

Wakened from her trance by his rough rapturous embraces, the child Gladys slowly raised herself, gazing at him
with dim eyes that were unconscious of him, and of herself,
and all around her: then she put out her hands feebly, and
felt and grasped him by his loose brown curls: then started
and looked at him with a strange fixity of gaze. At last,
with a cry that pierced my heart, she flung her arms around
him, and buried her face upon his neck, and wept in a very
passion of tears. "O Bronze, dear Bronze, good, precious
Bronze!" she murmured wildly. "You are come, you are
come!—then he is near!"

Bronze crouched in silence at her feet.

"He is here? He is well? O, tell me, Bronze," she
gasped. "Dear, dear Bronze, *do* tell me!"

Bronze could only gaze at her with tender hazel eyes, that
seemed to look love into her very soul.

"Take me to him, Bronze!" she cried. "This moment—

this moment! Look! I am quite strong!"—and she darted to
her feet, and stood erect, quivering all over with hope and
dread and longing.

Bronze crouched again at her feet, as though to entreat
pardon for a disobedience he could not help; and moaned—a
piteous heart-broken and heart-breaking moan.

She sank down once more, being far weaker than she
knew, and on her face there came a ghastly terror.

She seized him, and held him, and gazed into his eyes.

"Bronze—Bronze!" she gasped. "O God!—is he dead?
You are alone!"

Bronze lifted his head, and sent forth on the still morning
air a long wail of anguish, terrible as the Irish coronach over
an open grave:—then down he crouched afresh before her,
and silently caressed her feet, her hands, her dress, her hair.

She knew the meaning of that one long note of woe; and
without a cry, without a sign, she fell back senseless on the
stones.

There came down the street at that instant a girl who
sang as she went a snatch of a music-hall ballad.

The voice was fresh and gay and very full of melody, the
mirthful slang words rang out in strange contrast with the
gloom and the silence around her. She was a pretty creature
with flushed cheeks and round limbs, fantastically though
cheaply attired, whilst her chestnut curls were tumbled in
picturesque disorder out of a tiny Watteau hat with a bunch
of moss-rosebuds in its front. At a glance I recognised in
her the little Wood-Elf of the Coronet's Burlesque. Would
a little dancer of hornpipes and singer of slang songs be more
merciful than the pious youth on his way to his canticles, and
the buxom milk-woman with her swift judgment?

Little Courcey was coming no doubt from some casino-
ball or theatrical supper, that had been prolonged till sunrise,
and the devil himself would be strong in her, and utter through
her mouth some coarse and cruel jest.

As she approached her eyes fell on the child Gladys and
on Bronze, who was vainly trying all he knew to recall his

recovered treasure to 'life and consciousness. She looked, paused, then crossed the street.

"Mercy on me! what is the matter?" she cried. As none of us gave answer, she stooped and raised the girl's insensible form against the steps, and loosened her dress, and fanned her with her little hat. These efforts failing, she darted swiftly, with more regard for charity than honesty, towards one of the little milk jugs standing before the door of the nearest house. It was a slender white china pitcher, and she forced its mouth between Gladys' lips, and poured some of the still warm liquid down her throat.

After a few moments it revived her; her eyes opened with a dull dreamy stare in them. Through want, and exhaustion, she was still unconscious of where she was or of what had happened.

"Are you better, dear?" asked the Wood-Elf very kindly, "can't you hear me? won't you speak?"

"I do not know," she muttered. "He is dead,—he is dead."

"Who is dead?"

Gladys put her hands to her temples, and gazed about her with the look of a hunted deer.

"He is,—look!—Bronze would never have left him, and Bronze is all alone. He must be dead, you know, he must!" In the simple words there was an unutterable heartbroken certainty of an irreparable woe. Nellie, quick of thought, answered to the truth as she guessed it.

"Are you only sure 'he' is dead because the dog is alone? That is no proof. Dogs stray, or are stolen, very often. Do not think 'he' is dead only from that."

The girl glanced up at her with eyes in which a swift radiance of sudden hope shot through the dulness of stupefied senses. Then her lips quivered, and she burst into a passion of tears; the spirit which tyrannous and vulgar brutality could not bend, broke now at the first touch of kindness.

Nellie let that tempest of grief somewhat exhaust itself, then she spoke again.

"My home is close by here. Come along with me if you can walk; you are not fit to be out in the streets. Or shall I go home with you; is it far?"

"I have no home."

"None! then come along with me and rest a bit. We will see for 'him' afterwards, whoever he is. Come along. I live close by."

Gladys strove to rise.

"You are very good," she said gently, as she lifted her hands to her forehead again, and looked about her with that pitiful, wondering, uncomprehending look. Her limbs trembled; she had very little strength, and scarcely any knowledge of where she was or of what she said.

"Come, then," said Nellie simply, and she took her hand in hers, and half led, half supported her through that street and the next, Bronze and I following them close at hand. He had made no objection or opposition to the Wood-Elf's possession of his treasure, nor had he as yet taken any notice or given any recognition of myself.

Where Nellie went was to a vegetable shop in a little street to the left of the one in which she had found us. It was a small place, dingy, dusky, smutty from the sacks of coal that were also sold on the small premises; but with a certain fresh and pleasant smell from cabbages, and lettuces, and lemons, and thymes, that brought vaguely to my senses the memory of the little herb-garden in the Peak.

Early as it was the shutters were down, and a white-haired, brown-faced old woman was washing some sage and marjoram in a wooden bowl of water.

"Lawk a mussey, Nell, why when'll be a-bed next?" she cried, catching sight of her late returning wanderer. "Ten to six, as I live; I doan't like it, I doan't like it."

"Don't you, grandmother?" said Nell indifferently. "Well, I do, and that's all about it. Do the kettle boil yet?"

"Kittle was on the bile beautiful half-a-hour agone, but she's off agen now. Kittles can't be looked for to bile for ever," responded the old woman with a little asperity. "In my young days if wenches had come in at six o'clock, after trapezin and flamickin about all night, they'd ha' had to go down on their bended knees 'stead o' axin, like a queen, if kittles biled. But, Lord's sake! who've ye brought in with ye?"'

"A girl I know, that wants a bit of breakfast. I met her hard by, a pretty girl, gran', and a deal more respectable than I am. Now, look sharp, there's an old dear, and get me some tea, and put a dash of the craythur in it, for I'm dead tired, and so is she."

And Nellie therewith half-drew, half-forced, up the stairs and into a little room at the head of them, the still half-senseless, half-stupefied form of Gladys. Bronze and I followed of course.

"Dogs!" screamed the old woman below, "two dogs, Nell —Nell—them nasty, dusty, ugly beasts sha'n't go up on my clean boards."

But we were up, on the newly-scrubbed stairs, and Nell called out with careless answer to the clamour that the dogs might do as they liked, her grandmother wasn't to bother.

The little chamber, like all about the place, was scrupulously clean; it was a small square white-washed room, with deal furniture and a truckle-bed, and a latticed window that looked out dolefully on chimneys and on roofs. But there were touches of grace about it, despite its nakedness, as there were about Nell herself, despite her impudence; about the little window the golden-drop creeper grew out from a pot, and "made a sunshine in that shady place." There was a canary in a bright brass cage, canopied with white-blossomed chickweed and the amber tufts of groundsel. There was a heap of bright-hued things in a corner, which, though only the trumpery satins and tinfoil glitter of stage costumes, still made a glow of colour and a shine of silver. And on the bed was a short full skirt of rose-hued tarlatan, that was fresh and dainty and unworn, and gave something of the grisette's grace to the barren attic. This new ball-robe Nellie cast aside, as roughly as though it were an old piece of sacking, and with a gentle force pushed her guest down upon the pallet, and bade her lie there and not speak.

Gladys obeyed, her senses still but half-awake and incapable of resistance; and Bronze, flinging his huge form on the bed at her feet, kept watch and ward over her safety.

In and out of the room the Wood-Elf darted, some half-dozen times, noiselessly always, and brought by degrees tea and toast and bread, and a cluster of round radishes white and smooth as ivory, and a green fresh crown of dewy cress. All the while the voice of the old woman below was grumbling, in a running chorus of blame and of complaint; but Nellie paid no heed. Indeed, as I learned later, she was justified in this, since her money paid the house and all that was therein.

Vainly did she entreat the girl Gladys to touch food; she could not eat. Food was loathsome to one who had been without it for four-and-twenty hours, and who for a month past had well-nigh starved. Not so her good Samaritan, who, having eaten four hours earlier a hearty supper of lobster, oysters, ices, and confectionery, attacked with a will the radishes and bread-and-butter. The infusion of brandy in the tea, which she had put unknown to her young wayfarer, acted like a soporific on the child, who probably had never tasted the spirit in her life. It flushed her face, it warmed her chill and trembling limbs, it made her eyelids heavy, and drop with sleep, against her will or even her knowledge.

Deep dreamless slumber, like the slumber of an infant, came over her, and she lay on the narrow bed with all that beautiful unconscious colourless repose you see in a dead child who has died painlessly.

Bronze, crouching nearer, and also refusing all offers of food, since they involved the leaving of his post, stretched himself on guard.

Nellie, munching her radishes as rabbits munch clover, sat and looked at her with curiosity.

"By the looks on her she'd do for the profession," the

Wood-Elf muttered to herself. "But I guess she'd go and break her heart in it, as that D'Eyncourt woman did. You honest loyal thing," she went on, laying a quantity of broken bread beside Bronze, "your bones are half through your skin, and you're fairly perished, and yet you'll go without eating rather than leave her. Hang me, if you dumb uns don't beat us hollow!"

·Then, without noticing me, she threw off all her finery, dipped her face into a pan of cold water to take the rouge off, wrapped herself up in an old blanket, and, curling herself up in a corner of the room, was soon fast asleep like a dormouse.

In something less than three hours, by the tolling of the clocks, she awoke. All women are not at all pretty when they awake; some look very stupid, some very cross, some very pallid and untidy; but Nellie looked pretty, with her cheeks as red as roses and her eyes as blue as forget-me-nots, and her chestnut waves of hair all tumbled, and her ruddy mouth half-pouting and half-yawning.

She splashed about in her cold water like an otter or a salmon; came out of it ruddy and fresh, and dripping like a rose in a shower. Then she dressed herself very softly, wrote on a big card with great, sprawling, ill-formed letters, " *You are with a friend; do not fear!*" put the card where the sleeper's eyes would fall on it if they unclosed, and then left the room, locking the door from without.

"What d'ye know o' that wench up-stairs? Next to nothing, I'll be bound," I heard the old woman's grumbling voice ask as she went down.

"Less than nothing, Gran," the Wood-Elf answered gaily. "But I'll wager she's a good girl, and that's more than I am!"

"Y're good enow," grumbled the old dame, "if yer wouldn't stop out so long a nights; and if ye wouldn't spend such a power o' money on yer victuals and yer finery; and if ye wouldn't be allays a givin' credit to all them trapezin' poor as asks yer, and a wastin' apples and nuts and pennorths o' baccy on all the young uns and the old uns o' the street."

The Wood-Elf only laughed, and (by the more distant echo of the laugh) disappeared, I think, into the street.

As for me, I was in high dudgeon to be unrecognised and pent in durance like this; and Bronze would not enter into any sort of converse, nor permit me to utter a sound or move a limb, lest I should disturb the sleep of Gladys.

I felt deep interest in her; I could not help it; but I also wanted greatly to return to Beltran, and I thought with a sort of anguish of the delicious minced chicken on which his servant was wont at this hour of the day to regale me. One's regrets for a lost friend are never so poignant as when that loss also entails a limitation of one's daily dainties.

So I withdrew myself in a corner and sulked, having an erroneous notion, caught up from humankind, that sulkiness was a fine vindication of dignity.

With noon the Wood-Elf returned, having been down, I daresay, to the theatre in that toilsome routine which forms the most laborious part of the profession. To skip and sing and spout at night in the blaze of the light, with the stimulus of the crowded house, and the flattery of the clapping hands, —that is well enough, even when one is not a star but only a little fifth-rate performer with a guinea a week. But to tramp down to the house at noon, in snow, or rain, or heat, or tempest, and go through all the dreary repetitions in the ugly darkened daylight; to be scolded by shrill voices, and to be pushed about by rough hands, and to stand till your legs ache while scenes are shifted and elaborate sets are arranged, —ah, think twice, my good maiden, unless indeed you be a Rachel or a Mars, before you refuse the comely village-carpenter's marriage troth, or leave the old father's mill-house in the woods, or fling away the homely peace of life on the moor farm, for *this*.

Gladys once during her absence had awakened and started and gazed about her, then beholding Bronze and reading the kindly words on the great card, had sighed and smiled as in a dream, and fallen once more into slumber.

The opening of the door aroused her now, and aroused her fully.

She sprang up on her bed, and turned her beautiful wild eyes on Nellie.

"Who are you that are so good to me? And where am I? And how is he? And why is Bronze alive, yet all alone? O tell me! Pray do tell me!"

Nellie sat down beside her and regarded her with perplexity. She scarcely knew what was best to say; and she was absorbed in gazing with all her might at this creature, still younger and far more desolate than she, whom yet she felt was as widely different from her as though she had come from one of those distant worlds of stars which she, who dwelt in the gas-glare of cities, scarce ever even saw.

Gladys caught both her hands.

"O, do tell me! You are so good, and you wrote yourself there my friend. What is it that has happened? and why is Bronze here? and where is Harold?"

Nellie was forced to answer something.

"My dear, I don't know," she said slowly. "I found you in the street. You had fainted. I brought you home with me. That's all. Whose dog is Bronze? and who are you?"

The splendid flash of hope paled out of the girl's face. It grew white with vague fear.

"I am Gladys Gerant," she answered breathlessly; "and Bronze belonged to my brother, who took him away with him a year ago. And I came to London some weeks since, and I went to the house where Harold had written his last letters, and he was not there. They only knew that he had left them—long ago; and I never have learned more. And Bronze rushed on me to-day, and then I found he was alone. I was sure that Harold must be dead, or the dog would never have left him."

She spoke in an agony of dread, her slender hands locked hard in one another.

It was an inarticulate slight fragment for Nellie to gather any sense from it. But she had tact, and said the first thing that seemed best to her.

"Dead?—because Bronze is alone? What nonsense, child! Who put such fancies in your head? The best of dogs gets lost over and over again. Why, if he was half as fond of your brother as you says, he'd never have left his grave,—that you may take your word on."

"That is true," murmured Gladys. "You would never have left his grave, would you Bronze? dear, good, patient, precious Bronze?"

"That I would not, could I have found it," said Bronze's wistful eyes as he listened.

"That he would not," averred Nellie. "This Harold of yours is alive—depend on it; the dog got astray somewheres, and smelt you out, as those clever beasts always does. What was Harold?"

"Harold? A poet."

There was a superb glory and pride on her young wan face as she spoke those words. Nellie, like the practical, shrewd little worldling that she was, gave a significant shrug.

"A poet! Wants a deal o' money to be of that trade! Was he rich?"

"O no. We have been very poor."

"And he come to town to seek his fortune? And to make a great man of his-self?"

"He came to London for that—yes."

"And what did you come for?"

"Only to find him."

"Whew! Without an address!"

"I had that one. But he had not written for so long that I felt certain something had happened. O, something has—something must!"

She hid her face upon her hands, and shuddered. The dim shadow of an unknown woe is worse still than the presence of a calamity whose worst is told.

"Nonsense!" cried Nellie imperatively. "You must not

fret yourself like that. Young men have a hundred different
lodging-houses in a twelvemonth. For you to come to look
for him in that sort of way is just madness like—you might
as well set to look for needles in a bottle o' hay. He might
be within a stone's throw of ye, and you never know it.
Never think a man dead for that little. We'll try and find
him. Poets isn't so common as women; and I'll ask some
gentlemen I know as writes in papers. But come, tell me a
bit more about yourself, dear. Are you all alone in this
place?"

"I am all alone in the world."

"Goodness! Well—a many is. Only you look as if you'd
never roughed it like. How did it come about, if one may
ask?"

Gladys, by one of those strong efforts by which she had
restrained all emotion when she had given the locket to her
tyrant, looked up with dry, calm eyes, and spoke with a low
and steady voice.

"Of course you may ask everything. You have been so
good—"

"I aren't good," said the Wood-Elf pettishly, while the
colour sprang ruddily in her cheeks.

"You are to me. That is all I know. It happened in this
way: we had a farm in Sussex, such a fresh, lovely, quiet
place. My father was never rich; but he was better than
rich; so wise, so gentle, so God-fearing, so loving to his men,
and to his beasts. I always think that Isaac must have been
just such a man as he. And we were very happy—very—
though troubles came. You know farming is but uncertain
work; the sun, and the wind, and the rain, and the snow,
are all its ministers; but they rule very ill for it sometimes.
When I was quite a little child I think we had no want; but
I can hardly remember the time that there was not some
anxiety in the house. My father was very generous, and always gave much to the poor; he could not sit down and break
bread for himself knowing that another wanted it within his
reach. And the sheep would sicken, and the lambs die, and

the wheat rot, and the hops wither—so often, so often! Not
from any fault of my father's, but just from the cruelty of
things, as it seemed. And yet the life was so happy—at least
I thought it so. Harold, I know, grew tired, and chafed because of the stillness, and would leave us, and go forth to
make the world ring with his name, as he said. My father
took blame to himself because, he said, that it had been his
reading aloud of Shakespeare, and Milton, and Massinger,
and Ford, and Jonson, and all of them that had first moved
poor Harold with this spirit of longing and of unrest. I do
not think it was that Harold was born to dream dreams. But
I must not trouble you with this—you only want to know
why I am here. Well, Harold left us; and my mother seemed
to droop ever after. In a little time she died; of the cold,
they said, since she was delicate in health; but I am sure
what killed her was the absence of Harold. He was full of
grief when he heard of it; but he did not offer to return. Nor
did my father press it. 'If the lad can do for himself it will
be well,' he used to say. "To come back hither is to be
buried under the timbers of a falling house.' He meant by
that, things were very ill with us, and that he had no heritage
to bequeath to my brother. The land had been mortgaged
many a year, had been mortgaged when he came to it by my
grandparents. But he had always paid interest to the day;
and those who held the mortgages had promised solemnly
never to call for more. The year that Harold left us was one
of misfortune from seed-time to harvest. The cattle died, the
hay failed because of the drought, the hops did not yield,
and two of the best horses were struck by lightning; nothing
fared well of it all. It was a terrible summer; terrible, and
yet so beautiful. Thus, at last, my father for once could not
pay all the sums that were due, and the mortgagees broke
faith with him, and claimed the old house and all the lands.
My father was a proud man, and just, and upright; and—it
killed him. He died of paralysis, they say; but it was only
his heart that was broken. When he was dead, they took
all. They said that there was nothing for Harold or me; it

might be so, I cannot tell. I only know they thrust me over the threshold the first day that he was laid in his grave."

A convulsive shudder shook her, and the veins of her throat swelled like cords; but she kept calmness still, and ended her tale in a few brief phrases.

"A woman who lived in a village near took me to her home through the winter. A good, old, tender creature, blind, to whom I read, and for whom I wrote. She said my father had been good to her in her youth. But when the spring came I could not live on her charity. It was not possible. I served her in the rough cold season; but with the bright weather a young niece of hers always arrived, and then I knew she could really need me no more. Besides, I longed to see Harold. So I came hither. I had a little money; five pounds in silver that my godmother once had saved for me, all in bright sixpences, and I thought it would last well enough till I had found my brother. But you see—it went so little way. It was almost all gone, it seemed, in a week or two. Then I bought some flowers and tried to sell them; but I did not get again so much as I paid for them; and—and—the people were so rude, so jeering, so cruel. And at last I had no money, and the woman of the house turned me out, and—there is no more to tell. Only that now I have found Bronze all alone, I am sure that my brother is not with the living."

She ceased, and was very still; still with that quiet of absolute grief which is far more intense in its desolation than all more passionate and eloquent emotions.

Nellie had listened with great tears gathering in her bright eyes that had the sunny azure of the little cuckoo's-eye flowers.

She was touched, she was awed, she was subdued, she was for once at a loss for all words.

"Don't wed yourself to that fancy, dear," she said softly at last. "Maybe after a bit the dog will help you find him. As I told you, them poor beasts never leave their masters' graves; and it's more like by far that Bronze have been stray. Whose dog's that other little white un that was with you?"

"One that I found last night. And now,—may I not know who you are that have been so good to me?"

The Wood-Elf flushed a little hotly under the short locks of auburn that fell over her forehead in thick waving fringe.

"My name's Nell Browne. Leastways I was baptised so in the poorhouse. My mother came tramp, they say; she died the day I was born, locked up, I think, in a sort of a damp hutch. Nobody knew she was in trouble till they looked in in the morning and found me—and her dead. There's a many dies that kind of way. They never knew no more about me, nor who my father was. I daresay he wasn't no good. So it don't matter. Gran' here is no grandmother of mine. They farmed me out to her when I was seven, as a kind of little maid like. The old woman kept a little tea-shop in a village down in Berks; and she was very good to me; never beat me; not once. Well, you see, when I grew up a bit I was pretty and lissom; and I thought as I might do better nor go on sweeping out a little stye of a tea-shop all my days. So I bid good-bye to gran', and the noddin' chiney figures, and I come up here to seek my fortune—"

"And they were not cruel to you?"

"Bless you, my dear!" answered Nell hastily, with the colour still hot on her face, and her eyes wandering a little away to the speck of gold that the canary made against the light. "*You're* the sort Life's cruel to—not me. I got all my banging about in the workhouse. I've done pretty well since. You see I've a knack of singing and jigging about, and I've the go of it in me, and so I took to it natural, as it were, and I've fared very well as things run. I've been five years at it, though you wouldn't hardly think so; I'm twenty come July, and I was fifteen when I left granny and the chiney nodding-men."

Gladys looked bewildered. "I don't understand," she said softly. "What is it that you do?"

"Stage, my dear," said Nellie, a little curtly; "the theatre, you know."

Gladys' eyes opened in mute awe, and radiated with a solemn wonder.

"The stage! What, do you play Beatrice?" she murmured breathlessly, "and Victoria Corrombona, and the Duchess of Malfi, and Imogene, and—"

"Dear heart, no!" cried Nellie, laughter back on her lips, though her tears were not dry on her cheeks. "*Me* take leading business? Not a bit of it. I just dress as a boy, or a sprite, or a devil, or something queer, and jump about, and sing, and talk balderdash, and look pretty; that's all I have to do. It was awfully hard at first, you know. One could only begin, of course, with penny gaffs, and—"

"Penny gaffs!"

"I beg your pardon; I mean low places of amusement, where the poor people come."

"Poor people need not be low."

"O, of course not, but they mostly are. And that's how one has to begin. But that's over now. I'm at a fashionable house, and—and—it's all right enough. A year ago, when I'd made some money, I thought I'd go and have a look at the tea-shop. So I went down by return one Saturday to the little old village, and I asked after granny. The chiney men was there, nodding fit to kill themselves, and looking as wise as judges; the street was there, and the trees were there; and an old cat, as was our kitten when I first went to sweep out the shop, was there too, a-sunning of herself on the doorstep. But poor old gran' wasn't there. She'd come to grief; got in debt, you know; and all the plant and the things had been sold right over her head, and she was living on the parish in the wretchedest old almshouse, hard by the church. So I just said to her, 'Come along, gran', and keep house along of me;' and I took this bit of a place, and set her up in business like, because she's happier thinking as how she does something for her own living. And she's a good deal of use, the old woman is; she gives cads right down facers when they come after me; and it makes it feel a bit like a home you know, having her, though she's cranky as cranky can be. It's a sort of fancy one has—that of getting a home, when one hasn't had none but a workhouse."

In the expressive eyes of Gladys Gerant I saw a hundred changes pass whilst Nellie spoke. There was shrinking distaste; there was wondering non-comprehension; there was an instinctive sense of wrong, and yet there were the swift sympathies of a noble nature with that gratitude which had thus paid its debt to an old and helpless creature, and with that wistful desire for a life denied, a love unknown, that thus broke out in Nellie's latest words.

She did not answer for a moment; these two young lives, so widely sundered by training and temper, bewildered one another. They had only the common ground of their mutual trust.

"Are you happier than I, never to have loved any—never to have grieved for any?" said Gladys softly. "No, I think not; I wish—I wish you had such memories as mine."

"O God, so do I wish!" cried Nellie with a curious passionate cry; she rose impetuously and crossed to where her canary hung; she felt, I believe, as though she would have died in the streets on the morrow only to have such memories of the beloved dead, as this child possessed and cherished.

"But you see," Gladys murmured, with a strange sad tender smile upon her face, "I have had all my summer in my spring; it is all over now. There are nothing but the night and the winter. While you—you have had the cold and the darkness first; your sun has yet to dawn."

Nellie turned quickly and stared at her. She had never heard any one speak like this. "Are you a poet too?" she said suddenly.

"I? O no! Harold could tell what he felt, I can only feel; but I am rested now, I must go. I cannot thank you, only—"

"Go! what do you mean to do?"

"I do not know. I am not afraid. God will give me some friend as He gave me you."

"Nonsense! ravens gobble up worms on their own hook, and sew up the rents in their own nests: they don't go about on heavenly messages nowadays."

"But *you* must have found friends when you came hither, quite alone?"

Nellie's cheeks flushed. "That's neither here nor there. Friends! a woman has no friends unless she has two thousand a-year. She has only—but that's no odds to talk about. Just you stay there, stay as long as you like—stay till you are strong; and then we'll set about seeing for Harold."

"I could not live on your charity."

There was that singular dignity in the answer with which this delicate, terrified, desolate child had awed her vulgar tyrant; a pride lofty, stainless, incapable of accepting alms.

"Charity!" cried Nellie, quickly catching the tone and translating it aright; "it wouldn't be no charity of mine. You're so different to me—so gentle-born like, and uses such fair language; and I dessay so clever, and book-learned, and all that. There's a deal you might do for me, for I ain't no scholar; and if I could only read hard words off quicker, and speak 'em with a nicer accent, as it were, why, they all say as I've a deal of talent, and there isn't the least atom of reason why I shouldn't take a much higher line of business. And all that you might teach me; only by being with you I'd pick it up like; and then one day, perhaps, when you've found your brother (for I'm sure as he may be found, and shall be found), he'll write a great play for me, and I'll make a grand hit in it, and then we shall both say what wonderful good has come of Bronze's hollering out, and bringing of me to you on a spring morning, all by chance like, don't you see?"

Gladys looked at her with a look of infinite comprehension and gratitude.

"I see how nobly you try to make me think your charity a selfishness; but I see no fit return that I could give you for

18*

living at your cost, and I must beg of you to let me have my way, and go."

"Go to death or perdition, you innocent creature!" muttered Nell. Then at that instant she caught sight of the collar on my neck, and darted at me, and read the inscription, glad of some diversion, as her eloquence failed of its point. She dropped me on the floor, with that curious disregard of our bones and feelings from which we dogs perpetually suffer, as she read.

"Why, as I live, it's little Puck!" she cried.

"You know the dog?"

"To be sure I do! Why, here's a run of luck! there's five pounds reward out for it this forenoon, offered on hand-bills in the shops, you know, and one never thought once of this little beast of yours and Puck being one and the same, I was so busy wondering about you."

"You know its owner too, then?"

"Why, gracious, he's the lord as owns our theatre. Here, I'll take it back this minute to him, and bring you the five sovereigns, and if you pays me half-a-guinea a-week, you'll treat me like a queen, and you can stay on here two or three months, anyhow."

"Take the dog to him, but do not bring me back any money; I am not a thief, to take payment for honesty."

"What! But he's offered the five sovs. for the dog; you've a right to it—where is the harm?"

"There may be no harm, but I would not take it. My father would have never let me accept a reward for doing such a little simple thing, so plainly right as that."

"No wonder your father's farm was swallowed up in mortgages," muttered Nellie. "Well, shall I take Puck anyhow, and will you wait till I come back, certain sure?"

"I will indeed, thankfully. But I beg of you to tell that gentleman that I am very glad to be able to restore his dog, but that if he were to send me any money, I should at once return it. Do not tell him either that I want money, or he might think himself bound to give it, please remember; I trust you."

Nellie turned, a little uneasily, from the grave sweet gaze of those thoughtful and pleading eyes—eyes half prayer and half command.

"I'll be careful," she murmured; "but I'll go at once, for you aren't strong enough, and I know as he'll be pleased to see the little un safe back."

And with that she carried me forth, and closed the door once more upon her guest.

"What a queer lot of chances!" she murmured. "I am at my wits' end, little Puck, what to do for that child. She's a lady bred, if she aren't a lady born; she's not fit for our life; she makes one feel so good-for-nothing like with that look of her two big eyes. I'll tell *him* anyhow, if I can see him; he's generous, and he's a gentleman, and I know he aren't one-half so wicked as they says. Maybe he will do something for her; I never believe he'd go for to hurt her—an innocent thing like a fawn or a kid."

Then, with myself under her arm and her little rosebud crowned hat on her head, Nellie set forth into the streets again, followed by a grumbling valediction from the old woman to the effect that "gells as was allus a flauntin' and a trapezin abroad i' that fashion, and a takin' of low mawthers to gie 'em bed and board, couldn't look to kip a roof over their heads a week longer, with taters at two shillin' the quarter, and every blessed head of broccoli eyelet-holed wi' worums." To which dismal prophecy Nellie paid no heed; but wound her way through the streets which led from her own little home in the low purlieus of Westminster to the aristocratic places wherein the Coronet and its patrons were to be found.

When we reached Beltran's chambers it was six o'clock, and his night-brougham with its pair of bays stood before the house; with a certain shyness Nellie, who lost her hardihood with her entrance into his neighbourhood, rang the door-bell.

No sooner was the door opened than I wriggled out of her

hold', dashed up the stairs, and bursting through the apartments, danced and whirled round Beltran, where he stood before the mirror in his dressing-room. He welcomed me kindly, whilst they told him who desired to see him.

He was already dressed for dinner, and soon passed into his reception-room, where Nellie was standing, looking for once shy, and ill at her ease. Nellie was not promoted to that standing from which a burlesque dancer can hail lords and gentlemen as Fred and George and Jack, as old fellow, and old cuss, and old hoss; perhaps because she "kept straighter than most of them;" the glories of drag-seats and of little dinners were as yet unknown to her; and a peer was to her still only a very great and terrible person. For Nell no brougham waited as yet; no stalls clapped approval with delicate lavender gloves; and no Richmond repast was ever ordered at three guineas a head. She was as yet only a little dancing-girl,—unpromoted.

"I am very much obliged to you, Nellie," said Beltran, as he gave her a kindly good-morning. "I am glad the dog found so pretty a guardian. Won't you sit down, and have some fruit or some tea?"

Nellie blushed, and fidgeted. The very languor and ease of Beltran's manner—a manner as natural to him as it was to breathe—only increased her unusual perturbation. It was easy, no doubt, to chaff, and flout, and exchange impertinences and puns with young university-men or boy-soldiers in at casinos; but it was very much more difficult to her to speak out to and look straight at this thorough-bred, indolent, weary-looking employer, whose consummate insolence, when he was displeased, had, she knew, passed into a by-word even among his own set.

"I didn't find Puck myself, sir," she murmured. "It was a young girl as is at mine now, my lord; and she was almost dying this morning; and I took her in, though gran' made a fuss, and she's gentlebred, I'm sure, though it seems as how she be all alone, and hasn't not a shilling in the world; but she told me not to say a word about that to you, because she

seems so proud like, and she won't accept of no reward, and
she trusted me not to tell, and now I am telling; and I feel so
mean, and yet I don't know what to do. She is so helpless
and seems so innocent, and with it all she is as proud; and
you see, my lord, for a girl like me to work for her living
aren't nothing; but this one—"

And Nellie broke down in her flood of disconnected and
involved phrases, stammering very much, and entangled in a
web of words. Beltran smiled as he stood by the hearth, but
only kindly, with no touch of contempt.

"I don't quite understand. Tell me all about it, Nellie.
Don't suppose I'm in a hurry. I dine down at Greenwich to-
night, but I needn't start for half-an-hour. Who is it that is
too proud to take these five pounds for the puppy?"

Thus encouraged and reassured the Wood-Elf told her
own tale, and that which she had heard also. Told it, too,
rapidly indeed, and very brokenly, and with not any eloquence
save that of feeling, but pathetically for all that, by reason of
her quick, ardent, honest sympathies with its subject; and
Beltran listened, yielding her far more attention, and indeed
more respect, than I had seen him show to the elegant no-
things of a marchioness, or the coquettish repartees of an
ambassadress.

"And you see, my lord," continued the girl eagerly, her
awe of him fading away in the excitement of her genuine
pity and desire to do good, "my sort of life's well enough for
the like of me. I've always roughed it, and I'm fond of the
business, and I never was eddicated nor nothing of that kind;
but this one,—she may be a farmer's daughter; she says so;
but she's a lady, if ever I see one, and she's proud, and so delicate, and so coy-like, she couldn't do as I do, she couldn't.
She'd just go mad with the rudeness, and the bustle, and the
—the—shamefulness, as one may say. And I haven't a notion what on earth to do for her,—and she won't touch them
sovereigns as you've offered for little Puck; and I shall never
be able to stop her from rushing off again right into starvation and her coffin, and I thought as how maybe, if it wasn't

making too bold, you might take a kind of pity on her, and know some great lady or another as might know of something as would suit her!"

And she paused at last, fairly out of breath, and frightened at her own temerity now the words were uttered. Beltran smiled again.

"Great ladies are not very easy to persuade, I fear, in such cases. But I will do anything that I can for this child you have so generously befriended. She will not take the five pounds, you are sure?"

"No, sir; I am sure she will not."

"But you can take and use it for her?"

"No, sir, I couldn't. I don't tell a lie well at no time, and I never could tell one at all with her big eyes a watching of me."

"Well, it is difficult then to help her. Of course if she were fit for the theatre I might give her a place; do you think she would be?"

"She has the looks for it, sir; and she fired up like a wild thing about Imogene and Juliet and that lot. But you see, my lord—I mean—as she'd have to begin—being so poor, and so young, and nobody not knowing about her—as she'd have to begin like I did, just with hard, hard work, and a shilling a night, and a miserable tramp every morning and evening to and fro; she'd die off, I think, of cold, and worry, and hardship. And—and—she's that coy, and dainty, and proud; her heart would break on the stage, I think."

Beltran laughed.

"Do you think hearts break on the stage, Nellie? I don't."

"I don't know, sir. They says as Mrs. D'Eyncourt's did. I don't suppose there's a many as keeps on the stage as cares a hang; but some few as is drove off of it, as one may say, sir, do."

"Perhaps so. I never considered the question. If your protégée would not like the stage,—what is her name, by the way?"

"An odd name, sir,—one as don't sound altogether English—Gladys Gerant."

"Gerant! It is English enough, very old English. Her brother must surely be the same lad that wrote those verses which I—which the world has taken to praising."

"She did say as her brother were a poet, sir."

"That is very curious," murmured Beltran, stirred for the moment out of his habitual indifference to all created things. "There is not much doubt, I should think, but that they must be the same. However, there is small consolation for her, Nellie, in this: the boy is dead."

"Dead!" echoed Nellie. "O, dear heart!—how sorry I am. I have told her so to keep on believing he is alive, and that she'd find him and be happy with him, and all that! Might I make so bold as to ask what you know of him, my lord?"

Beltran walked to the other end of the room, and gave her a pretty green volume.

"Nothing in life," he said carelessly. "But these poems are a little the talk of the town, and you see by the inscription that the author is dead."

Nellie turned the leaves over reverently and helplessly! the dirty pages of Lacy's "acting-editions" were the only ones she ever strove to read.

"'To be clever enough to make a book as big as this, and then die!" she murmured. "Lord! how sad it seem! I never can tell her; O, never can tell her! Couldn't I hear something of him, sir, where this was printed?"

"I think you had better not try. You see you know nothing of her."

"O sir!" cried the Wood-Elf eagerly, in her zeal forgetting her awe of him. "You'd never say them sort of suspecting things of her if you could only look in her face! If ever I see a face as was all innocence, and loveliness, and pride, and light, and sadness like, all mixed up together and changing every minute, I see it now in hers—I do indeed. There's that about her, sir, as do seem to make me feel so common,

and so coarse, and so good-for-nought beside her. My bit of
a place aren't fit for her, and my talk will only do her harm
and—and—O! I know as every word she says is gospel-true.
I'd swear it!"

"I like to hear you, Nellie," said Beltran kindly. "It is
good and generous of you. I am not doubting in the least.
But at the same time you could not satisfy the publishers that
she was any connection of this writer's; and if you did there
would be very little good in it. Poems never pay: these are
no exception to the rule. The town may talk of them; but
five hundred people, at the outside, buy them. Leave the
matter with me. And until you hear from me again, tell this
child that you have lighted on her brother's work at a book-
seller's—take her that copy, it may give her pleasure—and
persuade her to stay with you till you can hear of him. It is
not worth while to tell her he is dead."

As he spoke he twisted out the front leaf or two which
bore the record of the young poet's brief life and death, and
handed the volume back to her.

"But what shall I tell her, sir, please?" murmured Nellie.
"She's not a one as I could tell false to; and she'll ask me,
and ask me, and say she won't live on charity."

"Tell her the truth, then, not all of it, but just so much as
this:—That you told me her name, and that I gave you this
book, and that I will see her myself to-morrow. She will not
leave you then, unless she be an utter little fool."

"She's no fool, sir; but she's dreadful proud."

"She's all the better for that. Leave me your address.
I'll try and get to you at noon."

"'Tisn't a fit place for the like of you, sir; 'tisn't, indeed,"
stammered Nellie. "It's nothing but a little old green-stuff
shop, and in a horrid part of the town, too."

Beltran laughed.

"My dear girl, I have been in fifty times worse places, I
will warrant. I'll see you at noon."

Nellie took the hint that her interview was ended, and
rose.

"You're very, very good, my lord," she said earnestly. "I don't know how to thank you. She'd do it better nor me. I was sure as you was kind and pitiful, though—"

"Though what? Come, out with it!"

Nellie looked for once up in his face, and took courage from its look.

"Why, in the theatre, you know, my lord, they're very afeared of you; and they calls you very hard, and very indifferent, and very full of scorn like. But I never thought that they spoke as was all true about that."

"Didn't you? Well, I suspect they did. Good-bye. And, for your own share in bringing back that little rascal, do me the pleasure to wear this."

He tossed lightly into her lap as he spoke a pretty necklet of quaint Roman beads, which lay with other trifles of the sort in an old Vernis Martin dish on a table near him.

Nellie coloured as brilliantly with pleasure as she had done with embarrassment. For a moment she held it, gazing at it in blind bewildered adoration. Then, as though the green scarabæi which were in it had life and sting, and sharply wounded her, she started and shrank a little, and put it quickly down upon the table near.

"If you please, sir—no," she murmured. "I'd rather not. I'd rather you'd not think as I could have come for sake of such a thing. I'd nothing to do with finding Puck. Nothing —nothing, indeed."

And then she turned before he could reply, and darted swiftly from the room, as though if she tarried longer in sight of those glittering scarabæi with their golden clasp, her continence would perish, strangled by desire.

"Wonders will never cease!" said Beltran to himself. "'The town talks of a dead poet instead of kicking him as a dead ass;—a dog comes back without a thief catching hold of him;—and one of my dancing-girls refuses to take my jewelry!—I thought that I knew the world, Puck; but I suppose after all that I don't."

And with that soliloquy he lighted his cigarette, and went down-stairs to his brougham.

CHAPTER XXII.

Par-ci; par là.

On the morrow he went out alone, and did not permit me to accompany him.

Hence I knew nothing of how the fates of Bronze and the child Gladys fared in the hands of a man whom the town called a gamester and libertine.

Ascot followed almost immediately on the night in which I had found her with her dying blue-bells; and we were the guests of its prettiest *maisonette*, all through those gay pleasant sunny days of early June. I often thought of poor Bronze as I watched that brilliant scene from the box of Lady Otho Beaujoluis, in which Beltran occupied his accustomed place, ignoring or defying, with his natural indifferent recklessness, the furies that he thus awakened in Avice Dare, whose box, though he had given five and twenty guineas for it himself, he almost entirely neglected.

She took her vengeance in a curiously characteristic manner. She went shares with the most unlucky and reckless plunger that she knew in all his maddest ventures, and as he (the merest lad) left off a loser by about five thousand, she involved her friend into the payment of one half of that amount: Beltran of course being obliged to disregard the poor boy's courteous protests that "ladies' losses never counted."

Altogether that Ascot cost him very heavily, and the social gaiety at his *maisonette*, where the champagne-cup seemed to flow in perennity under the lime-trees, and cards to come out of their own accord at evening on the laurestinus terrace, it seemed no marvel if he had altogether forgot his promise to serve a friendless child.

I remarked this to Fanfreluche, who was of course at Ascot with her mistress, and was made much of by her old masters, the First Life.

"My dear," returned that sapient moralist, "a gentleman may forget his appointments, his love vows, and his political pledges; he may forget the nonsense he talked, the dances he engaged for, the women that worried him, the electors that bullied him, the wife that married him, and he may be a gentleman still; but there are two things he must never forget, for no gentleman ever does,—and they are, to pay a debt that is a debt of honour, and to keep a promise to a creature that can't force him to keep it. Now, Beltran is a gentleman,—core through."

By this I suppose she thought that the cause of Gladys and Bronze was safe with him.

We often judge very differently from what you human beings do.

I was once taken into a night-club, where some of the highest play on the town is to be had; where the men who lounge outside its doorway, on a hot night in the season, are the maddest plungers of their time; and where those quiet soft-toned patrician voices name the biggest *coups* of their generation.

"Pick out the best fellow amongst us, little one," said my patron of the night, who was Clyde Paulette, of the S. F. Guards.

All the men were, as it chanced, almost entire strangers to me; of none of them did I know the character beforehand; but I studied them all one after another, comprehending what was asked of me.

At last I selected one--I cannot tell why—by that peculiar instinct which leads us instantly to a correct diagnosis; and I was greeted by loud shouts of laughter from all present, including the man I signalised.

It seemed that he was known as "Ruthless Rhy," from his duels, his intrigues, his fatality to married women, and many other wicked sports and pastimes; was indeed looked upon as the very worst lot, in a set as wild as it was thorough-bred.

But though they made such mockery of me for my choice, I adhered to it, and would not alter.

Well—two years later on, this man Vaughan Rhysworth, was martyred in China, when he was on his travels; killed by the most lingering and hideous of deaths. He might have saved himself—might have been living now—if he only would have told one lie. He would not; and he perished. Then men in England, hearing of that death, began to tell to one another many buried things of this lost life; and many who had owed him much were full of shame at their long silence, and spoke out their great debts to him; and the world thrilled strangely at this grand and simple heroism in one who had so long been calumniated and half shunned in its midst. And so it came to pass that they found at length how wisely I had made my choice, and how blindly they had mocked it, in that late summer night in the billiard room when steadfast in my selection I had trusted Ruthless Rhy.

But I wander too far a-field again; if I stray over all my recollections I shall have you as impatient of me as was Gil Blas of the archbishop's sermon.

Our Ascot week was a very pleasant one—bar its losses in money. These were not limited to the losses on the turf; they were increased by those at the piquet and écarté tables that stood out after dinner on the laurestinus terrace, which over-looked the close-shaven lime-shaded lawn; with the cosiest of arm-chairs beside them, and the mellowest of lamps burning near them.

The play was higher and more continual than common in consequence of the presence of the Prince de Ferras, one of Beltran's guests; a handsome and witty person, who was the most inveterate and the most fortunate card-player it has ever been my fortune to know. Beltran rather fancied himself at écarté, and with justice; for there were few better players than he in his set. But either the Prince was in reality far his superior, or else the run of the cards was too strong for science to change them, for it is certain that in the five Ascot days M. de Ferras won from his host some very enormous

stakes. He was a very rich man too, which made it more
provoking.

"The French were very stupid when they fixed Play in
the masculine gender," grinned Fanfreluche, sore of heart for
her hero. "How can it be anything but a woman? see how
it smiles on the fullest purse."

Avice Dare, however, was not like hazard; she did not
smile on the courtly de Ferras, who for his part treated her
with a cool and even ceremonious manner, which seemed to
argue a profound distaste for her.

I remarked this to Fanfreluche; who tilted her ears over
her nose with her accustomed gesture of satiric scorn.

"My dear! how can one tell! I saw a man once, the whole
London season through, so insolently rude to a married woman,
that everybody wondered she did not strike him off her
visiting-list. Well, when August came, he eloped with her
in his yacht to South America. O, you can never tell. Men
in love are often most intensely disagreeable. They are so
mad with themselves for being such fools that they take it
out in hard hitting all round."

"But M. de Ferras,"—I began in a maze.

"O, pooh, my dear!" cried Fanfreluche. "He has robbed
his host at cards, and abused his host behind his back: to
fulfil the whole duty of a nineteenth century guest it only re-
mains for him to betray his host in love!"

"You think very ill of men?" I muttered; I was, indeed,
slightly weary of her sceptical supercilious treatment of all
things; your pseudo-philosopher, who will always think he
has plumbed the ocean with his silver-topped cane, is a great
bore sometimes.

"I think very well of men," returned Fanfreluche. "You
are mistaken, my dear. There are only two things that they
never are honest about—and that is their sport and their women. When they get talking of their rocketers, or their
runs, their pigeon-score, or their *bonnes fortunes*, they always
lie—quite unconsciously. And if they miss their bird or their
woman, isn't it always because the sun was in their eyes as

they fired, or because she wasn't half good looking enough to
try after?—bless your heart, I know them!"

"If you do you are not complimentary to them," I
grumbled.

"Can't help that, my dear," returned Fanfreluche. "Gracious! whatever is there that stands the test of knowing it
well? I have heard Beltran say, that you find out what an
awful humbug the Staubbach is when you go up to the top and
see you can straddle across it. Well, the Staubbach is just
like everything in this life. Keep your distance, and how
well the creature looks!—all veiled in its spray, and all
bright with its prismatic colours, so deep, and so vast, and so
very impressive. But just go up to the top, scale the crags
of its character, and measure the height of its aspirations,
and fathom the torrent of its passions, and sift how much is
the foam of speech, and how little is the well-spring of
thought. Well, my dear, it is a very uncommon creature if
it don't turn out just like the Staubbach."

I have since seen the Staubbach myself, and don't consider
it any finer than the Kinder Scout* of my birthplace; at
that time I was mute; I was thinking that there were some
waters, deep, cool and silent, hidden from human sight, that
no man ever fathomed, and that there were such characters
likewise.

"Yes, there are," said Fanfreluche, divining in her curious
fashion my unuttered reflection. "And there are men like
them. And I will tell you what there is too: there is a torrent that flings airiest foam-bells on the wind, and sparkles
with gayest colours in the light, and seems to dance and sing
all its mirthful hours through, as lightly and as emptily as
though it were but a sheet of froth; and yet beneath, all the
while, it is so dark, so deep, so sad, so still, and it only flashes
with colour and foam, so that none may probe its depths, and
none stir its dead that it hides.

---

* Puck means a fall of water in the wild country about the Kinder
Scout, the highest summit in the hills of the Peak range. Allowance must
be made for his patriotic prejudices.—ED.

"But, goodness me, I shall be too late to dine at Maiden-head!" she cried, interrupting herself, as though ashamed of her momentary earnestness. "You know the Brigades have taught them simplicity there, and the dinners are very good; I don't care for simplicity as a rule, it's the biggest bore and impostor that ever existed, and with women always means limp muslin, weak tea, and a thatched cottage full of rats and earwigs. But when simplicity has the Guards for godfathers, and takes the form of ducks and green peas, or a perfect haunch of venison, I do like her. She's worth all the foreign cooks in the universe."

And off she went to enjoy it, perched atop of one of the drags of the Household.

Ascot fell very late that year; and as I overheard that we were shortly to go yachting, and afterwards to the German gambling-places, I trembled for the fate of Gladys Gerant and Bronze, notwithstanding the assurances of my little Mentor.

The day she spoke thus was our last day under the lindens and acacias of this pleasant little cottage—a cottage with a billiard-table and a croquet-ground, a conservatory, half-a-dozen men-servants, nine o'clock dinners, and a drawing-room in blue velvet.

There are few things more pleasant, I am inclined to believe, than the mixture of Town and Country, judiciously managed. You like the purling murmurs of a brook all the better, if beside you a delicate Burgundy also murmurs out of its jug. You find the odours of the sweet briar and the roses all the sweeter, if they be crossed by the spice-like perfume of your favourite cigarettes.

The song of the nightingales comes more purely and clearly than ever as you sit by the open windows, pushing the wine and the olives around. The hay never smells so fragrantly as when the wind tosses it to you where the five-o'clock tea is passing from hand to hand, under the golden-starred pyramids of the blossoming lime-trees.

And when the great white moon goes sailing through the

dark clouds above the woods, you think how lovely the night is—as lovely as nights used to be in your boyhood—when leaning over the balcony you are fanned by a jewelled hand; and lightly chiming across your thoughts come breaks of song, murmurs of laughter, fragments of the world's idlest talk, from those bright chambers within, that you see through the lace of the curtains, and the screen of camellias and myrtles, as you look away from this starry still night, and this fan that stirs like the wing of a bird.

O yes; it is well to talk of the mountains and forests in solitude. Take your tent if you will and live roughly, aloft on some barren plateau; cook your snared bird in a bed of ashes, and lie down to sleep on your pile of heather, and stare at the stars through the rent in your canvas, and stalk out alone in the mists of the dawn. That is very well; and it is very well you should think so, if you cannot afford any other; and it is simple, and solemn, and grand, and all that. But for pure amusement, my friend—combine the Town and the Country.

A certain friend of mine went not long ago to pass his *villeggiatura* in one of the fairest spots in all Europe. There is a poetic calm about the place that is beautiful exceedingly; great snow-clad mountains enclose it; deep darkling lakes sleep in its shadowy woods; wild pine-woods tower against skies of deepest blue; boats glide all through the day dream-like upon its waters; there is the sound of falling torrents everywhere, and now and then the chime of bells.

He spent seven weeks there. When he lounged into Arthur's again, another man asked him how he had enjoyed his time in that happy valley of the Oberland.

"Well," he made answer slowly, with a big cigar in his mouth, "we made the time out pretty tolerably. We used to breakfast late; and we'd get to whist about three in the afternoon, and we'd play on till about two next morning—bar dining, of course. We did that every day. It wasn't half bad fun. Never had such a steady innings in all my life;

and we'd first-class players. I don't know that I ever saw better: not even here, nor at the Arlington."

Now this man, whatever you may think, is neither of an unpoetic temperament, nor of an inartistic mind; he has, on the contrary, a great deal of feeling and of perception in him; and for athletic powers, whether in climbing, boating, or walking, he has few rivals. It was not therefore that he was a Peter Bell, to whom every primrose was but a stupid weed; it was only that he wanted his town in his country, and took it—in the form of a pack of cards.

I think that is the reason why, of all your human pastimes, yachting is the most charming to you.

You have the freedom of the seas, the freshness of the winds; the width of the waters is round you, and above flashes the silver-winged gull; life and its worries lie behind you with that low white shore that has died out of sight; all debts and all difficulties have been severed with the rope that moored your row-boat to the pier-head. You are away, and are afloat, and are free.

And yet all the luxurious pleasantnesses of the world you have left, are still with you. On the cushioned bench there lies the newest novel, just cut. In the big goblet the lumps of ice float on the golden wine. Screwed upon your deck your whist-table shows its green, tranquil, familiar face. The silky nectarines and the purple grapes lie lazily together on your plate. In the pretty mirrored cabin a choice little dinner will wait you, when the sun goes down; and, if you be one not happy without this additional toy, there can be also beside you some feminine form clad in the richest and coyest of dresses, that with gold buttons and azure satin and snowy silk so amusingly copies your own sailor's attire. You can strike right across an ocean, and yet can carry the town with you.

Here is the real charm of yachting that makes it the prince of all your pastimes.

To that pastime we went from Ascot; to the beautiful, graceful, gleaming schooner Bonniebelle, that called my

19*

master master also, where she lay on the smooth gray narrow
ribbon of the Solent water.

It was such a picturesque existence, I am ashamed to say
I forgot everything else in it. Lady Otho was queen on board
the Bonniebelle—charming Lady Otho, with her pretty
haughty head, and her gracious imperial ways, and her soft
patrician languor that was sweet as the south wind, after the
brusque tyrannies of the *cocottes*.

It was so pleasant there.

Resting all through the night, with the lamps of the op-
posing shores glistening through the gloom like glowworms
through a twilight. Gliding all through the day, with
laughter and music and song, and the scent of cigarettes
and the sound of gay careless voices, just crossed by the
sailors' shouts and the splash of the severed waters. Staying
now and again at nooks in the little Island, where some
pretty house was bowered in a nest of red tangled creepers,
and a green shadowy lawn sloped down to be lapped by the
waves; and quaint balconies, all leaf-covered, leaned over
the white foam-crests. Waiting far into the midnight, while
the waltz tunes rang over the beach, and the white dresses
here and there flashed through the aisles of syringa and
myrtle; and the lights shone out through dark festoons of
foliage, and thickets of tall fuschia; and the glad good-
nights were called, gaily from voice to voice; and the cigars
were lit, and the boat was pushed off, and the waters rippled
under the oars, and the harvest-moon arose, broad and
bright, above the silvered sea. Ah, how pleasant the life
was!—the old sweet life that is dead!

In it I could discern no sign that my master had remembered the child Gladys. Only once did I fancy that he had
spoken of her.

The Bonniebelle had run far down Channel; it was a very
sultry afternoon; the sky was cloudless, and the sails hung
motionless in the hot dry air. Lady Otho reclined under her
awning, lovely beyond compare, with a gorgeous feather fan
in her hand.

Beltran had been talking more seriously to her than usual; and those two, whose attachment was of the serenest and the most passionless sort, now seemed for the moment almost to have approached—a quarrel.

" *You* turning knight-errant, Vere!" I heard her say, as I drew near to listen; and there was a smile on her lips new there, and not sweet. "*Ah, je ne crois pas les miracles excepté en foi!*"

"Believe or not, as you like," answered Beltran, as he rose from his seat and lighted a cigarette.

"Some women are awfully good to us, Ned," he muttered a few minutes later to Lord Guilliadene. "But how bitter bad the best of them are to their own sex!"

"Awfully bad," assented the handsome Earl, brewing himself a pick-me-up. "What's amiss with Alice Beaujolais? You've ruffled her somehow, haven't you?"

"Not I," said Beltran. "It's the weather."

But I do not think it was the weather, oppressive though the heat and the calm might be. I think he had been speaking to her of the story of Gladys, and seeking to interest her in it—vainly.

I suppose I shall be considered very heterodox if I write a thing that I really believe; but I do believe it, and it is this—that men are much softer at heart than women.

O, I know men can be hard enough; they can swear savagely on occasions; they can hit mercilessly when they are minded; they can be like steel or granite to a woman whom they have ceased to care about; I know that. But for all that they are never hard with the chill, contented, egotistic, lifelong brutality of women. *Après moi, le déluge!* —that is a woman all over. If the Pompadour did not say it, she ought to have done.

Lucretius has said how charming it is to stand under a shelter in a storm, and see another hurrying through its rain and wind; but a woman would refine that sort of cruelty, and would not be quite content unless she had an umbrella beside her that she refused to lend.

I get very out of patience when I hear of the tenderness
of women; they are only tender just for themselves and their
belongings—as tigresses and bears are. They have no notion
of any impersonal sympathy. Men you can move by a thousand things—their imaginations, their affections, their chivalries, their follies, their intelligence, their perception,—what
you will. But a woman can only be moved by just one thing
alone—her own private interests.

Women always put me in mind of that bird of yours, the
cuckoo.

Your poetry and your platitudes have all combined to
attach a most sentimental value to cuckoos and women. All
sorts of pretty phantasies surround them both; the springtide of the year, the breath of early flowers, the verse of old
dead poets, the scent of sweet summer rains, the light of
bright dewy dawns—all these things you have mingled with
the thought of the cuckoo, till its first call through the woods
in April brings all these memories with it. Just so in like
manner have you entangled your poetic ideals, your dreams
of peace and purity, all divinities of patience and of pity,
all sweet saintly sacrifice and sorrow, with your ideas of
women.

Well—cuckoos and woman, believe me, are very much
like each other, and not at all like your phantasy:—to get a
well-feathered nest without the trouble of making it, and to
keep easily in it themselves, no matter who may turn out in
the cold, is both cuckoo and woman all over; and, while you
quote Herrick and Wordsworth about them as you walk in
the dewy green wood, they are busy slaying the poor lonely
fledglings, that their own young may lie snug and warm.

Allons! I shall be told, I suppose, that it is very easy
(and therefore ignoble) to satirize woman. It *is* easy, no
doubt—just as Pasquinades were easy in the corruption of
Borgian Rome; just as epigrams were easy in the vileness of
Bourbonic France. Had Rome been virtuous or France pure,
Pasquin's pillar would have been blank, and Figaro's mouth
been silent.

After the yachting there came the playing places in Germany; and after those there came the shooting: the latter at a variety of houses, in a variety of counties. Our servant, who was, as I have said, a notable exception to his class, and had taken me greatly into his affections, bore me about through all these manifold changes; and though his master and mine laughed at him for cumbering himself with me, Beltran never offered any serious opposition to my presence wherever he went.

It seemed to me the hardest work that ever men set themselves, that inveterate "gunning" from sunrise to sunset: that incessant unremitting assiduity with which they devoted themselves to the slaughter of birds without any pause or breathing space, save in that one hour when the hot luncheon smoked under the nut-coppice, and the champagne-cup was drunk where the great curling ferns shielded the mouse and the wren

But the share that I had in it was pleasant enough. Sometimes we were at great country-houses, filled with fashionable gatherings; sometimes we were at those grand ducal mansions that stand amidst the gorse and bracken of the midland shires; sometimes we were at his own place, a gray rambling old baronial pile, set in the heart of the green meadows, and the beechen woods, and the drowsy hawthorn lanes, of Bucks.

There were always women, of course; dainty dames and demoiselles of the world of fashion. Alice Beaujolais being always invited with the same circle of guests as Beltran, with that curious tacit recognition and condonation of such a *liaison* which people always accord while the woman is "in society," and which contrasts so comically with their virtuous ostracism of her if she once be fool enough to blunder into an open scandal and the columns of the newspapers.

"My dear, she goes everywhere; she attends the Drawing-rooms, you know; and her own people visit her. It would be ridiculous for us to object."—I have heard titled women say this hundreds of times of great ladies of their own order, whom they know to be guilty of the vilest of intrigues and the foulest of sensualities, and whose "connections" were as notorious to their own set as though they had been pilloried in a market place. And they never did object accordingly, but asked each aristocratic sinner with her favourite "friend" of the moment, in the very kindest and most charitable manner possible.

If a silly idiot mismanaged her matters, and created scandal by getting into the divorce court, or by irritating a long-suffering society with some folly that it is quite impossible for society to be blind to, of course it was a different thing. They "objected" then with all imaginable severity, and combined their forces to drive forth the foolish one from the sacred precincts of an outraged community.

Lady Otho, therefore, being a woman of an exquisite tact, and taking care to be always *au mieux* with her husband (a sensible creature likewise, who thought that in the matter of condonation it was always best to "give and take"), went to all the houses that Beltran went to, and carried on her "platonics" with him with the most admirable ease. She deigned to take much notice of myself; and though she declined to accept me when offered to her, petted me habitually very much, as she usually did the youngest and sauciest addition to her "pretty pages," from the cornet-list of the Brigades.

I never knew quite whether I liked her—how can you with those women of the world? She was kind and insincere; she was gentle and she was cruel; she was generous and ungenerous; she was true as steel, and she was false as Judas —what would you?—she was a woman of the world, with several sweet natural impulses, and all a coquette's diplomacies.

She tended me with the greatest solicitude one day that autumn, when I had run a thorn into my foot: and the very next day, when I was well again, she laughed to see me worried on the lawn by a bull-terrier. If you have not met a woman like that, I wonder where you have lived.

However, as a rule I enjoyed myself amongst those fair

patricians in the various houses we visited. I played with
their wools and floss silks; tore their yellow-papered novels,
and stept on their velvet or silken skirts at my fancy, in the
mornings; strolled after them in the conservatories and rose-
gardens; was curled on their folded plaids when they graced
the pheasant or grouse drives with their presence; and
learned to care for the bang of the breech-loaders, and the
risk of a shot, as little as they cared when a brave old cock
bird staggered dead through the smoke, and they watched
how the wagers they had laid in gloves went.

Then when luncheon came on the sturdy gray pony's
back, and they dispossessed me of their plaids to stretch
themselves thereon, they would toss me *foie gras*, and truffles,
and biscuits; while nonsense, "delicious thing, like the
bubble from a spring," and laughter, and stories, and half-
gay, half-sad fragments of vague sentiment, floated with the
smoke of the cigarettes, and the scent of the delicate bur-
gandies, amongst the yellow furze and the wet mosses, and
the big dock leaves of the bank, up to the branches of the
nut-tree hedge, where amongst the half-reddened foliage the
linnet would be singing her latest, and the robin his earliest,
song.

It was pleasant, very pleasant, and in these bright, careless, sport-filled days of autumn, there seemed no time in
which to remember Bronze and Gladys. I forgot:—and I
supposed that he forgot also.

When I met Fanfreluche again, she scoffed at me severely
for this. She came to stay with her mistress at that old place
of Beltran's in the beechwoods of Bucks. He was seldom
there except in the shooting season; it appeared that his
fortune was too impoverished for him to be able to sustain
the enormous expenses which a nobleman's open house and
great establishment involve.

When he went down to the place it was in a half-bohemian, half-bivouac fashion, that yet was perhaps pleasanter
than any other, in the old dim, picturesque, historic house,
with its oak-panelled rooms, and its stained windows, and its

shady grass terraces with their dark cedars. For though he called it roughing it, the roughness was only of the most artistic sort; with a perfect cook, and perfect wines, and perfect cigars; with wondrous old gold plate, and fabulous antiques, and paintings, and china, all around; and a grand piano in the Elizabethan drawing-room, and the clash of billiard-balls under the painted arches of the Chapel entrance, and whist-tables in the little garden room, that looked through oriel windows on to the terraces and the cedars.

Here Lady Otho came not; and the society somewhat scandalised the county.

I suppose he thought that the *demi-monde* best suited that indolent, irregular, half-bohemian existence; and that when his guests and he came trooping in through the twilight, from the golden woods, and the broad bistre fallows, into that strange old place, it was easier to be able to lounge into dinner in their velvet shooting dress; it was easier to be able to talk whatever impudent mischief came uppermost; it was easier to be able to brush a kiss from a cheek so coolly, and with as little pardon asked, as when brushing the bloom off a peach. It was easier certainly: and they were wont to declare that the ultimate practice of both *mondes* was the same, it was their theories only that differed. And when you come in tired from a long day's shooting, and indisposed for more exertion than to drink your wine and to light your cigar, it is easier to have to do with women who have no theories. For, at any rate, the theorists expect you to put on your dress coat, and to keep awake after dinner.

By the way, permit me, in parenthesis, to say that one of the chief causes of that preference for the *demi-monde* which you daily and hourly discover more and more, is the indulgence it shows to idleness. Because your lives are so intense now, and always at high pressure,—for that very reason are you more indolent also in little things. It bores you to dress; it bores you to talk; it bores you to be polite. Sir Charles Grandison might find ecstasy in elaborating a bow, a wig, or a speech; you like to give a little nod, cut your hair very short, and make "awfully" do duty for all your adjectives.

"*Autres temps, autres mœurs*." You are a very odd mixture. You will go to the ends of the earth on the scent of big game; but you shirk all social exertion with a cynical laziness. You will come from Damascus at a stretch without sleeping, and think nothing of it; but you find it a wretched thing to have to exert yourself to be courteous in a drawing-room.

Therefore the *demi-monde* suits you with a curious fitness, and suits you more and more every year. I am afraid it is not very good for you. I don't mean for your morals; I don't care the least about them, I am a dog of the world; I mean for your manners. It makes you slangy, inert, rude, lazy. And yet; what perfect gentlemen you can be still, and what grace there is in your careless weary ease, when you choose to be courteous; and you always *do* choose, that I must say for you, when you find a woman who is really worth the trouble.

Fanfreluche, who came thither with Avice Dare, took me to task, as I say, for my supposition that Beltran had forgotten his promise. She insisted that he had not done so, however appearances might betoken.

"He hasn't forgotten," she assured me again and again, and with much force, one Sunday afternoon, when there was no gunning, and everybody was out on the terrace in the warm golden October afternoon, reading novels, playing *écarté*, drinking seltzers, chanting glees, sauntering under the great old cedars, while the crimsoned woods stretched away in the sunlight, and the creepers glowed scarlet where they trailed over the stone balustrade.

"Gentlemen, don't forget—not that sort of thing, I mean. Now, you look there at Neil Strathbalan—there—he's pouring out the claret-cup for Laura. Beastly stuff, that those tomfools of the butler's pantry poke cucumber, and lemon, and spice, and brandy, and every abomination into! As though wine weren't bad enough by itself."

I looked at Neil Strathalan as she spoke; he was one of

the men staying with us, an ex-guardsman; a duke's son; a handsome, worn, reckless, indolent-looking man of the world, of whom I had seldom heard anything good.

"I know what a bad fellow everybody thinks my Lord Neil. And he does go awfully fast, that I grant. Plunges; turns night into day; makes love to no end of married women; does everything that he ought not to do. Well, I'll tell you a thing I know about Neil. It happened a long time ago, when I belonged to the Brigades. There was a man alive at that time called Maurice Drysdale; he was a great friend of Neil's, and they were always together. Poor Maurice was thoroughbred all over, but he was fearfully poor; he went the pace like all of them, and he hadn't stay in him for it; and he broke down—utterly—fortune, and body, and mind. He got abroad to avoid arrest, and he died abroad at a little fishing town in Norway.

"Neil Strathalan was yachting at that time in the northern waters, and he just reached in time to see the last of one of the handsomest, bravest, truest gentlemen that ever was killed by plunging. I was with him, and I saw Maurice too lying in that little, pent, dark, close chamber, with its scent of fish, and of tar, and of salt water, and with the endless sound of the sea coming in through the square hole in the wall, which was all that served him as casement.

"I can see him now, with his frank fair face, and his bright chestnut curls, and his great massive limbs that had, so little a while before, owned all the strength of giants, and now were stretched there powerless as a child's, and with the life ebbing out of them as the tide ebbed off the shore. His eyes were growing very dim, but he knew Neil.

"He looked up at him with his old sweet smile, and found force to grasp his hand. 'You'll take care of Ailie,' he murmured. 'Poor little Ailie! She'll be safe with you, Neil? You'll look after her, won't you? her and the child?'

Neil clenched his hand in both his own: 'By God, I will!' and as he said it the last wave of the tide rolled off the shore, and the last breath died on Maurice Drysdale's lips. And Neil—ah! do you know what a man's grief is to see?

"Allie Grattan was a mere girl—eighteen years I think at most—and she had loved Maurice with all a woman's passion, and much more than most women's fealty. He had met her in a summer-tour about the Irish lakes; it had been the old story, the Faust story that the world loves to condemn, whilst it leaves unarraigned the Messalinas of its palaces. She was far lovelier, truer, and more tender than most Gretchens are. Dying there, his last thought had been of Ailie—poor little Ailie—as defenceless, as lonely, and almost as innocent as any one of the heaths on her native mountains. For he had kept her in perfect seclusion, and had never let a gross word or a coarse glance light near her. Yet he had died alone—well, because such men will; they drag themselves out to solitude like stricken stags.

"Do you think Neil forgot his promise, or not? Perhaps you will confess that I know something more of men than you do, when I tell you that no sister was ever dealt with more loyally, tenderly, and reverently than is his dead friend's darling dealt with by Neil Strathalan. Ailie lives in utter solitude, giving herself up to the care of her son, and to the memory of her lost and unforgotten love. All want, all hardship, all anxiety are spared her; and she, absorbed in one remembrance, hardly heeds, scarcely knows all that she and her child owe to Neil. As for words of shame or passion, he would no more breathe them to her than he would lift his hand to slay her.

"Once when his visits to her got bruited about (for all things are seen and told in this day!), the world, which is always so vile of thought that it deems all men must be vile of deed also, said that this man was worse even than it had called him; that ere his comrade was cold in his grave he sought the dead man's mistress as his own. Neil smiled when he heard that they said this. He knew—I know—that sacred

to him as the name of his mother, were the trust of his friend
and his promise."

I said nothing; I felt that she spoke truth; although
of Neil Strathalan I saw nothing save an evil, careless, hard,
good-looking man, whose speech was very caustic, and whose
life was very lazy, and whose ways and works were, as the
world said, all of wickedness.

Fanfreluche, ashamed again of having suffered herself to
feel—unwise shame, that she had caught up from her friends
of the Clubs and the Row—trotted off, shaking her bells to
beg for bonbons from Beltran. Whether she was right about
his memory of the child Gladys, I knew not; and events
soon took place which thrust all speculations on it out of my
head.

CHAPTER XXIII.

Vendetta.

THE Coronet was of course far too fashionable a theatre
to be open during the months when the town was a desert.

Hapless amateurs would indeed now and again disport
themselves upon its stage, and some crazed creature would
perchance ruin himself with a "Shakespearian revival," or
an "Opera for the Million," in those dusty desolate months
when the clubs were tenantless and the park was a prairie.
But its own people knew it no more.

Mrs. Delamare went to the baths, sweeping from Spa to
Homburg, and from Homburg to Baden, at her fancy, changing her dress three times a day, wearing the costliest of
Worth's costumes, throwing the Astolat gold away at the
tables, and holding her pretty classic head as proudly as any
queen regnant or empress amongst them all. And so did
likewise such of her wise sisterhood, as, nominally dancing
at the Coronet, actually spent in three months the fortune of
any young baronet, or coronet of the brigades, who thought
it manly and fashionable to have their brazen chignons beside

him in his phaeton, and to pay for their ball at Willis's Rooms
or their big dinner at Richmond.

As for the luckless ones who either had not a pretty face
to attract the stalls, or else were foolish enough to cling to
some poor shred of self-respect and honesty, they of course
went in the dead season to east-end theatres and music-halls,
or to a toilsome tour about the provinces; and spent their
sultry summer amongst the grit and dust of stifling cities,
paying thus in murk and misery, and continual toil, for their
ignorance in not perceiving that the only horn of plenty is
held fast in the hands of vice.

With the early days of November the glories of the
Coronet revived, and were to revive with more extravagance
than usual this season; with a new burlesque, gorgeous in the
extreme, and of enormous cost, in which the darling of the
public was to delight it with even less drapery and more jigs
than ever.

It was much talked of during the shooting-time, and as no
pains or expense had been spared in the preparation of it, so
great results were expected from its production.

Denzil had often urged my master to sever his connection
with the theatre, but Beltran had never been induced to
do so.

"Amateur management is worse than plunging," Denzil
had said one night on the grass-terrace in the shooting
season. "Farquhar of the old Royal Buskin makes his fortune by a theatre, and why? Because he is a clever man of
business, who supplies the town with amusement as a mere
matter of commerce, just as a publican does beer. He has
been at it all his days, is not troubled with scruples, and is as
hard as nails to boot. He would never allow a pretty pale
piece of inanity to murder a fine bit of 'leading business,'
as I have known you to do, because the piece of inanity was
young and poor, and wept bitterly, and prayed of you to treat
her like a star. And he would, on the contrary, take his
twenty or thirty sovereigns a-week from any dainty dame of
casino celebrity, whose 'friends' would pay to get her on to

the boards, whose dresses would be ninety guineas each, and
all stiff with golden brocade, and whose admirers would fill
the stalls and muster strong and often in the private boxes.
Now, as for you—you bade Wynch keep on that wretched
woman Berthald because the woman was old and was ugly,
and could ill find engagements; you insisted on little Lacy
being retained because she was only seventeen and had not a
shilling in the world, when you knew she broke down in the
mere letter with every fifth word she spoke; you allowed
that wild German, Waldenvorst, to rant in Kotzebue and
Shakespeare, because you found him a scholar, and a poet,
and a beggar, and God knows what all besides; you never
give yourself the trouble of having the accounts audited by
any public accountant; and you never give yourself the
chance of making money by the only paying places in the
house, because you are always lending stalls to any man that
wants them, and always offering the boxes to every pretty
creature you meet.   Night after night I have seen every
private box filled with women of our set, to whom you had
given them, and who only came there to flirt, and to chatter,
and to yawn a little, and to have cups of tea sent them in
from your room."

Beltran smiled.

"Go on, pray: the recollection of the tea seems to excite
you rather. As far as I can remember, the wine that the Press
drinks is the bigger item."

"And I have seen," pursued Denzil, regardless of the
interruption, "the very best actresses you ever had snubbed
out of the theatre by that woman yonder. I have known the
poor girls actually surrender their engagements rather than
endure the insolence of her abominable injuries.   When she
is called at rehearsal, she is always absent. Inquire, and you
find she is 'bored,' and gone to her brougham, and so are
Dora Delany and Vic Villiers, just because you give them
high wages to oblige Annesley and Fred Orford, though
neither of the girls has a grain of talent, or sense, or decency
even; and both have their 'brougham,' and can snap their

fingers at fines. Then, when the first night comes, you wonder
they are not letter-perfect, and that the prompter's is almost
the only voice heard."

"You are hard to please, Derry," said Beltran with a
smile. "I am wrong when I take penniless virtue, and wrong
when I take independent vice! Pray go on; it is delightful
to hear you. In Gertrude d'Eyncourt's time you weren't so
severe on that poor old Roi d'Yvetot—the stage."

"Like most Rois d'Yvetot, it pays its ministers with a
senile laugh, and starves its public while it crams its courte-
sans."

"Don't be so fearfully epigrammatic. An epigram is a
truffle of truth, dished up in a soufflée of superciliousness.
Your antagonism to the poor theatre—"

"I have no antagonism to any theatre. I have a very
bitter antagonism to women who order their lover to take
one, as they bid him buy them a 5000l. diamond locket, careless how he may pay for their toy with his ruin; women who,
without one shred of talent, grace, or learning, seek it simply
as the arena on which to show their forms, and display their
diamonds, dress at their rivals, and put themselves up for
sale. It is as utterly disastrous for a gentleman to become an
impresario as it is for him to become a builder. Where the
adept makes a fortune, the amateur only rushes to ruin. A
theatre is a most ruinous toy for any man of your temper and
tastes. Is the game worth the millions of candles you burn
at both ends for it? For the life of me, I can't see what you
get in return for your money? Only the obligation to give
dinners and suppers to actresses whose genius lies in their
legs or their hair, and comedians whose facetiæ are even
staler and more intolerable over the claret-jug than before
the floats; only the necessity to mingle in a society inferior to
your own, composed of people who, whilst they supplicate
you with unblushing impudence for your invitations, curse
you behind your back, because you are what they call a
swell! People who submit to your contempt for the sake of
your champagnes, and who tout you for Richmond or Green

wich dinners, while they hate you like poison for the mere
tone of your voice, the mere cut of your coats, the mere cost
of the flower in your buttonhole!"

Beltran laughed, and got up from his seat.

"You're awfully good fun, Derry, when one does get a
rise out of you. Perhaps I shall please even you with an
actress one day—*qui vivra verra.* There's the dinner-bell.
The cook sent me word that he's invented a new style of
jumping mushrooms in wine, which he thinks we shall pro-
nounce very great in its way. Come along."

In this wise was Denzil's advice always disregarded, and
we went to town for the first night of this splendid piece;
many of Beltran's own set—men and women both—did likewise, although it was early winter, and fashionable London
was still desolate. It was to be produced on a Saturday
night, and he went up in the afternoon of that day, having
asked some score of critics and *litterati* to a dinner on the
morrow at the Leviathan—the one hotel in London where the
clarets are what they call themselves, and the innumerable
nuances of choice fish are studied, and the artichoke and the
tomato are comprehended to be as equal in import, and as
different, as a fugue of Bach and an overture of Rossini.

Laura Pearl had been in London some two weeks or so,
rehearsing; and the extravaganza was entirely to her glory;
for notwithstanding its magnificence, its cost, and its reputed
worth, as a thing actually of *esprit*, it was well understood
that its chief attraction for the town would lie in the fact of
its being written chiefly to exhibit a soulless, shameless,
mindless woman, who had a fairer face and a more notorious
infamy than any other; or at least had the good fortune to
have them more talked about.

"If there were a Garrick on the stage, the stalls would
vote him bad form, yawn, and go away to their carriages or
their clubs. But they will flock night after night to see
Pearl, half-dressed, jump about in a breakdown," said Fanfreluche. "The fascination Pearls, or anything at all treating of them, possess for society is a very odd feature of said

society.* It is a fact—there is no disputing it—that the public are as eager to see the worst woman of her year as they would be to see the greatest hero that ever lived. A theatre will fill from pit to roof, if only a cruel courtesan will show on its boards. A girl's photograph will sell like wild-fire if she be only known to be absolutely infamous. People in the park gaze after Laura Pearl or Lillian Lee with as curious a wonder and reverence as if they gazed after a Jeanne d'Arc or a Vivia Perpetua. Honourable women name them openly, and study their dress, and put their pictures in their albums. They have their opera-box and their pew at church; they are copied in their coiffures, and they are asked for their patronage to charities. It is awfully odd, this deification of degradation! Where will it end, I wonder? Ah, where will it, indeed? Well, I suppose it will end in their apotheosis. They have got to the Lawn; they will get to Hurlingham; and then I suppose there won't be a reasonable doubt but what they'll get also to heaven!"

Which was profane of Fanfreluche, but pardonable; for if she placed heaven latest and highest in her estimate of the triad, it is certainly more than most ladies seem to do.

I contrived to slip unseen down to the Coronet on this Saturday night. We arrived there towards the end of a witty, graceful old comedy, which formed the *lever du rideau*. Beltran went almost at once to the box of Alice Beaujolais, and thence to other people he knew in the house. I stayed behind.

The comedy soon came to an end. Maude Delamere swept off in a superb dress, and an injured frame of mind; martyred indeed she might well feel, as the house had been only one-third full until her last act; and she was well worth seeing in her comedies, despite the *Midas* sneers at her.

It was half-past nine—the time for the burlesque.

"Where on earth is Laura?" said Beltran, coming in from

* This was in the printer's hands before the *Formosa* audiences gave fresh evidence of the accuracy of Mlle. Fanfreluche's observations.—ED.

the front of the house, where he had been conversing with some friends.

"It's a quarter past her time," said Denzil, who was flirting a little with Mrs. Delamere as he put her carriage-cloak round her.

Beltran went across and rapped on the panels of the Pearl's dressing-room door; silence following, he pushed it open. The little chamber was empty.

The music had burst out afresh, and succeeded in amusing the audience. They played through the whole of the *Bronze Horse* overture; when it was ended she had not made her appearance.

Beltran smoked a cigar with apparent indifference, but his eyes grew angry.

The gods of the gallery began to raise an uproar; they stamped, and kicked, and whistled, and screamed snatches of song.

"'Time's up!" they holloaed.

"''Tis, by Jove!" muttered Denzil. "Shall I go and look for her Beltran?"

"Let the call-boy go."

The call-boy went.

The orchestra—gallant defenders of the stormed breach—burst bravely into a ringing waltz of Offenbach.

But the gods had heard enough of melody, and preferred their own tuneful screechings; they would not hearken to their Orpheus with his flourished bâton. They shouted, and hissed, and swore, and kicked, and screamed out snatches of the vilest music-hall comic ballads.

The stalls yawned visibly; the women in the private boxes rose.

Beltran, with his cigar in his teeth, looked pale with anger. But he said nothing; silence was his second nature in any crisis; he abhorred people who "ruffled ill."

"Let me go on and sing, sir!" said a little musical, feverish voice at his elbow. "They cotton to me, you know, my lord; and p'rhaps I'd keep 'em quiet?"

He looked kindly down on Nellie as she approached him. She had been allotted a good part in the coming burlesque, and was radiant in the gauze and gold, the glittering wings, and the starry crown, of a fairy's best Paris costume.

"You're a good child. Well—go."

She tripped on to the stage at his order, and burst, without preface or trepidation, into a charming little slang-song. It was utter nonsense, but it had gay, airy music to it; the musicians knew it, and took up its burden at her first bars; the gods welcomed her with rapture and growling intermixed. The song was a success, and a truce, for the moment.

"While they're quiet I'll get Alice away. They may grow noisy," murmured Beltran.

A second or two later I saw him, through the flies, in a private box where sat, with her party, Lady Otho Beaujolais.

"What an ass!" swore Denzil, regarding him as he placed her Cashmeres round the great lady's shoulders, and led her from the box. "To give the signal himself to empty his own house!"

"What on earth did you do that for, Vere?" he asked, when Beltran, returning to the scene of warfare, calmly re-lit another cigar.

"Lady Otho hates rows," he said briefly.

"And you think there'll be one?"

"Must be."

He leaned his back against one of the upright beams, and waited.

There were a frightful confusion and tumult around him; prompter, scene-painters, old Wynch, the luckless players, all the numberless supers and machinists of a fashionable theatre, were wild with exultation and agitation. Still he said nothing; but his face grew pale, and I did not care to look up at the gleam in his darkening gray eyes.

There was still no appearance of Laura Pearl, nor of any apology from her.

"Surely must be ill?" hazarded Denzil.

"She'd have sent in that case," said her lover, his feelings undisturbed by the suggestion.

To commence the piece without her was impossible; the first scene entirely, and almost solely, depended on the absentee.

The gallant little Wood-Elf, a heroine to the core, recommenced her singing with a daring and persistence worthy of the Vieille Garde itself. But her charming could charm no longer; almost all the respectable part of the house had followed when Beltran had led out his peeress; some men in the stalls alone remained. But the crowd in the two upper tiers and the pit still were there; and their howling and hooting sounded as though demons themselves were unloosed.

The Wood-Elf ran off breathless.

"O, my lord! I'm afear'd—I am indeed—that they'll get chucking something at me!"

"Dress and run off home," answered Beltran. "I'll thank you to-morrow, Nellie."

The girl's eyes flashed and danced, and her young cheeks were in flame beneath their rouge.

"I don't want thanking, sir," she whispered. "Might I, please, stay and see it out?"

Ere he could attend to or answer her, the call-boy rushed in, gasping for utterance.

"Well?" said Beltran imperiously.

"If you please, sir," palpitated the hapless Mercury, who was in mortal terror at the message he brought; "if you please, my lord, she've a bin out since five, and she ha'n't bin back, my lord. But they see as how this here was left, and was to be sint when you sint arter her."

And the boy tremblingly tendered a note.

Beltran, with his face as calm as an alabaster mask, tore open the letter.

Long afterwards I knew that letter ran thus:

"You're a clever fellow, Beltran; but you're a fool all the

same. Don't tell a woman again you can get as good as her
for breakdowns with whistling for 'em. When you get this I
shall be off to Paris with the Prince de Ferras. If you think
me worth fighting about—well; he's a deal better shot nor
you, I saw that with the rocketers. I hope your new piece
will be a hit to-night. But I guess it won't work very smooth.
Yours no longer,

"LAURA."

As he read his face changed terribly; but it was only for
a moment; he recovered himself instantly, and crushed the
note up in his hand.

"She will not be here at all to-night," he said simply to
the men around him, without a tremor either of passion or
emotion in his voice. "Tell the people, Wynch, that the
piece is put off, and return them their money—doubled—at
the doors."

Wynch only stared anxiously at him.

"Damn you, sir! do you hear me?" said his master,
calmly still, but with an accent in his voice which sent the
wicked old man to obedience as fast as his legs could carry
him.

"You may all of you go home now," Beltran continued to
the actors and actresses, who stood like scared sheep about
him. "Attend here to-morrow, at noon, as usual. Your
salaries will continue.

Then he put his hand on Denzil's arm.

"Come out with me, Derry."

They turned to go; but at that moment the announcement
that Wynch was making, in lieu of conciliating the people,
only exasperated them. In the tumult of their rage they
scarcely heard the offer of the double money, but only in-
censed at the deprivation of their evening's amusement—for
at this house the drama counted for nothing, and the burlesque
for everything—they became utterly unmanageable in the pit
and gallery, and howled like a herd of hyænas.

"Clear the house!" cried Beltran, his voice ringing firm

and imperious out as he paused, and abandoned his intention
of quitting the scene.

"Easier said than done!" muttered Denzil.

"We shall have a free fight," laughed Page Desmond.
"I'm agreeable."

"Call police, and clear the house," said Beltran again,
unheeding alike the terror of his actors and the chaff of his
friends.

Old Wynch, before the fallen curtain, continued to shriek
his entreaties to the public, all in vain. The roughs were
strong in numbers, and rampant in injured feeling. They
saw an exquisite opportunity for their vengeance, and the
temptation to seize it proved irresistible. Pit and gallery rose
on one impulse, hooting like owls, roaring like tigers, and
set to work to damage and demolish everything that they
could reach and seize.

The half-dozen men remaining in the stalls left their seats
and came round to us by a passage which, as they were
privileged frequenters of the wings, they knew by heart.

"House will be wrecked," muttered Denzil. "I'll swear
she's sent a score of lambs in here on order."

As he spoke, Beltran—forgetful that his name had never
appeared to the public in connection with the Coronet since
it was ostensibly licensed by the Chamberlain to old Wynch
—left the flies, and, displacing his manager, stood himself
before the footlights.

"At the doors you will get your money doubled. I regret
you have lost your night's amusement; but I will make you
what amends I can," he said to the infuriated mob, while his
voice penetrated to the farthest corner of the theatre. "As
to your rioting, I shall not permit it; quit the house at once,
or the law shall force you."

For an instant they were too amazed at his unexpected
and unexplained appearance to speak; but the pause lasted
only that one fleeting second; the next the very calmness
and contempt of his attitude and address infuriated them the
more.

"Curse the swell," roared a gigantic bully, who seemed to urge on the affray. "Will ye give over a rare lark just for *his* cheek, lads?"

The words were the signal for a terrific onslaught. The men became lunatics, possessed and loosed; they tore the curtains down, they wrenched away the gilded scroll-work of the balconies, they broke the glass of the gas-burners, they pulled up the benches, and used them as levers and as mallets to work more destruction; they wreaked their rage upon the inanimate, harmless things, as a mob, once seized with the devil of ruin, always does in its blind rabies.

"The beasts!" swore Beltran under his breath. In another instant he and the four or five men of his own class who were behind the scenes had sprung across the orchestra-box, vacated in a rush by the terrified bandsmen, and were in the midst of the crowd and the worst of the combat.

I, as though the blood of all the mastiffs flowed furiously in my veins, stood with leonine courage before the floats, and barked my loudest, till I thought that I should shake the house down, Samson-like, on friends and foes in one.

I have since been told that my loudest does not rise one note higher than the smallest wail of a penny trumpet; but this I do not believe. Fanfreluche has said it, and, besides the notorious fact that no female creature ever acknowledges excellence in what she has not done herself, it is well known that all earthquaking thunders, whether of the orator's voice or the hero's cannon, are invariably pooh-poohed by those jealous of them, as the mere collapsing crack of broken windbags.

I must, however, in veracity, grant that the fulminations of my wrath took little perceivable effect on the combatants. The roughs, of whom there were this night unusual numbers in pit and gallery for this fashionable theatre, had begun wild work, and appeared only the more resolved to prosecute it to its worst issues, because "the swells" endeavoured to prevent them. No scarlet-clothed matador ever more furiously enraged an Estremaduran bull than did the sight of these eight or ten men in evening dress infuriate the sweeps, and costermongers, and butcher-boys, and counter-jumpers, who had commenced the sack of the Coronet. "The gentlemen," hitting out straight with their old Oxford science, looked so cool, so tranquil, so contemptuous; and the roughs, hot, and dirty, and clamorous, and clumsy, were so thoroughly conscious of that immeasurable difference betwixt themselves and their adversaries, and hence grew only madder, fiercer, coarser, and more brutal. It was a duel of Class in its way; and bitter as class warfare ever must be: with disdain on one side, and hatred on the other.

Beltran and his friends were but as one against a score, a little knot of silent scornful men forcing their way, shoulder to the shoulder, against a furious, yelling, tumultuous crowd; levelling their blows with fearful force when they did strike, and thinking, it seemed, less of saving the theatre from its wreckers than of chastising the audacity of the mob towards themselves. There were only ten of them, and there were some three hundred of the rioters; yet I felt the little Courcey girl was right as she cried breathlessly to the prompter, crouching terrified in his den, "Ten thousand to nothin' on the swells, Davy; they'll beat, they'll beat!"

But Davy, crouching in his hood-like box, was far too white and frightened to accept or even hear the wager.

Meantime, every available weapon that could be torn or twisted out of wood and metal work, the mob seized and used. Fragments of gilded mouldings, of shattered glass, of coloured plaster, of carved decorations, flew hurtling through the air. There was not an unbroken gas-globe left in the whole house. The central chandelier hung unhurt indeed aloft; but all its glittering glass stars and rays fell crashing to the floor under the missiles hurled against it. Howling, stamping, and struggling, they wreaked their passion on all things within their reach.

Never a word spoke Beltran; but he acted as his Order always acts when, out from the serenity and impassiveness of habit and of temper, the fire of a sudden furious scorn breaks

into flame. The roughs went down like felled oxen before
him; no stroke went home surely and so cruelly as his, and
here and there a rioter, glancing up and catching the look in
his eyes, crouched, though unstruck, like a lashed hound before him. The mob knew by instinct that this man con-
temned them utterly, and would never fear them,—knew also
that though his property was being destroyed before his eyes,
there was a certain fierce, cool, sweet delight in the mere
sense of combat that had both pleasure and passion in it for
the quiet aristocrat.

The actors and actresses had all fled away aghast by the
stage-doors; the workmen and other people of the place hung
aloof amongst the wings, unwilling to come forward. No constables had as yet arrived; there was only Nellie, who kept
her ground and watched the issue of the fight with an intense
absorption into which no selfish fears had power to intrude.
In all her fluttering gossamer, and golden glisten, and winged
fairyism, painted and tinselled and spangled, she yet stood
there with so much of youth, of eagerness, of fear, of vivid
feeling and of tortured pain upon her face, that all the art and
artifice, the coarseness and the commonness, seemed dead,
and all tenderness and courage that were in her the only
living ruling things that had their dominion over her.

Laura Pearl could never have been transfigured by emotion as this poor child was. She was only a little common
girl, with a pretty baby face, that was her only fortune, and
an ignorant little mind, that had slang songs, and obscene
jests, and evil knowledge, and vulgar trickeries as its sole
store of wisdom; she thought it fun to show her shapely form
in posture dancing; she bared her pretty rounded limbs un-
thinking, to the gaze of the populace; she had never heard a
gentle word, or caught the echo of a holy thought throughout
her brief hard life, whose laughter was more sorrowful even
than its sobs.

Yet for the hour standing there, she was transfigured,—
because she had not fear, and she had love.

The conflict probably had not endured ten minutes; but

its uproar, its oaths, its ferocity, its insane frenzy of destruction, its noise of splitting wood, and trampled plaster, and
falling glass, made it seem like a long-drawn-out battle. The
broken benches were already slippery with blood, the ground
was already cumbered by the prostrate bodies of some half-
score of the mob; the roughs employed every missile they
could lay their grasp on, the gentlemen only used their
science of attack and of defence; yet those neat, straight,
calm blows were very pitiless, and took unerring effect. From
the moment that the struggle had commenced, Beltran had
striven to reach the ring-leader of the affray,—a huge brawny
bully, who, standing erect at the back of the pit, had been
the first to shout forth the signal for the wrecking. He appeared to perceive the efforts of "the swells" to reach him,
as he dodged them repeatedly, forced himself behind wood-
work, or amongst a thick knot of his companions, and escaped
that direct vengeance which he saw hung over him. At
length, however, Beltran, with a leap like a stag's, sprang at,
and reached him, and caught him by the throat.

Although the big brute was a giant, the gentleman in
height outmatched him; but where Beltran was of slender
build, and had lost strength from the manner of the life he
led, his foe was of massive form and sinew; a mighty brawler,
all made of bone and muscle. The conflict looked utterly
unequal,—the delicately-fashioned man of pleasure looked to
have no possible chance against the bully of the populace,
strong as any bullock. As they closed, their faces were in
as wide contrast as their forms—the one colourless, calm,
intent, with the pale curved lips pressed close; the other
flushed and swollen, and big-veined, with the great teeth
locked like a mastiff's. I shuddered and closed my eyes
for a moment—only one, when I looked again the man was
down, and Beltran, with his hands still at the rioter's throat
shook him to and fro as though he were a child, and beat
his great shock head against the iron pillar beside which he
stood.

I saw then what the rage of a man, habitually calm and

indifferent to an excess, can be when it at length is roused. All the pent passion in him, to which he had permitted no utterance, poured itself out now in physical violence.

The iron column was the one nearest the stage of all that row of fluted gilded metal shafts which ran the whole semicircle of the house, and gave it half its elegance and lightness. Thus he was very near to me and to the Wood-Elf. The girl gazed on in that wrapt fascination which the ferocity of physical struggles exercises over all women; and I shared it with her. The writhing of the huge ruffian's body; the impotent convulsions of his gigantic limbs; the swelling of the black veins of his throat; the gasping of his open mouth for words that would not come; the dull thud as his skull was again, and again, and again dashed against the iron; the contrast of the furious onslaught which thus dealt with him, and the look upon Beltran's face, which never lost its pitiless and immovable repose!—these had an awful fascination for both myself and her; one which held us breathless, wonderstricken, spell-bound.

"You will kill him, my lord," gasped Nellie.

Beltran did not seem even to hear her voice.

"You will kill him, sir!" she cried out, her pretty chiming voice grown shrill and tremulous with fear;—not fear for the death of the man of her own class, but fear for the issue of the passions that she for the first time saw roused and loosed.

The cry passed over the head of the one she supplicated, unheard or unregarded. The girl, beside herself with agitation, and nerved by the strong impulsion of an impersonal terror, sprang down the six-foot depth that severed her from the ground-floor, and seized with both her hands the sleeve of Beltran's coat.

"You will kill him—my God!"

"Why not?" said Beltran, without looking up;—and he struck the man's skull yet again against the iron column: driving it home upon the metal as though he drove a nail in with a mallet.

The girl gazed with her great blue eyes dilating.

"Is he worth it, sir?" she dared to whisper.

Her instinct led her to say the only thing that could have touched him to attention in this hour.

His old, quiet, contemptuous smile came on his mouth in an instant.

"I doubt if he be," he said indifferently, rather to the sense of her words than to their speaker; and he flung the man down with a crash upon the floor, where the huge body lay motionless, and the beaten brain throbbed slowly into stupor.

At that instant one of the many gas jets from which the glass globe had been shattered, flaring higher, caught one of the lace curtains of the pit tier boxes. There were a sheet of flame; a scent of burning stuffs; a puff of smoke;—they were enough.

The rioters, dominated only by the one sovereign impulse of self-preservation, ceased from their work of violence and ruin, and rushed pell-mell to seek their outward way through the narrow doors and passages.

Beltran saw the danger; it was in a favourite box of his own, where he would lie perdu sometimes after dinner, with only the jewelled arm, and the bouquet, and the lorgnon of his companion of the hour visible through those very draperies of blue silk and white lace, which were now consuming under flames. As he saw, he caught up a breadth of green baize which had been torn off the pit benches, reached up, grasped the burning curtain, and wrenched it down with no other cost than a scorched wrist. In two more seconds the danger which had threatened the theatre had died wholly away, and only left the odour of charred wood lingering after it, and the naked framework of the box exposed.

But the terror it had inspired endured much longer; the crowd were blind and deaf to the fact of their own safety; the alarm of fire had killed all other memory in them. Like terrified sheep one moment, and raging wolves the next, they huddled together, and fought, and tore, and shrieked, and swore, and trampled one another underfoot in mad competition for pre-eminence in egress.

"They will do their own killing now!" said Beltran with that placid contempt which men of his character always feel for the excited agony and maniacal terror of a populace. And he stood with that old quiet smile on his face, looking on at the plunging, shrieking, struggling mass of his enemies as they fought their way out through the portals of the house which they had ruined.

It was no vengeance of his own seeking; but it was vengeance curiously swift and sure. That wild throng pouring from the doors, the stronger trampling down the weaker, the more ruffianly brutally forcing their passage over the trodden bodies of the feebler in the fight, the whole stream rushing outward, pent-up, broken, mad with fury, like a swollen mountain-stream hemmed in a narrow gorge, drew at last attention in the street without; and constables coming to the rescue were met by that screaming, terrified, maddened, living river.

At length the building was slowly cleared of the last of the mob that had disfigured, and striven to destroy, it. That last was the big bully. As they raised him his eyes opened and glared stupidly, yet with returning consciousness, around him.

They fell upon his conqueror.

He made a sign for Beltran to draw nigh him, and drew his breath tightly.

"It was all along o' *her*," he gasped. "Look'ee, ye've bit me hard, but I don't hate yer as I hate that devil, now all's said."

"She set you on to this to-night?"

"Damn! I ses she did," gasped the wretch, his voice hoarse and almost inarticulate. "I warn't no worse nor most; and I bore yer no grudge, though yo're a swell; but I seed her night after night in yer theayter, and I was mad on her, right on mad. She's the buxomest blowan as ever—"

"Never mind that, go on."

"Yer minded it, as well as me! I ain't got no breath, I can't go on; not rightly. Yer see, them huzzies that yer swells take up with, they lags yer ready, but it's us as they sets their eyes on; they aren't never true to you swells, they allus git a lover somewheer out o' their own kind. It's a fact, don't go for to doubt it. You swells keep my lady, and my lady keeps Tom, and Dick, and Jerry unbeknown to ye! Lord, what game I've made of yer with her—"

He stopped, his breath failing him, and the great veins in his throat swelling like cords.

"Go on," said Beltran simply; but the look in his eyes, under their lowered lids, was darker even than that which had been in them when he had hurled this man down at his feet.

"Go on! ye'd go on, choking like this," gasped the other. "She made a lord o' me for an hour or two—'tis them women's way—I'd yer wine and yer gold, and yer victuals and yer baccy, and you warn't never no wiser! Ye never are, none of ye. Ye dainty swells, ye're poor trash to wenches like her, they takes strappin big blokes like me as'll beat 'em as soon as look at 'em. Eh? what was I telling ye? My head —he do buzz so. Handsome—ay, she's a rare un to look at, but a bad un to beat. She got sick o' me, she kep me on and off like: I was a awful fool. Not such a fool as you, though. Well, days agone she seed me, just a minute like; and she telled me as how, if I'd wreck yer place to-night, she'd take me back to favour, and not never look at you no more. She sed she'd be in the theayter, and when the smash was done, she'd have me round in her own room; and we'd get dead drunk together and nobody'd come anigh her never agen but me. And I sed I was game for't, and I'd do it, and I'd get my pals about me like, so that there'd be the damndest row. And there hev been—eh? And now she aren't here, curse her —and they sed awhile agone close by me as she've a stole away with some other lord, and cheated you, and me, and all on us! And they'll give me the stone jug, and hard labour, just for this 'ere spree—damn her, damn her, damn her."

And with the savage oaths rushing fiercely in a torrent of

blasphemy from his purpled lips, the man once again lost all
sight or sense of where he was or what he said. No one had
heard the strange confession.

"Take him away," said Beltran quietly, turning to the
police, "and have him as well cared for as you can, at my
cost."

Then he turned to his own friends: "They can do without
us now; and we have had enough of it, I think. Won't you
come and have some supper?"

The other men assented willingly, they were heated and
bruised, two or three of them had contusions; and all were
thirsty and tired.

"It's a happy thing they did not know where the wines
were," said Beltran with a little laugh, as he motioned his
friends to precede him through the familiar ways. "There
was something worth wrecking in them, if they'd only
guessed it."

He lingered behind the rest, and approached the Wood-
Elf who stood by, very pale, so that her rouge burned with a
hectic fire, and her large blue eyes looked black and humid
in her little plaintive face.

He took her hand, with a grave and gracious respect in
the action.

"I thank you sincerely, Nellie," he said gravely, "you
saved me from a passion that disgraced me."

It was very gracefully said, this acknowledgment from a
man commonly so contemptuous to his kind, and so reticent
of all manifestation of feeling; and it took a strange effect on
the poor little dancer.

She trembled in all her limbs till her bright silvery wings
shook like those of a frightened dove. If a season earlier he
had given her a jewelled trifle and a flattery she would have
received both with a saucy laugh; the touch and the words,
that had as much reverence in them as though they were
given to his sister or his wife, moved her curiously to a passionate sense of pain and of unworthiness.

"It was a rough scene for you, Nellie," he continued gently, noting her embarrassment and her emotion, though not witting of their cause. "You were a brave little soul to stand by us through it. Come to supper with me, and have some claret cup to shake off those horrors."

The girl shrank back.

"Not now, my lord," she murmured; "not to-night. I couldn't, I couldn't!"

He looked at her quietly, and understood something of what was moving her—moving a little ignorant, childish, burlesque dancer whom he paid ten shillings a night—to reject an honour and a pleasure that a week earlier would have raised her to the height of ecstasy and triumph.

He dropped her hand, and did not press her further. But he stooped to her with that graver sweeter accent in his voice which Laura Pearl had never heard.

"You are as well away, little one. Go home; and keep your bright and honest courage untarnished if you can. When you want a friend—rely on me."

Then he went on his way to his supper-room.

The customary attendants had fled in terror; but the supper was set forth as usual on the table, and he bade them welcome to it. He was easy, tranquil, indifferent, in no way altered from his habitual manner; and but for the disorder of his attire and his inability to use his left arm, there appeared no sort of change in him. I shivered at what seemed such almost inhuman self-possession. It is true, I was famished and unnoticed; all things look dark to us in such a case.

As they sat down there was a buzz of voices crossing one another in a fiery fury of excited talk; when it lulled a little, Paget Desmond's ringing mellow voice came straight athwart the table in a point blank question:

"Vere! You have never told us—what's amiss with Laura?"

"Nothing is amiss with her."

The voices fell; all the eyes of his guests turned wonderingly on Beltran.

"Nothing!" echoed the guardsman in amaze. "Nothing? Then why on earth didn't she show?"

"Caprice!" put in Denzil hastily, divining that there was something wrong with his friend. "Last winter, in Paris, Ysaffich paid a forfeit of twelve hundred francs, and, what was more astonishing, left her great part to be filled up by her most detested rival, for a mere piece of obstinacy and ill-temper, and the determination to spend that particular evening in a dinner with Russians at the Café Madrid, as she had made a wager to spend it."

"But that wasn't a first night, surely?"

"It would have made no difference to Ysaffich if it had been. She would have beggared herself of everything she possessed to carry out her caprice, and win her wager."

"The wager was a big stake, then?"

"The wager was a box of sugared chestnuts from Siraudin's! Nothing more on either side. Paget, on my word, you don't know women if you can't estimate the overwhelming ecstasy that lies for them in having their own way, even when their own way is their own ruin."

"Well—is Laura dining anywhere, then, like Ysaffich?" persisted Desmond, who was the biggest and most good-humoured of guardsmen, but slow to comprehend or to follow a hint. "It's deuced cool and ill-natured of her if she be—making all this row!"

"What on earth will poor Beaufort say? He begged me to telegraph how the piece went," said Dudley Moore. He spoke of the author of the extravaganza—a clever, graceful jester, who was imprisoned by a sudden attack of illness.

"Beaufort need not despair," said Beltran, with a certain inflection of coldness and of authority in his voice. "It is only a question of delay. His interests will not suffer."

"Pardon me. It is not in your power to promise that. The public—"

"The public! Well! What of the public?"

"Is not a turnspit dog that will come at your bidding to roast every joint you may put to the fire; and it certainly won't be inclined to perform its good offices for one of which it has once been balked as a meal."

21*

"No? And yet how contentedly it lives, famished on the crumbs which the Press scatters to it from the begged crusts of borrowed opinions! At any rate, Mr. Beaufort shall have what justice I can procure for him; and what compensation money can offer."

"That is very amiably said," interrupted the great editor. "But it seems to me that you utterly ignore the fact that it was the absence of a favourite actress to-night, not any hitch or fault in the presentation of the piece, that caused the *émeute* yonder. Now it will be exceedingly difficult to please the public with that same piece anyhow. It is as bad as champagne that has been uncorked but not drunk; whatever vintage it might be from, whatever sparkle it might once possess, it is flat and flavourless now. To produce it at all will be of very doubtful wisdom; not in your interests, I fancy, certainly not in Beaufort's; but to produce it without Laura Pearl in it will be sheerly and simply an impossibility."

"Why so?"

Beltran asked the question coldly and curtly, and a darkness came into his gray, tranquil eyes.

"Why so! Can you ask? And you have known the theatrical public all these years!"

"And so have I," dashed in Denzil. "And I could see your meaning fast enough if you were talking of an actress of mind, of talent, of taste; but we are only talking of a handsome woman who dresses well, and does breakdowns. There are scores of them to be had at the music-halls."

Dudley Moore laughed a little, grimly.

"We are talking of a woman who—be it through beauty or breakdowns—ingratiates herself sufficiently with her audience for them to pull the house down because she don't appear. This popularity of hers makes her as necessary to the success of this establishment, as though she were a Grisi or a Ristori. I am not paying her a compliment. If the public get accustomed to seeing a performing monkey at a certain house, and like the monkey, and find salt in its antics and tricks, it will make a fearful row if the monkey be absent from any piece performed at that theatre. It considers itself cheated, in point of fact; cheated out of its pet spectacle and diversion."

"You are not very gallant to the absent!" cried Denzil.

"I am not seeking to be gallant; I am stating a fact. You say she is of no consequence because she is only a burlesque actress; I say she would be of just as much consequence if she were only a monkey. However, I am talking on the premise that either her caprice of non-appearance (whatever its cause) is to continue, or that our friend here is irritated enough by it to resent it by her future exclusion."

"O, hang it!" cried Desmond in dismay. "I say;—we can't do without Laura. She's no end of fun in those flip-flaps. He won't cut up rough with her for this—will you, Beltran?"

"Colonel Desmond, you forget that we are all of us unenlightened as to the cause of the lady's absence, and consequently so as to the extent of her offences and the duration of her exile," said Dudley Moore, with dry cruel unction.

Beltran himself, thus directly appealed to once more, could no longer evade answer.

"I don't fancy you will any of you be likely to see her in this place again," he said very calmly; "as for the cause, —I don't think that much matters to anybody. Ysaffich's sweetmeats only concerned those who had to pay for them."

There was the strange quiet smile about his mouth as he spoke, with which he had watched the rioters rush on their own destruction; everybody at the table felt that the subject was not one to be pursued with him; even Desmond gathered that it might be best to drop the topic, and even Dudley Moore's bitter tongue remained for once inactive.

Beltran, with his easy languid laugh, changed the theme by a brief and witty story. It was very seldom that he ever took the trouble to amuse people; when he did no one could do it with more effect or greater charm. He chose to do it this evening, and succeeded.

The conversation grew brisk, and gay, and bright with genuine mirth; the wines were admirable, the men's tempers were heated. They drank perhaps a little more than they ought to have done; but the laughter if continuous was always good-natured and always genuine.

I no longer thought Beltran callous and heartless; he seemed to me a very marvel of self-command and of courage.

To be sure, by this time, he had given me food in abundance and a drink of water, which made me regard him through Claude glasses. But, my very dear people, you do just the same: when your master, the world, keeps you starving, you, in your cynical hunger, murmur at its coldness and harshness; it is a Saturn that devours its children, it is a Nero that fiddles while you are shrieking in agony, it is a Commodus that sees men tear each other to death for his pleasure, it is a Judas that betrays his Master, it is an Israel that crucifies all divinity! But if the world only toss you a cake, only keep you well fed and well fattened, what a good and a fair world it is, how full of all sweetness and light, how true in its vision, how pure in its excellence; fruitful as Ceres, smiling as young Hebe, tender as the virginal mother of Krishna, many-breasted as the Carthaginian goddess by whom all the multitudes of men might be nurtured!

And you are as sincere in your worship as in your curses, only you are an optimist in both.

When the supper-party broke up it was noisily and joyously; there had been no gayer or pleasanter night at the Coronet than this which followed on so wild a combat.

Beltran saw his guests out by the private door, and laughed them a careless good-night.

It was only one in the morning when he reached his chambers; but two and three and four were chimed by the clocks, and he never moved from the chair into which he had cast himself.

Once his lips quivered with rage, though they had laughed so lightly and so listlessly all the past hours through. His heart indeed had not been pierced by the blow dealt him that night; he had never loved this woman save with the slight, soulless, inconstant passion which a loveliness purely physical evokes. But he was deeply wounded in his pride, and in that form of self-love yet stronger than pride, which make a discovered infidelity so bitter to any man, even in a wife or mistress who has lost all charm, and from whom release is ardently desired. It was horrible to the haughty and exclusive gentleman to be thus cheated and betrayed; to be thus cast to the jests of the town; to be fooled like any boy in his earliest youth; to be made the dupe and the laughing-stock of a woman drawn from the dregs of the populace!

When his ignoble rival had panted out his confession of hatred and treachery, Beltran had suffered one of the keenest indignities that a man of his temperament could have endured.

For the opinion of the world, when he himself chose to provoke it, he cared not one straw; but the opinion of the world when he knew himself a fit subject for its mockery was a very different thing to endure.

He had been universally successful in his intrigues; he had been uniformly more the sought than the seeker of women; he was unsparing in his contemptuous ironies on those who were the fools of their own amours; he was given to believing, and to imbuing others with his own belief, in his perfect keenness of vision, and infallibility of judgment; he had as little of vanity and as much of it as a man of fine instinct and cool sense, but spoiled by a society that has too greatly deferred to him, usually possesses. Above all, he was intensely proud.

The blow fell on the most sensitive nerves of his nature, and the curse that he breathed through his teeth upon his traitress could hardly have been deeper or fiercer if a cheated idolatry and a wronged worship had spoken in it. His pride had been pierced to the quick and abased in the dust; it is a less forgiving and a more terrible enemy than the most cruelly outraged love, for its wounds are far slower to cure, and its scars far slower to fade.

. When five o'clock struck, and the last spark of flame died out from the gray ashes in the grate, he was still there; cast backwards in the great depths of the chair, and gazing out at the dead embers of the fire, as though in its dreary shadows he saw the ghosts of his own dead years: years whose strength had been spent, and whose resolves had been stifled, and whose purer dreams and whose higher desires had breathed out their faint life for ever, under the murderous embraces, and the poisoned kisses, of harlots. ·

END OF VOL. 1.

PRINTING OFFICE OF THE PUBLISHER.

May 200 6969

www.ingramcontent.com/pod-product-compliance
Lightning Source LLC
Chambersburg PA
CBHW020948030726
47496CB00005B/1407